A WOMAN SCORNED

A WOMAN SCORNED

Wendy Robertson

headline

First published in 2004
by HEADLINE BOOK PUBLISHING

10 9 8 7 6 5 4 3 2 1

Cataloguing in Publication Data is available from the British Library

ISBN 0 7553 0942 1

Typeset in Times by Avon DataSet Ltd,
Bidford-on-Avon, Warwickshire

Printed and bound in Great Britain by
Mackays of Chatham plc, Chatham, Kent

Headline's policy is to use papers that are natural, renewable and
recyclable products and made from wood grown in sustainable forests.
The logging and manufacturing processes are expected to conform to the
environmental regulations of the country of origin.

HEADLINE BOOK PUBLISHING
A division of Hodder Headline
338 Euston Road
London NW1 3BH

www.headline.co.uk
www.hodderheadline.com
www.wendyrobertson.com

For Bryan with love

Acknowledgements

The story of Mary Ann Cotton has long fascinated me but it was at the urging of Gillian Wales that I embarked on this dynamic combination of pure fiction and documented fact: the most challenging work I have ever tackled. For this I thank her. I thank Gillian's library staff for so willingly helping me with the sources for this novel. I thank Grahame Robertson for inspiring me on this historical journey, joining his historian's eye with mine as we tramped the back streets and lanes of West Auckland in search of historical traces of the nineteenth-century village. I thank Bryan Robertson and Debora Robertson for their unfailing support in what are challenging times. Finally, heartfelt thanks to my excellent editor Harriet Evans, for her expert support and encouragement in weaving together this fascinating story, and to Juliet Burton, my friend and agent, for continuing to understand what I am about and helping me to keep the panic at bay.

Prologue

Durham Gaol
March 1873

My Dear Child,

How fitting that my last letter from this dark place should be to you, even though I've known you for such a short time. But on that day we met didn't the very sight of your poor face cut through me like lightning? Didn't we know one another from that first second? It's the thought of you and your faith in me that's kept me going. But now, dear child, the shade of those black gallows looms right into this small room and even I lose heart.

Perhaps it's as they say – that I am the angel of death, that wherever I go people fall like fading poppies in the field. At first, child, I thought it might be all that dirt rolling through the streets, piling up against the houses. Or perhaps it was the bugs that crept into my rooms from their subterranean lair. Or even the poison in the wallpaper, as that man said at my trial. But it was not me, child, never me.

I'll tell you about those men in my life, honey. In the beginning, certain of them that got to know me – well, they'd eat out of my hand. They'd never known such joy, such <u>participating pleasure</u>, and they loved the dance I made for them. The doctors too, they liked my lively quality . . . saw me as different. But none of the men I pleased stood up for me – for whatever reason – in my darkest hour: not Quick-Manning, nor Robinson, nor Kilburn. And certainly not that Thomas Riley.

1

Ah doctors! The best doctors treat you like an equal. You join them as one of the company of healers. There you are, the doctor on one side of a sick person and you on the other, and there's proper work to do. Great work! I've met many doctors but I've never come across a real bad one until I had to listen to that Dr Scattergood spewing his poison in the court. Scattergood? Scatterbad, I say.

In the early days, child, when my own young ones faded to death, it wrenched my heart so much that I had to learn to stem that dangerous flow of love. Perhaps my worst sin is that after those early deaths in Bristol I learned to withhold my deepest favour because a heart can only take a certain amount of wrenching.

I am a religious woman. Did I tell you this? I taught regular at Sunday school. I know my Bible. If I'd really done those terrible things they say I have don't you think I'd repent? What have I now to lose? Won't I soon be brought to the hangman's rope and go meet my Maker? And then won't I need the comfort of His mercy while I contemplate His just punishment? To enjoy this comfort a person needs to repent of any ill he has done. But I'm certain that when He meets me He'll welcome me warmly to sit at His right hand, because He knows I am innocent and, like Him, have suffered the unjust rage of the mob.

So, child, in sorrow I must leave you to this earthly toil. Sitting in this place, it has dawned on me that at the very end at last my heart has flowed with love again, and that love was for you. For that I thank God and in that I am redeemed. But I'll not see you again. Not in this world, anyway. My gaolers here whisper that what's to come will not be easy and I must stay strong.

Kind regards, beloved child,
Marian Cotton

One

February 1872

I first saw the extraordinary woman called Marian Cotton on a train. That crucial meeting led directly to a time when I was healed and she was struck down. Perhaps it was foreordained: a savage exchange on the part of an Almighty who cares little for true justice. Marian, with her strange power, healed me and brought me to my true self, and yet – despite all my efforts – I failed to save this woman from her sad fate. How very slender were my powers compared to hers.

I must admit that I learned early in life how powerless I was meant to be. Take a look at that portrait on the first landing of my father's house in Lordship Park, Stoke Newington! See what a small, slight figure I make as I stand at the very edge of the painting, looking away from the others into the golden curlicues of the frame. The artist, a Mr Seebold, stayed at the house in Lordship Park for six weeks. He shared meals with us; took whisky with my father in the evenings and tea with my mother and my sister Lottie in the afternoons.

Mr Seebold did not paint us all at the same time. The maid would call us one by one to the garden room whose north skylight allowed the artist to use it as a makeshift studio. How I dreaded my visits to that room, with its bruising light. I had to stand there while Mr Seebold fiddled with my clothing, pulling it down, hitching it up. He would touch my chest and underarms and the backs of my knees, and call me 'naughty girl' as he adjusted my pose before he began to paint. I would look right away from him as he did all this, welding my gaze to the bowl of early roses on the small table by the long window. In this way

3

I could pretend that this fussy man who smelled of turpentine was *not* there and was *not* touching me.

In this family portrait even our dog, Lancer, is more central than I am. Perhaps my father, ever genial, had spoken to Mr Seebold of my self-consciousness (meaning *his* self-consciousness) regarding the bad skin on the right side of my face. I can just hear him. 'No need to make a show of the poor child, old boy. She is shy, understandably so. Worried at what people say when they see her.' Perhaps that's why Mr Seebold felt free to cup my knees in his hands and pinch the upper parts of my leg, and call me 'naughty girl'.

In the painting my father stands to the right. My sister Lottie stands in the centre, at my mother's elbow. Their arms are linked and their wide skirts wind together in a swirling tapestry of red, pink and blue. Lottie looks directly at Mr Seebold, a flirtatious glint in her eye. I'm quite certain he never felt *her* knees. She'd have screamed to high heaven and brought the household running.

Beside Lottie is my brother, Rollo, with his arm round Pixie, my little sister. She has her hand on the glossy nut-brown head of Lancer. Then there is a clear space, where you can see right through to the butterfly cabinet at the back of the room. I am to the left of that space, looking out into the picture frame.

Past me, through a window to my left, Mr Seebold offers us a glimpse of our own house in the background. The paradox of being *inside* the house, and looking *at it* through a window is for me the most interesting aspect of this painting.

Our house is no great pile but stands foursquare, its eight windows set symmetrically around the central door, with its decorative arch, that faces the clear spaces and wide paths of Lordship Park where Rollo walks with Lancer every day. On the wide windowsills of the drawing room sit the tiny but unmistakable figures of my dear cats, Whisper and Grouch. Like me they look away from the centre, not belonging.

They do say that sisters are a blessing but I have never been sure of this. Lottie has grown from that flirtatious girl in the portrait into a very fine woman. She was so very pretty as a child, so very beautiful as a young girl. These days she has the blossoming, voluptuous look of a married woman. And she is the proud wife of a husband who knows his prize and the mother of a child of her own, who, thank Heaven, favours *her* beauty rather than *his* long-jawed saturnine visage.

I've heard it murmured in our family that her husband Jacob's religion, his tendency towards intellectualism, his long jaw and his laconic style are 'unfortunate', but this is much compensated for by his family riches and his fine connections. This is the *ideal* bridegroom who kissed me very hard on the mouth the day before he married my sister. He told me (in the secret quiet of the back downstairs corridor) that at least I should savour this chance of a kiss. After all, marriage was not my destiny and it was unlikely that I should ever be kissed again. That said, he pressed into my hand a package, a book by a woman called Frances Power Cobbe called *Essay on Intuitive Morals* and a pamphlet with the title *Wife Torture in England*.

He watched me flinch as I unwrapped the package and peered at the titles.

'This will show you, my dear, what nonsense is this superstition called religion, and some ways in which a woman might escape its thrall.'

At first I thought these volumes were an invitation to immorality, but they proved much more interesting than that. My bruised lips tingled for hours afterwards and I had to put on some salve at bedtime before I opened the package again and glanced at the pages and became absorbed in this woman's unusual ideas of the dilemma of a woman in a man's world.

Anyone will tell you – repeatedly – that my sister Lottie is kindness itself. I should know, as I've been most often the object of her kindness. My burden was that I'd been regarded as a 'sickly crippled thing' (my mother's words) since I was born. I was supposed to be a boy but I was not. Then they had Rollo and they were satisfied. I ended up being a shadow resting on a chaise longue or a bed, depending on the time of day.

Young Pixie and Rollo, at first confined to the nursery, always kept their distance, entering my presence uncertainly. Perhaps they thought they would catch these things that made me so different from them. We have certainly never been close.

My problems were manifold. This was not just because I had a crippled left foot, twisted by an eager doctor as he tried to pull me feet-first out of my mother because I chose to be born the wrong way round. It was not even the skin on the right side of my face, just below my cheekbone, which has the appearance of dried, occasionally suppurating porridge. As well as this, every noxious vapour, every stray germ has always insisted on having its way with me. My mother blamed my illnesses on the bad air released by the turned earth and the rash of new building all around us in Lordship Park, so she kept the doors and windows locked and kept me inside. Then, to cap it all, when I took on the burden of 'being a woman' I was regularly cursed with agonies of backache ten days in any month.

How many weeks of my life have I spent in a darkened room with the beautiful Lottie coming every hour, on the hour, to plump my pillows with her dimpled hands and discuss my case with Mother. The two of them would talk as though I were insensate, as deaf to human intercourse as were Whisper and Grouch, who always lay on the eiderdown at my feet.

My mother and sister would insist, with pressing hands and lowered voices, that I stay still, move little and conserve my strength. In the end, as the years ground by, a hard voice inside me started to say, *save my strength for what?* For more lying down with drawn shades and my feet weighed down by two cats? To sleep even longer than the twenty-four hours that comprise a day?

But then things changed. Lottie was married to the man with the hard mouth, who had just undergone a very convenient conversion to the Church of England. Soon afterwards the happy couple were entraining for Paris *en route* for Venice, then on to settle for a long stay in Tuscany where Lottie had the baby whose conception – it was never mentioned openly – precipitated the nuptials.

Despite being waylaid by the bridegroom on the back corridor I was not allowed at the wedding, as *they* thought I might faint during the ceremony. I suppose I should have been grateful that no actual mention was made of the fact that the flawed side of my face might be rather difficult to cover with a veil, and a hobbling attendant might spoil the wedding picture somewhat.

My only glimpse of the wedding was the sight of Pixie and Rollo in their children's finery as they stood in my doorway with Nanny, who said, 'We thought you might like to see your little brother and sister dressed in their best, Miss Victoria.'

I sat up straight on my couch. 'You look splendid!' I said faintly.

'Now, children!' she said, releasing their hands.

At that point they performed a perfect curtsy and a perfect bow.

I clapped my hands. 'Bravo!'

'Now, children!' Nanny repeated, and the three of them vanished down the landing.

So I missed the wedding.

In spite of this, my mother – an earnest Pixie now replacing Lottie by her side – assured me afterwards that it was a magnificent ceremony and would be the talk of all their friends for many months to come. They sat me in a chair and made me watch as my mother's maid, Joan, packed the magnificent wedding dress and veil into a velvet-lined box. I had to sit there and listen yet again to the story of the wedding: who wore what; the roses nestling in trailing ivy in the church. Above all we had to dwell on the beauty and the perfection of the bride.

After that grand event, without Lottie and her intolerable fussing, my life became much quieter. I passed some of the time reading the volumes by Frances Power Cobbe, coming to appreciate her ideas of a God who is a kind of mother-father with endless wisdom and kindness. She inveighs against the burden of marriage and asserts that it is designed by men to keep women innocent of their true subjugation. She talks of the delights of the single life, says all women should be educated on a par with men, and even, incredibly, that they should vote and go into Parliament! It was very strong stuff and I hid it under my pillow so that no one might see it and destroy it with a comment.

Of course her ideas of a good life are a kind of fairy tale but they were so invigorating to read in my stuffy, overheated room! In my excitement my blood heated up and I began to notice more clearly the colours of my curtains, the smell of the roses that Joan arranged for me, the touch of velvet on my dressing gown. I breathed in more deeply, and hugged these impressions to me. Oddly enough, I began to feel better each day. The time seemed to pass more quickly.

My mother failed to notice my improvement during these months. She would come into my room from time to time, pat my shoulder and tell me how well Rollo was doing at school, how Pixie was doing with her piano, or about the approving looks Pixie had drawn when they went to Mrs Wentworth's reception for her cousin from Africa. When our Dr Fennel made his weekly visits, my mother would talk with him in whispers about how concerned she was about me and how *very* much 'dear Victoria' missed her sister Lottie. This was not the case. Wasn't I noticing more? Didn't I feel more alive? My view was that my mother talked like this because she was bored to be the one doing the caring all by herself. It was *she* who missed Lottie, not I.

In what I came to realise was my extreme good luck, the outcome of all this was that my father and my mother decided that I really needed a change of air, a change of scene. My father came up with the idea that I should be sent to stay with his cousin William in the North.

I'd overheard my mother and Lottie, more than once, talking about this William. It seemed he had contracted a scandalously early marriage to a rather unsuitable local girl of sixteen, but this had not put him off his medical studies and he was now a well-established village doctor, like his father and his grandfather before him. My mother agreed with my father that in the house of a doctor I'd get every attention, and *surely* the country air would do me good. She brushed aside Dr Fennel's protestations that the air of the industrial North might not be salubrious, and continued to insist that *this* was the solution to the problem. She talked yet again of all the new building in Stoke Newington and that dangerous turned earth.

Whether my going north was a solution for her or for me was never really made clear. Whatever the reason, I welcomed this strange proposal. With this new life of the senses rising in me I had begun to feel entombed in that cluttered London house. Any change would be for the better.

At first my mother tried to insist that I should be accompanied on the long journey by her maid, Joan, who would return to London by the next train. But I gathered my new strength (inspired by Miss Cobbe!), and had a very rare tantrum. I even resorted to stamping my good foot, and said one would think I were six, not eighteen. I insisted that I should travel on my own. My mother blinked at my uncharacteristic revolt. Then, being too weary, bored or too lazy to insist, she gave in.

Despite the weariness of the long journey (when, to be honest, I would have welcomed Joan's company) I was to learn that to travel alone is a good thing. I liked being the stranger, watching the whirl of passengers as I was escorted from train to platform to train again by solicitous porters. I relished the sight of the land rolling past and the eerie beauty of the high chimneys, tangled skylines and glittering canals in the smoky towns through which we moved so quickly. I opened the train window to take in every sound, every smell, even every taste in the air as I travelled the length of the land. Wasn't all this giving me a sense of England that no bland book, no words on a page could provide? Wasn't I being free, independent and strong, just as Miss Cobbe advocated? And in the end, wasn't it on the very last leg of this unchaperoned journey – from Darlington to West Auckland – that I met Marian Cotton and, effectively, my real life began?

Two

The porter has taken my hand luggage and settled me in the solitary first-class carriage. I am sitting here in secluded splendour when the door is wrenched open and a pale-faced woman peers in. She pushes in a heavy bag and a basket, and lifts into the carriage a fragile boy of eight or so. Then she leaps lightly up the steps herself and settles into the corner opposite to me. My breath is taken for a second by the scent of fruitcake and almonds, with some kind of back-smoke of lavender and honeysuckle. This person fills the compartment with her perfume and warmth.

I turn to stare out of the window, but not before I have taken in the image of a woman of thirty or so, of taller than average height with thick glossy black hair under a rather becoming bonnet. She wears an unusually fine paisley shawl and – highly polished, although stitched and mended – small button boots. Instinctively I pull my own ugly boot, with its built-up instep, further under the hem of my skirt. Her dress, unlike the shawl, is plain – a working woman's garment. Yet she has a refined presence that compels my attention.

Staring at the puffs of steam dissolving into trails of vapour that stream past the window I wonder at the audacity of this unlikely woman in entering a first-class carriage. I can feel her looking at me. It takes all my strength not to turn and catch her gaze.

Then her voice, low and surprisingly well-modulated, cuts through the air between us. 'And how have you been these past days, honey?'

Now I do respond to that compelling look. I turn my eyes to meet hers, the darkest, brightest blue eyes I've ever seen: eyes alive with interest and humour. This woman is quite beautiful, despite the workaday clothes. I have to battle with the desire to smile broadly and my cheeks feel hot as though I am in a fever.

'Well, honey?' she says. 'Do I suit?'

'Why do you speak?' I murmur faintly, my breath rolling finely from my mouth. My lips tingle, like that time when Lottie's husband kissed me. How this woman affects me. 'And why do you ask how I am?'

'You're as pale as paper, honey, and I've just seen you limp along the platform like a weary old man.' Her voice, locally accented, is brisk, energetic.

'I've not been well,' I mumble. 'And I've always had the limp.'

'Why, honey, you need to get yourself a better shoemaker. You've no need to limp. No one with a good shoemaker needs to limp.' Her tone is warm, affectionate, her smile is irresistible, but her words are threaded with assurance, with authority.

'I know this shoemaker fellow that works magic with the crookedest feet. And he can keep your shoes goin' for ever, which is convenient as shoes are so dear to buy in the first place. I tell you what, honey, I'm gunna tell the shoemaker all about you. I'll take you to him. He'll enjoy the challenge.'

I have to blink. I am so mesmerised by this woman that I seem to have allowed her a measure of impertinence that my mother would never have permitted. I glance again towards solidifying steam on the streaming window, longing to escape from her close attention. The train clatters and counts the rails beneath its wheels. The woman's soft, low voice drags me back into the plush space of the compartment.

'You're not from round here, honey,' she persists, her gaze capturing mine again. 'I can see that.'

I stare at her. I've never had such a frank conversation with anyone of her class. Never in all my life. Of course, I have talked with Effie, the maid I shared with Lottie, and listened to the chatter of Joan, as well as all the other maids and housekeepers who have passed through the house on Lordship Park. But none of these women has ever looked at me so directly, nor demanded my attention as does this woman.

She persists. 'You come from away, don't you? Now where would that be?'

I sigh and then, almost happily, surrender. I even smile. 'I come from London. Well, just north of London. A place called Stoke Newington. I've come to the North for a rest. For some fresh air.'

She nods. 'I don't come from this place neither. Been here in South Durham less than a year. It's quiet enough, but quiet like a nest of snakes. I was once in Bristol.' She settles back and sighs a little. 'Big dirty place, that. A port, d'you know. Ships coming in like flocks o' pigeons. But I was happy as a lark there, with the lad I was married to then. After that I was in Sunderland. That was not long before I came here. Another place with ships. I liked it. The sea is clean and fresh.' She leans across, puts a hand on my knee. I can feel the power in her touch through all my petticoats. 'Us outsiders have got to watch out for ourselves,' she smiles, 'in places like this.'

I stare down at her hand. The fingers are long and tapering – surprisingly unworn for such an evidently working woman. Strangely, it's not unpleasant to be in her grip. 'That's very kind of you,' I say faintly. Her confiding, her smile, her touch – never have I received such attention and such consideration, even from my own family.

She nods and sits back against the padded backrest and closes her eyes. I am, for the moment, set free. But one part of me is bereft. I want her to go on talking, to be with me again.

Suddenly the boy sits up as though stung. 'Mother,' he gasps, 'I'm gunna be sick.'

The woman's eyes snap open. She reaches out and puts an arm round him and places the other long-fingered hand on his brow. 'Breathe deep now, son, breathe deep. You're not gunna be sick, I'm telling you.'

I sit and watch as the boy relaxes against her arm and his face becomes less blue and wretched. Despite his distressed state you can see he is not a bad-looking little fellow, though he does not share his mother's fine bone structure. Her pretensions as a mother reveal themselves in the velvet cap that is perched on his thick thatch of hair. Rather grand for a boy of his class.

Her gaze meets mine. She shakes her head. 'This young'n's not my own, poor wretch. He came part and parcel with the man I got married to a while back. And I was not married for long when *he* was taken. This one will not make old bones.'

I glance hurriedly at the boy, but so deep is he in his corporeal distress that this means nothing to him. I wonder if my mother has said this about me to Dr Fennel or anyone else who will listen: 'She will not make old bones.'

Now this woman reads my thoughts. 'Not like you,' she says. (Anyone else of her class would have added 'miss' to this statement.) 'No doubt about it, honey. Once your head clears of its fog and your body gets to know itself, you'll surge on – past the century's end and into the new times. I see this.'

Then the strangest thing happens. I feel a great charge run through me as though my blood has really started to flow: as though for years I've had this thick sluggish treacle in my veins that has now softened and is starting to move. The feeling makes me smile and the woman grins straight back at me, a dimple showing in her cheek and her bright eyes shining and urgent.

'There, didn't I tell you, flower?' she says. She *knows* what has just happened to me! No doubt about it. She knows that our conversation, our meeting here on the train, has wrought some kind of magic that has made a deep change in me. Thinking about it much later, I will compare it to falling in love. I will also come to understand that I am not the only person to whom this has happened.

Five minutes later the train pulses into West Auckland station, where the water from a recent downpour still drips from the wrought-iron canopy. The woman lifts the boy out of his seat, plants him on the platform and gets down after him. She reaches back into the compartment for her shopping and puts it on the ground, causing a sugar packet to spill out. Then she turns again to help me down with my hand baggage before striding away and returning with a porter.

'You need to tell this feller where you're going, honey. What d'you say your name was?' she says. 'Just where are you going?'

I have not told her my name. 'I am Victoria Kilburn. Miss Victoria Kilburn. My boxes are in the guard's van, all labelled,' I gabble on, striving to take charge of myself. 'I'm visiting my uncle who lives on Front Street in this village. Western House.' The porter nods and trundles his barrow through the puddles to the guard's van to get the rest of the boxes.

The woman is smiling broadly. 'Dr Kilburn, is it? I know nobody better. A fine man.'

'He's my uncle. Well, my father's cousin.'

13

'He's often at my house, the doctor. Tended my Fred Cotton – my husband that was – right to the bitter end. And now he's treating my lodger, who's near as bad. No wages coming in, that's a big problem for me, with sickness in the house. The parish officer here is good enough to me, and he and the doctor get me some nursing. They're both a big help. Their work's cut out, of course. There's so much sickness in this place. So much dirt. Typhoid and smallpox common as the cold. Only last month I was nursing this man with smallpox.'

It is starting to rain again. She looks up at the grey sky. 'You came here for fresh air, you said? I don't know how healthy that London o' yours is, but all I can say is this village might be quite a pretty place but looks isn't everything. It's no healthier here, I'm telling you.'

Suddenly my blood clots again in my veins and I feel faint. She catches me as I crumple and holds me up in a powerful grasp.

'Now then, honey,' her soft voice whispers in my ear. 'Let's get you to your uncle. He'll have you better in no time. I've never seen a better doctor and I've seen a few doctors, I'm tellin' you.'

And here he is. William Kilburn, whom I will call 'Uncle', strides through the wide station gates, wielding a recently furled umbrella like a walking stick. He's a tall man, younger than I thought. No more than forty. He has the reddish hair, the same sandy side-whiskers and pale skin as my father, but his face is more alive, and he smiles with more genuine warmth.

'You must be Victoria!' As he strides towards me, I can feel the pleasure – like heat from a fire – in the woman beside me.

'Why, Doctor,' she says, 'here's your relative fainting with pleasure at the sight of our little village. It seems she comes here for her *health*.' Her tone is ironic and her manner with him, as it was with me, is surprisingly familiar.

He doesn't take offence. 'Well, Mrs Cotton, you and I see the worst of what happens here, but neither of us knows the perils of Stoke Newington nor the dire diseases that lurk down in London. Here we have the moors up behind the village and the river flowing through it. West Auckland is pretty enough for any Londoner. I have always thought it so.' His tone brooks no argument. He takes my right elbow as she releases my left. I feel like nothing so much as a parcel that has been passed from one hand to the other.

14

She retrieves her stray sugar packet from the platform and picks up her shopping basket. Then she nods at the boy and, silently, he takes one side of the handle. 'Well, I told that lass of yours, Doctor, she couldn't be in better hands.' From any other mouth this would have been obsequious but here it has the feeling of a compliment between equals.

He looks across at her son, who is still standing holding the basket, his head bowed. 'And how is Charlie today?' he says.

She answers for the boy. 'Better, Doctor. Not bringing up so much. I gave him a bit of arrowroot before I set out. An' I thought the fresh air of Darlington would do him a bit of good.'

'I was really sick on the train, Doctor.' The boy's voice is thin and reedy. 'Really sick.'

'But we sorted that out, didn't we, son? Nothing to worry about.' The woman called Mrs Cotton smiles down at him and the two of them set off ahead of us along the platform and out of the wide gate.

Uncle William waylays the porter and tells him that his groom, Jonty Sanderson, will be along any second with the trap, to pick up the luggage. Then he turns to me.

'I thought we might walk, Victoria,' he says, glancing down at my awkward boot. 'Walk'll do you good. Jonty'll pass us on the way. But if you want to wait for him . . .?'

'No thank you, Uncle,' I say. 'I am stiff with sitting. I could do with the exercise.' I say this because this is what he wants me to say and, anyway, I think I might be able to make it to the village. Even so, the five minutes it takes is very tiring. My uncle distracts me with questions about my parents and Rollo and Pixie, and enquires whether Lottie is still abroad. Of course, my father, always keen to keep in touch, writes regularly to my uncle so he has told Uncle William all about the wedding.

'Would that we'd made the journey to the wedding,' Uncle William says. 'But my dear Mary has her hands full with the *babes* and I had my hands full with a rash of enteric fever, then the incidence of smallpox, not to mention an accident in the pit that called for an amputation.'

I shudder at the thought of my uncle sawing away at someone's calf bone.

'That woman, Mrs Cotton, said she'd worked for you, Uncle. Nursed someone with smallpox.' I want to talk about her. The woman is under

15

my skin. I want to mention her, to get my uncle to talk about her. I don't want to leave her behind.

'Mrs Cotton? Now there you have a strange woman, but quite a gifted nurse. Scrupulous. Fearless. Even intelligent. She worked a time ago at the Sunderland infirmaries. Useful experience. A cut above the ordinary, is our Mrs Cotton. And she knows it, which means some of the good folk in the village don't care for her, if I were to be honest with you. Around here they don't lightly take to someone who puts their head above the parapet. The people of this district are modest, even reticent, and Mrs Cotton's directness can set some hackles rising.'

We cross over the bridge and make our way alongside a looming mill where the road opens out into the wide village green. Today this is an entirely fresh panorama, but in the coming months I will learn this village off by heart. West Auckland is a pretty place, mostly cottages with a sprinkling of fine buildings set against a backdrop of rising moor. I like it from the start but even at this first glance I can see it as inward-looking, crowding round two wide fields that do the job of village green where, I will learn, children play, chickens roost and sheep graze. And, of course, men play football.

A small trap jingles towards the station and my uncle waves to the driver. It seems this is Jonty, going to collect my luggage.

The village houses sit at the edge of the greens, on which narrow pathways have been threaded through the lumpish grass by the boots of miners on their way to work. At regular intervals through the day and night these sturdy men surge silently towards the colliery on the hill beyond the river. In the daytime this same greensward is crisscrossed by lesser clusters of workers making their way to the brewery at one end of the village or to the big corn mill at the other.

Dotted among this tumble of houses round the green are drinking houses, narrow taverns and inns. Such places, as well as quenching the mighty thirst of the local people, cater for travellers on their journeys westward towards the Pennines or eastwards on their way to Durham or the Tyne. In these establishments the men are beered and the horses are watered and sent on their way.

Scattered among the houses are shops (some no more than a narrow front room), which cater for the needs of the heaving populace here (some say up to three thousand). Apart from the occasional clerks or the customs men and, of course, the doctors, the working population in the village, though sometimes ruddy-faced and often sturdy, is characteristically of the lowest and most needy sort.

Coming from Lordship Park in Stoke Newington, where we have the park and the gardens to sift the sounds of the trains on their way to the city of London, I will come to find this village to be full of noise: the jingle of harnesses, the clatter of hoofs on cobbles, the shrieks and shouts of children at play, and the hum of the voices of inhabitants who lean against their doors and reflect in their lively fashion on the affairs and the scandals of this strange village. Nothing escapes their eyes and, at times – as I come to know only too well – they are mistresses and masters of fantastic invention.

Still, I like the village from the first. The grass is green and the air is good, and the people, if Mrs Cotton is anything to go by, seem quite kindly although amazingly forthright. As my first step on the road to freedom, West Auckland will do very well.

Three

Western House, sitting at the east end of the green opposite the post office, is rather larger than its neighbours. A tall, thin woman of about thirty stands at the open door, directing the young man in a baize apron, who overtook us on his return journey, as he unloads my luggage from the trap. She smiles warmly at Uncle William and bobs the faintest of curtsies towards me.

He turns to smile easily at me. 'This is Mrs Grey, Victoria, who is our irreplaceable housekeeper. And you saw Jonty on the road. What he doesn't know about horses is not worth knowing.'

Mrs Grey looks up at Uncle William. 'Jonty said you went to the station straight from your call on Mr Vart, Doctor. Mrs Kilburn and Miss Emily are not yet back from the river with the little ones. Didn't we make them a fine picnic, sir?' Her voice has an Irish intonation, quite common in the serving classes. 'They've took young Lizzie with them to help. Aren't I managing on my own here?'

He hands her his hat and cane and turns to me. 'I'm afraid my wife is determined to make fishermen of my children, Victoria. Even Eric, who's not yet five years old.'

Then I have another fit of dizziness and am compelled to lean hard against the wall by the door. Uncle William takes my arm and we squeeze by my own piled boxes, and on past two doors with 'Surgery' and 'Dispensary' etched in gold on their glass panels. Shadowy figures move about behind the glass and the buzz of voices comes from the room.

My uncle calls over his shoulder, 'I fear Miss Kilburn is exhausted

18

from her journey, Mrs Grey. A refreshing cup of tea, I think? In the drawing room.' I look despairingly up the steep stairs and he puts his arm round my waist and half-carries me up.

The steps up to the first-floor drawing room seem endless, as does the wait for the promised tea. In the end my uncle takes out his watch, peers at it and excuses himself, remarking that I may have seen the number of people waiting in the surgery. 'Can't leave Chalmers to cope alone. He's a good fellow but a body can only do so much.'

Thankful that he has gone, I close my eyes. When Mrs Grey finally arrives with the tray I am too exhausted even to tackle the tea and before long she is leading me up another staircase into a large front bedroom. She stands a moment in the doorway, surveying its gleaming surfaces and flickering fire.

'Doctor says you were to have the best spare room.' Her tone suggests she can't think why. 'Didn't I have young Lizzie give it a special clean?'

'Thank you,' I say faintly, and sit down very hard on the high plumped-up bed.

'I've turned down the bed, miss, and there's warm water in the jug. Supper'll be at six. Mrs Kilburn and the little'ns'll be back long before then.' She pauses. 'You'll find the food at Western House is very fine, miss. Mrs Kilburn is very particular about that. Will there be anything else, miss?' Her tone is mild enough but her eyes are watchful.

I haul myself to my feet. 'I travelled from Darlington with a woman from this village,' I say. 'A Mrs Cotton?' That strange, attractive woman is still on my mind.

She frowns. 'You want naught to do with that one, miss. Some folks here like her, true enough, but the woman can be a nuisance. Never off the poor doctor's doorstep. Didn't she have a husband that died and now the "lodger", as she calls him – he's poorly. And if it's not him, it's those children, or it's some question about the people she nurses for the parish. Any excuse. Or isn't she bothering the poor assistant relieving officer? Notes for the Guardians. Advice. Getting on to Dr Chalmers for some medicine or other.'

'She told me she is a nurse, Mrs Grey,' I venture. 'I think she might be concerned about all those things.'

'So *she'd* say. Like *I* say, miss, I can't think what someone like you'd want to do with someone like her.'

19

I am relieved when the door shuts behind her. Her faint distaste for Mrs Cotton fills the room like sour air. I shrug myself out of my jacket and go across to open the window. However, the sash is already pulled up, the damp February breeze lifting the lace. One of my Uncle William's idiosyncrasies is his obsession with fresh air. My father has told me that William has written about it in learned journals: the curative properties of fresh air. Of course, he is not alone in his beliefs. Fresh air clinics are springing up everywhere these days.

With the woman Mrs Cotton on my mind I lean out of the open window, looking past the tipsy bulk of the post office to the row of houses on the other side of the broad green. How much nicer all this is than the continuous new building and dusty bustle of Stoke Newington. I savour the freshness of it all, even in this fading light, and take a second to gloat on my luck at being here, away from that stifling house on Lordship Park. I peer across at a grocer's shop on the opposite corner of the green. Brooms lean up against the impressive plate-glass window. A rack of clothes flutters in the breeze. A barrel of potatoes stands stiff sentinel beside the door.

Then my eye catches the unmistakable upright figure of Marian Cotton walking into the shop. The boy Charlie is not with her but in her arms she carries a younger child, a baby in long petticoats. I feel a small thrill go through me at seeing her again. I recall her soft voice, her concern for me on the train. I smile to myself at the thought of her hand on my knee and the lavender-almond smell of her. She is certainly a very remarkable woman.

I turn to my right and observe the sweep of the houses that line and encircle the green. I wonder where, in which of these houses, Mrs Cotton actually lives. That woman has so caught my fancy in such a short time. How I revelled in her attention on the train, her caring demeanour at the station! I will most definitely find out where she lives, from my uncle or Mrs Grey. And I will seek her out. I can't think why I am sure of this, but I am.

Four

At six o'clock, as I make my way down to the dining room in response to a gong, my ears are assailed by the joyous din of children's voices in the back regions of the house. My uncle sits alone at the stout dining table, and Mrs Grey is leaning casually against the wall next to the sideboard, waiting to serve.

He stands up as I enter. 'Victoria! My dear wife says we must start without her while she settles the brood. She'll be down anon; declares she's agog to meet you.'

Mrs Grey stands upright and presents the dishes for us to serve ourselves before she slips from the room. The food is plain enough: boiled ham and potatoes and a mess of vegetables. But the ham is succulent, aromatic, the potatoes are buttery and cut through with strands of parsley, and the carrots and turnips are beaten together as smooth as cream. And yet, despite the fact that I'm so hungry after my day's exertions, the sheer quantity of this repast defeats me.

My uncle, having cleared his own plate, goes to the sideboard and pours three generous measures of port into waiting glasses. He places one by his wife's plate, then, ignoring my protests, he places one beside my plate, which is still half full of pushed-around food. He sits down again and nods at my glass.

'Some fresh air and a glass of port each day will put roses in those waxy cheeks of yours. Perhaps it will mend your appetite. From what my dear cousin says, you tend to be a bit of a lay-a-bed.'

My cheeks grow hot and I take a sip of the wine to dull my anger. 'Lay-a-bed! That was where they wanted me, my mother and Lottie.

Out of the way, lying down somewhere where I may not make a show of myself.' I push my half-empty plate further on to the table. 'Mrs Grey is very generous in her portions.'

'My dear wife will have ordered it.' He takes a cigar from a box on the table. 'Do you mind, dear girl? This is my relaxation. A relief from a hard day and a preparation for further labours.'

I shake my head. Country ways are so informal. My father always retires to his study to smoke. I rather enjoy the way that Uncle William clips the cigar and lights it with a frowning concentration. He draws on it and exhales in a gasp of satisfaction. I have never before thought of smoking but now I can see that it must be very relaxing. One day I should try it for myself. Lottie whispered to me once that her friend Virginia Lockside smoked cigars in the privacy of her bedroom. I wouldn't be surprised if Miss Frances Power Cobbe smokes a cheroot in the privacy of her study as she writes her books.

My uncle stares hard at the glowing tip of his cigar. 'Mrs Grey is used to doling out generous portions of food. My wife insists on it. I think this comes from her early days when her own family had little money for the table.'

Then his face breaks into a wide gap-toothed smile as his wife bustles into the room. He stands up to greet her. She's much smaller than he is, dark in complexion, with lively eyes that seem too large for her face. She is slender and girlish but obviously carrying within her the child which will, I think, be her fifth. According to my mother she is just twenty-nine years old. I have to say she looks even younger than that.

I stand up to receive her warm embrace. 'At last! Dear Victoria,' she says, kissing me first on one cheek then the other. I can smell milk on her and the sickly sweet smell of some kind of ointment. 'How wonderful to welcome you. Best to get the *babes* stowed first, don't you think?' She turns to her husband. 'Naughty John fell on his nose in his scramble to get up first from the beck and I had to find salve for him. Lizzie's up there giving them their bedtime milk, although dear Emily has vanished into the corner with her nose in a book as usual.' She turns back to me. 'I said perhaps you'd go up after supper to meet them, Victoria.'

Not waiting for an answer, she moves across to the sideboard and begins to serve herself. 'Now this ham should be good, best shank from Mr Cruddace. Such a wonderful man . . .' Her accent is different from my uncle's: less clipped and schooled. Her humble origins are very clear in her voice, as they are shown in her open reference to food, which my mother would consider vulgar.

In the months to come, I will learn that my aunt has a way of filling a room with sound and laughter, much of it her own, which makes all there feel better about themselves. In her company one is excused the need to perform and may sit back and enjoy the fun. I will also come to know how passionately she loves my uncle: he is the sun and the moon in her life and she lets him know it, in private and in public, at the least opportunity (another thing my mother would consider vulgar). It is clear that the feeling between these two is mutual although Uncle William is not as expressive as she is. Now I understand how, with this strength of feeling between them, they met each other when she was only sixteen, and ploughed through all the difficulties of difference in wealth and class to stay together.

Now she's telling me, in detail, just how one gets the ham to such succulence and the importance of herbs in the vegetables. My mother would be horrified at such talk at the dinner table. I am charmed and agree most willingly to come to her kitchen tomorrow so that she can show me just how to get the potatoes right.

'I am a good teacher,' she says, spooning potato into her mouth while still speaking, 'and Rebecca Grey, though a bit stiff and unwilling at first, is a good pupil.'

I am sure Mrs Grey could not, in the end, resist.

I take another sip of my port. 'I'm afraid I will make a slow pupil, Auntie. I'm not in the least familiar with any kitchen. I can't cook at all.'

'No such thing as *can't*,' she says, spearing the last bit of ham. 'That's what I always say.'

We are interrupted by a crash and a scream upstairs, and she leaps to her feet and is gone, clashing the door behind her.

'So that, my dear, is your Auntie Mary,' says my uncle, dabbing his moustache with his napkin. He looks at me blandly and we both burst into laughter. When this subsides I feel easy enough with him to ask again about Mrs Cotton.

He draws on his cigar and the aromatic smoke drifts through his teeth as he answers. 'She has been in this village less than a year but one might say she has indeed made her mark.'

I reflect on the fact that she has made her mark on me in the space of an hour. I thrust my bad foot under the table to ease it a little. It has been a hard day. 'And what kind of mark is that, Uncle?'

'Well, I have to say she's somewhat different from the women of her class in these parts. She has a little education. She can read and write, for one thing, although her spelling is somewhat unique. She has a curiosity about things.'

'Your Mrs Grey says she's never off your doorstep.'

'Mrs Grey is indiscreet. Although one shouldn't be surprised at that. This village sails on a sea of indiscretion. Don't take me wrong, there are some fine people – hardworking and decent. But sometimes I get the feeling that distrust and blame are sports here; gossip an entertainment. It must be something in the air. One must be careful not to indulge oneself. It can be very seductive.'

I've never in my life heard such open talk. My blood is racing. I take a gulp of my port. 'And *is* she never off your doorstep, Uncle?'

His shoulders move in a shrug under his broadcloth coat. 'This woman deals with the sick in their own homes. Her husband, Frederick, died quite painfully last September. She has a sick lodger. And Fred Cotton's son, Freddie, is not well. And then you will have seen for yourself how frail is the child Charlie, who was on the train with her. A lot of sickness in one house and, in that, much need for a doctor. In that, of course, the Cottons are not unlike other families here. Typhoid – enteric fever – it flies from door to door. And now there is smallpox. It's impossible to get anyone to tend these people. Their own families flee. Mr Riley, the relieving officer, asserted when Mrs Cotton arrived she was heaven-sent. He uses her a good deal.'

'Mr Riley?'

'He has the grocer's shop across the green from here. On the corner. Is a farmer and merchant of sorts. An upstanding man. He also works for the Board of Guardians as assistant relieving officer apportioning relief to the poor. The poor call him assistant overseer. This, of course, makes him a person of standing here in this village. He is the gatekeeper to survival for some poor folk.'

'I just saw Mrs Cotton go into that shop. I was watching from my bedroom window.'

He throws his head back, the cigar smoke leaking from his mouth. 'Well, no doubt Mrs Grey will say she is never off *his* doorstep either!

As I told you, my dear, distrust and blame are sports here. And never more so than when the object is an outsider.'

Of course this makes me think of myself. I am truly an outsider here. I take a gulp of port from my crystal glass. 'And does Mrs Cotton live close by? In one of the houses on the green?'

He raises his eyebrows at my persistence.

'It's just . . . well . . . she is a strange woman. But interesting.' I am defensive.

He laughs, belches quietly, excuses himself then says, 'It's true that the woman has a certain fascination. Not just for you, my dear. She lives on Johnson Terrace, the road down past Riley's shop that leads to the Darlington Road. She has been asserting to me for some time that that house is far too dirty and inconvenient and is looking for a house on the green, out in the open. I have to tell you, my dear, that she'll get it. Mrs Cotton usually gets what she wants.'

My face is suddenly far too hot and I stand up, somewhat unsteadily. 'I think perhaps I should retire, Uncle. I think the journey has taken something of a toll.'

He stands up, folds his napkin neatly and places it on the table. 'How good, though, to see some roses in your cheeks, Victoria. I should go too. I have work to do in my dispensary – some preparations to make up. No rest for the wicked.'

I fight back the desire to yawn, knowing perfectly well that the burn in my rosy cheeks is caused more by the port than surging health. My peculiar state makes me forward. 'I would really like to learn more about that, Uncle – how you make your medicines, what you do as a doctor.'

He holds open the door for me. 'Perhaps I could show you how to mix some of the easier preparations,' he says thoughtfully. 'A little activity will be efficacious in your recovery from this London malaise your father describes. Just as the devil makes use of idle hands, germs tend to rampage through an idle body.'

This is so true of me that I want to cry. Tears climb from my reddened cheeks into my eyes. As I make my way back up two flights of stairs in tears, I think of the hours I've spent lying too still in shaded rooms. Then my heart gives a leap and I blink back my tears. No more of that. Perhaps this quaint village with its moorland and its wide greens, its little houses and its black circlet of pits will turn out to be very good for my health. Tomorrow, perhaps, I'll take a walk out of the village past the corner shop and call upon Mrs Cotton. After all, I think muzzily, we are both outsiders.

On the top floor I'm waylaid by the young maid, Lizzie, who tells me I'm to go and greet the children. In the nursery they sit up neatly in bed, one in each corner of the long room.

Auntie Mary, storybook in hand, leaps to her feet. 'Ah, here we are! Victoria! This is my beautiful clever Emily, who's twelve going on twenty; my serious John William, who's seven; my dizzy little Maggie, who's six; and my baby Eric, who's only four. Have you ever seen such fine children, Victoria?'

We all shake hands gravely. I feel drawn to Emily, who, with her sandy hair and pale face, is the image of her father. I hang on to her hand a little longer than the others.

Auntie Mary looks on, smiling. 'Such fun, children. Victoria is to stay with us right till the autumn.' They all nod and, as is usual, I think, leave Auntie Mary to do the talking. 'I was just saying, Victoria, how nice it would be if you would read a story for them . . .'

I look round wildly for escape. Then Emily says quietly, 'I think cousin Victoria looks far too tired to read to us, Mama.' Here and now, in my muzzy state, I would like to hug this child, to kiss her on the top of that little braided head.

Auntie Mary examines me closely. 'How observant you are, Emily. As always, the voice of common sense. Away, Victoria, away to your sleep! Tomorrow, after all, is another day.'

Five

Before Thomas Riley took off his jacket and put on his apron he glanced at himself in the long mirror in the back hall behind the shop. Tall, rosy-faced, with a full head of hair, clean-shaven except for the obligatory moustache: every inch a merchant, benefactor, relieving officer, an elder at the chapel, a governor of the school; a leader in this admittedly small and impoverished parish. Thomas was quite a modest man. Very occasionally he wondered how someone like himself had managed to achieve such social heights. After all, he'd been an ordinary enough lad until an accident at the pit drove him above ground to take up farm work. Once there, he'd been prudent enough, eventually, to buy a patch of land to farm for himself. After that he worked in shops and, still prudent, he bought a shop and set up in business himself. So here he was: a respectable man, a tradesman who talked on equal terms with other tradesmen and businessmen and was patronised in the best way by the gentry. Now and then he reflected that if he'd tried to rise to such heights while still at the pit he'd soon have hit his head on the low stone ceiling.

In the early years of his worldly success he used to think the Good Lord would forgive him a certain amount of pride. But the Good Lord was not so kind. It was only ten years since his secure world had been cracked to pieces by the savage, self-inflicted death of his son Teddy. When Teddy 'did that thing' to himself, any vestige of pride had been scrubbed clean from Thomas's soul. Thomas could never even bring himself to use the true words out loud. *Killed himself.* Wasn't 'kill' too strong a word for what poor Teddy did? Too emphatic, too deliberate a word. How many sleepless nights had Thomas revisited the image of his son staggering down these very stairs, blood spilling over the fingers that clutched his throat? How many times had he pressed his fists to his ears to shut out the echo of his daughter's screams that had so penetrated the thick stone walls of the house and rolled down the length of the green?

These days, in Thomas Riley's life there was no room for pride: just work and service, and his duty as a significant person in this village.

He sighed as he shrugged off his coat and shook it out. He removed the snowdrops from the buttonhole and a stray fair curl from his collar before he hung it up. Then he took down his apron and tied it neatly round his waist.

Work to be done. The tray of tinned beef stacked in the back shop had to be ticked off in the delivery book. And there was the basket to be put up for the Manor House and another delivery for the Edens at St Helen's Hall. Thomas took personal pride in the wrapping and packing of these important orders: he always made sure they were delivered exactly as requested.

He squared his shoulders, took a deep breath and prepared for the encounter with his wife, Margaret. He could hear the click and bustle of her as she moved around the front shop. Sharing the same bed, the same house with Margaret had not been easy since 'that thing' happened to Teddy. The boy had been her beloved child and her *bête noire* rolled into one. His charm was counterbalanced with sometimes ugly perversity, and it was some little spat with his mother that led him, defiantly, to take up the razor that day.

Thomas knew from that last, surprised look on Teddy's face as he stumbled down the stairs that it had indeed been an accident; that the boy had not intended to *kill* himself, and was as shocked as were they all at what he had done. Thomas tried to say this to Margaret but this was no comfort to her. She blamed herself for the tragedy and always asserted that Thomas also blamed her, no matter what his protestations.

Sometimes in his heart Thomas thought she might just be right.

Thomas was just starting to fill the Manor basket, ticking off each item, when Margaret appeared at the curtain that separated the front shop from the back room. Her face, once so dark and pretty, was somewhat bloated now. Deep lines had cut their way into her broad brow.

'It's that Mrs Cotton, Tommy,' she said. 'Says she *needs* to talk to you.' Her voice was bleak, drained of any feeling. But she could not disguise from him just how much she disliked the Cotton woman. This was despite the fact that Mrs Cotton had never been anything less than civil to her. Excessively so, as far as he could see. Perhaps Margaret saw it as a criticism, this politeness without subservience.

Thomas wiped his hands on a convenient towel. 'I'll just finish this, Marg. Tell her to sit a minute.'

When he came out to the front shop Margaret was dealing with another customer. Mrs Cotton was sitting on a seat by the door, her baby on her lap. 'Now then, Mrs Cotton. What can I do for you?' He had to admit to a soft spot for this woman who'd brought a little life to the quiet village, who looked at you with a direct gaze and had an open laugh. But he was not blind to the fact that these very qualities were the cause of annoyance to some of the women who gathered at his counter. He had mentioned it more than once to Dr Kilburn, adding most recently, 'You don't work in shops without finding out how women think, Doctor.'

Thomas surveyed the child on Mrs Cotton's knee. Not for the first time he noted how like Marian this child was. The same dark hair and high forehead, the same dark blue eyes. He too would grow up blessed by fine looks.

She stood up respectfully, pulling the baby's legs round her so he was supported by her jutting hipbone. 'Now, Mr Riley.'

'What is it today, Mrs Cotton?'

'I called on old Mr Lanister, bottom of Johnson Terrace, and he's right over the pox. You'd have thought him a gonner at one time. But he's up and about. I thought you'd need to know that, so I came to say.'

'Some good nursing you did there, Marian.' His wife and her customer looked up at his use of Mrs Cotton's Christian name. 'I'll put it in my report to the Board.' He felt suddenly that he was looming over her. He sagged his knees to lose an inch or two in height, so their eyes were on a level. She was gazing at him with that bright-eyed deep look of hers, a dimple hovering to the left of her full mouth. He decided to have a bit of fun. 'And how is Mr Quick-Manning?' His tone was measured but he could feel behind him the sharp attention of the women at the other end of the counter. One spectacular thread of gossip in the village at present concerned the 'goings-on' between Marian Cotton and the excise officer whom she'd just nursed through smallpox.

Marian didn't blink. 'Feller's come through well, Mr Riley. Back working at the brewery now. I did tell him he must do light work, not strain himself. I left him some of my ointment for his face, like. That's still a bit of a mess. He could've paid Dr Kilburn for that ointment of his, but he wanted mine. Says it does more good.' She ignored another splutter and hum of talk behind them. 'I was wondering, sir, if you'd any more work to put my way? My lodger's off sick and I've both to take care of him and to support him. And I've these bairns to feed. I wouldn't care, but two of them are Fred Cotton's – rest his soul. They're not mine. I've only known them a year.' She jiggled the child on her hip. 'This one here, though, Robbie, he's my own. The only one.'

Thomas shook his head. 'As you know, Marian – Mrs Cotton – there's been plenty sickness round here. Dr Kilburn and his man, Chalmers, have been run off their feet. But it seems like just now we're in a bit of a lull. Unless you want to travel up to Bishop Auckland to do some work? I could put a word in.' Bishop Auckland, the large market town nearby, was a five-minute train ride away.

She shook her head. 'Train fare'd swallow up any money I made. And there's my lodger, Mr Nattrass, to look after. He's still abed, can hardly lift his head. Might not even make it.' She switched the child to the other hip. 'Thank you for the thought, though, sir. So if you've nothing for me in terms of work maybe you could just let us have a couple of mousetraps, sir. Mice! Hate them, I do. Bring filth and germs right there in your home. Any amount of scrubbing doesn't get rid of them germs.'

He reached the traps down from their high shelf, wrapped them, and took her pennies. He might have let her have the mousetraps free but for the watching women at the other end of the counter.

As she went out the doorbell pinged behind her, and Thomas made his way quickly back through the curtain.

He'd just finished the St Helen's Hall basket when Margaret came through the curtain. She stood watching him. 'I'm surprised you encourage her,' she said. 'A woman like that.' Her lips, once so full and innocent, curled down now in a thin line.

'A woman like what?' he said wearily.

She shrugged. 'You know, but you're as soft as the other men. And women. Plenty have time for her, but they'll learn. You're soft on her, admit it.'

30

'You know I shut down her "tick" . . . ' At Margaret's urging he had stopped Marian Cotton's credit when her debt reached twenty-nine pounds twelve and seven pence – an enormous sum. One of his services in the village was to extend credit when men were laid off or between jobs. But with Marian, whose husband had died and whose lodger was off sick, the debt had got dangerously high. It was no service to any villager to give them credit that they would never pay.

'You *gave* her some arrowroot, remember! Didn't charge her a penny. I checked in the book.'

'She had a sick man and a child at home. Anyway, it was the very last of that box from the old chemist's stock I bought for nowt.'

She charged on. 'You. The doctors. The excise man. They're all taken with her bold looks and her simpering. Everyone knows it.'

Thomas shrugged and tucked a snow-white cloth all around the goods in the grocery basket. 'Plenty folks get on with her. "Everyone" must be those gossiping women that gather round your counter, Marg. They should have more to do with their time.' He turned away from her and shouted for his son Pat to come and get on with the deliveries.

Margaret flushed, bestowed on him a look of pure malice and moved back through the curtain.

Having given Pat his instructions Thomas thought perhaps he'd take a walk down the village to see old Mr Lanister. He'd need to put in a report on him for the Board: a home visit would be in order. As assistant relieving officer he knew home visits were seen as good practice. It would be convenient. He needed some fresh air. The atmosphere in the house and shop was just too stifling.

He put on his coat and tucked the snowdrops once more into his buttonhole. Then he picked up his hat and, without calling for Margaret to tell her of his intentions, he left the house, striding briskly.

Across the green he could see the light on in Dr Kilburn's dispensary. Mixing up his pills and potions, no doubt. The man worked too hard. That assistant of his was rarely there, and there was more than two men's work here, with so much sickness about the place.

As Thomas strolled on down the village, thoughts of his son surged back into his mind. Teddy had always been such an attractive child, full of that kind of laughter and charm that brought indulgence in its wake. Beside him young Patrick was stodgy, workaday. In those early years, as Teddy grew up, the shop began to do well and the farm flourished.

There'd been no need to deprive the boys or their sister of anything. Margaret scolded him for spoiling the children but he insisted that he was happy to give his children what he'd never had himself.

As he grew, Teddy showed himself to be clever and quick, so they sent him to the old grammar school in Bishop Auckland and he'd flourished there, even though his high spirits earned him a lot of beatings. But his spirits were not always high. The boy had his gloomy, lethargic moments, but they were more than paid for by the moments of delight: his music and singing; his fast-paced excitement at being alive. Thomas himself was indulgent regarding all this, but Teddy's quick reversals of mood unnerved Margaret and she began to focus her motherly feelings on young Patrick and Teddy's sister, Jane, who was a much quieter and more amenable soul. Rather too late, Margaret began to try to exert hard discipline on Teddy to bring him into line. She was eternally frustrated that the boy, once her golden child, perpetually defied her and had latterly begun to frighten her.

Teddy had been defying his mother on the morning of the accident. That Sunday, against her wishes, he'd just ordered a fine new suit from Geoffrey White, the village tailor. And then, instead of coming down for his dinner as instructed, he stayed up there in his room playing wild music-hall tunes on his accordion, a Christmas present from his father.

His mother called upstairs for him twice. Then she sent Jane up to tell him to get down for his dinner. Then there was that awful silence. Then the house was filled with the sound of young Jane screaming. Then there was Teddy staggering down the stairs, clutching his neck like a bit player in some cheap melodrama at the Eden Theatre. At first Thomas had thought it was a typical Teddy-joke. But it was no joke. Never a joke.

After that day nothing was ever the same.

Thomas dragged his mind back to the present. The evening was damp and quite cold, but the village was busy. The public houses across the green and the Eden Arms down at the bottom had a steady stream of customers. A trickle of miners, just off shift by the colour of their skin, were making their way down the village in twos and threes, vanishing into their narrow houses and entries as though peeling off in some kind of dance. It was starting to rain: needle-points of that February rain that brought cold more than damp to a man's bones. Thomas jammed his hat further down on his forehead and quickened his pace.

Mr Lanister, as Marian Cotton had said, was out of bed, sitting beside a bright fire in his cluttered room, which smelled of urine, drying wool and burned food. He was very cheerful. 'Never thought I'd see the light of day again, Mr Riley. There's me dreaming of my young days as a bairn and seeing my old grandma open her arms for me from the centre of a bright light. But that woman brought us back here to the land of the living. Slow at first, but very steady. That Mrs Cotton! She's got her buttons fixed on tight. Other folks kept right away – even that doctor, who's not a bad feller, like. Even he doesn't cross the doorstep, though he peers in. Me own daughter has kept away, fear of catching it. But not *her*. Not Mrs Cotton. Fearless. Those poultices of hers took care of the sores. And once yer gettin' better those tonics of hers kind of bring yer round, I'm tellen yer. How she never caught the thing herself I don't know. She's a wonder of a woman.'

Thomas entered three neat sentences on the new page and put away his notebook. 'I believe she suffered from it once. She told me that she had it as a child. And once you've had it you can't get it again.' That, of course, was the reason she was such a useful nurse. Others would go nowhere near these cases. Cursed pox.

'Wouldn't'a told she'd had this. She's a fine-looking woman. Skin like a young'n.'

'So she has,' murmured Thomas. He looked around. 'Mebbe you could do with this place cleaning, Mr Lanister.' He wrinkled his nose. 'Fumigating.' He wouldn't get Mrs Cotton to do that. She didn't clean. It was a sore point with Margaret that Mrs Dodds, the woman's next-door neighbour, cleaned that house of Mrs Cotton's. Marian even put her washing out to other women. According to Margaret it was no wonder she was always in debt.

Thomas opened his notebook again and wrote a further note. 'I'll get a woman round to make a start and send a note to your sister. In my view the Parish has made enough of a contribution to your wellbeing, Mr Lanister. That sister of yours needs do her bit.'

'And grateful I am to you, sir. I praise the Parish in me prayers every night, Mr Riley.'

It was a relief to get out into the clearer evening air. Duty done, Thomas's step lightened.

He was halfway down the village when a voice behind him said, 'So, Mr Riley, d'you find the old man well?' He turned quickly to see

Marian Cotton close behind him. 'I've seen that you called on him there. Old Mr Lanister?'

'He's remarkably well. He speaks highly of your nursing.'

She shrugged her shoulders. 'As he might. I brought him back from the brink, the very brink.'

'So he said.' Thomas made to move on.

She put a hand on his arm and a lit spark charged through him. 'I wondered if you'd help me, sir?'

He glanced round and took a step back, extricating himself from her touch. 'What is it, Marian? About the nursing? I told you I'd nothing to offer. Not just now.'

'Naw. It's about a house. I'm sick of that house down Johnson Terrace. Nothing but a dog kennel. I noticed that there's this house on the green empty. That tall house, right next the Rose and Crown. They say you have the say-so on the tenant.'

'That's right.' He had the say-so on many things in this village.

'What say you put in a word for me? There's room for the children, and even poor Nattrass at a pinch. It's more out in the open than that hole I live in at Johnson Terrace. That one faces the wrong way. Looks out over stagnant water. No wonder the little'ns are ailing, never mind poor Nattrass.'

He'd helped less needy cases than this. He assured himself it was not favouritism. 'I'll see what I can do.' He'd have to face Margaret's wrath over this, but he was used to that. Water off a duck's back.

'Why, thank you, Mr Riley.' Marian Cotton swept him a deep curtsy. 'I'm in your debt, and I won't forget it.'

Then with a rustle of skirts she'd swept past him, leaving in her wake the warm scent of nutmeg and lavender. Thomas watched her stride briskly, almost mannishly down the green before he carried on his way. There was surely something about the woman. She made you feel brisker, better for meeting her. No wonder she was so good with patients. When he got back to the shop he was whistling.

Margaret, who was tugging at the potato barrel in an effort to roll it inside, looked at him. 'There's no moving this barrel,' she said, her mouth very thin.

He whipped off his coat, handed it to her and rolled up his sleeves. 'Leave it to me, old girl,' he said. 'This is man's work.'

Putting the coat under one arm, Margaret Riley used the other hand to pick up the brushes that were leaning against the rail Thomas had nailed up to protect his precious plate glass. She wondered what had got into him today. He was usually so glum and serious you couldn't get a smile out of him these days. And here he was, whistling. A turn-up for the books to be sure.

Six

My uncle and I are just sitting at breakfast the next day when a prim-faced Mrs Grey announces that Mrs Cotton is here at the house with *something* for Miss Kilburn. 'The woman come round the front, but I sent her round the back and she's in the back lobby by the surgery.' Then she marches to the door and bangs it behind her.

My uncle is pouring himself a second cup of coffee from the battered pewter pot. He smiles slightly and says he sometimes thinks perhaps he should do something about Mrs Cotton's curious brand of importunity, but he's used to her behaviour and, anyway, her heart is in the right place. 'You go down and see what sweetmeat Mrs Cotton has for you. She's forever bringing peculiar gifts. That is her way.'

I hesitate a moment, wary of my uncle's indulgent tone, which reminds me too much of the way Lottie and Mama speak to me: as if I am eight years old and very slightly deaf.

Uncle William takes a sip of his coffee. 'Of course, if you don't wish to see her I'm sure Mrs Grey would be delighted to send her away.'

This makes me stand up very quickly. 'No. I'll see her.' I am dying to meet her again, if only to ascertain if that great impact she had on me yesterday was just some illusion of exhaustion on my part, some strange symptom of travel sickness.

Mrs Cotton is leaning against a dusty glass cabinet lined with empty pottery jars and glass containers. She stands away from it and smiles broadly at me. It is a genuine smile of stunning beauty.

I feel a lift, a warmth inside me. Now I know yesterday was no illusion. 'Good morning, Mrs Cotton.' I smile my welcome.

36

'Oh, go on, honey. My name's Marian and you should use it. I never liked that name Cotton, which isn't me own anyway, me never being married to Fred Cotton proper. To be honest, if the law were served I'm still tangled up with a fellow called Robinson, though I haven't seen him in years. Now I'm telling you, child, there *was* a man, that James Robinson. You just need look at him to love him.'

I almost flinch at this confidence, then I relax. It occurs to me that this strange warmth I feel for this woman will permit almost anything. 'Mrs Grey says you have something for me,' I say. 'My uncle tells me you are very generous with your gifts.'

'I suppose I am, but only with them I care for,' she says easily. 'I tell you what, honey, I took one look at you and knew I had just the thing for that cheek of yours. No offence, but it's a right mess.'

I put up my hand and finger the familiar nasty rough patch. 'I don't think you should say things like that . . . er . . . Marian. It could hurt a person's feelings.'

'Like I say, honey, I mean no offence. But shouldn't I mention it if I think I can do summat about it? If I can help you? Do you not wish for health?'

'Well, if you think you can . . .' I can hear murmurs from further in the house and suddenly this is all too intimate. I push open the nearest door, which leads into my uncle's study. 'Let's go in here. It's quieter.'

It is a narrow room, crowded with furniture, piles of books and the laid-out instruments and implements of his trade. The morning light streams through the window and glitters on a tough-looking steel-toothed saw.

'Won't you sit down, Marian?' I say.

Marian sits down and looks around, and I can tell that her stillness does not quite disguise a certain excitement. 'That uncle of yours works hard without appreciation for the benighted folk around here,' she says.

I nod vigorously. 'I'm very proud of him.'

'Is he really your true uncle? Or is it a thing your kind of people say?'

I can't think what she means. 'Well, he's my father's cousin but I call him uncle.' I look into those bright eyes and try to bring the talk to more immediate matters. 'What was this thing, Marian? The thing you wanted to tell me about?'

Marian lifts her basket on to the desk and carefully raises the embroidered cloth covering. She takes out a jam-jar filled with a grey paste. 'Daub that mark on your face with this six nights in seven. Make a nice thick, even spread. Don't forget to cover your face with a clean cotton rag before you lay down. And a towel on the pillow lest you scare the life out of that witch of a housekeeper the doctor puts up with.' She smiles slightly. Her teeth are small and very even.

I stare at the jar. The mixture looks disgusting. 'It's very kind of you, Marian, but I can't think that this will do me any good. Some very great doctors have treated my poor old face to no avail.'

She laughs. 'Doctors don't know everything, honey. Not by a fine chalk. This is ancient healing that's come down through time. All things off the hedgerow.' She counts them off with her fingers: powdered roots of bryony and mallow of the marsh, mashed garlic, blackberry wine suspension. 'You do what I say, honey, on six nights without fail, then leave off one night. Do it regular and you watch. That thing on your cheek will fade like steam on a windy day.

'Now . . .' She takes a bottle out of the basket and places it beside the jar. It is half full of a dark liquid. 'As well as the poultice you should take a teaspoon of this stuff in a cup of water when you get up. It'll brace you up, give you some fizz for the day. You'll need to give it a shake.' She shakes the bottle so the sediment rises and suffuses the liquid. 'Here you have a whole load of things: galwort, meadow pimpernel, marsh marigold, barberry, infused in the same blackberry wine. Take it once a day and it'll raise your spirits and make your courses less of a curse. You have trouble with them, I think.'

I have to blink at her prescience. 'How d'you know about that?'

'It shows in your face. It all shows in your face.' She laughs then, a gay appealing sound in my ears. 'Drink it in the morning, honey. That's after you've washed that clart off your face, like. You'd look a fine mess walking down to breakfast clarted up like that.'

I can imagine Mrs Grey's face.

'Now, honey, you promise me you'll take the stuff. It's all natural stuff but it does wonders for a person's skin and spirit both.'

I shake my head a little. I don't want to give up without a fight. 'I don't know . . .'

'Go on! Could you be much worse? You'd be a lovely lass without that mark on your cheek like a smear of white moss. Look at my own skin.' She holds her face to the light from the window. It is smooth and clear, and to my astonishment I have to fight back the desire to stroke it. It is a lover-like feeling entirely strange to me.

Marian nods. 'I started using all this stuff after I got the pox myself, when I was down in Bristol. This old woman down there showed us how to make it.' Her face darkens for a second. 'Oh, honey, at first it was marvellous down there. I thought I was set fair. Then I had such a bad time! I lost this bairn when I was laid low unto death myself. And that poor little one was the first of a few. Like I wasn't meant to keep them. No justice in this life.' Then she shrugs and strokes a hand down her cheek. 'See my skin? Did you ever see clearer? I use it six days in every month. Clean as a whistle and that's how you'll be. Mark my words. Clean as a whistle, smooth as a baby's bum. You believe me, honey.'

I fiddle with the bottle and the jar, lining them up on the bench. For me this honesty and directness that Marian puts forth is almost a physical thing, like the light streaming through the window or the snowdrops in the jar on my uncle's desk. I do believe Marian and feel I always will.

As I show her out and watch her walk away from the house until she is out of sight, the strange thought occurs to me that this must be what it is like to fall in love. Of course it can't really be that, as she is a woman and so very different from me and my kind.

Seven

I've had three days of settling in now in this sunny household, talking with my uncle, getting to know my lively aunt and making friends with twelve-year-old Emily. These days in their company have bound me into their family and I feel I have never been happier. My days here are lively and busy, and the memory of the chaise longue in the curtained room becomes distant and unreal. I am sustained in high mood by these dear people, this bright village, and perhaps the underlying presence of Marian Cotton, represented by her paste and her potion on my dressing table. The only element of shade in my life is Mrs Grey, who is rather glum around me and laughs very little, unlike almost everyone else in this merry household.

On my fourth morning here Mrs Grey knocks on my door to tell me sourly that I'm to come down again to the surgery where '*that* Mrs Cotton' awaits me yet again. I smile to see Marian sitting on a chair outside the narrow waiting room. She sits tranquilly, her basket on her knee, the pale, patient Charlie at her side. She smiles widely when she sees me, a dimple emerging on her cheek. This makes my heart lurch in a way that reminds me of a very unique time, when I was a child, when my mother endowed me with a rare smile of approval rather than pity.

'That Mrs Grey said you'd be busy, honey, but I told her you'd not be too busy for me!' She stands up and Charlie stands up beside her. 'I thought I'd take you to see that shoemaker feller that I said'd make you better boots and stop you walking like a cripple. Are you ready then? Let's get along there now.'

She is so certain I will go with her. I stare at her, feeling Mrs Grey

behind me willing me to dismiss this woman, to dismiss her impor-
tuning. This decides me. 'A minute, Mrs Cotton! I'll get my cloak.'

I follow a muttering housekeeper back into the hallway and allow
her to hold my cloak for me. 'Thank you, Mrs Grey.' I smile very
sweetly. Then I put on my little straw hat, checking its angle carefully
in the mirror.

'You watch that woman, miss,' Mrs Grey's voice breathes fiercely in
my ear. 'Watch her, I tell you. That woman neither knows her place nor
cares.'

Mrs Cotton – whom I must now call Marian – leads the way down
the dusty village road to the cluster of narrow dwellings just before
Brewery Cottages. One door is standing open, the sun cutting a bright
line on the worn stone step. She knocks politely and waits. A deep
voice bids us enter and she turns to Charlie. 'You stay here, son. Sit
down there in the sun.' She thrusts him towards a peeling makeshift
bench that stands up against the wall.

The doorway leads straight into a low room that – with its iron range
and fireside cupboard – could be a living room. But here it is most
definitely a workshop: the meaty smell of cured hide fills the air,
intermixed with the peppery scent of newly cast iron nails. Underneath
the window, set to catch the slanting morning light, is a long wide
bench, neatly spread with leather swatches and tins of nails, brown
paper patterns and iron shoe-lasts in three different sizes. At the far end
is a pile of newspapers and periodicals. The wall above it has a single
shelf with much-thumbed books. The opposite wall is busy with
methodically stowed tools. Beside them is a wood-turner's lathe, with a
flush of firewood shavings like fallen snow at its foot.

'I do hope it all meets with your approval.'

I blush. In savouring the detail I'm avoiding the gaze of the occupant
of the room, sitting on a lower stool by the bench. 'I am sorry, Mr,
er . . . I've never been in a shoemaker's shop . . .' My glance finally
settles on the face of the shoemaker and I blink with surprise. First, he
is much younger; secondly, he is a much bigger man than I expected.
Even seated, you can tell he'd be nearly six feet tall: thick golden hair,
streaked extraordinarily with bright silver, springs from his high
forehead, and his large eyes gleam so much that it's difficult to make
out the colour. At this moment they appear to be enjoying my discomfort.

41

Marian saves me. 'This is Aaron Whitstable the shoemaker, Victoria. The man makes proper shoes, not clogs. Even riding boots for the gentlefolk. This is the lass I told you about, Aaron. Niece to Dr Kilburn,' she adds. 'You can see the child needs a very special pair of boots.'

'Does she now?' He stands up and the room shrinks in size. He puts out a hand and shakes my limp paw heartily. 'My name is Aaron Whitstable, Miss Kilburn. I make shoes and boots, as did my father and my grandfather. Like Marian says, I make proper shoes, not clogs. Clog-makers are ten a penny. So, you need me to make you a new pair of boots?' He speaks to me directly.

'Mrs Cotton says you're very skilled. Perhaps a new pair of boots would be a good idea?'

'Perhaps it will.' He nods at the chair he has just vacated. 'Sit yourself down, won't you?'

I sit down on the worn leather chair. He kneels in the shavings and pulls across a very low wooden stool. 'Now then, Miss Kilburn, will you put your feet up on this cracket?'

The two of them are eyeing me like a pair of wise owls. I wait a full minute before I lift my feet up on to the stool, being careful to pull my skirt down tightly over my calves and ankles. The shoemaker pulls up my feet, one after the other, on to his upper thigh. I can feel the taut muscles under the hessian of his breeches. 'And where'd you get these things from?' he says, very ungraciously in my view. 'These boots?'

'My sister Lottie obtained them in London, from an establishment that deals . . . that makes shoes for people who . . . have problems.' In fact Lottie bought three pairs: one in black, one in brown and one in pale kid. They all look ugly and heavy and are painful to wear.

He grunts, then slowly turns my feet this way and that, lifts them up to see the sole, then tucks down his head so he can see the back of my heels. He grunts again. 'An' would it bother you if I took off your shoes, Miss Kilburn? I can tell from the start they are far too big and heavy.'

How could taking my boots off make any difference, after all this mauling? I glance at Marian, who is watching the proceedings with a rapt face. 'Yes, Mr Whitstable. That would be all right.' I try to sound lofty and gracious, and fail.

He unlaces and unbuttons my boots with great care, easing them off as skilfully as any lady's maid. He runs his fingers over my feet, prodding and pinching them through the cotton-knit stockings. He glances up at Marian, his thick brows raised. 'I canna do anything with the sock on, Marian,' he says.

'Could I take them off for yer, child? Those stockings?' Marian smiles down at me. 'Aaron knows his trade. You should trust him.'

He watches me with those large brown eyes as though he is interested in, but not too dependent on, my answer. 'Yes,' I say faintly. 'If it will help.'

He stands up and glances out of the window while Marian kneels to peel them off. Then he is there again, kneeling down before me. He lifts my bare feet into his large palms and moves them from one hand to the other very slowly. I am hot with shame. I know how I am with this horrible mark on my face, but this terrible twisted foot is the source, the essence of all my ugliness. He turns my feet this way and that, strokes the length of them above and below. This sends ripples of alarm right to the core of me and brings even more blushes to my face.

'Bonny little feet,' he says thoughtfully. 'Bonny.'

The hair on the back of my neck stands up. How can he say this?

He grips the left, turned foot. 'Relax, miss, or I can't do my work. Breathe deep, very deep.'

I force myself to relax and he begins pressing and stroking both feet again. Then an amazing thing happens. I find myself engulfed in a new, wonderful feeling of connection to the whole human race through being touched so softly, so tenderly by another human being, this stranger who makes shoes.

At last he places my feet back on the stool and stands up. 'Now,' he says, 'I need to see you standing.' He glances towards Marian. 'An' I'll need to see the ankle and calf proper.'

She nods, her bright eyes shining. 'It'll be worth it, honey,' she reassures me. 'Don't worry.'

Now I must stand on the footstool and the shoemaker kneels down again. Marian pulls up my skirt to mid-calf. Now he has his hands on my ankles, running them up to the calf and down again. I have an overwhelming desire to laugh out loud. My mother and Lottie would have had this man put in gaol for this, for just exposing my foot. Their desire is to have my ugliness always out of sight. Rollo and Pixie have never even seen it. Out of sight, out of mind. Now today it is so much *in* sight, so much *in* mind. In my mind, anyway. And in the mind of the shoemaker.

He stands up again. 'If you would sit down, miss . . .' he says. He goes to the cupboard and brings out something wrapped in chamois leather: he peels it open to reveal some kind of clay or dough. First he lifts my feet on to two beautifully crafted wooden pattens. Then he rolls the dough into balls, which he smoothes on to my bare feet and right up above the ankles.

'It'll take ten minutes or so to let it set on,' he says. 'I need to go out and feed me hens,' and he vanishes through the shadowy door into the back places.

I relax a little, thinking briefly how mannerly it is of him to leave. He can see I'm already embarrassed enough. To sit here in this tiny space wearing these dough clogs, with him looming over me, is almost more than I could bear.

Marian's voice invades my thoughts. 'It wouldn't be so bad if he were a little wizened old feller of sixty, would it? But such a well-set-up lad . . .' She has the same tone in her voice as when she talked about that husband, James Robinson.

I try to shrug in a dignified way, but am somewhat let down by the sight of my dough boots. I meet her sparkling glance and we both collapse into laughter. She knows exactly the torrent of feeling I have just endured.

'You knew that about me? No one has touched me like that since I was four and my last nursemaid was given notice,' I splutter. 'It is very strange.'

'Not to be touched! An' that's a great pity,' she says, 'you being so bonny.'

My mood calms down and I grow silent, a little uneasy now at the impropriety of this whole thing. At last I manage something neutral. 'Will young Charlie be all right outside?'

'I could send him home, I suppose. But like me I think he gets weary, tarrying in the house of sickness. His older brother and Mr Nattrass, my lodger, are gloomy with fever. It's our duty to succour them, but it's very hard. A body needs to have some light relief now and then.'

'And I am your light relief?' Being so strangely drawn to her I find myself eager to define just how she sees me, just what she thinks of me – again, an astonishing mimic experience of being in love.

She laughs at this and stands up, away from the bench. 'I knew you'd be something to me, honey, the minute I saw you on that train. It's like you and me have been together before, in another place.' She stares at me for a moment and then says, 'I'll just gan out and see if young Charlie's content. Mebbe I'll send him down to Riley's for a penn'orth of Spanish. He has a weakness for Spanish.'

'Spanish? What's that?'

'Spanish liquorice root. Children like it round here; find it soothing. They just call it Spanish.'

I scrabble in my purse, select a silver sixpence and hold it out to her. She reaches out and closes my fingers over the coin. Her hand is soft. 'No need for that between us, child. You know that,' she says, and glides through the doorway.

I sit there in the cluttered workshop listening to the pleasant mutter of their voices outside. I am still alone when Aaron Whitstable returns carrying a battered tin pan full of eggs. He puts them carefully on the shelf to the right of the fire range, then comes again to kneel at my feet.

To gain some power in the situation I take the initiative. 'I thought perhaps you might be something of a radical, Mr . . .' I indicate the pile of journals on the bench, the bookshelf on the wall.

'Didn't you know, Miss Kilburn? All cobblers are radicals? Comes from working on our own and realising that everyone only has two feet, and may only wear one pair of shoes at a time.' He brings a sharp knife from a pouch at his belt and starts to cut at the hardened dough to loosen each foot-shape into two halves. I hold my breath but his cut is sure and his hands are gentle. He lifts the dough casts on the pattens carefully across to the bench, where they stand: the left one is a weird facsimile of my disability.

He takes my feet in his hands again and rubs off the remaining flakes of dough that still adhere. He rubs a hard spot on the ball of my foot and looks up. 'You walk a little in your bare feet?'

I nod my head. 'Only when I'm alone. I have never been encouraged to flaunt my bad foot to others, even servants.'

He takes the guilty foot in his hand. 'It's a canny little foot,' he says. 'Like a leaf not yet uncurled. And it's doing you service despite its own inadequacy.'

I catch my breath at the sheer kindness of what he has just said. I want him to hold my poor little foot for ever.

Just then Marian crashes into the room. 'There, Charlie's off to get Spanish an' I've told him to stay at Mr Riley's till I go for him.'

Aaron Whitstable stands up. 'I'm done here, Marian. If you could help Miss Kilburn with her stockings . . .' He has the manners to stand with his back to us, examining my foot-casts on the bench, while Marian helps me with my stockings and my boots. Then, as I stand up, he goes to the dresser and wraps three eggs in a bit of chamois leather, tying the top to make a kind of basket handle. 'Here you are, Miss Kilburn, eat them soft-boiled. Nothing better.'

He comes to the door to see us off. 'Walk barefoot as much as you can, miss. Strengthen that bad foot,' he says. 'I'll have a plain pair of indoor boots ready in three days. An' a proper outdoor pair in seven days. They'll hurt at first, you being crippled by the rubbish you got on your feet now. But you'll walk straight in the end an' it'll be worth it.'

Walk straight? How can that be possible? Walk like other people? Without the rocking gait that has drawn glances the few times I have walked in public? My heart is dancing as I walk along with Marian to Riley's corner.

Marian reads my mood. She puts her arm through mine. 'Didn't I tell you the lad was a magician? Just you watch! He'll have you walking straight in no time. An' if you keep using my potions we'll have that face clear in a month.'

I say nothing to her now, but that is already happening. I looked in the mirror this morning and already the patch is less lumpy, less inflamed. Everything is changing, I know for the better. I am changing. My life is changing.

I hug Marian's arm to me. I feel I am walking on air and she knows it. I am right to believe the words she says and am beginning to recognise that our meeting on the train will change not just my body but my life.

We stop at Mr Riley's on the corner. Through the plate-glass window we can see Charlie on the high stool by the counter. A florid woman in a neat white apron is standing behind the counter serving a customer. I recognise the customer as Mrs Grey and take another step forward so I am out of her eye-line.

Marian leans against the plate-glass window and looks at me. 'Mr Riley, whose shop this is, is very fond of our Charlie,' she says. 'Not surprising, if the tale I've heard is right.' Her face takes on a knowing look, which for a second I find rather a shock. It's a side of her I have not seen before.

'What tale is that?'

'My neighbour Sarah Shaw told me. Seems poor old Riley's son killed hisself years back. Slit his own throat. There's another son, and a daughter, but the one that killed hisself was Riley's favourite son, according to Sarah. Mebbe the old boy looks on our little Charlie and thinks on that lad.'

The good feeling I brought from the shoemaker's house drains from me. 'How terrible. Heartbreaking.'

She stares at me a minute, then slowly shakes her head. 'Heart-breaking? Don't I know all about heartbreaking, honey? Nothing worse than losing your own child. I should know, having lost more than one myself.'

There is something blind, troubled about her gaze, but her tone is level, almost neutral. There is not even a thread of grief, merely a kind of dry anger in her voice. I wonder if you get like that when you suffer too much. I think Marian must be very strong inside to hold all that grief to herself. Many women these days suffer such dreadful loss but surely none can be the stoic that she is.

Eight

The customers never found it easy to reach to the counter in Riley's shop. For a start, although it was a proper shop (not somebody's front room like so many other shops in the village), it was still quite small. Despite its corner windows, even in the middle of the day it was dark and shadowy, as though each item in the clustered space sucked out its own bit of light and left the centre of the room in shadow. The floor was crowded with battered flour bins, only one of which contained flour. The others were filled with all kinds of goods that Mr Riley would sell on to other, smaller shopkeepers and traders. The shelves behind the counter reached to the ceiling and were stacked tightly with every kind of thing any modern housewife could desire to keep her family tended and her man happy.

Charlie was sitting on a high stool next to the window. Mrs Riley stood at the spotless counter serving Mrs Grey. Neither looked up when Marian charged through the door, making the bell tremble furiously on its spring. Young Charlie Cotton went on licking his Spanish stick and watching. At the sound of the bell his gaze turned to watch his stepmother but he kept licking his Spanish. The sheer dense flavour of it made his jaws ache with pleasure.

Mrs Grey made a great play of referring to a neatly written list as she gave her order. She had just been expressing her disapproval to Mrs Riley of the 'cut' made by the doctor's niece walking down the green arm-in-arm with that woman Marian Cotton. The housekeeper told Mrs Riley quite firmly that she would have to report this to the doctor. Nothing else for it. Yes, the doctor would hear of it word for word.

Matches. Oven black. Half a dozen candles. Cough mixture 'for the Young.' Beeswax polish. Fly papers. Half a pound of lemon drops. Mrs Riley entered them in a ledger; no money changed hands.

As Mrs Grey turned to leave, basket in hand, she banged into Marian, recovered her balance, then glared at her. 'Isn't it time you was taught your place, lady?' she said grimly, and pushed past her.

Marian moved to the counter to face a sullen Mrs Riley. With any other customer Margaret Riley would have made a comment on the day, uttered some kind of pleasantry. But now she fiddled with things on the counter, straightening the ham knife, putting the tick book under the counter.

Finally Marian said, 'Is the master about, Mrs Riley?'

At last Mrs Riley looked up, her apple-clean face shining beneath her neatly parted hair. 'I'm not sure that Mr Riley is in, Mrs Cotton.'

'Well, why don't you call him and see, Mrs Riley? No better way, I'd say myself!' Her tone was grim and she held the shopkeeper's gaze until the other gave in. Marian turned to Charlie. 'Not much in the way of manners in this place, son, is there?'

Margaret Riley went to the doorway that divided the shop from the back of the house. She looked back at Marian. 'And I'll thank you not to leave your brat here when you've nobody to mind him,' she snapped. Then she vanished through the curtain.

Marian put her hand under Charlie's arms and jumped him down to the sawdusted floor. 'That lady has a nasty mouth on her, Charlie. You're not to mind her. She's showing her broughtin's up.'

Charlie stood still beside her and continued to suck on his Spanish. She adjusted his velvet cap and patted him absently on the cheek. The curtain moved to one side and Thomas Riley glided into the narrow space. Marian beamed at him.

'My, Mr Riley you're lookin' fine today. Always spotless, that's what I say to anyone. Nipping clean, that Mr Riley.'

Thomas Riley put a hand on his smooth cheek, a finger trailing down to smooth his sandy moustache. 'Marian, I don't think . . .' This was what set people against the woman: her openness, her directness. He admitted to himself again that for him, here in his own chill house, there was refreshment in it. He judged her actions differently from other people. He could be put out, even embarrassed sometimes, at the deferential way people would treat him, knowing as they did that he

49

could assign the favours of the Guardians. Whatever they really thought about him they'd act out like whipped curs, whining and pleading for what, if they were honest, was their right. 'What can I do for you, Mrs Cotton?' He had a slight smile on his face.

'Well, sir, I'm in a difficult way. You'll know already that my lodger, Mr Nattrass, came off work at the pit and has been off some time now? So I've had nothing coming in. And if things go right for me now, seems I'm to have the expense of moving house.'

'Come on, Marian. Everyone knows Mr Cotton's workmates made a generous donation when he was taken bad. Didn't I hear that?'

'Aye, so they did. That and the insurance saw me through. But that money's run out now. There was stuff to buy and I had to pay the women who helped me in the house when I was doing my nursing. You know yourself that I work hard for my nursing money, but that dribbles away. Now I've got Nattrass lying bad, and have him to feed and take care of. I cannot throw the feller out. Then there's Fred Cotton's oldest, young Freddie, and he's off colour. And even young Charlie here comes and goes like a will-o'-the-wisp and takes nurturing.' She sighed. 'And neither of them my own. And even my own bairn is down with teething. I'm being sore tried all round here, I can tell you. I haven't a single penny in my purse. These bairns'll starve when they need sustaining.'

He hesitated, well aware in this public arena of what others thought of his leniency towards this woman. His wife had related tales to him, with relish, of Mrs Cotton haring off to Darlington and coming back with silk dresses and fine shawls. Of her paying women to clean and wash for her. 'The woman's feckless. A spendthrift,' she'd mutter in that way of hers that so irritated him.

Margaret had not taken it kindly when he protested that Mrs Cotton was always neatly turned out. She retorted that the woman could hardly be a pauper, then, if she was so well turned out. When he said that Mrs Cotton earned what she could herself, with the nursing she did for the doctor, his wife snapped that there was something funny about a woman visiting men in their houses. Even old men. Even if they were sick unto death. Thomas insisted that someone had to do it; not everyone would go into a house where there was typhoid or smallpox. His wife pursued her point. It was not decent; no decent woman would do such a thing. She repeated that everyone knew that the woman used the money to

50

pay Mrs Dodds to do her cleaning and other women to do her washing. Who did she think she was?

It occurred to Thomas now that perhaps dealing with death every day might be what made Marian so forthright, less mincing and falsely modest than most women. It could be such a merry thing, talking to her. He tried to reassure her. 'Your work is well respected, Marian. That must be a comfort. And your friend Quick-Manning? You did well with him,' he added slyly. 'Like you say, he's back at work.'

She didn't bat an eyelid. 'Oh, yes. The feller's right as rain.'

He glanced at the boy, still standing there holding his Spanish to his nose, breathing in deeply. If the boy hadn't been there he might have had a little joke about the excise officer 'paying his way' a bit further. His wife and 'everyone' in the village knew there was more than nursing between Marian and Quick-Manning. This was the case even now when, if Margaret was to be believed, the lodger Nattrass had been more than a mere lodger. The word was she had been engaged to him.

'Well, Marian,' he said softly. His back was to his wife and her customer. He slid out the shallow drawer under the counter, took out a silver florin and put it on the counter. 'I'll enter the need with the Guardians, Mrs Cotton, and you may have this on account,' he said under his breath. 'I'll enter the fact that you made every effort to find work but that you have a sick man and a poorly boy on your hands, as well as the baby.'

'Aye, the baby,' she sighed. 'At least *he's* my own.' Almost casually, she put her hand on the coin. His hand came on top of hers, pressing it to the worn counter. 'You're a rare woman, Marian,' he murmured. 'There's sommat in me that envies old Quick-Manning.'

She looked at their hands, entwined on the counter, then slowly extricated hers. Then she looked him full in the face, her eyes sparkling, a dimple showing on her cheek. 'Now, Mr Riley, that wouldn't do, would it?' she whispered. 'It wouldn't do at all.' She grasped the coin and slipped it into her apron pocket.

She turned to the child. 'Now, Charlie,' she said loudly, 'let's get ourselves home. That bairn'll be screaming and old Mrs Dodds'll be straining at the bit. She's a canny help, but she likes to let you know it.'

The bell trembled on its spring as she shut the door behind her. Thomas felt rather than saw his wife standing to his left.

'That woman is a powder keg,' she said. 'Just needs a flint. It's the bairns I'm sorry for. I always say that.'

Thomas didn't know whether she had observed the exchange of the florin and thought perhaps he did not care. There had been no significant exchange of any kind between his wife and himself since the thing with Teddy. That wouldn't change. Not ever.

Along in the house on Johnson Terrace Marian took the bawling baby from a sour-faced Mrs Dodds and calmed him down.

'Has the bairn been all right? I can see you've got the kettle boiling there. I tell you what, love, I'm clamming for some tea.'

Mrs Dodds, flat-footed, still broad of beam and breast despite her age, busied herself with the kettle while Marian sat down on the spoke-backed chair by the roaring fire with the baby in her lap. She wriggled her feet out of her boots and held her toes to the fire. She put one arm out to the boy, Charlie, who was standing by the door, chewing at his last shred of Spanish. 'Come you here, pet. Sit by me and give us a love. You've been a good lad this morning for your mother.' He came to sit by her and she pulled him to her. She looked over his head at Mrs Dodds, who these days was the closest she had to a friend in this village. 'I tell you what, Mrs D.! That Mr Riley has a fancy for himself.'

Mrs Dodds scalded the dry tea leaves. She smiled. She enjoyed Mrs Cotton's near-the-knuckle talk. Apart from its entertainment value it was always worth a penn'orth of ale at Halloran's: a gift from some eager listener. 'Has he now?' she said. 'Me, I'd'a thought he was a respectable type, what with the chapel and the Guardians and that.'

'Respectable or not, they're all the same under the cloth.'

Mrs Dodds put the tea on the iron hob to brew. 'You're a bad'n, Mrs Cotton,' she chuckled. 'I seed you walk down the green, arm in arm with that Miss Kilburn, bold as brass. Her Dr Kilburn's niece and all.'

Marian shrugged. 'Like I always say, Mrs D., folks like that are no different from us. I've been in their houses, washed out their piss-pots. I've read their letters, tried on their clothes, their shoes . . .'

'Their husbands and sons too, I'd bet,' chuckled the old woman.

Marian put her hands over Charlie's ears, nearly dropping the baby from her lap. 'Mrs D., how could you say that? You are *in-decent*.' But her broad grin took the edge off her reproof.

At that point a crash rattled through the house, making the ceiling above them shake. They both looked upwards.

'Oh, His Majesty calls,' said Marian, standing up and looking. 'Either him or the lad.'

Mrs Dodds glanced at Charlie. 'The word about the place is that you and your lodger were – well, more than that . . .'

'Me and Nattrass?' Marian laughed heartily. 'Not so, Mrs Dodds. Once, a long time ago, in another world, our gazes met. But now? Whatever the scandal-hags say, the feller's just a lodger, helping me make ends meet. Or not, now he's not working,' she added drily.

She placed the baby on the rag rug on the stone floor and loosened his clothes so he could kick freely. She told Charlie, whose Spanish was now a string of fine black straw in his mouth, to go out again to play.

'I tell you what, Mrs D., poor Nattrass up there is not a patch on Fred Cotton, and *he* was no great shakes. There was this other fellow across in Sunderland . . .' She paused. 'Now then, Mrs D., is there some water left in that kettle?' She took a small, handleless teapot from the chimney shelf, spooned in some dry leaves from a battered red tin and scalded them with hot water. Then she mixed some white powder to a paste in a shallow bowl. 'Arrowroot. Nothing better. This should settle his belly a bit, poor feller. I'll give young Freddie a spoon or two while I'm on.' She stood there a second and shook her head. 'D'you know, I've got this fear, Mrs D.? I'm afraid they'll go the same way as poor old Fred. It's too much.' She sighed deeply. 'How much can a body stand?' Then she pinned her skirts up into her waistband and, balancing the teapot wrapped in a cloth in one hand, she made her way up the ladder that did the service of a staircase between the two floors.

Mrs Dodds poured herself a cup of tea and went to sit in a seat by the table under her window. In the road outside, Charlie was throwing some stones at a gaggle of hens. Beyond him, men in pit clothes were making their way down the road in clusters of three or four. The boys, dressed for work like their dads, kicked a ball between them, ever forward through the houses towards the green and up the hill for the afternoon shift at the colliery. 'Poor old Fred?' she murmured. 'Like Nattrass, a fine figure of a lad once.' She looked up at the unplastered ceiling, listened to the patter of Marian Cotton's feet above. 'Death seems to follow you like a faithful dog, lass. Queer thing, that.'

Nine

Young Emily Kilburn favoured her father in character as well as looks. She too was fair-faced and sandy-haired, with a quiet, direct manner. Bookish and clever, she seemed and acted older than her twelve years. Underneath her modest demeanour lay something of her mother's sparkle, as well as a self-confidence that came from years of being treated as her mother's equal and never routinely chastised. Her parents' unusual tolerance meant that she could move about the village freely, and go on errands for her mother on the train to Bishop Auckland. Each week she even took the train there alone to sing in the town choir. Such licence was looked on quite benevolently in the area, as something on a par with her much-admired father's obsession with fresh air.

It was Victoria Kilburn's good fortune that young Emily took her under her wing; she sat beside her at breakfast and enquired after the wisdom of Miss Frances Power Cobbe, which Victoria was still reading in the evening.

When Victoria described Miss Cobbe's ideas, Mary Kilburn raised her eyes from her sewing. 'I can only say that that sounds blasphemous,' she said. Her tone was severe. 'Quite unchristian.'

Emily laughed. 'Oh, Ma!' she said. 'All we have here is a plea to take note of your senses, your intuition. Pa is always saying we should do that. That and take note of the evidence. "Note the evidence that is before your eyes." He's always saying that.'

'He'll make a scientist of you yet,' said Mary gloomily. 'And then where will we all be?'

Emily turned to Victoria. 'I have been thinking, Victoria. You should come to choir with me, in Bishop Auckland. Thursday evening. The choirmaster is Pa's second cousin Mr Nicholas Kilburn. That's why they let me go. He is quite a musical genius. Do say you'll come. You would enjoy it. There are so many fine people and the singing is divine. All the young people will be there.'

Victoria shook her head. 'I've never sung, Em. Don't know how to. I never even went to church or chapel to sing unheard in a crowd.' She said it placidly, without self-pity.

Mary, stitching away at a shirt for young Eric, wondered at the morality of bringing up a child as a heathen simply because she had an unsightly foot and was burdened with the role of family invalid.

Last evening, as they retired to their bed, William had confirmed the evidence of her own eyes: that apart from the problem with the foot there was nothing wrong with the girl that a little fresh air would not cure. He also muttered darkly against his cousin, who had so weakly allowed one child to be favoured over another and had stigmatised the child who was burdened by nature.

Now Mary Kilburn said brightly to Victoria, 'How do you know that you can't sing, dear? I always say that Nicholas Kilburn could make a corncrake sing with his sheer enthusiasm.'

Victoria surveyed the eager faces of Emily and Auntie Mary, relishing once more the feeling of being at the heart of a family whose members cared so deeply for each other. She smiled. 'Then I must go along with you, Em, and "note the evidence that is before my eyes".'

Emily jumped up then, and hugged Victoria, while Aunt Mary smiled her delight, her fingers still flying over the hem of Eric's shirt.

Ten

So the following Thursday, I find myself in a church hall in Bishop Auckland with Emily, under the sharp eye of Mr Nicholas Kilburn, who shakes hands very seriously.

'And what are you, Victoria? A contralto? A soprano?' His own voice is soft, unemphatic. He is so much less definite, distinct than my Uncle William, though one can see the family resemblance.

I shake my head. 'To be perfectly honest, sir, I don't know whether I can sing at all.'

He nods. 'Then you must come with me.' He leads me down a corridor to a small cluttered room with a piano in the corner. We spend a quarter of an hour in which he strikes notes and I hum and *lah-lah* in an attempt to match the key. Eventually he seems satisfied enough. 'A contralto,' he says. 'You have the beginning, the very first threads, of a fine contralto voice.'

When we get back to the rehearsal room his assistant has assembled the choir and is standing in front of their ranks of chairs and, directing from the piano, is taking them through their scales. Nicholas rearranges the seats of the women in the front row and finds me a place centre left, away from Emily, who is obviously a soprano. He sits me beside a tall woman with a slightly reddened face and watery eyes, who smiles broadly.

'Miss McCullough, this is my kinswoman Miss Victoria Kilburn.'

She nods and whispers, 'Welcome, my dear.'

Nicholas shuffles the papers on his lectern and says in his soft voice, 'We'll begin tonight with the Irish air, which will loosen up our throats

56

a little. Miss McCullough, will you kindly ensure that my niece Miss Kilburn can see your copy?'

She opens her copy and points at the first line. At first, I just can't sing a note. I just stare desperately at the sheet with its alien dots and swirls. Then I feel Miss McCullough's elbow dig in my ribs and, wavering at first, my voice begins to follow her warm fruity tones and I manage to start to sing the words. Then magically our voices seem to blend and she carries me with her. Her lovely voice makes the singing much easier.

Now we move on to a lullaby and I feel safer, following Miss McCullough's voice like a lamb after her mother. Song follows song. Sometimes Nicholas stops us and makes us try again. Always better. Then too soon, the last notes of the piano fade and Nicholas is pulling together his sheets.

Miss McCullough turns to me and shakes my hand warmly. 'Welcome to our merry band, Miss Kilburn. You have the most tuneful voice.'

I smile my gratitude. 'You were pulling me along the whole way. I couldn't have tried even a single note without you.'

Miss McCullough is very talkative. By the time we get to the back of the hall for tea and scones, I have learned a good deal about her. It seems that she is not from round here. She comes from Somerset. She came some years ago to keep house for her dear sister, a schoolteacher, who unfortunately passed away last year from influenza. Now she is the matron of the house where the schoolgirls board. 'And I do so like it, Miss Kilburn. Those girls can be naught but *buggages* but in fact are quite sweet.'

She tells me all of this in one breath and I find myself trying to breathe for her. Everything she says makes me warm to her. She is so open and without an ounce of guile.

Then Nicholas comes up and takes her away from me, voicing a query about a visiting singer. Emily vanishes to talk to a friend and I am only alone for a minute when a rather stout, quite good-looking young man approaches, a tray of scones in hand.

'They say you're Mr Kilburn's cousin? Miss Kilburn?' He puts down the plate and shakes my hand. 'He is a great man. A wonderful musician.' He is not much taller than I, and has bright eyes and a keen, curious face. He goes on, 'I felt I should come and introduce myself.'

He takes up the plate and offers me a scone. 'Kit Dawson. Baritone. I work for Mr Chapman the solicitor.' His voice, accented rather like Auntie Mary's, is rich and deep and not unattractive. I take a bite of my scone, quite pleased with the attention of this polite, rather nice-looking young man.

I have to say finally, 'I don't know whether I am Mr Kilburn's cousin to be honest, Mr Dawson His cousin William, with whom I'm staying in West Auckland, is his second cousin. And William is cousin to my father.'

'Ah, families!' he says lugubriously, and we break into laughter.

'Mr Nicholas Kilburn is a very great man,' he repeats, when our laughter fades. 'A force for good in this town. A legend around here. It's an honour to know any relative of his.'

I am at a loss to know what to say next but here is Emily bustling up, obviously in a hurry. 'Victoria, we have to run! If we miss the eight twenty train Ma will not be best pleased.'

Kit Dawson insists on shaking hands again, and Emily and I button up our capes before we walk briskly up Newgate Street, with me hopping and skipping to keep up with her. We catch our train just in time.

As we collapse, laughing, into our seats, I have to reflect on the fact that three weeks ago, at this time of night, I would have been tucked up in bed for an hour, and Mother would have drifted through my open door, fussing around and insisting that I must put out my light soon so as not to tire my eyes.

How much my life has changed. I have gained Marian for a friend, allowed a shoemaker to stroke my feet, joined a delightful new family at Western House and now, just in this one day, I have met another cousin, learned how to sing and made the acquaintance of a delightful lady singer and a very personable young man.

When we get back to Western House, we find a neat parcel on the hall table addressed to me in copperplate writing. Some instinct makes me resist Emily's pleading to open it there and then, and instead I take it up to my room and unwrap it very carefully. Under layers of tissue are the indoor shoes, accompanied by a neat note from Aaron Whitstable. 'Miss Kilburn. These should fit all right. Will you call tomorrow to say so? The "out doors" ones are nearly ready. Yours faithfully, A. Whitstable.'

I take off my cape and jacket, sit in a low chair and try on the boots. They are made from dun-coloured kid, soft and light, and fit my feet like a second skin. Lower on the ankle than my normal boots, they are much lighter on the sole. They fasten with cream cord laces and three neat leather-covered buttons. They are objects of beauty.

I stand up and move round the room, up and down seven times. I walk towards the long wardrobe mirror and note the steadiness, the straightness of my gait. No rocking from side to side. I stand there, just stand looking down at my boots. Under my skirts they look like perfectly ordinary boots. Somehow Aaron Whitstable has built up the left one inside to take my twisted foot, but it looked exactly like the conventional right boot. I give a little skip and laugh at my own reflection. Suddenly my eyes fill with tears. I put my hands to my face and let the tears roll down over my fingers. I lift my hand away from my scarred cheek so I can see again how much the unsightly patch has smoothed out. It is barely there. Then I move about the room again, walking on air.

I keep my boots on when I go back down into the drawing room, led there by the murmur of voices. My uncle and aunt are sitting on either side of the blazing fire. He is reading a medical journal taken from a pile by his chair. Auntie Mary is knitting.

She beams up at me. 'My dear! Our Em says you were quite a hit at the choir. She tells me that Nicholas says you may have "*A Voice*".'

'He is very kind.'

'And you received a parcel as well?'

It suddenly occurs to me that at home in Stoke Newington such a parcel would have been opened by my mother and the contents passed on to me – or not – with appropriate comments. Here, no less than Emily, I am treated with respect.

'They are boots, Auntie, made for me by Mr Whitstable the shoemaker.' I raise the hem of my skirt so that the boots are fully in view. 'They are special. I can walk straight in them.'

'Oh, how sweet. How dainty,' says Auntie Mary.

'Walk!' my uncle commands. 'Walk to the far wall and back again.'

I obey him, tripping across the room on light feet.

'Amazing!' Aunt Mary says.

'And again!' my uncle says.

I do so again and return to stand before him.

'Are they comfortable?'

'Well, no, to be honest. There is a kind of pull on my good leg. But Mr Whitstable said there would be, until I became accustomed to it.'

'That is so. Your other leg has been so used to compensating. Now it seems to me that you almost walk straight.'

The flare of delight races through me. 'Yes, I do, don't I?'

'The man's a genius.' My aunt takes up her knitting again. 'And here's the evidence.'

'These are only for indoors,' I have to say. 'He's nearly finished the outdoor pair. They're in brown leather. I'm to pay for both together.'

'They'll be cheap, whatever his price. How can you put a price on straight walking?' my uncle says.

'Mr Whitstable will not overcharge, William. He made the children's shoes. He never overcharges.' My aunt has her say.

I sit down on a wooden chair beside my aunt's more comfortable seat. 'And I have Mrs Cotton to thank for this, Auntie. She took me to him. She knew what I needed.' I find myself insisting that Marian is at the centre of all this.

Uncle William takes up his cigar and his journal again. 'I did tell you she was an unusual woman, my dear.'

'I can't say I like the woman myself,' says Aunt Mary, flourishing her needles. 'She always looks through me. As though I do not exist. And to be honest, when I listen to her talk with you, William, I think she thinks she knows more than she really does. Rather too full of herself for my taste.'

I hear her words but the heat from the fire makes me drowsy and I take little note of my aunt's criticism of my new friend Marian. I'm afraid I am too busy wriggling my toes in my new boots and feeling quite content.

Eleven

In no time at all my life at Western House has fallen into something of a routine. Each day I get up with the family at eight o'clock for an occasionally riotous breakfast. This meal around the table in the breakfast room is rather strange to me, as usually in London I am served breakfast in bed and told afterwards to rest till lunchtime to conserve my health. No chance of that here. Too much laughter, noise and movement.

By nine thirty I am back downstairs in the dispensary, weighing and mixing to my uncle's prescriptions under the supervision of Mr Carr, a young dried-up sort of man here from Australia to train as a surgeon.

The walls of the dark, narrow dispensary are lined with shelves of brown and blue containers, each labelled in the diverse, neat hands of the apprentices who have worked for my uncle in the last fifteen years. On one broad shelf are fatter jars filled with viscous liquid that contain the more interesting specimens harvested by my uncle in his role as autopsy surgeon. Mr Carr numbers them off for me (enjoying, I think, the slight shudder that I feel unable to suppress).

'Here's the hand of a miner who got his arm in the way of a falling rock. And a babe no bigger than a kitten born too soon to a mother who died. And here's the double head of a monster that was born full term but died soon after. At the far end there are the two stomachs of a man who was born with them and lived seventeen years without knowing it. Only discovered by Dr Kilburn when the man died suddenly without warning and an autopsy was required.'

At one end of the dispensary is a high bench where the autopsies are carried out. It has a special lamp on a pulley to give the doctor light at his work. Behind that, in open leather cases made especially for the purpose, are blades and hacksaws and scalpels that still glitter menacingly in the limited light that reaches the room through the narrow window.

After the flare of enthusiasm in showing me the tools of his master's trade, Mr Carr pulls on his black apron and cuff savers and goes about his measuring, labelling and pouring into small phials. He becomes weary of me watching him and gives me a safe job of mixing cough mixture.

One day when my uncle comes in from his surgery and sees my neat rows of cough mixture, he applauds my hard work and asks if I would like to come out with him on a visit. He's had a call to a farm three miles up the dale where two children in a family are in difficulty. I jump at the chance, rushing, in my still slightly lopsided fashion, to find my cloak.

As I clamber up into the trap my uncle smiles at me. 'So where is this invalid I've heard so much about, then? I've seen little sign of her since you arrived.'

I grin back at him. 'I think perhaps she was lost somewhere on the train between London and Darlington.'

Then he takes my face in his gloved hand. I flinch a little but he holds on tight. 'I note that those eruptions on your face are almost entirely faded. This sooty Northern air must be doing you good.'

I can't think why I don't mention Marian's poultice, or her bitter tonic, but I don't. Later on I will regret this, as I will regret other omissions of mine that contributed to the blight on Marian's cause. As it is, Marian and I seem to come across each other quite often in our movement out and about in the village. We stand and talk, or take a stroll along the edge of the green, talking, laughing, confiding. Sometimes I can't recall what we have said but I always know I feel better when we part.

It takes my uncle and me half an hour's bumpy ride to reach the farm. It is set peculiarly in the elbow turn of the River Gaunt, surrounded by scrubby mounds that can scarcely be called hills, which are etched here and there with a line of new broom. We are met by the stench of the farmyard before we see the farm. When we see it, it is running with mud and pigs. Hens and geese roam freely around the yard and in and out of the house, finding food where they may. A boy, forking slurry from a handcart on to the dung heap that dominates the yard, disturbs a rat, which flees like a flutter of black silk into the corner and down a crack in the wall.

At the far end of the yard, two watchful children of indeterminate sex pursue desultory tasks, staring at us with protuberant eyes as we alight from the trap. Another barefoot lad darts out from a dark doorway, takes the reins and stands by the horse's head. A tall man, who has been filling the doorway, moves into the light. 'Aye, Doctor.' There is a trail of mud on one side of his face.

'Good morning, Mr Staincliffe.' My uncle shakes hands with the man with his usual cordiality. 'This is my niece, who has come from London to find out how we do things in the North.'

'Aye.' The man barely looks at me. He is a tall old man of rakish, spare build and deep-set eyes. His voluminous trousers are held up with rope and his jacket, too small for him, is moulded to the creases and folds of his body. 'It's not just the bairn's gone. Our lass is bad as well, like. Worth it for you to come. Dinnet want to lose this one too. The new bairn's gone already. Need a note from you for that.'

He leads us to some kind of back room, which is bare except for a bed in a corner with a wooden cradle beside it. The room is suffused with a soupy, sour smell that turns my stomach. A crocheted blanket is pulled right across the cradle, entirely covering a bundle that is lying there. The woman on the bed, covered in a tumble of grey wool, could be any age from twenty to fifty. Her skin is taut against her bones and there are bruise-like shadows all round her eyes, which glitter in the dim light of the room.

I stand still, trying to make myself invisible as my uncle draws back the blanket and peers into the baby's face.

'He was right sick, Doctor. Couldn't keep anything down.' The woman's voice, light as a wisp, comes from the bed. 'I tried to feed him but I was sick meself and he wouldn't suckle. Then my oldest, Tessie, she fed him with a bottle. An' then he got worse.'

My uncle strips the baby down, prods the tiny body with gentle fingers. Then he grunts, wraps it up again, pulls the blanket up over its face. He turns to the woman. 'And how are you, Mrs Staincliffe?'

A ghost of a smile flickers over her face. 'I've been better, Doctor. If I could get rid of this sickness I'd be all right.' She presses a hand on her mouth to stop a convulsion.

He takes her pulse, then puts a hand on her brow. 'I'll give your husband something to steady your bowels. But you must try to take something. Some beef tea. And you need washing and cleaning to help you fight this infection. You need some air in here. And something that you can keep down.'

He turns to her husband, who shrugs. 'No time here to fettle fancy stuff,' he says.

Then I see anger ripple through my uncle like a wave, making his mouth taut, his cheeks red. 'Then you should find time, Mr Staincliffe. Or you'll lose this wife just as you lost your last.'

The farmer looks at him under lowered lids. 'Nay stamina, these women. I've said it before an' I'll say it again.'

My uncle moves back into the kitchen and I follow. He clears space on the cluttered table and sits down to write on a piece of paper that he takes from his bag. The farmer stands at his shoulder, waiting for the form that will allow him to bury his dead child.

'I wouldn't'a bothered you, Doctor,' he says. 'I knew babby was dead enough. But I need the paper for the insurance, like.' He puts his hand out, palm up. I can see the ingrained dirt in his palm.

My uncle keeps his hand on the paper. 'Mr Staincliffe, you *will* take that dead child out of that sick room. You or your daughters *will* attempt to clean your poor wife up. You *will* open that window and get some air into that room. As I said, you are in danger of losing this wife just as you lost the last one. Are you still taking the water from that filthy well?'

'Only place round here, Doctor,' says the man sullenly. 'We gotta get watter somewhere.'

'You have the river fifty yards away, man! Fresh running water. Use that.'

The man shrugs. 'Like I say, too much to do. Kids is willin' enough but have no stamina, like their mothers.' He looks my uncle in the eye. 'Now, Doctor, what do I owe you for that note? I gotta get on. There's the pigs to see to.'

My uncle casts his eye round the desolate room. 'There will be no charge, Mr Staincliffe.' He sighs. Then he holds out the paper.

The farmer grasps it. 'I'm right sorry about the babby, Doctor. It was a boy. Five girls and three boys I've had. Only two of each surviving.' His look is bland, displaying no shred of contrition.

My uncle stands up with a movement so violent that the chair on which he has been sitting falls to the stone floor. He charges out of the room and down the lane to the trap, making cockerels fly and pigs run squealing before him. I hurry after him, trying to find less muddy places to put my boots.

Mr Staincliffe bowls after us. Then he stands by the wall, the paper still flapping in his hand. He looks up at my uncle, the very ghost of a smirk on his face. 'Bit of a surprise, Doctor, you bringing a cripple round with you. 'S all right with me, but some'd be worried about—'

My uncle pulls up his whip to tickle the horse into movement and it whistles inches short of Mr Staincliffe's nose. 'You take care of your wife, Mr Staincliffe. If anything does happen to her I may have to have a serious talk to the coroner. You may be liable.'

I say nothing to him until I know that the sway of the trap, as the horse pulls us down the lane, soothes his fury.

'Not a nice man, that Mr Staincliffe,' I say finally.

He shrugs. 'No worse than many. Living from hand to mouth, surviving as he may. Unsanitary conditions, dirty water, melancholy. Not an uncommon feature in these parts.'

'But that poor wife! The baby.'

'Well, this wife is his third one. This baby is his eighth, with only four surviving. As I say, in these conditions . . .'

'But Mr Staincliffe survived. How can he survive when they all die?'

That shrug again. 'He has the better constitution. I would guess he gets the best of whatever is available. After all, he is the breadwinner.'

'Will she die? The wife? She looks half dead already.'

'With food and good nursing she could very well survive. If we could send your friend Marian Cotton up here to nurse her, the woman would survive. But that man? And his rapscallion children? They cannot take care of her.'

Mention of Marian makes me think of the boots. My heart flips at the thought. Whether this is because of Marian or the shoemaker or the boots themselves, I'm not quite sure. Marian is often on my mind even when she isn't there. But then so is Aaron Whitstable. 'I have to collect another pair of boots from Mr Whitstable this afternoon.'

'You must bring them to show me. I am intrigued by Master Whitstable's particular design. I could recommend it to the Board for other people who need such a service. People who need some corrective for a foot problem.' Then he lapses into silence, and I leave him to his thoughts all the way home.

As for me, I am dwelling on thoughts of the shoemaker Whitstable and the fact that this afternoon I will again have to put my feet into his hands. Perhaps I will put the boots on and call round on Marian to show her them. It will be a good excuse to see her again. I have never seen her house, and the thought of calling on her is rather engaging.

Twelve

Like Victoria Kilburn, Mr Quick-Manning, the excise officer from the brewery, knew he had cause to be grateful to Marian Cotton. He was quite sure that he was still alive because of her ministrations. She had come with good recommendations from the doctor, as a last resort before Quick-Manning was sent to some isolation infirmary. He had imagined that it would be some old village harridan whom he'd have to endure until he got better. So Marian Cotton was a surprise: clean and quite fine-looking, she was brisk and efficient in her nursing, and had a sense of humour that was quite refreshing in the dull cycle of days of sickness. As Quick-Manning improved in health she had dosed him with various herbal pick-me-ups that seemed to bring him to better health and energy at good speed. As well as this, she organised a woman to cook and clean for him to ensure that the house was in good trim when he finally got up from his sick bed.

It was when he finally rose from his sick bed properly that his relationship with Marian changed. His gratitude to her turned to passion and when she kept coming to his house, also in Johnson Terrace, to enquire solicitously after his health they became close. In his first week of true health they made love in every room in his house except the bedroom, where she'd nursed him out of the smallpox and back to health. Despite the fumigation of the walls and the floor and the new bedding, it took some time for Marian to be happy making love to him in that room.

The thing that continually surprised Quick-Manning about Marian was her energy. Unlike other more orthodox lovers, Marian relished rather than endured these loving encounters. She even enjoyed being naked. As well as this, she played little love-games that quite intoxicated him. It all certainly made him look out for her, listen for her step.

Indulging in such a relationship was not so easy when he finally returned to his work at the brewery and members of her family became sick. Still, she made time in the darker end of the unlit evenings to slip in to his house, using the large key she'd kept from the time she had been his nurse to get in by his side door.

So, on the night that Victoria Kilburn went to the choir practice, Quick-Manning was not displeased to hear the click of his side door. He poured himself another finger of whisky and waited.

Then she was there in the room with him. 'So how are you, mister?' she said, smiling slightly, showing her even white teeth.

He held his glass up to her in a toast. 'Very well now, thanks to you, old girl. Why don't you pour yourself a touch of this? It'll warm you up. It's damp out there. I was chilled when I got back from the brewery.'

She sat down opposite him and shook her head. 'I never take such stuff. You know that. Who knows what a person may do with that inside you to make your head fizz?'

He took a sip from his glass. 'So, how have you been, dear Marian?' he asked placidly.

'I have to admit I'm pleased to be out of that sick house of mine. Ma Dodds is there watching out for them all. I felt the need for clean air.'

He put down his glass, and patted his broad knee. 'Come here, Marian. Sit on my lap and sing me one of your songs.'

She stood up and settled herself in his lap. He pulled her towards him and buried his face in her bodice, one hand reaching down to pull up her skirts. She let him go so far, then pulled his head away in a strong grasp. She had surprisingly strong hands. He looked up at her, astonished. Marian was no prude and usually she enjoyed these preliminaries.

'What is it, Marian?' He untied her bonnet strings and tipped off her bonnet, his hands busy at her pins and braid, so he could loosen her thick glossy hair.

She took both his hands in hers. 'Mister, I've sommat to tell you.' She paused. 'It seems I'm with child . . . with your child.' She said it calmly, definitely. There was neither panic nor pleading in her voice.

He stiffened and his hands dropped loosely to the arms of his chair. 'What's this you say? I thought I'd no need to worry about such things . . . that you'd prevent—'

'What's this *you* say! You allow me magic powers? You are only a child yourself. Things that happen have sure consequences, don't you know this? This body of mine's made for making life. I lose them, granted, but that's the savage world.'

He stood up, hauling her to her feet with him. 'This makes a big difference, Marian. So it does.'

'How many times did you tell me that you loved me? That you couldn't do without me? How many times?'

'That's in the way of what we were doing. A man is driven to it. To do those things, to say such things. At those times.' He was defensive.

'Are you sayin' you won't marry us, like you said you would? I'm free enough, Fred being gone. "Just a decent wait." ' She looked at him hard and he sat down again. 'That's what we said, "a decent wait".'

He relaxed a little. 'I suppose we did. A decent wait. That's what we said.'

Her face softened and she put a hand on his shoulder. 'You're tired, old man. Maybe back to work too soon after that bad time you had. You sit quiet, old boy, and I'll make you a nice cup of tea.' She glided through to the kitchen and he could hear a scrape of the kettle, the clash of cups.

He began to think about how he'd got tangled up with her. It was true that he'd been grateful for her close attention when he had been ill unto death. It was true also that he'd found her presence comforting in a way he had almost forgotten in his wanderings from clerk's job to clerk's job. And when he'd first drawn her to him and removed her bonnet so he could kiss her, it was quite a relief, a letting go. He had felt suddenly energised by her. As though their conjugal contact had been the final part of her cure. He had been lonely, and then he had been ill. Then, because of her, he was better. There was so little other company in this village that looked askance at outsiders like him: a step up from a miner or worker; more learned than a shop man or tradesman; but not on a par with the brewery boss or the doctor. He didn't fit in here, any more than she did. And if he had to stay here in this safe job at the brewery, why not be married? Was it such a bad idea?

He stood up as she came through the door carrying a tortoiseshell tray with two china cups and saucers.

'That one's yours, love.' She nodded towards the steaming cup on the left-hand side. 'I put cold water in mine. I cannot abide hot drinks. Never could.'

He waited for her to sit down and sat down himself. He blew on his tea and took a sip. 'I was thinking we should still wait awhile, Marian, just for the decency.'

She took a gulp of her tea. 'I never was in a hurry, old boy, but if there's a bairn inside me that belongs to you, I couldn't think you'd like it born the wrong side of the blanket. Your own flesh and blood. I thought, you being such a decent man . . .'

They sat in silence, drinking their tea and watching the fire in edgy silence. Quick-Manning put down his empty cup. He dabbed his moustache with the napkin she'd placed so conveniently on the tray.

'We . . . well,' he said, 'perhaps we could do this, but discreetly. Be married in Bishop Auckland or even Durham City.' His head was swimming slightly. She must have put something in the tea. He wouldn't put it past her.

'I'm not against that. For this bairn's sake,' she said kindly, as though he were the urgent one. She stood up and went across to him and put her hand on his shoulder. 'Well, old boy. How about it? Shall we go upstairs now?'

Thirteen

One afternoon, my Auntie Mary, pleading severe backache, asks me to take young Maggie and little Eric out for some fresh air. I sport my new outdoor boots; Lizzie pulls on the children's galoshes, as there is a heavy dew. We're all wrapped up against the wind but the sky is bright and clear and the new spring green is showing through in the dry, tired grass that has survived the winter. We make our way through the back door of the house, over the lawn and through the stunted apple trees, beginning to bud; past random clumps of daffodils; past the garden hut at the bottom of the garden, which has smoke curling from its crooked chimney; past the stable where Jonty is polishing the black lacquer trim on my uncle's trap; through the gateway to the narrow stretch of wild grass alongside the weir that feeds the busy flour mill downstream. The children, ever optimistic, carry fishing nets. My pockets are full of dusty apples from the stable loft.

My right side is aching but this is a cheap price to pay for the fact that, in recent days, as well as being lighter in spirit, I've been walking much straighter. In the privacy of my own room I often dance a little to celebrate. And in my mirror I relish the almost smooth, almost clear skin on my cheek. Inevitably when I do this, Marian comes into my mind and I bless the day I met her. I owe her so much and always look for her as I move about the village. My heart lifts when I see her and I treasure the moments of talk we share. Her open smile warms me, but her news is not good as all around her seem ill and she seems weary of it. I also watch out – in vain so far – for Aaron Whitstable.

He must stick close to his workshop. I passed there one day but could see only the top of his bent head.

I think I am so much changed. And it's not only I who think this.

Last night after choir Miss McCullough commented on it. 'This is a funny old place, which has its dark corners, as you may have discovered. But I do remember that I too became more content when I came to live here. I believe I too may have begun to walk straight – well, on the inside – which must be why I stayed when my dear sister passed on.' I have become used now to Miss McCullough talking all in one breath. This habit of hers makes me smile, just as her warmth makes me feel comfortable.

Last night she went on to invite me to tea at her school boarding house: any time I was in Bishop Auckland I was to knock on her door and I would be made welcome.

Then the nice young man called Kit Dawson came up to me, a plate of home-made biscuits in his hand. He put his head on one side like a sharp-eyed sparrow. 'I can't place my finger on just what it is, Miss Kilburn, but there's something quite different about you these days. There's a queer change in you. You light up the room.'

I'm ashamed to say that I smiled then and became the coquette – a new role for me – and asserted that I could not think to what he alluded. In fact I'd noticed him watching me as I walked the length of the hall to take my place beside Miss McCullough. He could not miss how much straighter I walked in my new boots. And as he handed me my cup of tea he must have seen that the right side of my face was almost clear now of the terrible blemish.

As he sat beside me he told me of his day's work in the office of the solicitor Mr Smith, who also works for Mr Chapman of Durham City. He confided that although much of the work he has to do is somewhat dreary and has to be executed standing up, the law is a promising profession. Mr Chapman is a man of affairs in Bishop Auckland and Durham City, and has evidently inspired his young clerk to emulate him. Mr Dawson began to press on about his own virtues rather too much for my liking, confiding that his prospects in life are very good. 'I feel there are no heights to which I may not aspire.' He seemed rather pink-faced and excited.

After filling my tea cup for a second time from the large silver teapot, he'd just ventured to suggest that the next week before choir we might meet for tea in the Kingsway Rooms – with Emily as chaperone, of course – when Emily herself intervened in her usual headlong rush for the eight twenty train. As she hustled me out, Kit Dawson mouthed, 'Four o'clock!' at me like some pantomime mimic, and made me laugh.

Perhaps that is why today, as I walk down by the river with my small cousins, my mind wanders back to my saturnine brother-in-law and that assault of a smacking kiss that occurred on the day he married Lottie. Now, almost guiltily, I start to wonder whether I'd like Kit Dawson to kiss me in that fashion. This thought makes me blush here and now, on the mud path. Even so, I guiltily allow myself to dwell on Kit Dawson even further. He has a smooth, whiskerless young face and a full mouth. I imagine that his skin is very soft, like a girl's.

Then, unbidden, my mind wanders on to contemplate the face of Aaron Whitstable. He has soft side-whiskers and his long upper lip is covered by a moustache. His skin is faintly brown, as though it has been tanned like his leathers, and is set off by those bright watching eyes. The thought of his face makes the smooth young face of Kit Dawson less attractive and suddenly I feel less nervous at the thought of Kit's company. He's only a boy, after all.

On the other hand my thoughts of Aaron Whitstable do the reverse. With these thought I've made myself feel rather *un*easy about the fact that at last I am to go to his house this afternoon so he can check the fit of some new boots, and – my delighted uncle demands it – order yet another pair, this time in black patent, for Sundays.

'Victoria! Victoria! Stop daydreaming!' Young Maggie is tugging at my skirt. 'Look! There is Mrs Cotton in the water!'

So she is. I almost laugh with pleasure at the sight of my friend. Down there in the water, her skirt pulled up almost to the waist, she wades in the shallows, plucking plants and tucking them into a canvas bag she carries on her back. She looks up and a broad smile crosses her face. She is like an image out of some painting. Natural beauty.

'Now, Victoria! Is this morning fine enough for you?' She squints up at me against the sun and I know she is as pleased to see me as I am to see her.

'Dear Marian, that water must be freezing,' I call down. 'What on earth are you doing in the river?'

'Gathering mallow roots, fresh and young, honey. Good for matters of the urine. Maybe they'll release the humours in them invalids of mine. I need sommat more radical to tackle the sickness in that house. The doctors dose them and dose them and they only seem worse.'

I glance down at the children. They are dipping their nets in the water and I am relieved to see that Marian's vulgar reference to a very low human function has gone over their innocent heads.

She makes her way to the bank, shakes down her skirt and thrusts her bare feet into her boots. She puts a damp hand on my sleeve. 'Nice to see you, honey,' she says with some warmth. She shakes up her bag and peers inside. 'I have this old book written by hand that says young mallow and rushes by the door and on the sills will purify the air. But the rushes have to be straight from the river, not too close to the bank.'

'Are your patients no better, Marian?'

'Well, poor Nattrass is failing now and Cotton's lad is not much cop,' she says. Her smiling demeanour falters. 'What point is there in gettin' close to anyone?' She shakes her head. 'Even if they are so easy to get you have to tune yourself to losin' them all the time . . .'

I put my arm through hers. 'Walk along with me, Marian. You have me. I am your friend.'

Linking arms, we walk as far as the curved wall that protects the garden of the Old Hall. We sit down on the stone bench that some inspired stonemason has cut into the wall and embellished with gryphons. Maggie and Eric follow disconsolately, their nets drooping like puppy dogs' tails. I shoo them towards the river to find tadpoles. No doubt they'll run to their mother with stories of me sitting around the riverbank with my friend Mrs Cotton, but I cannot trouble myself about this.

Marian smells of the river, damp and very faintly rotten. Even this, now, is not unsavoury to me. It is part of her natural self, the self that I am so drawn to.

'Can my uncle not help you?' I think of his shelves of coloured bottles. 'Surely he has something for your invalids?'

'He's a saint, that uncle of yours. He's called round mine every day, checking on Nattrass. Him, or that Chalmers, like. I can't say I take to that fellow as much as your uncle. But they ask no payment, which well they might. They do give the poor lads medicine, but it's no better than my purges. Not strong enough, if you ask me.' She sighs deeply. 'I've told them, like I've told that Thomas Riley, that it's all about that house in Johnson Terrace. The walls're teeming with wet. Even the bit of wallpaper I put on the wall to cheer it up when we first moved in, even that's peeling.'

'Is there no better place? No other house for you?'

'Well, I've had words with Riley and there's a house on the green that I'm promised. At least that'll be better than living by that filthy Oakley Beck.' She sits in silence, then begins to brighten entirely. She turns to face me, puts a hand on mine: an intimate gesture that I enjoy now . . . 'I watched you walk down the lane there, honey, and you can't half tell Master Whitstable's fixed the problem of that foot. You hardly rock at all.'

I have to laugh. 'Well, Marian, we can't say he's really fixed it. My foot still twists. I do rock a bit.'

'But you're walking just about straight now.'

'It doesn't fix the foot,' I insist. 'Just makes me move better.'

'Oh, honey, what d'you want?' she says, her brows raised to the sky. 'Jam on it? Surely good enough is good enough?'

I have to laugh at this. To placate her I put my hand down my own nearly smooth cheek. 'But the poultice and the potion,' I say, 'they have both been a great success. The mark's nearly gone and I've never had such energy, never felt so good.'

She leans over and runs a still-damp finger down the cheek. 'Seems like,' she says. 'And how are your affections, child? Those that surge within?'

A savage charge runs through me and I pull my face away from her. 'Marian!'

She shrugs. 'The potion works in all kinds of ways. Makes you notice others, makes others notice you. I bet more than Master Whitstable's taken notice of you.'

'What on earth did you put in that stuff?'

She shrugs. 'I told you clear enough when you asked before. I made a list for you. It's nothing really. All it does is make you who you really are and that's what draws people to you.' She stands up and slings her bag over her shoulder. I wish she would stay.

She takes my hand in hers and pats it. 'I need to go and see my invalids. That Ma Dodds'll be champing at the bit. On top of the sick ones, my baby Robbie's teething and is getting to be a handful.' She looks me in the eye, bringing her face close to mine. 'It's good that Aaron did such a fine job for you. Nice lad. Keeps cheerful, considering.'

'Considering what?'

'He told me once that before he was here in West Auckland he was up in Morpeth and his house blew up in a fire. Feller lost his leathers, half his tools.' She pauses. 'Lost his wife and bairn too. That finger of fate never lets up. I know it, he knows it.' She shakes her head slightly then turns sharp right, almost like a soldier, and marches away. I watch her for a moment as she strides across the green, looking neither to the right nor the left.

I don't think it's the potion. I think it is Marian herself who has somehow shown me who I am and made my life what it is now, made people like Aaron and Kit and Miss McCullough take to me so. I have come to the conclusion that it's a kind of healing, a kind of love that's outside potions.

This morning at breakfast – I can't remember for what reason – my Auntie Mary mentioned Marian. 'The woman craves for excitement. She's always on the road. She's always leaving that old woman to cope with the sick children and that so-called lodger of hers.' She grimaced. 'At one time I thought she was eccentric, amusing even. But these days she gives me the shudders. I am puzzled why you have this fancy for her, Victoria. I see that she seeks you out. And perhaps you seek her out?' She looked at me with earnest, bewildered appeal: a kindly woman who hates to be seen to be unkind. All I could say, quite lamely, was that Marian Cotton had a lot of life about her; that she'd helped me with the matter of the boots. (The poultice and the potion are still a secret, although Auntie Mary has commented on my clearing skin, giving credit to her fine food and the country air, sooty though it is.)

'Mrs Cotton has this wonderful spark,' I ended, my voice wavering. 'You can warm yourself on it. Such energy . . .'

My aunt laughed then. 'She's laid a spell on you just as she has on my dear William.' Then she went back to her kedgeree. To be honest, she didn't sound too troubled by Marian. Not really.

Fourteen

On her way back across the green, Marian Cotton came across Thomas Riley, well turned out in his broadcloth coat, a jaunty daffodil in his buttonhole. 'So what is it, Thomas Riley?' she said. 'Smart as a carrot, you are. Going to see the Queen, are we?'

He smiled slightly. 'Not quite that, Mrs Cotton . . . Marian. I'm off to Bishop Auckland to see my solicitor about a new bit of land that I've taken a fancy for. Then on to a meeting with the overseer.'

She shifted her heavy herb satchel so that it sat more comfortably on her shoulder. 'It's all fixed then, for that house for me on Front Street? I'm hoping you'll keep to your promise.'

'Aye. On its way. It'll take a few weeks to fix.' He looked at her closely. 'I'll need further details to fill in the papers. Just how old did you say you were, Marian?'

'I didn't say. But if yer must know I'm just past forty. Born eighteen thirty-two. My own father was coming up seventeen when I was born. I was the child of children. No good can ever come from that.'

He nodded. Then he coughed. 'Me own son – the one we lost – he was seventeen when he died.'

'I heard tell of this. Nothing is kept quiet in this place. Must have been hard times for you, though, Mr Riley, losing a young'n like that. Don't I know that? You have them, you lose them. Sometimes it seems to me like God's forsaken the lot of us. No point, is there, in being good?'

He glanced around the green. Only a few feet away from them three children were playing 'kick the cog' with a bashed-up old bucket. A

77

group of women in aprons clustered around the gaping back of a butcher's wagon on the far end of the green. 'We-ell, I don't know. Maybe you should watch that, Marian.'

'Watch what?'

'Watch that talk, Marian. Tongues like vipers, round here. It'll be even harder when you live on the green. It's even more in the open here.' A smile flickered briefly across his face. 'You won't be able to nip round Quick-Manning's under cover of dark like you can now. You'll need more discretion than that.'

She looked him straight in the eye. 'That Sarah Shaw has been gabbin' again. Nosy neighbours, save me from them. But I've more to worry about than what the likes of her thinks. Do you reckon I care about her and those idle chatterers?'

He shook his head. 'Not in the least, Marian. That's the problem.'

She looked up at him, her eyes gleaming. 'And that's why you like us, Thomas. I'll bet you on that.' She smiled at him, her eyes bright, her white teeth gleaming. 'Me not being discreet. And knowing that I know how to be grateful – grateful, that is, to someone that does me favours.'

He glanced round at the busy, watching edges of the green. 'And that's why they'll get you, Marian, the people you offend. My advice to you is to watch your back, like any good soldier.' He changed tack. 'And how's young Charlie these days?'

'Well, *Mr* Riley, he's better than his brother Freddie and much better than poor Mr Nattrass, who's fading fast.' Her tone was neutral, measured. 'He's not the man he was.' Then she smiled slightly. 'Did you know we were sweethearts once? Not here, not now. But years ago when we were both quite young.'

Riley had known Nattrass when he was a strapping miner who called every week at the corner shop for his tobacco. He had seemed a good enough fellow, genial, even. And clearly fond of Marian, thinking he'd got a good billet when she took him in as a lodger before he was cast down by this sickness. That was not so long ago. How things had changed.

'But young Charlie's holding it off?' he asked now.

'Aye. I think so.' She cocked her head to one side. 'I'd swear you have a soft spot for young Charlie, Mr Riley.'

'He reminds me of . . . someone.'

'Aye. That struck me.' Her gaze moved beyond him to where she could see Margaret Riley standing in the door of the shop. 'I'd better go,' she looked up and winked at him, 'or your lass'll have the evil eye on me.' With her free hand she lifted her skirts just a little too far above her slender ankles and made her way across the deep grass towards the edge of the green that led to Johnson Terrace.

Thomas didn't turn back to the shop, but continued on his way to the station. He was looking forward to his meetings today. He relished the knowledge that in the district he was known as a 'coming man'. And with all that land freed up by the bishop for new shops and houses for the prosperous tradesmen, Bishop Auckland was a coming place. They were made for each other.

Fifteen

This is the third time I've been to the shoemaker's and I still relish the peculiar atmosphere of Mr Whitstable's workshop. I love its neatness and its smoky warmth; the bench with the self-made tools; the small shelf by the fire loaded with his radical journals and books; the cold pipe in the old saucer.

He gets to his feet as I enter and gestures for me to sit on the leather-topped stool he's just vacated. 'I've been sittin' here watching you as you move round the village, Miss Kilburn.' He nods at the long low window. 'Walkin' straight. Takin' the children home with their tiddlers in jars. Goin' down to the shop. Consortin' with Mrs Cotton. You're walkin' well. And I see now where the skin on your face is clearin' up, on that side that was blighted.'

'I have our friend Marian to thank for that, Mr Whitstable. She gave me a poultice to put on it. I'll thank her for ever.' I peer through the window. 'Yes, there's that house Marian wants to move into. And there's Western House. You must see everything from here.'

'So do all the folk round here. The green's a cockpit.' He laughs. 'It's been a bear-pit more than once. There *was* a bear here in the village once, on a chain. Brought by travellers. The villagers had their dogs up at it, poor ragged beast. Brought to earth, it was.' He pauses. 'Aye, they see everything. Their windows are their newspaper, Miss Kilburn, their penny-dreadfuls. Everything is recorded and made sommat of. A person needs to watch themselves in this place.' He leans forward to poke the fire and the light flickers across his brown arms. I clutch my hands to stop them reaching out and touching that soft skin. What is happening to me? I know there is something, *something* in Marian's potion that's making me do this. These days I find myself savouring thoughts that my mother and Lottie would never have recognised in me. In fact the girl called Victoria who languished on my mother's chaise longue would not have recognised these thoughts either.

Such changes.

He reads my mind. 'She's had a great impact on you, hasn't she? But Marian Cotton's a strange mate for you, Miss Kilburn. If you don't mind me saying, like.'

'That is my aunt's view, but I can't think why you'd say that, Mr Whitstable. She's your friend too.'

' 'S easy to be friendly with Marian. She's needy in a way but doesn't let you see it. And she's direct, straightforward, not like any woman I ever met. Nor many men.'

'And you really like that?' I am curious. 'The way she is?'

'It's a perverse thing, maybe, but many men do. It's a . . . change.' He kneels down suddenly and without ceremony undoes my buttons and laces. He eases off my boots and holds them up to the light of the window to scrutinise the wear. 'Like I say, you're walking well, Miss Kilburn. Have you aches on the opposite side?'

'Not so much in the leg. On my . . . up here.' I place my hand over my petticoats roughly where my hipbone is.

'Well, miss, manners say I can't feel you there, but my guess is that the muscles will be having to change their habit: be short where they would be long, long where they would be short. And this shoe needs just a bit more compensating. See that wear on the edge of the sole? I'll keep hold of these now and adjust them a bit for you.'

'Mr Whitstable!' (I am astonished at my own arch tone. I am teasing him. Being arch with Kit Lawson, teasing Aaron Whitstable. Where does this come from?) 'I cannot walk home barefoot. Where would be my reputation then on your cockpit of a green?'

He stares at me for a second, and then smiles slightly. 'You should take no notice of what people here say. They will crush you in their vice. I have your second pair of outdoor boots ready. And I have more.' He turns to unwrap a parcel that stands on the dresser beside the fireplace. 'I was going to leave these at Western House for you if you didn't come today.' He pulls the paper away to reveal a pair of patent leather boots that glitter like tar in the flickering light of the fire.

I am amazed. 'I was calling specially today to ask you to make me another pair for—'

'Sunday. I thought of that.' He kneels down, puts my feet into them, then ties and buttons them for me. 'Now, stand up and walk to the door,' he orders. 'Now, back to me.'

I do as I am told and come to stand before him. 'Is this all right?' I say, looking up at him.

'All right?' He ducks his head until his face, his lips, his cheek are too close to mine. I can feel the heat of his skin and I want to reach up and touch it with my lips. To touch his lips with mine. I imagine his lips will be cool, soft and gentle. So very different from the searing touch of my brother-in-law. And yet I am melting inside at the thought of it.

He pulls away and I must put on the new outdoor boots, which fit perfectly. These I will keep on. He fastens them for me, then he pulls away quickly. He goes to the bench and picks up the boots he has just removed from my feet. He holds them towards the afternoon light. 'Like I say, this pair need just a little adjustment,' he says. 'That should fix them. I'll do that this afternoon and leave them at the house in the morning.'

'I'll call for them,' I say quickly. 'Here.'

He turns round and very slowly shakes his head. 'Oh, I think not, Miss Kilburn. I think it's too dangerous for you to come here again.'

I make a play of surveying the neat aromatic space. 'I'm in no danger here,' I say. 'No danger from you, surely!'

He looks at me then, from the flowers on my bonnet to the tips of my new outdoor boots. From anyone else – even Kit Dawson – this would have been insolence. But I don't feel insulted, not here. Not today. Finally he says, 'It's me that's in danger here, Miss Kilburn, not you.' He parcels up the patent boots and thrusts them in to my hand, then he turns away from me towards his bench and throws words over his shoulder like crumbs to a starving man. 'I'll just get on, if you don't mind. Can you close the door tight on your way out, d'you think? There's quite a breeze blowing up out there. Unpredictable, April weather.'

And I'm outside the door, tasting that chilly breeze and vowing to take no more of Marian's potion, which, it seems, has made me so light-minded and free that I'm embarrassing myself.

'Don't worry about it, honey.'

I swing round to see Marian, about to go into Aaron's house.

Of course I am blushing. 'Worry about what?'

'Whatever is on your mind. You look worried.' She glances at Aaron's door and back at me. 'Aaron can wait. What say I walk you back home and I tell you what to do when a man gives you the cold shoulder?'

This makes me laugh. I hold out my arm and she takes it. We walk down the village arm in arm, like the friends we are. As we walk she sings the praises of Aaron Whitstable in my ear, telling me that perhaps I have punched the poor lad in the heart and he is a bit giddy. 'But give him time, honey. Just give him a bit of time.'

We pass two women who stare at us and mutter to each other but we are too busy laughing to care.

Sixteen

The woman, young and rather plump, with an open bright-eyed face, stopped at Marian's gate. 'Oh, Mrs Cotton, can I have a word?'

Marian was standing leaning against her wall, savouring the fresh air, delaying the moment when she had to return to the house, which she found stifling, not just because of the competing neediness of those inside, but because she always kept her sick rooms hot, trying to burn away the fever that lived there. Such heat was hard-won, being the product of end-loads of coal she obtained from the colliery coalman in return for small favours after dark at the back of the wash house

'Mrs Edwards, is it?' she said to the woman. 'I've seen you down here.'

'Aye. I live down the bottom of the terrace.' The woman paused. 'They say you know about things.'

'We all know about things, honey.'

The woman took a deep breath. 'They say you know how to stop a bairn and start a bairn.'

'I can't think why you'd say that. Though I can see that some people'd like to stop a bairn if they've strayed. Or more likely if their man's given them another one too quick.' In fact she had secretly done that favour for one or two benighted women, but such things, naturally, were secret.

The woman shook her head. 'Nah. I wouldn't stop any bairn. What a sin that would be. My trouble is, I've been married seven years with neither sight nor sign of a bairn and my man is none too pleased. I thought you might just have sommat . . .'

Marian was already shaking her head. 'Really hard, that one, honey. I can give you some tonic to make you and your husband strong, so nature may take a better course. But that's it. Easier to stop than to start, babies.'

The woman sighed. 'I thought it would be too good to be true. I've this yearnin' for a babby to teck care of, to love. Ever since I was eleven I wanted me own bairn. And here I am, thirty year old and barren.'

Marian stood up straight and put a hand on the woman's arm. 'Aye, a bairn is a wonderful thing,' she said softly. 'But fragile. So easily lost.'

Mrs Edwards shuddered at the insinuation. 'Mrs Cotton, I don't think . . .'

But Marian was already turning towards the house. 'I'll just go and get you this herb tea. Remember to teck it morn and night, you and your husband both, never miss. You never know, you might just fall lucky.'

Seventeen

Despite my misgivings about my feelings for Aaron I have not stopped taking Marian's potion, which I still think has something to do with how open and easy I feel about things. So, despite his troubling rejection of my presence in his shop, I intend to return to see Aaron.

My routine of helping Mr Carr with the medicines in the morning continues. Occasionally, Dr Chalmers will come and join us, mixing his own medicines for his pauper patients, who seem to mill in a muttering crowd just beyond the window. He is always in a hurry, throwing the medicines about with a flamboyant hand, filling in the poison book with a flourish.

Mr Carr and my uncle are more measured in their work. Working down there, just next to his surgery, I am becoming more and more conscious of the high regard in which my uncle is held in the village. I am proud of his hard and unremitting efforts to establish a level of civilised care among these poor people. I relish the affectionate note in the buzz of voices in his surgery as he bustles in and out, replenishing the stocks of drugs and potions that weigh down his ever-present black bag.

The day after I acquire my new patent shoes, my uncle – bustling in yet again – catches sight of me and frowns for a second as though I am a stranger, then his vision clears and he says, 'I have a call for your friend Marian Cotton, Victoria. That stepchild of hers, Frederick, is failing. I must say, I saw him only yesterday and Mrs Dodds is back again for me.' He jams on his hat and whirls out again, leaving a trailing scent of pipe smoke and chloroform.

Mr Carr stares after him. 'I can never make out why the doctor does it, chasing so assiduously after those ne'er-do-wells. They die, they always die and never do they pay. And here's the doctor as poor as a church mouse himself.'

I think of my uncle's house and its large garden, its groom and gardener and its two servants. He may not be as rich as my father but my uncle is not so very poor.

I nod briefly at Mr Carr, take off my black apron and cuffs and hurry out of the dispensary to get my bonnet and cloak. Perhaps I should do something for Marian. Be on hand to help in some way.

On Johnson Terrace, I duck through lines of chilly washing, past stinking privies, almost tripping over a squealing pig that darts out of one of the gates. Although it's nearly noon the clouds are lying very low, reflecting an eerie daytime twilight that in some strange way masks the distant sounds of the village green. A woman with dense black hair in a pigtail down her back is leaning over a gate. She directs me to the back of the terrace and the mean door of Marian's narrow dwelling. Charlie, wrapped in a long scarf with his strange velvet cap on his head, is sitting inside the back gate on the small stool they call a cracket, playing his penny whistle.

Marian's door is ajar. I am engulfed by a draught of dense, sweet-smelling heat. The kitchen beyond the door seems crowded. I can hear the high keening cry of the teething baby. Through the spotless window I can see the bulk of Mrs Dodds and the towering height of my uncle, who, as I watch, sits down at the table and takes out his pen. Marian is standing, rigid as any statue, by the mantelshelf. I don't know what makes her do this but she looks up, into my eyes. Her stare is blank. Her normally blazing eyes are opaque. She looks sad or angry but I can't quite understand which.

In a second she is outside the door, standing beside me, holding my arm quite roughly in a strong grasp. 'What are you doin' here, child?' Her tone is low, almost growling. She seems like a stranger. Gone is the merry friend who walked down the green with me arm in arm. 'D'yer want to catch it too? Can't you smell it here? The sickness? The seamy mire of the beck? The rank sweat of folks living too close? That's what's just now taken young Freddie Cotton from us. Now my own bairn's in hell with his teeth. The fever's got Nattrass in its death grip. Get yourself away. Don't add yourself to that black list. Or you'll find yourself six feet under like the rest of 'em.'

She thrusts me towards the gate and I stumble out into the lane. I stand still and wait there, under the curious eye of a rooster hopping about on a midden heap and the blank gaze of the dark-haired woman, who stands there, her arms folded under her armpits. Seven ragged children sit in a row on a broken wall like baby crows, watching me with their bright eyes.

My uncle emerges from the house, clashing the crude plank door behind him. He grasps my elbow and marches me down the back street out on to the comparatively broad reaches of the Darlington Road.

'Are you mad?' His rage is a match for Marian's. 'That is no place for you. Filthy. Insanitary. The sewer's overflowing. There are ten diseases within ten feet of here that could kill you. Your father would never forgive me if anything happened to you. He sent you here, entrusting us to bring you back to health, and you place yourself in the middle of a stinking unhealthy mire.'

I hurry alongside him, hopping a little to keep up with his long stride. 'The boy?' I gasp.

'Gone,' he says bitterly. 'I just signed the certificate. I will never get used to it, how easily they slip away. How cheap is life.'

'What was it?' I say breathlessly. 'How did he die?'

'Enteric fever. Very common. His father, Fred, died of it and he was a strong man. This boy's been fighting it off almost since then. How Marian's kept him alive I don't know. Her nursing skills, I suppose. Now that battle's over for him. Poor Mr Nattrass is just hanging on. And young Charlie is fragile. And the baby there is in convulsions from teething. Good God! There's no end to all this.' His voice is wretched. In his anger against fate my uncle has almost forgotten me.

I hop along beside him, ashamed of my selfish pride now I walk straighter and my skin is smooth, mortified by my sensual thoughts about the shoemaker, even ashamed of my childish delight in the advanced ideas of Miss Cobbe.

Later that day I wonder how right it is for me to go to choir as usual. But I feel so helpless to do anything about Marian and her plight. She made that quite clear. And when he got home my uncle crashed around the house in an uncharacteristic bad temper and looked at me as though I were a stranger.

But Emily has saved the day by insisting that we should go to choir as usual. So I find myself singing quite happily under Nicholas Kilburn's enthusiastic baton and joining my voice with the warm contralto of Miss McCullough. As I do so I can feel my own optimism rising again. Marian's rough treatment was understandable, a consequence of her own despair. It had nothing to do with our friendship, which will, I am sure, survive even these events.

As well as this I find my bruised feelings soothed by the attentions of Kit Lawson, who insists on sitting beside me when it is time for tea and biscuits. As he talks away, gossiping indiscreetly about things going on at the court, I am forced to reflect that, eager, charming and suitable as he is, Kit does not have a shred of the magnetism of Aaron Whitstable. The problem is that Aaron, by anyone's count, could not be called a suitable object for my growing affection for him. Affection! That's what it is. I will not deny it even to myself, any more than I will deny my affection for Marian.

But in the church hall I still smile and nod at Kit's chatter, rather basking in his obvious admiration and affection. I go so far as to agree to meet him for tea in the Kingsway Rooms. There is to be an extra practice next week and we agree to meet there for tea before we make our way to the church hall. Marian would probably be contemptuous of such teasing and Miss Cobbe would probably criticise me for playing a man's game. But, for this evening, this little assignation makes me feel liked and admired, and that will suffice.

Eighteen

Riley's shop was empty when Marian called to announce the news of young Frederick Cotton's death. The bell trembled on its spring for a long time. The curtain in the doorway to the back room shook for a second, then was still. After a full minute Thomas Riley came bustling through.

'Mrs Cotton!' he said with bright formality. 'What can I do for you?'

They both knew Margaret Riley was waiting behind the curtain. Her invisible presence filled the cluttered shop. Marian looked at Thomas, her eyes cold and lifeless as the still sea on a grey day. 'Did you hear young Freddie's been taken? I've lost him. Another of those Cottons gone now.' She paused. 'You know my situation, Mr Riley. The Parish will have to bury him.'

'You must have insurance, Mrs Cotton.'

'Aye. I'll walk along to Mr Young's with the doctor's certificate, soon as I've seen you.'

'Well, I don't want to sound brutal, Mrs Cotton, but you must bury him with that.'

She brought a hand down on the counter with a thump, making him flinch. 'That's not for *that*. I've debts to pay, things to buy back from pawn. And then I've gotta get my stuff fumigated and scoured of that sickness that is soaked into it so I can move into the house on the green.' She reached out and grasped his hand where it lay on the counter. 'Go on, Tommy,' she almost whispered now. 'Help me this way.'

There was a cough from behind the curtain. He rescued his hand. 'I'll see what I can do, Mrs Cotton.'

Her shoulders relaxed and she nodded, the faintest of smiles finally softening her face. 'Well, thank you, Mr Riley.' She turned to go. 'One thing, though. Perhaps we should hang fire a day or so? Might be better to make do with one funeral for two. My own bairn's fading too. He'll not last long.' Her tone was bleak.

He frowned. 'Not young Charlie?'

'No. Don't you worry about that. It's me own little'n, Robbie. The last of my own. Doctor says it's just teething but I've never seen teething like this. Convulsions. I sometimes think these doctors don't know everything.' She went out, clashing the door behind her.

Margaret pulled back the curtain and moved through to stand beside her husband at the counter. 'What a cold, uncaring *bitch* she is,' said Margaret, leaking the words through gritted teeth. 'You'd think she was talking about a pound of bacon. She's pleased to be shot of them. More time for her fancy man, no doubt.'

Thomas glanced at his wife. 'Careful now, Margaret. Language.'

'She brings us all down to her level. Does she care about that boy who's died, or the baby who's dying? Does she care about her so-called lodger who's breathing his last?'

He shrugged his shoulders. 'She's a nurse, Margaret. Used to death and all its trappings. She's used to keeping her feelings in. Covering up.'

'Too used, if you ask me. I think she *likes* all those trappings. She *likes* having them all cupped in her hands like that. Then she gets tired of them and gets old Mrs Dodds and others to do her work. Anyway, these poor souls are her own kin, not some smallpox patient in some scruffy hovel.' She turned away. 'She's unnatural. Too keen on 'ticing the men. Everyone says so. Now she cannot even show the natural grief at the death of her child.' She lifted the curtain and glided into the back room.

He turned and shouted after her, 'Not like you, my dear Margaret. Couldn't you show her how to grieve? Show her how to grieve for ten years and turn to stone in the process.'

The bell rang and Thomas turned to become the unctuous shopkeeper again. It was Mrs Grey from Western House, neat in a dun-coloured bonnet and carrying a basket. She was closely followed by Sarah Shaw,

Marian's neighbour, whose black plait was now wound round her head under a man's woollen cap.

He smiled blandly. 'What can I do for you, Mrs Grey?'

'We'd like to speak to Mrs Riley,' she said. 'We need a word.'

Nineteen

The Kilburn family had lived in the wider regions of South Durham for nearly a hundred years and were connected in various ways with the local community. Through his wife, for instance, William Kilburn was related to the old farming families around the ancient villages of Escomb and Newfield. Through his mother he was related to the Smiths, one of whom, Margaret, was married to Riley, the grocer in this village in which generations of Kilburns had served in the role of surgeon.

Though she treasured the Kilburn connection, Margaret Riley had never taken advantage of it before today. Now, with Mrs Grey and Sarah Shaw at her side, she stood before William Kilburn in his study, demanding his attention in the pressing matter of Marian Cotton. He told them all to sit down, including Rebecca Grey, who was reluctant to do so in his presence. Sarah Shaw bobbed a curtsy before she sat on the very edge of a hard chair and looked around her with barely concealed curiosity.

Kilburn listened to them patiently for a while, as their protests and tales overlaid each other in a chorus of dislike for Marian Cotton. He let them go on for a while, then he struck the scarred surface of his desk with a pencil and they fell to silence.

'Are you telling me that there is something wrong with the woman because people die around her? I have to tell you that people die around us all in this place. We have just survived an epidemic that took nearly three hundred souls around here, sixty-four in this little village alone. People die of accidents brought about by drink, they die in ill-kept

93

mines, they die in childbirth or in childhood. I see it every day of my life. What makes her situation so different?'

The room was charged with silence for a moment, then Margaret Riley spoke. 'It's her attitude to it, William.' Her use of his Christian name resonated in the room, setting up a transient atmosphere of equality. 'It shows in her attitude, the way she sets herself up.'

Sarah Shaw, encouraged, said, 'The woman sheds no tears, Doctor. She seems resolved that they will all die. It's unnatural.'

'She knows no containment,' said Rebecca Grey. 'She doesn't know her place.'

'The woman has no morals,' said Sarah Shaw. 'She was going with Nattrass when Cotton was lying ill. Now, with Nattras abed, she goes with the excise officer. And she gives herself for favours, even while she puts on airs. Beg pardon, sir, but there's no other way to say this.'

William sighed. 'Are you telling me that before she came there was no immorality in this village?'

Margaret Riley shrugged. 'We can't say that. The place is rife. Eleven public houses in a place as small as this? And so many miners coming in to work without a family to steady them. But—'

'But she flaunts it,' put in Rebecca Grey. 'It's not decent.'

'So what do you want me to do? Join you in making a scapegoat of this woman for all the ills that befall this poor village? A woman who struggles on in her own adversity and does work no one else will touch? A woman who is about to bury her child, perhaps her children?'

The silence ticked on. Then Sarah Shaw, the only one who had no real connection with the doctor, burst out with what they were all thinking. 'It's always the men, Doctor. She can make her case, no bother, with the men. They fall for it hook, line and sinker.'

William's normally pale cheeks were getting redder. Rebecca Grey grabbed the woman's arm to shut her up. 'What Sarah means, Doctor, is—'

He stood up. 'Well, I must thank you ladies for taking the trouble to come to see me, but I've patients to see and more to consider than such envious, spiteful tittle-tattle.' He picked up his black case and strode to the door. 'Perhaps you would see your friends out, Mrs Grey?' He glanced across at Margaret Riley. 'Perhaps you will give my regards to your uncle when you see him, Margaret?'

The three women sat in silence for a second before Rebecca stood up, her corset creaking, her stiff skirts rustling. 'Well, then, I'm sure the doctor will reflect on what we've said. We've given notice. Events will prove us right, have no doubt about it, ladies.'

Twenty

Today is extra practice day and I've managed to persuade Auntie Mary to allow me to bring Emily into Bishop Auckland early so that we can have tea in the Kingsway Rooms at four o'clock.

'I haven't yet been into the town during the day, Auntie, and I thought we might buy a book for Emily at Braithwaites, then have tea before choir,' I say to her. 'Emily's been so welcoming to me, has brought me such friendship. I thought I might give her a treat.'

I'm sure I look the picture of innocence, but am only briefly visited by guilt at my deception. Changes stirring within me – caused by this place, which is both wonderful and threatening at the same time, and the impact of my friendship with Marian – allow me not only to have wanton thoughts about two men of my acquaintance, but also to deceive my loving aunt with this less-than-innocent visit to town to meet one of these men. Fortunately, my sweet aunt (brought a little low this week by her condition) is very trusting, and waves us off with something akin to relief.

We are rather delayed by Emily's dithering around the shop before she chooses *The Legend of Sir Galahad*. When we arrive at the Kingsway Rooms, Kit Dawson is sitting there beside an enormous aspidistra with highly polished leaves. Smiling broadly, he waves a handkerchief to catch our attention. At the table, Emily opens her book and proceeds to ignore us. I am not clear whether this is due to the particular charms of *Sir Galahad* or her natural discretion. Perhaps, as normally she is forbidden to read at the table, she too tastes forbidden fruit today.

After the usual pleasantries about the weather (gloomy) and our own health (blooming), Kit Dawson tells me a tale about his day sitting at Mr Chapman's elbow in the local magistrates' court, making notes regarding a case about two women in West Auckland who came to blows over the abuse of a washing line, and renewed the battle again in court only to be fined five shillings each and bound over to keep the peace. He thinks this is very funny, but I am concerned at the fine. 'That would mean such a lot of money to these women. A week's wages for Lizzie, my aunt's maid.'

Kit Dawson is entirely indifferent about this. 'If they care about that, they shouldn't start bashing each other. They're barbarians, every last one of them.'

I shake my head. 'Mr Dawson, to be poor is a misfortune, not a source of barbarism.' I have to say I regret the primness of my tone but mean what I say.

To my surprise, he laughs. 'Ah, you live a protected life, Miss Victoria. You should see what I see in court. Drunken miners, low women, thieves and vagabonds, wife-beating husbands, husband-beating wives. For me it's like that first, most absurd circle of Hell in that courtroom.'

We pause while a neat silver-haired waitress lays out our tea: substantial cucumber and ham sandwiches; cakes on a tiered stand; silver teapot and water jug; china milk jug and sugar basin. She's slow-moving and we have to be very patient. The woman completes her task, glares frostily at Emily (who still has her head in her book), and bustles away.

This business gives me time to gather my argument. 'I'm in no way protected, Mr Dawson. We live right there in the village. I have been on calls with my uncle to the poorest of houses. I have seen the miners on their few hours off, streaming into the public houses, even sometimes fighting on the green. I have seen the spindly children and the anxious mothers at the surgery. My aunt takes food to paupers; my uncle tends them without pay. Only yesterday I was at a house where a child died—'

He's holding up his hands as though surrendering. '*Mea culpa! Mea culpa!* You share my insights into these barbarian hordes. I acknowledge it.'

I lean over and pour tea into his china cup. 'I must insist, Mr Dawson, there are no barbarian hordes around here. They are merely poor and without direction.'

'Without direction?' He claps his hand to his forehead in a melodramatic fashion. 'Miss Victoria! These days there are churches and chapels being built on every street corner. There are Temples to Temperance in every village. Every village hall has its programme of Improving Talks. Our own choir saves even us from straying from The Way Called Strait.' His speech is full of capitals.

His sheer bombast makes me smile and alerts me to the fact that we seem to be straying away from the safe waters of polite conversation.

I indicate the large blue plate. 'Those ham sandwiches look delicious. Would you care for one, Mr Dawson?'

I turn to Emily. 'Now, Em, perhaps you should put away your *Sir Galahad* and concentrate on your tea?'

Much later that day, as we settle down in the train for the short journey back to West Auckland, Emily turns to me, her eyes asparkle. 'Do you think Mr Dawson is very handsome?'

I consider the point. 'He is nice-looking, I think. He certainly looks well fed.'

'I think he's very enamoured. He looks at you as though you are a princess. Or like a jam tart he is about to eat.'

'You talk such rot, Em.'

'Would you walk out with him?'

I consider this. 'I don't really know. He looks nice and—'

'. . . he laughs a lot,' puts in Emily. 'That's a nice thing, even in spite of the big teeth.'

'Yes, it is a nice thing. But he has such unfortunate ideas, is so judgemental.'

Emily reaches into her velvet bag, takes out *Sir Galahad*. 'That's a relief. I thought he might bowl you over, paying for the tea like that and mooning over you in choir.'

'Not likely,' I say. 'He's not at all to my taste.'

'Good. He's not to my taste either.' Now her head is bent over her book and our journey is completed in silence.

As the pockmarked, shadowy countryside races by, I rather relish the notion that I've just, in my head, rejected the first man who has ever seen me as myself, not some fainting invalid. Then my mind goes to the village he has so much maligned. Then I think of Aaron Whitstable.

98

Then, inevitably, Marian Cotton. I decide I must go to the funeral of the child. It's the least I can do to support her. I can't imagine there will be many mourners there.

Twenty-One

'It's a present for you.' Marian held out the silver watch in her mittened hand.

Quick-Manning stood with his arms by his sides, not touching the proffered gift. Having heard the news of the death of the boy from Mrs Shaw as he came home from the brewery, he'd not expected to see Marian tonight. He had to admit that he'd felt a stab of resentment that something . . . anything . . . should keep her from him, but had then felt uncomfortable at his own selfishness. In his saner moments he recognised that Marian Cotton was like an addiction for him, like strong drink or opium. The more he had of her, the less he could do without her. 'It looks like a very decent watch,' he said. 'How . . .?'

'I was left it, fair and square, by Fred Cotton in his will. Today I just came into a bit of money and I got it out of pawn. I want you to have it.' She thrust it into his chest and he had to grab it to save it from falling. 'There, take a look at it in the light. It's a very good one. See the engraving on the case? Dragons.'

He did as he was told. He wondered where a miner might get such a watch. But these miners were odd men. Paupers one minute, rich men the next. 'As you say, Marian, a very fine watch. I can't think why you want me to have this—'

'Can't you see?' she interrupted. 'It's a pledge. For our marriage. Like a ring. You said you'd get us a ring for me finger. Do you remember?'

He couldn't remember. He stared at the watch.

'We can get one soon,' she said urgently. 'Nattrass won't be with us long. Signs are there. And then I'll move into this new house on the green.'

' "Won't be with us"?' He scowled.

'Well, it could be two things. One, he'll get better and'll be off about his business because he knows he's nothing to me. The other . . . well, you know what the other is. Nature will take its toll.'

He stared at her, the hair on the back of his neck lifting slightly. 'You're incorrigible, Marian.'

'Well, I don't know that word, but I'll take it as a good thing.' She took the watch from his hand and tucked it into his pocket, threading the head of the gold chain through his buttonhole. She patted his shoulder. 'There now! I've been waiting a long time to see it in the right place.' Her tone was warm, motherly. She lifted his hand – a soft clerk's hand – and kissed the palm. 'Now then, honey, shall wuh make tha one of my special cups of tea or shall we just go upstairs and get us another kind of comfort to keep the demons at bay?'

Twenty-Two

I am determined now to go to this double funeral to support Marian. Sadly, the teething baby has been taken as well as young Freddie, so there will be two coffins. Marian must be feeling so bad about it all. Unfortunately, my determination to attend the funeral has been the instance of a rare quarrel between my aunt and uncle.

This morning Auntie Mary told me she thought it a scandal, saying I've been led astray by 'that strange woman'.

My uncle berated her for listening to tittle-tattle and praised me for my charitable and caring attitude. 'It leaps the bounds of class and obligation. No bad thing in a young woman.' (He is so very advanced in his views!)

'I'm surprised you don't attend this funeral yourself, William,' my aunt said scornfully, 'if you feel this way.'

'I can't attend myself,' he said. 'I've a meeting of the Board of Guardians in Bishop and then urgent work in the dispensary.' He turned to me. 'Perhaps you'd care to use the trap, Victoria? The walk to the church at St Helen's could tire you. It's a fair lap.'

At that, my Auntie Mary rushed from the breakfast room, clashing the door behind her. I confess that I was surprised at my uncle's obduracy. But I suppose he as well as Marian suffers another dark disappointment. After all, his and Dr Chalmers' constant attendance on the Cotton family has been rewarded with this double tragedy.

I am determined to do this thing, not just in the face of my aunt's objections, but to insist to Marian herself that I have a right to try to support her as her friend. She has already hustled me away once when the boy died. Then when I heard the news of the baby, Robbie, I went to the house again and Marian shooed me away as though I were a troublesome chicken. Her face was hard and stiff, her low voice muttered about the bad drains and the 'terrible place'. 'This is no place for you. I told you before. Get yourself away. I don't need you here.'

All this, of course, has made me more determined than ever to go to the funeral. What kind of a friend would I be who deserted her at a time like this?

So this is why I stand at the window at Western House, watching the pathetic cortège make its way from the Darlington Road, across the green and down the road to St Helen's church. Tears prick my eyes at the sight of the pony cart, driven by a man in a dark cap, loaded with two small coffins. These caskets are both small but one is no larger than the top drawer in my dressing table. Behind the cart walks Marian, straight and steady, in a black-and-white shawl and a neat black bonnet. Beside her is Aaron Whitstable, in dark jacket and a black floppy tie, carrying young Charlie on his shoulders. Oddly, if you blanked out the image of the cart and the coffins they look as though they could be going on a family picnic. Charlie is wearing his velvet cap on his thick thatch, and his pale face gleams in the white light of morning.

Silence sits on the green like a fat white pigeon. Despite the early hour, people are standing at their doors and hovering on the muddy paths that crisscross the green. They stand still for the few minutes it takes for the sorry procession to cross. The men and boys remove their caps and the women stand in groups, their faces closed and forbidding.

I race downstairs. Auntie Mary and Emily are standing in the passage by the back door. My aunt puts her hand on my arm. 'Don't go, Victoria. It really isn't right.'

I shake off her hand. 'It can't be right that that poor woman's going to bury her children unsupported. What's the matter with people round here?' I turn to Emily, who's about to say something, but her mother glares at her and she says nothing.

In the stable I urge Jonty to make haste harnessing Patch. When he has done this I sit up behind Patch and look down at Jonty. 'Now what do I do?' I say.

'Yeh canna drive?'

I shake my head. 'Not yet.'

His face is mutinous. There is obviously no question of him volunteering for the task of driving me. In the matter of Marian Cotton he is evidently at one with Mrs Grey and the rest of the village.

'You just say "walk on", don't you?' I say desperately.

He shrugs. 'Aye, and "woah" to stop. An' pull his head off-left if you want to go left, and off-right if you want to go right. Pull down both hands if you want him to go slow. Let loose if you want him to walk at his own pace.' Suddenly he stops being difficult. 'Patch has a lot of sense, Miss Kilburn. He's a quiet enough lad. He'll take you where you want. I'll lead you out of the yard and set you on your way.' Good as his word, he leads me out of the stables and down the back road past the mill until we are out on the St Helen's road. Then he slaps the pony's rump and he sets away at a very sedate trot.

My heart is thumping and my gloved hands are clutching the reins tightly. Patch goes much faster than the funeral pony and we soon pass the walking mourners and catch up with the cart. I shout 'Woah!' and pull on the reins a bit, and we end up stopping abreast of the funeral cart.

I look back at Marian and Aaron. 'Would you care to ride, Marian?' I say desperately.

A grim smile crosses her face. She nods and climbs up into the trap. Aaron hands Charlie up and leaps up to sit beside me. The funeral cart is drawing away again. I look down at Patch's glossy rump, then take a breath. 'Walk on, Patch. Walk on,' I say too loudly. He does nothing. I shake the reins. 'Walk on, Patch! Walk on!' He shakes his head, rattling his harness. He takes one step, then another. I try to pull him to the left so we are walking properly behind the coffin cart, but he insists on keeping his line so we walk abreast of it for twenty yards. Then Aaron Whitstable puts his hand over mine and helps me jerk the reins hard to the left. 'Come on, old lad,' he says. 'Show some respect.'

The church has no spire, no pointing finger to God. It is squat and very old, more like a castellated house than a church. We drive right in to the church door. The churchyard is overgrown with long grass and littered with gravestones, some of them very old. In places both grass and gravestones are higher than a man. Here and there stones have fallen in the grass and been left where they fell. I wonder where, in this crowded space, there may be room for more coffins, even two very small ones.

The cart man goes into the church and comes out with a man in dusty black gear whom he introduces to me, not to Marian, as Mr Drummond the sexton. The cart man secures his own pony and goes to hold Patch's head, not offering any further help. Mr Drummond asks who will lift the coffins. Perhaps we should get some men from the road?

'We'll carry them ourselves,' says Marian. She lifts the smallest coffin out of the cart and holds it before her like an offering. Aaron Whitstable lifts the larger one and puts it on his shoulder as easy as if it were a garden log. I take hold of Charlie's small cold hand. The old man leads the way behind the church.

'Grief!' says Marian, standing very still. For a second it seems to me as though she will cry. Then she shrugs her shoulders. 'I had forgotten.'

A swathe of rough land stretches from the back wall of the church to the far stone wall of the graveyard. Here there are no gravestones, just hundreds of heaps of earth, some marked with crude wooden memorials, others with no markings at all. This place is full of the dead. I have the feeling of them in layers below us. We must be standing on the dead. Grief! as Marian says. 'So many,' I say.

'It's been a bad couple of years,' says Mr Drummond. 'They're falling like flies and all buried next to the Parish.' He tells us that our departed ones can't be buried next to each other, as the spaces will not allow it. He indicates two holes, already dug. They are fifteen yards apart and must have thirty graves between them.

Marian lowers the smallest coffin into the first hole. There is a rustle behind us and a clergyman, white stock flying, rushes to our side, a paper flapping in his hand. 'What is the name, what is the name?' he puffs, clearly out of breath with his rush.

'This'n's called Robert Robson Cotton and he was fourteen months old,' says Marian. 'T'other is Frederick Cotton. You buried his father some time back.'

'Were they christened?'

'Aye. This one by thee . . . *sir* . . . in this very church.' I admire her patience with this buffoon.

Immediately, almost without looking at her, the man puts his hands together and closes his eyes. We all follow suit. He holds his hands up high in front of him and sets his voice at a certain nasal, toneless pitch, very familiar to those who've had to endure the routine sermons of half-hearted parsons.

'*Dear Lord, look down on us in thy mercy. Forgive us our sins and the sins of this child Robert whom today in your infinite mercy you will welcome to your bosom. Today we think of the words of the Lord Jesus. Suffer little children to come unto me. Amen. We will now say the Lord's Prayer.*'

We keep our hands together and chant the Lord's Prayer, then we are briskly hustled on fifteen yards by Mr Drummond and, standing by that grave, the curate says exactly the same words in the same tone, only substituting the name Frederick for that of Robert. Then we all stand back. Marian splits a bunch of daffodils into two smaller bunches and drops them carefully, one on each coffin. I curse my own thoughtlessness at having brought no tribute.

The curate scribbles on his sheets of paper, whispers something to the sexton, gives them to him and scuttles away towards the grand vicarage close by the church. The sexton hands the papers to Marian and turns to follow him.

Aaron grasps his shoulder. 'What about the graves, marrah? Who will fill them in?'

The sexton pulls away. 'It'll be done this afternoon. We have two more funerals and all the graves will be done together.

'Have you spades?' demands Marian.

He looks at her directly for the first time. 'Aye, I have spades. Behind the porch.'

'Well, sir, you should go and get them for me and my friend Aaron here, and we'll do it ourselves. We cannot have these bairns exposed to the sky and the spring wind. 'T isn't decent.'

So this is what they do. Ignoring the fresh faces of the daffodils, Marian shovels the soil back over Robbie's coffin. Aaron does the same for Freddie. We stand there looking at the mounds of earth – first one, then the other. Then I raise my eyes to the rows and rows of the dead and see that what we have here are no longer Freddie and Robbie. They are just more of the dead, under a heap of earth, soon to be earth themselves, like all of the others.

Something occurs to me. 'We have no markers,' I say.

'Now that's a pity,' says Marian, hard-faced and dry-eyed, and she strides off towards the front of the church.

Tears are falling from my eyes now and they won't stop. I look up into the concerned gaze of Aaron Whitstable. 'It is all so awful,' I gasp. 'What can we do?'

Now his arm is around me and he is hugging me to his side, guiding me down the path round the church. 'We can do what Marian does. We can look to ourselves. We can get on with things, refuse to be crushed,' he says. 'We can embrace life. That's all there is.'

Twenty-Three

This is incredible. It seems never ending. Just a week after those first two children were buried it was clear that Marian had yet more trouble to face. Her lodger, Mr Nattrass, took the same track. He just followed the others: faded and died. This funeral was much more difficult than that of the children. Mr Nattrass had been a well-liked man. Before he was interred he was treated to a service in the low grey church, that was filled by his workmates from the pit, as well as quite a sprinkling of wives. The church bell tolled.

Marian seemed to welcome my presence this time. She sat in the front pew with me and Aaron on either side of her, and Charlie at her knee. The people in the crowded pews made no pretence of offering her even a little sympathy. You could not have accused them of being hypocrites. As she followed the coffin down the aisle, one woman hissed.

The thin curate was in less of a hurry. He was more thoughtful this time, introducing some dignity to the service. But in the end the burial was just as peremptory as that of the poor children. The hole was larger, but only a few mourners could get near to it, as it was cheek by jowl with so many other sad, unmarked graves. We waited by the hole until the graveyard emptied, then made our way to the trap, leaving behind two of Nattrass' 'marrahs' who were filling in his grave. Looking back, I sensed that soon this man's earthly space would be indistinguishable from that of hundreds of others in this dark place. It had been raining. Already it was impossible to see with any accuracy where lay the two little ones, buried last week.

Back at Western House I hand over the trap to the disapproving Jonty, and walk across the green towards the Darlington Road. Marian and Charlie walk between Aaron and myself. It is as though we are her sentinels, guarding her from the hard looks of those peering from their doors and windows. I sense now that this pleasant country village that I so loved when I arrived has changed. Or perhaps I never saw it as it really was.

We stop outside Riley's shop on the corner but Marian doesn't want to return to her empty house on Johnson Terrace. 'I left Mrs Dodds in there cleaning. Place is running with vermin; needs a good clean-out before I hand any keys over. What say we go round your house, Aaron, and lift a cup to poor old Nattrass?'

So we set off again at a steady pace. She takes my arm. 'I had a soft spot for that Nattrass, you know, even though it's a long time since I had a real fancy for him. He was a good lad. Hard-working. For a while I thought he was rallying but I knew there was no point in getting my hopes up. I sometimes wonder, Victoria, whether there's Someone around and about who's got it in for Marian Cotton.' I have never heard her speak in such wavering, pitiable tones. 'Perhaps not Jesus, meek and mild as He is. But I'm not so sure about that wrathful God I used to read about in Sunday school, the one who smote the Israelites and brought down the walls of Jericho. He has a lot to answer for, in my life.'

We stop outside Aaron's door.

Marian stands very still. 'I can't think what I've done to Him, honey, for Him to do this to me.' She looks down at Charlie. 'And what about you, child? Are you safe from this wrathful God?'

At this moment Marian is the saddest and most regretful I've ever seen her. She's usually hard and strong, difficult to read. Enigmatic. Defiant. But I think this last death – of someone she hardly cared for – has been somehow harder to bear than the demise of her own children.

Aaron pushes open his low door. 'Come on then, Marian. I have a bottle of navy rum in here that'll blur those jagged edges.'

Aaron must have anticipated Marian's wishes not to go home. The workbench has been cleared off and on it he's spread a rough white cloth. Standing on it are an odd collection of glasses and a bottle; a wooden plate with crusty bread, slightly burned at the edges; another wooden plate with a slab of spice cake cut in a falling line, like dominoes. He stokes the fire so it burns really brightly, then leans over the bench and pulls the woollen curtain across the window so we can no longer see the green or be vulnerable to its watching eyes.

'Let's shut that lot out,' he says.

I've known him and liked him for some weeks now and this is the first time I've heard the least thread of anger in his voice. He leans over the bench and fills three glasses half full of rum, and splashes a spoonful in the bottom of a white cup for Charlie.

'We'll stay standing,' he announces, 'and drink in respect for Nattrass, that died far too young, in his prime, no less. And for the bairns Robbie and Freddie, even younger, with their lives before them . . .'

'I never touch the stuff,' says Marian. 'But today . . .'

We all take a drink. They drink theirs off in one. Charlie and I choke and splutter on a mouthful.

'. . . and we drink an oblation to a vengeful God to ask Him to leave off,' says Aaron, pouring again. 'To leave off tormenting Marian Cotton.'

'Amen to that,' says Marian, sitting down heavily. She looks up at me. I'm still getting back my breath after choking on the navy rum. 'Take your weight off your feet, child. That bad foot of yours must be givin' you some gyp.'

She seems to have recovered her humour and is as bland and hard as ever. She sits and allows Aaron to give her a further glass of rum and a piece of spice cake. She talks about her plans for the new start in her new house, and her faith that Mr Quick-Manning will come through 'with the goods'. By this, both Aaron and I know that she means an offer of marriage. Then suddenly she stands up.

'Well, friends, I need to get back to that Mrs Dodds. She's not a bad soul if there's money involved. But she needs watching.' She takes Charlie's hand in hers. 'An' I've a letter to write about this'n. Fred Cotton has this brother in Ipswich. Charlie's uncle that will be. Mebbe he'd take on this'n here. His kith and kin, like, after all.'

I glance down at Charlie, who looks quite unconcerned at his fate being discussed in such a manner. But I am concerned.

'Charlie? But—'

She shrugs. 'I like young Charlie. You can see I do. He's a good'n. But he's Fred Cotton's son, not mine. I've only known him a year. I need a clear start with Quick-Manning. New house, new start.'

110

'Really, Marian . . .' I don't know how I dare to challenge her but I do.

Aaron puts a hand on my arm.

Now Marian is glaring defiantly at me. 'Have you been absent in these last weeks? Haven't you seen them all smitten down? Charlie here is the last. *The last.* You don't want that for him, do you? The same as happened to them. Do you?' And she's out of the low room, dragging Charlie by the hand and leaving the scent of fruitcake and lavender behind her.

The rum must have left me a little dizzy because I fail to get up to leave with Marian. In truth she gave me no opportunity. It's as though she meant to leave me there.

Aaron shuts the door behind her with a distinct click and turns to me. 'Now, Miss Victoria, would you like some more rum . . .?'

I laugh and shake my head vigorously.

'Well, tea, p'rhaps?'

I shake my head again. Conversation should help. 'I do like Marian, but there is something so . . . unpredictable . . . about her.'

He sits down opposite me and smiles slightly. 'She's a one-off.'

'One-off?'

'Unique, of herself.' He points to my left foot. 'That boot I made for you. Not another like it. That's unique. Not another like it in the whole of England. Nay, the whole of the Empire.'

I stare at my unique foot in its unique boot. 'They don't like her here. The atmosphere in that church . . .' I shudder. 'The woman hissing.'

He shrugs. 'This village is nice enough. It's like any village. But the people here – they've no time for anyone that's different. You might say Marian makes it worse herself, not giving a fig for what they think. Not being humbled by their rancour.' It is clear that his wide reading gives Aaron good words to say exactly what he thinks.

'She's had a terrible time,' I say, 'and yet they have no common sympathy for her.'

'No fear. They blame her. Say she brings it on herself, this bad luck.' He pauses. 'I think they're within a hair's breadth of saying she causes them, all these disasters.'

Now my flesh is pimpling up like an orange. 'That's so unfair . . .'

He smiles slightly and says, 'Dear girl, their dislike goes deep. In the mood they're in now, should their horses die, they'd say it was Marian Cotton's fault. Let the pit flood, let a thunder storm destroy the crops, and they'd lay it all at her door. In the last few weeks they've stopped coming to me for shoes because they know that I'm her friend. They tar me with her brush. It's very fortunate I've people further afield who like my work.'

I can't bear the thought of all this malice. It's spilling all over me and I don't like it. The tears start to pour unbidden down my face. Aaron stands up and takes a clean folded cloth that has been airing on the string over the fireplace and starts to mop my tears as though I am a very little girl. He is smiling slightly. 'She is lucky, Victoria, strange and unique as she is, that she has you as her champion and loyal friend.' He has used my name and it seems quite all right.

'And you,' I mumble, and grab the cloth and mop my own face. 'You are her friend.'

He drops to his knees before me and looks up. His eyes, streaked green and brown now, glitter in the firelight. 'Mebbe I should take a look and check on the fit of these boots of yours while you're here,' he says softly. Without waiting for a reply he unbuttons the buttons, unties the laces and takes off both my boots. He holds them up to the light then places them on the floor, neatly, side by side. Then he peels off my stockings and holds my feet in his hands, one on each palm. I can barely breathe. Then he lays my right foot on the floor and begins to stroke and pummel the left one, there, where it curls in his hand. Then the right. Then my ankles and calves.

My flesh is like golden treacle. The room is melting before my eyes. I can't stand it. I say, 'Stop!'

He stops instantly. He places my foot carefully on the ground and sits back on his ankles, looking up into my face. His skin is smooth and brown in the firelight; his hair, where it springs from his high forehead, is threaded with the purest gold and silver.

'Don't stop,' I say faintly. 'I don't want you to stop.'

But he doesn't pick up the foot again. He kneels up so we are eye to eye. He puts a long hand on each side of my face and lays his lips on mine. I cannot say how absolutely right this feels. It's as right as the sun coming up in the morning, as the moon rising at night. It is as right as the rain on a dry day, the wind on a still day. It is as right as snowdrops in spring.

Then he takes his lips and hands away and picks up my hands, which are scrunched tight in my lap. He opens these up as though they are the petals of a flower and kisses each palm very carefully. Then he looks me straight in the eye. 'Now I must ask you to marry me, Victoria. To be my wife. It's the only way forward, as far as I can see.'

I take my hand from his and touch the softness of the skin of his cheek, the fine sweep of his hair, the perfect curl of his ear. One inner part of me is astonished at the ease with which I do this, but an even deeper part of me knows that it's right. It's right because I love him. My intuition guides me. I have learned this here in this village.

He turns to one side, rescuing his mouth from my fingers. 'Well?' he says.

'Aaron . . .'

There is a sharp hammering on the door. He groans and stands up. As he does so I fumble with my stockings, slip my feet into my boots and pull down my bonnet where he has displaced it. He moves slowly to the door.

It is Emily. She walks into this humble place with the bold assurance of her class. She glances around with interest. Her glance settles on me. 'My mother was looking for you, Victoria. She sent me to ask Jonty and he sent me to Mrs Cotton's and *she* sent me to Mr Whitstable's.'

'We have been toasting the departed,' says Aaron easily. 'There's some spice cake left. Perhaps . . .'

Emily shakes her head vigorously. 'I have orders to bring my cousin Victoria home, kicking and screaming if necessary.'

I stand up. 'No necessity for that, Em. I'll come directly.' I turn to Aaron and bob a brief curtsy. 'Thank you, Mr Whitstable. Such a difficult day, even though so memorable.'

Later, as Emily and I walk down the village to Western House, I wonder what Auntie Mary felt like when she met and married William, so far above her in status. I wonder whether that made a difference. Most certainly no difference shows in the way they are these days. Except perhaps the difference is that they are even now so devoted to each other. So many people seem discontented, out of step with their mutual lives. Think of my own mother and father. But not Uncle William and Aunt Mary.

As we go through the back door Emily announces that I am to go to the kitchen, as her mother is making pigeon pie and she specially wishes to show me her method.

'In the matter of cooking she's given up on me, thank goodness,' says Emily, grinning.

Twenty-Four

Auntie Mary is at the big kitchen table, chopping steak. I can hear Mrs Grey clattering pots in the scullery. My aunt dismisses Emily, tells her to 'go and read your books'. Then she beams at me as though there is nothing amiss.

'Ah, Victoria, there's an apron for you on the hook on the kitchen door. Put that on and come by me. I'll show you how to make the best pigeon pie in England.'

She is clever. Here am I waiting for a dressing-down and I am to make pigeon pie.

I tie on the apron and come to stand by her at the table.

'Now, dearest girl, you take this cut steak and use it to line the bottom of that pie dish. Make sure that pie funnel is dead centre.'

I scoop the steak into place, patting it so that it covers the bottom of the dish.

'Now,' she says, 'a tablespoon of salt from the salt box there by the fire. And a bit of white pepper from the shaker. Now, the pigeons!' She points to the line of three cleaned and gutted pigeons sitting beside the dish. 'A tablespoonful of butter on each of those, outside and in. Use your fingers.'

This isn't as easy as it sounds. The dead flesh of the pigeons is cold and unpleasant to handle, and the butter on my hands makes them slippery.

'Now lay the pigeons atop the steak and on top of each of the pigeons lay a slice of that ham.' As she speaks she breaks eggs and slides the separated yolks into a bowl. These she beats vigorously, her

115

fork scraping and squeaking against the side of the bowl. Then she hands the bowl to me. 'Now pour this over the birds then fill the pie dish with stock from that jug. Just about halfway, mind.'

I do all this with fumbling slowness, very aware of her critical gaze.

Now she indicates the marble slab on which sits a fat disc of pastry. 'Now, dear, you must roll that out to be bigger than the plate.'

I need two goes to get this right. It seems my touch is far too heavy. Then she shows me how to put a strip of pastry round the edge of the pie dish, then settle the flattened disc of pastry over the whole thing like a hat, and she holds the dish up while I cut the hat to fit. Now I must learn how to cut and prink the edges together with a fork, cut round the funnel and let it rise through the pastry like a chimney. This, apparently, will let out the steam.

'Now, last!' she beams. 'The egg white!' This she does herself, smearing it over the entire piecrust, using the palms of her hands. 'Now, Victoria, you may put it in the oven!'

I stand waiting with the dish until she washes her hands, takes up a cloth for protection and opens the huge steel door of the fire-oven. The heat that blasts on to my bare arms is almost beyond bearing. I lift the pie dish cautiously on to the middle shelf and stand back to let her close the door tight.

'There!' I say. This is my first line in this whole drama.

She stands back, whips off her apron and smiles. 'Your Uncle William's favourite. I have to tell you he's putty in my hands after a taste of my pigeon pie.'

I don't know whether to laugh or cry at this.

She goes on. 'That'll be in there best part of an hour, which means you and me, dear Victoria, we can have a nice little talk.' She glances at Mrs Grey, who came into the kitchen while we were busy and is now decanting a basket of clean crockery on to the huge dresser that lines the far wall.

My aunt beams at her. 'A tray of tea, when you have a moment, Rebecca?' Then she leads the way up to her tiny slip of a sitting room, me following her like a lamb.

We sit either side of the flickering fire. She draws a small table towards her, ready for the tray. She looks a bit like a pretty pigeon herself, rather large and pouting now she's with child, settling her colourful clothes around her like a bird preening its feathers. Auntie

Mary is a strange mixture: cook in her own household and yet very much mistress of it too. She has been cunning enough to let me join her in the pigeon pie adventure before settling down for what is obviously going to be a serious talk.

She looks me directly in the eye. 'I'm embarrassed to say, Victoria, that I have to speak with you about Mrs Cotton. I've urged William to do so, but he has demurred. So I have taken it on myself.'

I meet her gaze, but say nothing.

'You must have been to Mr Nattrass' funeral?'

I nod.

'And then back to Mrs Cotton's?'

'No. Back to the house of Mr Whitstable the shoemaker. With Mrs Cotton and her son Charlie.'

She lets out a little '*Ttch!*' of exasperation.

I am a bit exasperated myself. I burst out, 'You are *such* a good woman, Auntie, such a kind woman. I'd have guessed you'd have thought more kindly of a woman like Mrs Cotton, who's gone through so much misery.'

She stares at me, as though trying to transfer the thought itself, rather than put her thought into words. Then she says, 'We *were* kind to her in this village. When Fred Cotton died there was a collection. And so much sympathy for his wife being left with his children and a tiny baby.'

I try to understand this. 'So sympathy is only for when you have one tragedy? If you have more of it, it thins out, transforms itself? It turns to malevolence?'

'It's not quite that. It's that . . .' she is straining after the thought, '. . . her attitude is wrong. She is too fancy, too forward . . .' Her voice trails off. Then: 'She is very free with . . . herself.'

I try to grasp this properly. 'Even if everything you say is true, Auntie, are all these reasons to have less sympathy when yet another tragedy strikes? Do you know, a woman in church today hissed at Mrs Cotton? In church. Hissed!'

She shakes her head. 'That's not decent. I will acknowledge that. But what they're saying is really bad, Victoria. They're saying she's dangerous. They're saying that it's no accident that all these poor people around her die—'

'*They?*' I interrupt. 'So many people die, Auntie. The graveyard is

117

full of them. Whole families. Uncle William has told me about the epidemic and the bad conditions here.'

'This is different.' My aunt's voice is hard, stubborn. 'She is different. She has an effect on people.'

Now I understand. 'You think she casts a spell on people? Auntie, these are modern times, not the Middle Ages.' I even laugh. But in the back of my mind I remind myself that even I think Marian has a kind of magic.

There is a knock on the door and Mrs Grey bustles in with the tray, which she lays on the table and prepares to unload. My aunt waves her away and she flounces out.

I glance at the closing door. 'You get all this from Mrs Grey? She's *they*?'

She shrugs. 'She's sensible. Very reliable. And she's out among people more than I am.'

'And you take your opinions from *her*?' I can't keep the contempt from my voice.

She goes bright red at this. 'That's quite enough, Victoria. You're a guest in my house and I'll have my say on this.' She stands up. The tea stays unpoured. 'You are forbidden to see, or have anything to do with Mrs Cotton, or with Mr Whitstable, who has chosen to be her boon companion. He too is under her spell, as you might put it. I can't have you under her spell. You are forbidden to see her.'

'You can't say this, Auntie.'

'*Can't?* I can. I have just said it. This is my house and you are my guest.'

'My uncle—'

'Will abide by my wishes. He will tell you it's rare that I insist on anything, Victoria. But when I insist, he concedes. That has been the pattern and there's no reason that it should change now. In addition, I shall request him to write to your father and voice my concerns. I shall insist.' Her tone is icy. I sense now the determination that has allowed her to climb into the role of doctor's wife and make a very good fist of it.

I stand up and face her. 'I cannot agree with anything you say about Mrs Cotton or, by implication, Mr Whitstable. It is just too unfair.'

Her full pretty mouth is closed very tight. 'That is your prerogative, my dear. Now you may go. Supper is seven sharp as usual.' Her mouth relaxes. 'You may try out your own pigeon pie. I'm sure it will be quite delicious.'

I walk steadily out of the room and stand outside the door, thinking yet again of my mother and father. I can see there will be much drama when they hear about my behaviour. They will probably send for me and deliver me back to my chaise longue. I can't have that. I walk down the corridor as far as the dispensary.

My uncle is there in his black apron. Mr Carr and Dr Chalmers are nowhere to be seen. Uncle William is weighing out substances into a narrow jar and mixing them into a liquid with a glass wand. Three empty, scrubbed bottles stand at his elbow, neatly labelled in his handwriting.

'What are you mixing?' I hitch on to a high stool beside him.

'In the solution I have mixed bismuth and hydrocyanic acid. In this one I am adding arsenic in the smallest quantities. Just a quarter of a grain. He holds up the measuring spoon to show me. 'And the third one, morphia, an eighth of a grain. Needs scrupulous care.'

'Is it so very dangerous?'

'Like the surgeon's knife. A fraction this way means cure, a fraction that way means kill. Arsenic is very much a case in point.'

'Ugh!' I shudder. 'I had not realised you use poisons. Arsenic? Ugh.'

He shakes the solutions vigorously and carefully checks the labels. 'They do say that arsenic occurs naturally. All around us. Harder to control in its natural form, of course.'

He has caught my interest. 'Where is it, naturally?'

'In some colour pigments, in water. It has been found in the soil of graveyards. I read one paper where the scientist was arguing that it was even to be found in the fleece of sheep. I must say I think that's far-fetched. But arsenic is used on common or garden flypaper to kill flies. There are women who soak it off the flypaper and use it quite widely to cure skin complaints.'

I think of the poultice Marian concocted for my own smooth clean skin.

He goes on, 'I read somewhere that Elizabeth the First used it in her skin cream. She said she had the heart and stomach of a king, but she had the vanity of a woman.' He screws the tops back on the containers and puts them in a high cupboard and locks it. He checks the tops of the new bottles and places two of them in a low locked cupboard. The remaining bottle he tucks in his black bag. He removes his apron and pulls on his coat. I notice the lapels are slightly shiny. There is certainly no money to spare in this house. This is what Jonty must see in his 'poor doctor'.

'Well, Victoria?' says my uncle. 'It's a pleasure to have the chance to give you an impromptu chemistry lesson, but I'm sure you came here for a reason.'

I nod. 'I've just helped Auntie Mary to make a pigeon pie.'

'We are having that for supper? My favourite, as I'm sure she has told you.'

'She says you're putty in her hands when she makes pigeon pie.'

He laughs at this. 'Perhaps you had not noticed, my dear. I am putty in her hands whatever we have for dinner.'

'She's also just forbidden me to spend time with Mrs Cotton or even Mr Whitstable, who has made me these wonderful boots.'

He clicks his teeth. 'Oh dear. I did hear mutterings in the wind. Perhaps you could desist from these friendships for a while? Till the wind blows over?'

'That would mean that Mrs Cotton would be on her own with all this bad feeling around her. I can't do that.'

'Not alone, surely? Mr Whitstable is there. And the mutterers mention this Mr Quick-Manning from the brewery who pays her attention. So she's not alone.'

The words burst from me. 'They seem to think she's a witch or something. It's ridiculous.'

'I must concur with you there, my dear. She merely has the propensity to draw attention to herself, to raise ire and jealousy. That doesn't give her supernatural powers.'

'Exactly! So why should I stop seeing her?'

He picks up his bag and puts on his hat. 'You should stop seeing her out of courtesy to your dear Auntie Mary. At least for the time being.' His tone brooks no argument.

'She says that you'll write to my father.'

He is at the door. 'Well, perhaps we might postpone that particular task until we see what happens here.'

I follow him to the hallway, where he puts on his greatcoat. He turns to me. 'Don't worry about such letters at present. Now then, my dear, would you tell your aunt I have one final call to make, but will most certainly be back in time for her delicious pigeon pie?'

At dinner I have to admit that the pigeon pie is exceptionally good and that my aunt and uncle are their usual benevolent selves. Sweetness and kindness are the most powerful magic in the hands of good people and there is no doubt that in the hands of my aunt and uncle – at least for this time – they win out for me against the darker magic of Marian Cotton.

Eating my second portion of pigeon pie, I decide reluctantly that I should stay out of the way of Marian and Aaron until I see 'which way the wind blows'. At the very least that will save me from thinking too closely about Aaron and his life-changing question, or remembering the warm touch of his hands, the soft feel of his lips. And it will also save me from contemplating a return to the chaise longue.

Twenty-Five

Marian Cotton sat up straight in the chair at the sound of heavy knocking. She unbolted her front door to see Thomas Riley standing there, holding a black umbrella up against the driving rain. She looked up and down the street before she closed the door behind him. All was quiet. Only one window showed a light. Early shifts and the expense of oil, and even candles, meant that most people in Johnson Terrace went to bed with the daylight.

Riley went to stand in front of the blazing fire, lifting the tail of his coat to enjoy the heat. 'By, it's hot in here,' he said. 'Locking your door now, Marian?'

She sat down at the table. 'I never locked me door before, Tommy, not anywhere where I've lived. But when I got back from burying Nattrass, all the doors and every single window in the house were open, wide to the winds. I don't know what anyone's thinkin' of, settin' about and doin' that. People round here, can you believe them? So I'll lock my door from now on.'

'Well,' Thomas reached into a pocket and pulled out a large key and threw it on the table, 'you'll need to lock the door of a different house. There's the key to number thirteen.'

She put a hand on the key. 'Mine?' she said, smiling slightly.

'Yours.' He put a hand on hers where it lay on the table.

'Why, thank you, Mr Riley. That's good news on a bad day.' She rescued her hand and stood up. 'Would you like a cup of tea? I have very special tea.'

He looked round. 'Where's young Charlie?'

122

'He's up in bed. Charlie sleeps with me. He's slept with me for months. That bedding that Nattras lay on needs hanging out and bleaching afore anyone else sleeps on it.'

Thomas grimaced. 'You should burn the lot.'

'You think I'm made of money? Good mattress, that was. Brought it with me from Sunderland, from my mother's house.' She pushed the kettle to the centre of the fire. He watched as she made the tea. Her movements were graceful, distinctive, like everything else about her. She handed him a cup and he caught her hand under his as he took it.

'Sit down,' she said. 'I want to ask you about something.'

He took a sip of the tea, which was very pleasant. Aromatic. 'So what's this, Marian?'

'It's Cotton's lad, young Charlie. I want you to help me to get in touch with Fred Cotton's brother down in Ipswich. Get him to take the lad on. His own kith and kin, after all. Blood relative.'

Thomas was shocked. 'Send him away? I thought you were fond of him?'

'Fond?' she laughed. 'Look, Tommy, I've lost bairns of my own and, nice as he is, that one's nothing to me. A year I've known him. He's another mouth to feed. Another back to put clothes on. And I've got nothing. I can't get proper work cause he's to watch. He's never well. An' as far as I can see he might go the way of the rest. I couldn't stand another one, another burial. I'm never outta that cemetery, if you ask me. And it all costs money. You know that. I've had to look to you time and again for that bit support.'

'You need to find a way of being independent, to support yourself, Marian.'

'A decent lodger might help. But a decent lodger would never come to a place full of children.'

He took his hand from hers. 'You mean a decent lodger like Quick-Manning?' His smile was knowing, hearty.

She smiled calmly. 'There's no saying what, Tommy. But to tell the truth, just now the boy's in the way.' She paused. 'Perhaps it won't matter – mebbe I won't be troubled long. Mebbe he'll go the way of the rest of them. He'll not make old bones.' Her voice was weary.

He shook his head. 'Not my business to help you dispose of him, Marian.'

'Then you can sign for him to go to the workhouse down Bishop Auckland. They can take care of him. He's an orphan, after all.'

'How can you be that hard?' He shook his head. 'I can't sign for him to go to the workhouse on his own. If you say you consider yourself destitute, and I can prove it, I could put you both down there. But not him on his own.' He put his hand again on the key, where it lay on the table. 'And if you see yourself as destitute, how can I give you a house where you'll have to pay rent?'

She wrestled the key from him. 'Give us that here. Haven't I waited long enough for that? To get out of this place?'

He kept his hand over hers. 'But you'll have rent to pay. You'll have to find the money.'

She shrugged. 'I've a little bit now from Nattrass. And a bit from me insurance.'

'So no one could call you destitute.'

'You might say that. But I will be destitute with that child to care for and no chance to work. What I want to do is set that house up real nice; a nice bit of wallpaper like I did this house up with; get a few bits and pieces to make it nice. Make it smart. I like things nice.'

He took his hand away from hers. 'So it's good enough for Quick-Manning?'

Her face hardened. 'I didn't say that.'

'My dear wife tells us you're engaged to be married. On the say-so of Mrs Dodds, I think.' He took another sip of tea.

'Ma Dodds should keep her mouth shut.'

He laughed, feeling quite warm now. 'She likes a chat, does Mrs Dodds.' He paused. 'So you're not engaged. Not really spoken for?'

'I speak for myself. I always have.'

He put the teacup down and pulled her out of the chair, clasping her roughly against his coat, his hand on the back of her skirt pushing her hard against him. 'Well then, Marian. Come on, lass.'

Carefully, she peeled herself away from him. 'Not here, not now. Not in this filthy house.' She put the key in her apron pocket. 'Wait till I get across there. Then we'll see.' She stood on the spot where he'd recently stood before the blazing fireplace, her hands behind her back.

He was dismissed.

He retrieved his umbrella from behind her door and shook it out. He looked back at her. 'At number thirteen, then?'

124

She nodded. 'We'll see. Mebbe if you help me with that letter to Charlie's uncle . . .?'

'I told you . . .'

She moved towards him. 'I'll lock that door after you. Nothing's safe round here any more. Not a thing.'

He walked briskly home in the rain to find, as he'd expected, that the lamps had been turned right down and the fire was merely a glow. He went to the smaller bedroom where he slept these days, feverishly tore off his clothes and pulled on a nightshirt. Then he went to the larger room above the shop, with the high white bed where his wife Margaret slept. He slipped into bed beside her. She was hardly awake when he pulled her to him and had no time to protest when he sank himself into her.

When he'd finished, she pushed him right off her. 'Get out of my bed. You're depraved, shameful.' She mouthed the words, as though the very walls might hear. 'And get out of my room.' He was dismissed for the second time that night. He left her sitting there on the side of the bed, pulling her voluminous nightgown back around her knees and adjusting her nightcap. 'Shameful,' she whispered after him. 'Depraved!'

Twenty-Six

Marian gave Charlie sixpence from the leather pouch that did service as a purse. 'Run along to Mr Townend's and get us sixpenn'orth of soft soap and arsenic. Say your mother wants it to clear bugs from the bed frame.'

Charlie put his whistle in his pocket and ran off, happy with his task, reassured that at last his stepmother was cheering up. It had been a grim fortnight. The funerals had been dark days but at least Miss Kilburn and Mr Whitstable had been there, which meant a ride in the trap from Miss Kilburn and a farthing for Spanish from the shoemaker.

And now things were looking up. He and his stepmother were moving to a new house.

On his way to the chemist's he passed Mr Riley, who was rubbing vigorously at his plate-glass window with a wash-leather. Mr Riley got down from his stool and beckoned the boy back.

'And how are you today, Charlie?'

The boy tipped his cap. 'Very well, Mr Riley,' he chanted.

'And how's your mother today?'

'Very well, Mr Riley.'

'It's certainly been a hard time for her.'

Charlie didn't know what to say.

'Are you still playing your penny whistle?'

'I can only clean it now, not play it. My mother says I must wait for the new house to begin to play again. There'll be better times there. I keep it polished, though.'

'There's the boy. Well done.' Mr Riley dropped the wash-leather into his bucket with a splash. 'Wait here, why don't you?'

In a minute he was back out of the shop, carrying a long stick of Spanish. 'Here you are, son. Run off now, and do your message.' He patted Charlie on the shoulder, picked up the sodden chamois from the bucket and wrung it out until it was nearly dry and had the consistency of damp velvet. As he started to rub at the window he began whistling a tune.

Charlie set off again. He had heard Mrs Dodds say that Mr Riley always cleaned that window himself. That window was his Pride and Joy.

Mr Townend the chemist was not so helpful. He shook his head when Charlie made his request. 'Can't do that, young man. Dangerous stuff. Has to be entered in the poison book. Takes a grown-up to buy stuff like that. Tell your ma to come back herself.'

When he got back to the house, his mother, helped by Mrs Dodds, was still scrubbing down the bed frame with lye soap. She was not pleased with the message he brought back from Mr Townend. 'Will you go down there for us and get us some, Mrs Dodds? No matter how much we scrub these struts, the little buggers'll get back in, an' that's the only thing to keep them at bay. An' I'm not takin' any of this filth across to my new house, I tell you that. New house, clean start, that's what I say.'

Mrs Dodds wiped her hands on a dirty towel, slipped out of her pinny and picked up her shawl. She took the sixpence from Charlie. 'That all, Mrs Cotton? Owt else?' She knew Mrs Cotton had money in her pocket, at least for now. Nattrass had left her twenty pounds. So tips were quite a possibility.

'Aye, you can find out if that old sourpuss wife of Riley's has a bit of spice cake. We can have it with our tea.' She fished out another shilling and put it into Mrs Dodds' open hand. 'Scouring this place is no easy game.'

In Riley's shop the chatter of the crowd of women stilled as Mrs Dodds came through the door. Sarah Shaw, a cap perched on top of her thick braid, was leaning against the counter. She raised an eyebrow at Mrs Dodds.

'I canna see how you can work for that woman,' she said. 'She's got death written all over her.'

There was a murmur of agreement from other women in the shop.

Mrs Dodds shrugged. 'Work's work and we dinnet all have a man to keep us, Mrs Shaw. Her money's as good as anybody's.'

'See?' Sarah looked round at the eager crowd. 'That whore doesn't even do her own work. Someone to clean for her, someone to wash for her, and her on the Parish. Winnet get her hands dirty. That shows yer.'

Another murmur of agreement.

'Mrs Cotton works out o' the house, nursing. Hasn't much time.' Mrs Dodds still defended Marian.

'Works elsewhere on her back, I know for certain,' said Sarah Shaw. 'That excise officer . . .'

'He's gunna marry her,' said Mrs Dodds quickly. 'They've got engaged.'

The women laughed. Even Mrs Riley, standing quietly at the counter, allowed herself a smile. These social times in the shop were her only pleasure. With her daughter away in Harrogate and her son, Patrick, either out with the wagon or hiding in his room, there were not many smiles day by day. Life with Thomas was not easy. He was getting very peculiar.

'Marry? Marry?' said Sarah. 'She's dirt beneath his shoes. Any man who marries her is making a great mistake. Ask Fred Cotton. Not that you can, him being six feet under.'

Again the room hummed with murmuring agreement.

Mrs Riley smiled thinly at the old woman through the crowd. 'Now, Mrs Dodds, what can I do for you?'

'Mrs Cotton wondered whether you had a bit of spice cake,' said Mrs Dodds, glumly. 'She usually gets it at Bishop Auckland, like. Shop there does good spice.'

'See?' said Sarah Shaw. Here was further proof. 'Bought cakes!'

'It so happens I do have a bit of spice,' said Mrs Riley. Business was business, after all. She lifted a large fruitcake from under the counter, weighed it, then cut a piece off and carefully weighed that.

Mrs Dodds handed over the money, took the cake and escaped from the shop, well aware that she'd been allowed to jump the queue so that the women already there could get on with the gossip after she left. Talk was rife in the village since Nattrass had died. The coincidence of four deaths within seven months in the house of a woman whom everyone loathed was too much to stomach. There *had* to be something going on. The tenor of the talk was becoming self-righteous, gloating. Those who'd never liked Mrs Cotton from the beginning were pleased to see their dislike – now dissolving into suspicion – vindicated. Mrs Dodds had even stopped going down to Halloran's as there was so much suspicion in there that her salacious little tales of Mrs Cotton's foibles were too thin fare for the appetites in that particular hostelry.

It was a relief to get to the chemist's shop, where Mr Townend could not have been more helpful. When she explained about the bed bugs, he nodded thoughtfully. 'Folks swear by it. My own wife has used it herself.' He mixed the arsenic and soft soap, and scooped it into a screw-topped jar before entering it into his poison book in fine, looping writing.

'You will tell Mrs Cotton she must use it up or keep it well out of harm's way? I tell all my customers this.'

'Aye. I certainly will. She's a careful woman. Precise, like. So there should be no bother as to that.'

When Mrs Dodds got back to the house Mrs Cotton had the kettle on and the teapot warm. She smiled cheerfully at the old woman and took the jar and put it on the high mantelshelf. 'Now then, Mrs Dodds. Let's have a bit of that spice. I've promised our Charlie he can have a slice if he plays us a tune on that whistle of his.'

Sarah Shaw, on her way back from the shop, heard the penny whistle and the laughter as she passed the house. She shook her head and hurried on, eager to recount to her husband this coarse behaviour in a house where there had been three deaths in a fortnight.

Twenty-Seven

This week, in my perverse desire now to avoid both Marian and Aaron, I have been helping my uncle in the dispensary and spending more time in the house learning how to make Manchester pudding, syllabub and clotted cream. I have become the model niece. By the time we get to clotted cream, Auntie Mary tells me she's now persuaded Uncle William not to write to my father, as I have so changed my ways.

On the Saturday I am invited to tea with Kit Dawson when there is no choir practice, and this time I tell Auntie Mary about Kit and say perhaps I might go on my own. There is no need to drag Emily away from her books. My aunt is unfazed by this request and says an outing away from the village might do me good. Perhaps she considers Mr Chapman's clerk to be a more salubrious choice of companion than Marian Cotton and the shoemaker.

Saturday is a fine day and the Kingsway Rooms are full of Saturday afternoon customers relaxing after shopping or a bracing walk in the Bishop's Park. After Kit and I have taken our tea under the watchful eye of the stern waitress, we ourselves walk along the thronging street through the market and into the Bishop's Park. We are very sedate. I tell Kit about my family and ask him about his. I cannot think up an appropriate picture of me chained to the chaise longue so I make up a few stories about my beautiful older sister and my funny younger sister and leave it at that. (I have to think hard on this: the events close at hand in my life are so dramatic and powerful that Lottie and Pixie and Rollo are fading right into the background. I can hardly remember their faces.)

As I chatter on, embroidering these stories, it occurs to me that perhaps we all invent ourselves with every new person we meet. Certainly the Victoria known to my family is entirely different from that same girl who is now the guest of Dr and Mrs Kilburn and the friend of Marian Cotton and Aaron Whitstable.

I wonder whether it is the same for Kit. He tells me of his father, who is a clerk in the Newcastle shipyards, and his brother, who is in the navy. As Kit did well at school and wrote with a fine hand, it seems his father capitalised on an acquaintance from the dockyard and obtained the place for him with the solicitor Mr Chapman.

'Your father must be proud of you.'

He leads the way across a narrow footbridge over the river and waits for me to reach him. 'Perhaps so. I'm the first of my family to join a profession, that's for sure.' He sounds rather complacent and the smile that I first thought attractive now seems just a little too cocksure.

I jump down to the path beside him. 'And you seem to like it? Working for Mr Chapman?'

'Well, most of it is for Mr Smith, who works for Mr Chapman. Some of it is tiring. So much copying. But it'll be the means whereby I better myself.' He takes my elbow in his hand. 'In the meantime I go to choir, and to the Eden Theatre. I walk the park with a pretty girl. I would count myself a lucky fellow.'

I have to say I regret the familiarity of his holding my elbow far more than the remembered, more intimate sensation of my feet in Aaron's hands. We turn a corner and I see a red squirrel scrambling up a tree. I wrest my elbow from Kit's hand and rush forward and take a closer look. When I have satisfied my curiosity I make sure that we walk with clear space between us, so Kit Dawson is unable to repeat his familiarity. It suddenly occurs to me that he may have seen my awkward walk as an opportunity to take advantage of me. Perhaps he thinks I should be grateful for any attention.

He has sensed my stiffness and his talk becomes more formal and clumsy as we make our way along the river and across the wider bridge to retrace our steps back into the town. Our talk fades and there seems nothing to say.

He walks me to the station and shakes hands firmly as the train steams in. 'I enjoyed our walk, Miss Victoria. It'd be nice if we could do it again.'

'Yes, that would be nice,' I say calmly.

'But in any case, I'll see you at choir on Thursday?'

'Yes, I'll be there.'

He tips his hat and walks away, his head down. For a minute I regret my coldness. But still, where would that touch on the elbow have led? How might he have construed any encouragement? Did he think because of my foot I'd be an easy mark? Grateful for the attention of any whole man? And if he were encouraged, where would I be then?

It is only when I am on the train that I begin to be more honest with myself, to realise that there is only one man in the world I want to touch me and he is one whose company is forbidden me. I wonder how long I can keep up this distance between me and Aaron Whitstable, how long I can sustain the role of the obedient, ideal niece.

Later, as I walk alone from the station towards Western House, I see the object of my loving speculation pushing a heavily laden hand-barrow across the green. Marian is walking alongside him with a sack on her back, and young Charlie is trailing behind, overburdened with what looks like a bag of laundry tied up in an old sheet. Our paths cross, so I am obliged to speak to them.

'What ho, Marian? Moving to the new house?' I keep my eyes away from Aaron.

'Aye,' she says, looking at me closely, her head on one side. 'And none too soon.' She puts down her sack and eases her shoulders, obliging me to stand still and talk. Aaron stops the cart and looks back. Charlie drops his laundry in the long grass and heaves a long grateful sigh.

Marian smiles faintly at me. 'And how've you been, child? A few days since I saw you, honey. I was wonderin' . . .'

'My aunt has been teaching me to cook, so I've been confined to the house. And today I went down for a walk in the Bishop's Park.'

She nods. 'I hear it's very fine. Never been there myself. I only get as far as the market. I suppose you took young Emily with you?'

To my annoyance I blush. I am aware of Aaron's cautious, steady gaze. 'Well, no. I went to have tea and a walk with Mr Kit Dawson, who works for Mr Chapman the solicitor.'

'I see. Well, lucky for some, I suppose.' She reaches down for her

132

sack and Aaron lifts the shafts of the barrow. 'You might take that laundry off our Charlie, Victoria, and bring it down the house for me. The bairn's passin' out. Real peaky these days.' It is an order.

I almost smile. She is incorrigible. She will *not* let me go. I am *not* to be allowed to cook with my aunt or go walking in the park with some young man.

'All right then,' I say. I lift up the bag of laundry, then we all troop on – Marian leading the way, followed by Aaron and the cart with me beside him. Charlie trails behind us, obviously much happier now without his burden.

The house and all its doors and windows are open. Inside, old Mrs Dodds has already lit a huge fire and is up on a stool, pasting rather smart green figured wallpaper on a stripped wall. I dump the laundry on the deep windowsill and Aaron unloads the cart with swift efficiency. Marian makes the boy stand outside 'until the dust settles'. He stays where he is put and looks away listlessly across the green as we all gather in the doorway.

Marian turns to Aaron. 'Now then, Aaron, why don't you take Victoria upstream to find this donkey I saw wandering there? I told you about it, didn't I? Well, I've seen it again. Get it back to the owner and he'll be grateful and pay up. And if there's no owner to find we'll sell it. Can't look gift money in a donkey's mouth.'

Aaron and I look at each other, both uncertain for a moment.

'And there's otters in the river down there, slinky little things. Victoria'll like to see those,' she ventures. It's as though she's offering children sweetmeats. 'You can get out of the back gate of this house. No nosy parkers. The back gate leads straight out on to the riverbank.' Marian so likes secrets and subterfuge.

Aaron glances at me quite coolly. 'I can easily do it myself, Marian – get you that donkey. Like you say, you can use the money. I can do it on my own easy enough.' The light from the window glows briefly on his smooth brown cheek.

She is quite firm. 'I'd say the child here could do with a fresh country walk. Been kept in the house cooking all week. The river's better than some old park, any day. You believe me.'

He starts again, 'Marian, I—'

My mind is made up. 'I'd really like to go, Aaron,' I interrupt him. 'The park was fine, but we have a nice park in Stoke Newington. I have seen parks. But I've never seen an otter before. I'd really like to see an otter.'

He shrugs and leads the way through a narrow back door over a cluttered stretch of land that is half-garden, half-store place for broken wheels, rusty baths and buckets. As we walk cautiously, quite separately on the narrow riverbank path, we pass the spot where I came upon Marian that day, wading for mallows. All that seems a long time ago.

I have to hop and skip to keep up with him until finally I stop and call breathlessly, 'The next boots you make for me should be seven-league boots, Aaron. How else will I ever keep up with you?'

He stops at once, turns round and waits for me. 'You stayed away,' he says. 'Away from Marian and away from me. P'raps we embarrassed you.'

I shake my head. 'No, that's not true. My auntie did chastise me and I thought I should stay close to the house for a while to keep her happy. Otherwise they'll send me back to London. I have to be careful.'

He stares at me, then nods and we set off again, this time side by side. We leave the village behind us and walk off the path through tall grass along the widening river until we reach a little stand of woodland.

Aaron stops, putting a light hand on my forearm. 'Now then, where is this creature?' We stand still and allow the rustling restraint of the wood to take the place of our crashing feet. The muttering chirrup of birds, calling each other or fighting over territory, comes from our left. The coo of doves or perhaps pigeons filters through from our right. I jump at the sudden sound of a barking scream deep in the trees.

Aaron clutches my arm tighter. 'Fox,' he whispers into my ear, laughing. 'Not dangerous unless you're a chicken.'

The barking stops.

'Here!' Aaron keeps hold of my arm and walks me softly into the denser part of the wood.

There, standing under an old spreading beech tree, contentedly munching away in a small clearing of grass, is the donkey. He is smaller than I expected and somewhat moth-eaten. It's hard to imagine anyone paying good money for him. He turns towards me and his round, long-lashed eyes gleam in a shot of light that has pierced the overhead canopy. I walk up to him and catch up his rotted rope harness.

'You poor thing,' I coo, like any dove. 'Who left you here? How did you stray?'

'Probably some travellers. They'll be well on their way north by now.' Aaron takes a coiled rope from under his coat and makes a loose halter for him, and removes the rotten rope that has done this service so far. He ties the rein to a low branch of a tree and turns to me. 'Now,' he says, drawing me right to him. My eyes are level with his chin. 'We need to continue our interrupted conversation.'

Then he kisses me, right there on the lips, really hard. Without my willing it, my hand comes up and touches his brow, his hair. And I kiss him back with a certainty I never knew was in me. He draws back, and I kiss him again.

The unearthly braying of the donkey brings us back to our senses. It is getting dark. We must have been here, kissing, just kissing for a long time. We realise we've forgotten to look for the otters but decide we may do that another day.

He grasps my hand. 'There'll be many good times ahead, Victoria. You can be sure of that,' he says exultantly. And for the moment I believe him.

When we get back, we tie the donkey to the gatepost and let ourselves in the back door. The only sign of Mrs Dodds is a whole papered wall. Marian is at the front door, watching Mr Riley make his way back across the green. She turns and grins at us. 'Just been graced with a visit from the Almighty Assistant Overseer. He's pleased to see I'm over what he calls my "bereavement" and that I'm settling in, and asks us if I can nurse another feller out of smallpox. I tell him, like I've been saying to him before, how can I do such things with this'n to take care of?' She nods at Charlie, who's sitting by the door playing cat's cradle with a loop of knitting wool. 'His uncle in Ipswich won't have him and Riley won't let him in the workhouse on his own, orphan that he is.'

'Marian!' says Aaron.

'Don't say such things!' My voice chimes with his. 'The child's sitting there.'

She laughs. 'Our Charlie knows his stepmama thinks sommat of him. But if I've learned anything in this crucifixion of a life I've learned to be practical. I cannot keep this house going on the one and sixpence out-relief I get for him. They won't take him into the workhouse. So I have to work.'

'There's Mrs Dodds . . .'

She laughs again, a hard, barking sound, like that of the foxes we've just heard in the woods. 'Ma Dodds'll take you for your last sixpence if you let her. I'd be robbing Peter to pay Paul if I paid her for the bit time she'd give to minding the lad. I've done that already and still they talk. I've had a feller called Taylor here asking if he could lodge with me, but I'd be off again, looking after someone, wouldn't I? He might get sick and we'd be back on the old nasty roundabout. And you know where that leads.' She looks around the room: even with the tangle of furniture she's brought from Johnson Terrace it looks bright and welcoming. 'What I want is a clear start here. That's all I want – a clear start. Charlie wouldn't want to stand in my way. Isn't that right, Charlie?'

Charlie looks up from his game with the string. 'That's right, Ma.'

She stares at us defiantly, with that marble-hard look of hers. Then her face softens and she smiles. 'Well, I can see that you two have made friends again. Did you get the donkey? Did you see the otters?'

'I'm afraid we didn't see the otters,' I say, relieved to return her smile. 'It got dark. But the donkey's tied up outside.'

'I'll give you two bob for the sighting of him, Marian,' says Aaron. 'An' I'll have him myself. Needs a bit of caring but will end up a fine animal. I fancy him for myself.'

'A donkey? What does a shoemaker want with a donkey?'

'I'm gunna feed him and spruce him up and give him as a present . . .'

I have to cough here.

'. . . to a friend.'

'A friend is it?' she says.

'I have to go,' I say hurriedly. 'My aunt will get angry all over again.'

'You don't worry about her,' says Marian. 'You get on with things yourself.' She pauses. 'Have you plenty stuff for the poultice, for your face?'

I put my hand up on my smooth cheek. 'I ran out. But my skin seems all right now.'

She shakes her head. 'No good. You need to put it on three weeks in every four to keep the thing away. You don't want that scabby skin back, do you?'

I shake my head. Then I frown, thinking of Queen Elizabeth and the arsenic. Would you go on a lifetime putting it on? Could it kill you?

She continues, 'Well, get down here tomorrow and I'll show you how to put the stuff together yourself. I'll not always be here to run after you, you know.'

She turns to Aaron. 'Now, son, can you give us a hand to get these beds upstairs?'

I am dismissed. Behind her back, I smile at Aaron and he cocks his head to one side in response. I wish we were back there in the shade of the old beech tree. Then I flee the house and race up the village, already rehearsing the excuses I will make to my aunt.

Twenty-Eight

'I see you've moved house.' Quick-Manning settled down to the cup of special tea that Marian had just brewed for him. 'You'll be comfortable there in your new house on the green?'

'I think so. It's much better. Already got me new wallpaper on. Fires in every room drying out nicely. No stinking beck to contend with. Cleaner water from the pant on the green. You know, the big stone thing that leads out the water?' She looked round his cluttered parlour. 'Perhaps my house is not so good as this, like. But even you still have that dirty beck to contend with out the back.'

'So you wouldn't want to live in a place like this?'

'With you?' She sat down on the little stool at his feet and sipped her own cup. 'It'd mebbe be all right. You've got some nice things here. But that beck? It's still there with its filth.' She put a strong hand on his thigh. 'You could bring a few of these nice things across there to my house and it'd be a grand little home for us. Nice for this bairn in here.'

He ignored her allusion to their joint offspring. 'What about Cotton's son? Is the old woman minding him tonight?'

She shook her head. 'No. I have to pay her every time. Mind you, he's not been so grand today. I'll need the doctor to him, I think. Tomorrow is soon enough for that. As for tonight, I just put him to bed with a little tincture of valerian to keep him sound asleep. Cheaper by half.'

'So it's the case that you're stuck with him?'

'Well, the uncle in Ipswich won't take him and I can't get him into the workhouse. He's not a bad lad, though. You'll never notice him.' She paused. 'We'll need to get on with that business of marrying, you know, so you can move in. There is the matter of this child of ours to do right. Or else I won't be able to keep the house.'

He stayed silent. Neither of them spoke for more than a minute.

'I suppose I could take a lodger,' she ventured. 'There was a feller enquiring . . .'

He put a hand on her shoulder. 'No more lodgers, I told you! No more lodgers!'

She stood up, took away his cup and saucer and perched herself on his knee. 'Well, you know what you must do, then, don't you?' She put her face against his, withdrawing only slightly at the roughness of his grey whiskers. 'Now then, what about a little kiss, old boy, for your Marian? And here, why don't you have a little feel in the place where you put this bairn of yours?'

Twenty-Nine

When I finally arrive back at Western House I can tell from her face that my Auntie Mary is not best pleased with me. I have turned up much later than the time I got off the train and she has come to her own, correct, conclusions. I am prepared to placate her but she barely acknowledges me. She's not enjoying the heat in her condition, and is busy with little Maggie, who's had some throat infection: a sore larynx that stops her sleeping and makes her cry. My uncle and Dr Chalmers have dosed her with all sorts of things but she seems not to be improving.

It's Emily who finds me in my hiding place in the window seat of the upstairs drawing room and settles down beside me with a rustle and settling of petticoats.

'So did your *rendayz-voo* with Kit Dawson come up to scratch, Victoria?' (My mother would have said that her French accent was execrable. *These provincial schools!* I can just hear her voice. She, of course, has made sure Pixie and Rollo have nice toned French accents by employing a French daily tutor.)

'It was no *rendezvous*, Em. We merely had tea in the tearoom and a walk in the park. I got the five fifty train back.'

'I know.' She smiles very wisely. 'Ma was watching out for you. She saw you joining up with Mrs Cotton and the shoemaker on the green. Then she stormed through the house like a hurricane, back up to our poor Maggie, who was howling her head off.'

'I would not hurt her feelings, Em. But I must see my friends.'

She gives this great, unladylike whistle. 'How wonderful to be such friends with bad people.'

I am so angry at this. 'They're not bad people, Em. Not at all. Mrs Cotton is not well understood round here. And Mr Whitstable is a fine craftsman. They have been good friends to me.'

'Yes. I see this. Mrs Cotton has mended your face,' I have confided in her about the ointment, 'and Mr Whitstable has mended your walk. But Ma says they are very unsuitable people. Both of them.' She pauses. 'But I think my dear mama has a special problem regarding this. Her father, my own grandfather, was a blacksmith and *his* father was a miner. What if my father had thought that *they* were unsuitable people?'

She has said it for me. 'Just so,' I nod.

'But why do you think everyone hates Mrs Cotton so? Mrs Grey and my mother are always on about her.'

I'm at a loss to explain it but I have a try, and in doing so try to explain it to myself. 'Mrs Cotton is a very unlucky lady, Em. No matter how she has tried, her loved ones around her have died. But instead of sympathising, people here seem to hold it against her. She's a newcomer and they gang up against her. And she doesn't help things herself because she's . . .' I have to search for the word, '. . . arrogant, uncaring of what others think of her. She doesn't care whether they like her or not and that really offends them.'

'But you like her. Does she care about you?'

I have to shrug my shoulders at this. 'I honestly can't say. She makes me smile, somehow. I feel close to her, as though I know her from another time, another place. I think she feels close to me. And I think she's amused by me, another outsider. And I'm sure she likes the fact that she could . . . can help me . . . with my face, and it was through her that I found the shoemaker. Stops her feeling powerless with all this bad luck that follows her around.'

Emily nods wisely at this. 'But would all this make her your friend? Because I'm sure she is your friend. You can see it in your bodies as you walk together.'

I have to stop this talk. 'You are extraordinarily wise considering how few years you have been on this earth. Now, tell me how many books you have read today? Are you all done with *Sir Galahad*?'

'I read nothing,' she says. 'My eyes are sore and my father says I must rest them. So I've been mooning around and, I tell you, I don't like it. I don't like it at all. I think I would like to go to a proper big school. Somewhere where I can learn some hard things.'

I am surprised at how much Emily's proposal discomforts me. She is an indispensable part of the web of my life here in West Auckland. She and Marian, and now Aaron, are the three fixed points in this web. I suddenly feel that if any one of these points loosens, my web will break.

I take her hand in mine. 'Don't go away, Em. I couldn't do without you. I just couldn't.'

Her face breaks into a smile. 'Well, p'raps I've still a few more hard things to learn here at home. Don't worry, Vic. I'll stay, if only for you.'

Thirty

During the following days I have to endure this new restlessness that occurs when one has a great deal of energy coursing through one's veins but cannot quite dissipate it through action, talk or any normal intercourse of life.

One day, to secure myself from Auntie Mary's close attention, I retreat to the upstairs drawing room to watch the to-ing and fro-ing in the village from the window seat. Sitting there I dwell for some pleasurable moments on every single movement and gesture of my walk with Aaron Whitstable.

Then I force myself to think more rationally of him and who he really might be. Aaron is not just the man who held my feet in his hands and then made me walk straight. He's not even the man who kissed me for so long with such strange power under the beech tree.

I have to face the fact that Aaron is quite, quite old. Don't grey strands thread through the gold of his hair? He might be as much as thirty-two years old! Didn't he once have a wife and child and suffer their loss? Is it not a fact that he works with his hands – clever, skilful hands that make him well known across the county, but nevertheless he works with his *hands*. In the eyes of people like my aunt, Kit Dawson is much more acceptable than Aaron because his professional involvement in the law and his skills in copying show he works with his brain.

But Kit is not half the person – half the man – that Aaron is.

There is no logic in it.

At two o'clock my aunt looks in at the door and says that she and Lizzie are taking the little ones by train to Bishop Auckland to have a

143

picnic in the park, would I like to join them? I shake my head and cry off with the excuse of a headache. She asks me to keep an ear open for Emily, who is staying at home with a new book about African missioning.

'She'll want to be a missionary next, though how that can be for a girl who never wants to go to church, I can't think.'

I watch them go off with Jonty in the brake. When they are out of sight my uncle emerges from the front door and strides down the green, black bag in hand. He, in turn, is followed out by Mrs Grey, carrying her basket. She makes her way across to Riley's grocery shop.

I am suddenly overcome with tiredness and am forced to lean my head back against the heavy lace curtain. For some seconds, perhaps minutes, I am in the smoky regions of sleep. I wake up suddenly, jerking my forehead so hard that it bangs on to the glass, which fortunately does not break. Now I can see Aaron walking briskly across the green. He's wearing a matching tweed jacket and breeches. A soft tie holds together his linen shirt-collar and a soft felt hat confines his flowing grey-gold hair. In his hand he carries a small package. He passes out of my sight, too close to the house, and then my blood freezes as the clanging of the doorbell echoes through the house. I sit very tight where I am, not having the courage to go and answer the door. I back away from the window, sit down on a chair, and wait for him to go away.

After an age, there is a little knock on the door and Emily, book in hand, enters, followed by Aaron. 'Mr Whitstable came,' she announces, a great beam on her face. 'And he has a present for you.'

I stand up. 'Emily, I don't think we should . . .'

But he's here, already in the room, breathing the air that I am breathing.

'Good day, Victoria,' he says, smiling slightly, very much at ease on this alien territory. 'I have something for you.'

I turn desperately to Emily. 'Em . . .'

She waggles her book in the air. 'I simply must check something about Africa in one of my father's directories. The route of the Zambezi,' she says. 'I think it will take me ten minutes. Perhaps fifteen.' She leaves the room, closing the door behind her with a decisive click.

He is smiling at me, with his eyes as well as his mouth. He takes wicked pleasure in my discomfort.

'You watched them all go, and then came to the house,' I accuse him.

He shakes his head. 'I've had my head down all morning finishing some shoes for a farmer from Toft Hill. Then a traveller called. I'd written to him to bring these.' He places his paper package on a low table. 'I thought they'd make a nice present for you.'

I stare at the package.

'I was going to talk to your uncle and ask if I could give them to you. I was going to tell him of my prospects and what I could offer you.'

My cheeks are burning red. 'He's not here,' I say stiffly. Privately, I'm pleased he's not here. What ructions would such an interview have caused?

'So your young cousin tells me. I was turning away and she assured me that you were here and she could bring me to see you.'

'She's a very mischievous girl,' I say crossly.

Oh no. Now he's turning away. I grab the package from the table. 'It was kind of you to think of me,' I gabble, undoing the string and almost tearing the brown paper in my haste. 'May I take a look?'

He turns back towards me, folds his arms and watches me as I take a pair of gloves out of a shallow velvet-lined box. The gloves are fashioned in a kid so creamy that they are almost golden.

'Try them on,' he says softly.

I pull them on to my hands. They fit perfectly. 'How did you know my size?'

'I know your little feet, so I why should I not know your hands?' he says.

I smooth them along my palms and down the backs of my hands. 'They are so soft.'

'Just like your skin.' He stays where he is, just inside the door. 'So soft.'

I am not sure, now, what to do. I can't ask him to sit down. I know that wouldn't be proper. But I don't want him to go.

'I *did* come here to see your uncle,' he says. 'I would have told him that I am a shoemaker, but a very fine one, with customers who come from as far as Yorkshire and Northumberland for my work. I would have told him that I have part ownership of a farm in Yorkshire that is farmed by my brother, and I own a shop and a furniture manufactory in Morpeth. That I live here alone because, after the tragedy of my wife and child – Marian says she told you of them – I needed solitude away from all those I have known formerly in my life.' He pauses. 'But your uncle isn't here and so I find I have to tell you all this.'

I take a step towards him. He puts a hand out, as though to ward me off. 'Stay where you are. We will do this right.' He pauses. 'The gloves are by way of signifying a betrothal. Gloves are bad luck as a gift except for this purpose.' He puts his own hands in front of him and grips the one with the other. 'Clasped together for ever.'

I put my hands in front of me and clasp them in the same gesture. 'Betrothed,' I whisper.

The dilemma as to what may happen next is solved by Emily, who charges through the door and skids to a halt. She looks somewhat disappointed to see us standing at the same distance, so far away from each other. 'Oh!' she says. 'I thought it might be like Lancelot and Guinevere.'

'With your father as King Arthur?' Aaron's laugh rings through the room. 'I think not, lass.'

I realise now that he's been nervous, is pleased that the declaration has been made, and would like now to escape. 'Perhaps you'd show Mr Whitstable out, Emily?' I look him full in the face. 'I will call on you regarding those new shoes, Aaron.'

He stares at me then nods. 'Very good . . . Victoria.'

Emily sees him out and comes leaping back up the stairs two at a time. 'It *is* like Lancelot and Guinevere!' she crows.

I nod, pressing my lips together to stop them smiling.

'And is it a secret?

I nod again, then peel off the gloves and lay them in their shallow box. 'A great secret.'

'Just like Lancelot and Guinevere!'

'You must keep the secret, Em.'

'Course I will. You don't think I tell *them* everything, do you?'

We move to the window seat to see my uncle and his colleague Dr Chalmers, walking back down the village street, their shining black top hats close together. For no reason I can fathom, the sight of this makes me shiver.

'Poor you! You still have that headache.' Emily's solicitous voice comes over my shoulder.

'No, no. I just had that chilly feeling. You know? When they say someone has walked over your grave?'

Thirty-One

I find that my foreboding is not displaced. I walk downstairs and meet my uncle by the dispensary door. 'You look worried, Uncle William,' I say, as innocently as I can. 'Such a hard task you have.'

He stares at me for a second as though he cannot quite remember who I am. Then his brow clears. 'Victoria! Always so concerned. I'm afraid it's young Charlie Cotton. In a really bad way. The things that woman has had to stand! Chalmers was there yesterday, me today. Poor child can't keep anything down, is quite wretched. Mrs Cotton can get no sustenance into him.'

'Should I take something for him?'

He frowns again. 'Some milk, perhaps. Or some beef tea? Your Auntie Mary usually has some to hand. Keen on the old beef tea, is my Mary. Says you never know when it might be needed. You could try taking that for the boy.' In his kindly concern for Marian he's obviously forgotten the ban he imposed last week. 'Tell Mrs Grey. She'll find you beef tea.' Then he nods briefly and vanishes into the dispensary.

Mrs Grey is not in the kitchen, so I go down into the big pantry and make my way along the shelves, turning round the preserves and the bottled fruit as I go. Right at the end, on the packed chill-shelf, I find a screw-top jar labelled in Auntie Mary's schoolgirl hand. It is beef tea, made two days ago.

When I get to her house on Front Street I'm prepared for Marian to rebuff me, as she did when the baby died. But she is preoccupied. Her normally immaculate hair is awry and her face is even whiter than usual. She nods at me, then retreats into the kitchen. I follow her. The boy Charlie is on a makeshift bed in the corner of the kitchen. His face is drawn and there are blue shadows under his eyes. Lying there, under the drawn-up blanket, he looks half the size he was very recently. A woman I do not know is standing by the fireplace, a jug in her hand.

'This is Mrs Tate. She cleans for us sometimes.' Marian nods in her direction. 'She was kind enough to bring some beef tea for the bairn. But I told her—'

Mrs Tate interrupts her in a strange voice that is both concerned and angry. 'Mrs Cotton here has told me that the bairn winnet take anything, nowt but what she herself prepares.' She nods at two teapots sitting on the hob. 'Herbs and all that stuff. Says it's easier for the bairn to drink out of them.'

I hold up my basket. 'That's what I brought myself. Beef tea. And some milk.'

'Well, you can take the beef stuff back,' says Marian grimly. 'P'raps leave the milk. That might help things later on.'

'Well, I'll get off,' says Mrs Tate. 'You don't want me cluttering the place, not with *Miss Kilburn* here.'

Being known by someone I do not know gives me a frisson of distaste. But I have come to understand that any niece of the sainted Dr Kilburn would be known in this enclosed village. Mrs Tate bangs the door behind her and I don't quite know whether she's angry because I'm here, or because her beef tea has been rejected.

I glance at the bed. Young Charlie lies there, undisturbed by the clashing door. On the floor beside him, his strange velvet hat lies like a cowpat. Beside that is a scrubbed enamel basin, chipped on the rim.

'Doesn't care if she wakes the bairn.' Marian glares at the door. 'Good riddance to bad rubbish,' she says. 'Only here for sheer nosiness. She's the third this morning.'

'People are only trying to help,' I say humbly, attempting to circumvent her potent anger. 'Really, Marian.'

She stares at me, then her gaze softens. 'Sit down, child, an' I'll make you a cup of tea with your own milk. Don't be deceived by them women, honey. I've had that Sarah Shaw in here as well as Mrs Tate. They've both been foul-mouthing me around the place. So why d'you think they'd want to come here now?'

I look around. The room is neat and clean, though very sparse. The fire is roaring up the chimney, making the room unbearably warm. 'I don't know why they would want to do that.'

'They want to see what I'm up to, to report back to their cronies at Riley's shop.' Her voice trembles slightly. This rare expression of weakness shows me for once how desperate she really feels.

'Up to? What could you be up to?'

Charlie groans suddenly and Marian glides across to the bed, lifts the boy from his grey-white pillow and dabs his sweating brow with a corner of her apron. 'There now, love. Sshsh! You'll be better soon. The fever'll break and you'll be right as rain.' She almost whispers the words.

He whispers something into her ear and she nods. 'Hungry, are you? Well, isn't that a sign?' She nods to me. 'Pass that small teapot to us, honcy. The one without the handle.'

I do as she says. She cuddles him to her and puts the spout to his mouth and dribbles some of the liquid between his lips. She must have heard the doubt in my voice.

'Will that feed him?' I say.

She shakes her head. 'Poor mite can't keep a thing down. It's the fever. More food – even your beef tea – 'll just torment his poor old stomach. Those ignorant women there don't understand that. This here is just something to keep him calm, keep him resting. Mayhap with this rest and with the doctor's medicine, he'll pull round.'

Suddenly her eyes are staring directly into mine. They are dull as marbles, just as they were the day baby Robbie died. I can't see a spark of hope there.

She goes on, 'But I doubt it. I'm fated to pull others through worse diseases than this and still to watch my own die. My own children. My own mother that I really loved. It's a punishment for something that I don't know what.' Now at last her eyes flash and there is passion and rage in her voice.

Restlessly, the boy pulls away from the spout and she settles him down again, pulling the thin stitched quilt back up under his chin. 'Yes. A judgement. Though what I've done wrong I can't say. Aside from marryin' Fred Cotton when I shouldn't.' Her voice, normally attractive and low toned, is rough and despairing. 'Me still being married to the other feller.'

149

Tears are brimming on to my cheeks. 'Marian, don't say that!'

She stands up and runs her hand down her apron where it has creased as she sat cradling Charlie in her arms. 'Why else would all this happen, child?' There is anger in her voice but no tears in her eyes. 'Why else?'

The door opens and Mrs Dodds crashes in. Instantly, Marian's demeanour changes. She is as flint-hard as ever. 'Oh, missis! I thought you'd never get here. I need to get across to Mr Riley's and check on something. Just mind the bairn, will yeh?' She looks up at me. 'I'll walk down with you, Victoria.'

The old woman leans over Charlie. She pokes him and he doesn't move. 'This bairn could sleep for England.'

As we walk down the green, Marian stumbles and then links her arm through mine. 'So,' she says, 'd'you like the gloves?'

Of course, I flush at this. 'How d'you know about the gloves?'

She ignores my question. 'That Aaron is an exceptional person. A special man. Reminds me of my first husband, the one who took me down to Bristol. My, we had a good time down there. He knocked all the others into a cocked hat.'

All the others?

We pass a huddle of miners who have just come off the fore shift. 'Now, Marian,' says one. 'How're yeh keepin'?'

She nods. 'Canny,' she says.

'I knaa this lad needs lodgings,' he says. 'Would yeh . . .?'

She smiles at him full in the face and shakes her head. 'Any other time, bonny lad!' she says, and hurries me on.

Behind us a spurt of laughter passes from mouth to mouth among the men. As we walk on Marian looks neither right nor left and her face is hard and set. It occurs to me that perhaps the village women would not pursue her so much if she did not persist in showing them that hard, flinty side of herself all the time. Or perhaps if she desisted from teasing and taunting the men. Perhaps she is her own worst enemy. Then I shake myself. Here I am, doing what they do: blaming her for her misfortune.

We come to a stop before Mr Riley's plate-glass window and I start to go on. She hangs on to my arm. 'Stay a bit, child.' She reaches under her shawl into a pocket in her skirt and pulls out a folded piece of paper and thrusts it into my hand. 'I wrote out the list of things for the poultice, and the potion. I'll not be here for ever and might be too busy to put up any more for you. And we can't have that face going off the corks again, can we? Not when that lovely face has caught our Mr Aaron's fancy.' Her voice is laced with humour and affection. She pats my arm and pushes me on my way.

I cross the green, catching sight of Emily's bright face peering at me from the drawing-room window. I have to run quickly up to my room to avoid her and smooth out the paper to read what Marian has written for me in quite fine looping writing.

Use Dryed herbs if Not in Season
Poultice for the skin
Mash together these with measure of wine vinager and trace arsenic water:
  Bryanny root
  Garlik
  Mash Maller root

Tincture for the spirit
Mix all these in half wine, half water.
  Dried Gelwart
  Meddow Pimpernel
  Mash Marigold
  Barberry

Victoria
  You can get trace arsenic water by soaking off one flypayper in a pint of water overnight.

Thirty-Two

Margaret Riley glanced at the grandmother clock wedged in by the cocoa tins, then peered past her other customers at Mrs Cotton.

'Mr Riley's not in,' she said firmly. 'Not due back till six from Bishop Auckland. Can I do something for you, Mrs Cotton?' The polite words were belied by the acid tone.

Marian stared at her for a second. 'No, missis. It's the master I want.'

'Well . . .' Mrs Riley's plump shoulders hunched up in a shrug.

The chatter started again even before the door had properly shut behind Mrs Cotton.

Marian walked across the green and met Thomas Riley off the five fifty train from Bishop Auckland. Fortunately he arrived on his own, although there were other people trickling off the half-empty train: women with shopping baskets and one or two clerkly men.

She smiled warmly at him. 'Ah, Mr Riley! I told myself I'd catch you here.'

He glanced around, but the yard was emptying rapidly and the porters were busy loading parcels on to the train for its onward journey. He set off briskly down the road and she kept pace with him on her long legs.

'What can I do for you, Mrs Cotton . . . Marian? How is that lad of yours? I hear he's bad.'

The smile faded from her face. 'Charlie's not too grand, seeing as you ask. I'm doing my best, and the doctors couldn't have been better. Everything's being done for him. Miss Kilburn – Victoria, that is – brought him beef tea and milk this afternoon.'

'Very kind. I've a suspicion that young woman's quite fond of you, Marian.'

She smiled slightly. 'I suspect the same. She's a nice child. Quality. Not a lot of that round here.'

'You judge us too harshly, Marian.' His tone was jocular. He'd enjoyed his afternoon. His solicitor, Mr Trotter, had confirmed that the deal on the land was completed and plans were afoot to build a pair of houses on it, to sell on at a tidy profit. After lunch at Mr Trotter's own house on Back Bondgate they had strolled down Newgate Street to look at the site, on a new street cutting through from the main street. The new road was to be called Victoria Street in honour of the Queen.

He slowed down slightly and looked at Marian. 'So what is it, Marian? Do you need sommat from the shop? No need to come down to the station for that.'

'I've seen you take a walk round the village every night, after you've shut the shop. About ten o'clock?'

'So I do.' It was no surprise that she knew this. In this village everyone knew.

'I just thought you might call into number thirteen, like. To see what I've made of the house. It's all clean now. I've got it all papered and dried out. Had fires on day and night. The house could do with a bit of work in there, though. Staircase, for one thing, instead of those ladders.'

'I can't promise . . .'

She put a firm hand on his arm and stopped his forward progress. 'I just thought that tonight when you go out on your walk, you might like a cup of my special tea, a bit of a warm,' she said. 'In my house.'

He flushed and glanced round at the empty road. 'Marian, I . . .'

'I'll leave you now,' she said, releasing his arm. 'I'll go home the back way. Now if you came this back way tonight, not a soul would see you. All nice and private we could be.' She turned off on a narrow lane by the mill and was out of sight in a second.

Thomas was relieved that he would not have to turn the corner on to the green with Marian Cotton beside him. Even so, as he crossed the green towards his shop there was a spring in his step and he was whistling.

At quarter past ten that night Thomas Riley let himself into the back door of number thirteen Front Street and walked straight into the single downstairs room. Marian was sitting on a low stool in the darkness, a mere outline in the late high glow of the fire, wearing a rather fine silk paisley shawl over a simple long shift. The room was very hot. She'd loosened her hair from its usual tight bun and it dropped in one heavy, oiled wave almost to her knees. In the firelight her face looked very white and her eyes gleamed.

'Now, Thomas,' she said. She put her fingers to her lips and glanced at the boy on the bed in the corner.

He came to stand beside her, one hand on her hair where it spread over her shoulders. 'How is he?' he whispered.

'Very quiet,' she breathed back, handing him a small china cup. 'He'll sleep now right through, with luck.'

As he finished his tea she stood up. The shawl fell to her feet and he could see now her slender white shoulders. 'Marian!' he groaned.

She put a finger on his lips and led him across the room to the ladder. 'I'll go first,' she whispered.

As he climbed the ladder behind her, his head swimming from her special tea, his senses filled with the woman-ness of her; he felt drenched in the scent of lavender and roses. He knew that sometime, somehow, he would have to pay for all this. But he was a starving man, and here, dark as it was, was sustenance.

Thomas awoke the next morning to the rasp of the curtain rail as Marian opened the curtain wide. Still half asleep, he lay watching her. She was fully dressed now, her hair neatly coiled, a clean apron over a brown day dress. He sat up and swung his legs over the edge of the bed in one heave.

'Great heavens, woman. Shut that curtain, will you?' he said groggily. 'Are you mad? What time is it, what time is it?'

She peered through the window before she closed the curtain again. 'Dawn, or just after. The men have just peeled up the hill for the fore shift, poor buggers.'

He was struggling with his breeches, pulling on his shirt, all at the same time. 'I meant to go, meant to go straight off after . . .'

She laughed. 'After you'd had your wicked way with me? Nay. You went off to sleep, Tommy. Slept the sleep of a babe. I tried but couldn't get you awake no matter how I tried.' She buttoned his shirt for him as though he were a small boy, then handed him his necktie.

'They'll see me. I'll have to go round the back way again,' he was babbling.

She held out his coat. 'Don't worry, honey. No one'll see you. People don't see what they don't expect. I think there's likely to be more worry for you when you get home.'

He stopped tying his necktie. 'You'd like that, wouldn't you? Me in trouble at home?'

She shrugged. 'It's matterless to me.'

'Well, you may be pleased to know that Margaret won't have noticed. We sleep . . . we have our own rooms.'

'I see.'

He pulled on his jacket. 'You probably do. But don't you go getting any ideas, Marian. And there'd better be no consequences from this . . .'

'A bairn, you mean?' she laughed again. 'No fear of that, Thomas. I'm already in that way.'

He stared at her, seething now with a revulsion which was as much for himself as her. 'You're a very strange woman, very strange,' he said dourly.

She stared him in the eyes. 'Aye, perhaps I am. And it's a very strange – perhaps a very unhappy – man as'd spend a night abed with such as me. Don't you think?'

She smiled her strange, knowing smile and he shot across the room and down the ladder as though he were escaping from a dangerous fire. Looking neither left nor right, he fled the house through the back door. Once out in the lane he peered all round him, but apart from the backs of one or two surface men making their way over the hill to the pit, no one was about. He walked along towards the mill, quickly at first, then he slowed down and swung his stick a little as he walked, as though he were merely out for one of his early morning strolls and this was a very ordinary day.

As he made his way past the millrace he contemplated his humiliation at the hands of Marian Cotton. There was no doubt the woman had trapped him. How she had plotted, how she had cajoled him into her company, currying whatever favours that might come her way! What black delight in their cavortings in the night! She was good at all that stuff, no doubt about that. Very eager and inventive. Playful and passionate. Groaning with a pleasure equal to his own.

But what good woman would do that? With another woman's

husband, even? And to do it when she was pregnant by some other man, probably by the excise officer. The woman was depraved. Margaret was right. There was something wrong with her.

Dwelling on Marian Cotton's iniquities brought calm to Thomas by the time he turned off the mill lane back towards the green. By the time he'd crossed the green and had taken out his little key to open the side door to the shop, he felt quite at ease. Margaret would never know. She slept heavily in her own room and he often went out for an early walk before opening the shop. All he need do was ruffle his bed to make it look slept in. She would never know. He put his key in the lock.

At that moment he heard a high-pitched, keening scream from the other side of the green. He turned to see Marian Cotton frantically waving at him from outside her house. He looked up and down the green. There was no one about. He raced across the green, galloping, leaping the high grass in his haste, disturbing the hens that had chosen the green for their night-time roost.

He was gasping when he got to her. 'What is it, woman? What is it? Shut thyself up, will tha? Tha'll have the whole village up.' He was no longer the suave near-gentleman who had left his mining roots so far behind.

She was pressing her hand to her lips; her eyes were red with violent tears. 'Tommy, Tommy . . .' She grasped his arm.

He shook her off. 'What is it? Get inside. Get inside.'

She took a very deep breath. 'He's dead, Tommy. The bairn's dead. His skin is like cold clay. Been dead for hours. Mebbe last night . . .'

While they were cavorting above? He shuddered, his blood turning to ice. He pushed past her and leaped across the room to the bed in the corner. The lad lay there, his face a whitish blue. He had thrown off the blanket in some kind of paroxysm, and there was a dribble of yellow stuff from his mouth to the pillow. Thomas touched the small claw-like hand and it was stone cold.

He turned round and looked at her with newly minted loathing. 'You did it, you wicked woman. How did you do that to him?'

She looked at him, face white as paper. 'You were there,' she whispered. 'I did nothing. Please, Thomas . . .' She put her hand on his.

He shook off her hand yet again. 'Mr Riley to you, Mrs Cotton. I'm going to get Dr Kilburn.'

'Aye. I need the doctor,' she whispered. 'The certificate . . .'

156

He stared at her. 'Is that all you can think of? There's sommat wrong with you, woman.'

He strode off along the green towards Western House, then broke into a run.

Marian stared at his back, her eyes, at last, filling with tears, her hands trembling. 'It goes on,' she whispered.

Thirty-Three

Having just been transfixed for a moment by the sight of Mr Riley striding down the village with Sergeant Hutchinson lolloping along beside him like an oversized rabbit, I return to my washstand and my morning routine of clearing Marian's noxious poultice from my face. Then a thunderous knock on the front door pulls me out on to the landing, where I'm joined by a gleeful Emily.

She puts her fingers to her lips. 'Drama!' she says.

The chatter of voices floats up to us from the hall. Peeping through the banister we see them clustered there: the policeman wrapped in his cape, the relieving officer with his beaver hat in his hand, my uncle in his morning coat clutching a copy of *The Times*; my aunt in her morning gown, clutching a shawl just below her bosom where the baby is really beginning to show. The deep voice of the policeman, the lighter voice of my uncle and the thready baritone of the shopkeeper merge together in an anxious rush.

Here is drama, no doubt about it. We learn that Mr Riley has gone straight from the house of Marian Cotton to get the policeman and has dragged him along to see my uncle. These two insist that *this time*, no automatic death certificate should be issued. Mr Riley's voice rises an octave. There is sufficient doubt to demand a post mortem. 'Sufficient doubt,' I hear the sergeant say.

'Sufficient doubt,' echoes Mr Riley.

A ripple of fear travels from my heels to the back of my neck, where it makes my hair stand on end. This can't be right. I thought Mr Riley was Marian's friend. Even her protector.

My aunt glances upwards, catches sight of Emily and me, and bustles up the stairs, breathing rather hard. She shoos us back along the landing as though I, as well as Emily, were only twelve years old.

'That woman!' she mutters crossly. 'That woman!'

I allow her to push me into my bedroom and wait for her footsteps to fade behind the door. Then I put on my outdoor boots, pull on my jacket and bonnet and make my way down the back stairs and through the kitchen. Thankfully there's no sign of Mrs Grey. She must be out in the back vestibule, eavesdropping on the row, just like Emily and me. Of course she'll be delighted, as is my aunt, at the thought of trouble for Marian Cotton.

I make my way out through the rear garden, along the backs of the houses, and then turn up on to the green near Marian's house. She's standing there before the door, her bonnet on, looking across the green at a boy who is sitting on the grass, playing mud pies.

'Marian, I heard about Charlie . . .'

She looks at me blindly, as though I'm a stranger.

I try again. 'I'm sorry for your loss, Marian.'

She blinks and her face clears. 'What was it, child?' she says. 'I was in another place.'

'I'm sorry . . .'

She shakes her head, her face curiously without expression. 'Don't worry, honey. I'm used to this, burying those who've slept under my roof. I tell you, child, it just has to be endured.'

Her words sound hard, but I am used to her now. Marian would never scream and rage at her fate. She is too strong for that. As her friend I am proud that this is so. The problem is that her very strength rebounds on her. This is why she raises such ire in those around her.

I take in the fact that she's wearing outdoor clothes. 'You're going somewhere?' I glance at the closed door.

'Ma Dodds is in there watching Charlie – though he's past watching, of course.'

Now her stoical endurance pricks my eyes to tears. 'Can I do anything for you, Marian? Can I come with you?'

She shrugs. 'I'm just going down to the insurance man. I'm owed four pounds ten shillin' insurance now, so it's not all for nothing.'

I frown. This sounds so mercenary. Even so, I am beginning to

159

understand that it's her way of coping. 'You'll get money for him? For Charlie?'

She shakes her head. 'Not yet, honey. I'm just telling the man so he'll come up later with the money. I cannot collect any money till I get the certificate, like. An' I cannot buy the bairn a coffin until I get that money. Though p'raps I'll get a coffin on the Parish.'

I think of the scene I've just witnessed in the hall of Western House. 'You're sure you'll get a certificate, Marian?'

She lifts her shoulders in that familiar shrug. 'No reason why not.'

'Marian, I have to tell you Mr Riley was at our house just now, with the sergeant. There was talk of *doubt*, an inquest . . .'

Now I have her close interest. Her jaw is set, her eyes blue pools of despair. 'That bastard!' she whispers disbelievingly. 'That bastard Riley.'

I'm red with embarrassment at her language but hold her gaze. 'So do you think you should go just yet to the insurance man, Marian?'

That shrug again. 'Fellow needs to know. The bairn died, like the other bairns died, like so many die. That's all there is. There's nothing more wrong here than the way they've made us live. That's all.'

I stare at her. I don't quite know what she means. She often uses 'us' when she means 'me'. Does she mean the way they've made *her* live, or the way they've made *everybody* live, those of her class and type? In poverty and dirt, the despair of easy death dulled by repetition? It's common enough, as I've seen since I've been here in this village. It must be so in London too. But Lordship Park, where my family live, is set at a distance from such despair. The funerals in Abney Park Cemetery are on a much grander scale than anything I've seen here.

Suddenly Marian's face clears and softens. 'Aye, but Riley'll not get his way. Your own uncle is a fair man, child, innocent of the nasty attitude that infects this place. He'll see us right.'

Through the corner of my eye I can see bustle and movement down at Western House. 'He'll be coming along soon, Marian. They'll be coming. You shouldn't be out of the house when they come. You know that.' It is rare in our friendship for me to take the lead, for me to tell Marian what to do, but now I do it.

She nods slightly and calls across to the child who is now scraping out a mud hole on the green and pouring water into it from a battered kettle. 'Would you like a penny, kidder?'

160

The boy comes quickly enough. She thrusts a scrap of paper into his hand, then reaches into her apron pocket and pulls out a coin. 'Take this to th'insurance man. Ha'penny now, son, and a ha'penny when I know it's been delivered.'

He hesitates a second, then grabs the paper and the coin. 'Aye, I'll dee that, missis. An' I'll be back.' He turns and runs, showing us his bare heels and a glimpse of his bare bottom through the ragged seat of his pants.

She turns to me and says gently, 'So, honey, would you like to come in and see poor Charlie?'

I hesitate. I've never seen a dead creature face to face except for Tilda, the mother of our present cats, who was trodden by a runaway horse in Church Street in Stoke Newington. I was reprimanded by my mother for crying about that. But I can see now from Marian's shrewd eye that she's waiting for me to refuse, waiting for me to fail her. I nod slowly. 'Yes. I'd like that.'

Inside the house, Mrs Dodds is drinking tea by the low fire. I look around the room to put off the inevitable sight of the makeshift bed in the corner. The room is very hot but spotlessly clean. Even so, it smells mousy and dank in a way that reminds me of that farmhouse I visited with my uncle. Unlike the farmhouse, though, this place is very decent. The walls have been decorated with a rather stunning green wallpaper. One chair has been graced by the draping of a very fine paisley shawl along its arm. At the back of the room is a ladder, which must lead up to the next floor. Not even a staircase! The way these people live.

Marian leads me across to the bed in the corner where Charlie lies. The thin quilt pulled up to his chin is quite clean. His face is moon white and gaunt, his eyes closed, his eyeballs showing blue through their translucent lids. He has a bandage under his chin like a bonnet strap. On his thick thatch of hair sits his velvet cap.

'Our Charlie loved his cap, like his big brother loved his. We buried him in his cap and we'll bury Charlie in his,' said Marian. 'Charlie was not my own, Victoria, but he'll be a miss round here.'

There is the faintest tremor in her voice but I know I must not respond to it. I long to take her hand, to give her some comfort, but am constrained from such action – by my own uncertainties, by the sharp eye of Mrs Dodds in her low chair by the fire, and by Marian herself, who seems in some kind of queer trance. I look back at Charlie and have a ghostly glimpse of him standing doggedly at Marian's side, sucking his Spanish.

We're brought back to the present by a thundering knock on the door.

Marian stands up very straight. 'That'll be your uncle,' she says. 'You don't want him to find you here, child. Take the back door.' She nods at a narrow door beyond the ladder. Then she looks me in the eye. 'Tell our friend Aaron about all this, will you, honey? All that's happened here?' Then she puts a hand on my arm and squeezes it softly. 'You are my best thought-of friend, Victoria. Best. Never forget that.'

In his low room across the green Aaron listens patiently to my tale and nods. 'I saw some commotion over there, as would many others.'

I raise a brow. 'The bear-pit?'

He nods. 'As you say.' He puts a hand on my shoulder and presses it, making me sit down on a stool. He sits opposite me. 'You say they talked of a post mortem? An inquest?'

'Yes. Mr Riley was quite insistent.'

'Riley? I thought the relieving officer had a bit of regard for Marian. Didn't he put work her way? And he fixed her up with that house, after all.'

'I thought so too.'

'Aye. I'd say he even had a bit of a soft spot for her.' He stares at me as though he's about to say something else, then desists. He stands up. 'We can't do anything for her until the doctor's gone. I've got the hens and the donkey to feed. Would you like to come to help?'

Outside, in his long garden, he puts his arms around me to show me how to scatter the millet in the hens' run. Then our fingers touch as we tip the meal into the manger for the donkey, whose coat is now silky and who eyes us through a dense fringe of eyelash in great contentment.

'We need a name for our donkey,' says Aaron, watching closely as I stroke the donkey's ears and tolerate his nuzzling nose.

'Tilda!' I announce.

'Why that name?'

'Because I had a cat once with that name. So there's continuation.'

'It sounds like a lady's name. He might not like it.'

'Change the spelling. Say T-I-L-D-E-R.'

He nods. 'Right.' Then he takes my hand, but I pull away. 'I have to go. They'll have missed me at Western House and will be blaming that on Marian too.'

At the door he nods across at Marian's house. My uncle must still be inside. Mr Riley is loitering outside.

Aaron says, 'I'll watch till your uncle comes away, then go across to see her.'

'Tell her if there's anything I can do for her, I will.' I press my lips together to stop them trembling.

He touches the back of my gloved hand. 'You're growing up before our eyes, Victoria.' I can feel him watching me as I set off across the green so I make a conscious effort to walk as straight as I can.

Thirty-Four

Thomas Riley looked down at the boy who had sidled up to him.

'D'you have the ha'penny, sir?' said the lad.

'What ha'penny is that, son?'

'The ha'penny Mrs Cotton promised us if I took a note to the insurance man.'

'And you did that?'

'Aye, I did.'

Thomas fished a ha'penny from his waistcoat pocket and handed it over. 'Here you are. I'll tell Mrs Cotton you've done the message.'

The boy tucked the coin in the pocket of his breeches, touched his forehead where a cap might have been, had he worn one, then ran off to a pile of mud ten yards away and settled down with his pot-pie making. Thomas watched him thoughtfully. The insurance man . . . That would be something to report to the sergeant when he emerged.

Thomas was dealing with the very surface of things: today, the fact of the boy's untimely death. What a good lad the boy had been. No bother to Marian Cotton, even though she wanted rid of him. The sheer heartlessness of the woman, entrapping men with her wiles, even while her own son – well, stepson – was dying down below. As though sons were so easily to be disposed of, rather than treasured. There had to be an inquest. Hadn't there, quite rightly, been an inquest for his own Teddy? They'd had to manage at that inquest without calling Margaret. With his connections Thomas had been able to ensure that. Margaret had been in such a bad way and was so wildly condemning of Teddy. Who knows what the coroner would have made of that?

It was obvious, though, that there should be an inquest in this case. His Margaret was right. There was something very . . . well, bad . . . about this woman. He'd been blind to it so far, but now the blindfold was off. Just wait till the sergeant heard about that note to the insurance man! That would strike a chord.

William Kilburn pulled the blanket back across the thin body of the child and up over his head, dislodging his cap. He glanced at the sergeant. 'Enteritis, I think. But I have to say I am not absolutely certain,' he said. 'The boy has been poorly but he didn't seem to be quite so bad when I saw him yesterday. And before I came along this morning I consulted Dr Chalmers—'

'That one's not much good,' interrupted Marian. 'Not half the doctor you are, sir.'

'Mrs Cotton!' grunted the sergeant, who was standing, helmet in hand, in the doorway. He looked at William. 'Not certain? You know that'll mean I'll have to see the coroner, Doctor?'

William continued, 'Dr Chalmers has seen Charlie three times this week. Said he thought the boy was pulling through.' He paused, then said sharply, 'So what have you been giving him, Mrs Cotton?'

She flushed angrily. 'He wouldn't take food. Just a bit of beef tea of my own making. No one else's stuff passed his lips.'

'Nothing else?'

'I give him all the stuff you and Chalmers prescribed but that seemed to make him worse, if anything. I did give him a bit of arrowroot to settle his stomach. And I thought that tincture of yours really took the stuffing out of him.'

William frowned. 'Nothing else?'

'I did give him a bit of valerian to help him sleep. Poor bairn had a job sleeping. Threshing about half the night.'

'When you say "a bit", what do you mean?'

'Same as I'd give anyone, to help them sleep. I used to give some to Mr Lanister. I gave some to Mr Quick-Manning. As you know, Doctor, sleep is the great healer.' The doctor and the sergeant looked at her hard at the mention of the excise officer, but she was quite tranquil.

William glanced at the sergeant, then exhaled a large breath. 'Well, I think you should see the coroner. I suppose an inquest is inevitable. And with this level of uncertainty I imagine I'll be obliged to do an autopsy examination before any inquest.' He raised his eyes to meet Marian's angry gaze. 'It's for your sake, Mrs Cotton. An autopsy should tell us what we want to know.'

'You'll cut into the child?' Her tone was filled with disgust. 'As if he hadn't been through enough. And when will this . . . autopsy . . . be? Now? This minute? Will you cut him now?'

He glanced at the sergeant. 'I would do it only at the coroner's request.' He took out his watch and clicked it open. 'Now, Mrs Cotton . . . Sergeant. I have a queue already at the surgery and ten visits to do today.'

'I'll check with the coroner. Would tomorrow morning suit? For the autopsy?' said the sergeant. 'Ten o'clock?'

Marian looked from one man to the other, and back. 'Does this mean I won't get my death certificate then?'

William shook his head. 'No death certificate just yet, Mrs Cotton. Not until after the inquest.'

Up to this point she had been dogged, responding to them in angry restraint. Now she seemed to collapse into herself, her shoulders bowed, her hands and arms wound round each other. 'It's too much, too much to stand. What am I supposed to do?' Her wailing voice penetrated the floors above her, to the very rafters of the tall house. Mrs Dodds stood up from her fireside seat and went to stand by her, awkwardly patting her shoulders.

William coughed. 'Nothing to be upset about, Mrs Cotton. This will clear the whole thing up.'

'But I've no money to do anything for young Charlie. Nothing. And that devil Mr Riley – even he's taken against me now.'

William clicked his bag closed and glanced at the sergeant. 'We'll leave you now, Mrs Cotton. I'll be here at ten o'clock in the morning to . . . do the autopsy should the coroner request one. In the meantime Mrs Dodds here will, I'm sure, be a comfort to you.'

The door creaked shut behind the men, and the women stared at it for a moment. Then Marian stood up straight, leaned across and lifted the paisley shawl from the chair. She vanished up the ladder and came down with two dresses. Very carefully she tied them up in a brown paper parcel.

'Here!' she said quietly to Mrs Dodds. 'You take this to the pawn man, will you? See what you can get. I'm going to need some money here. How can I face this, with no money to back me? Riley and the sergeant and now even the doctor are ranged on one side, and me on the other. Just me. So I'll have to conjure up something. You take that stuff, missis, and get me what you can.'

Mrs Dodds hesitated.

'There'll be something in it for you, never fear.'

The old woman nodded and pulled her shawl close around her.

Marian bolted the door behind her and turned back towards the child on the bed in the corner. She pulled the sheet down so that she could see his face and adjusted his cap so it was straight again.

'Now, Charlie,' she said softly. 'Poor old Charlie. First there was just you and me left in this world and now there's just me. Oh yes, there's Aaron and my young Victoria. But their paths are not mine. I know that. I think they know it. Really, like I say, there is just me to sort all this. Isn't that a pickle?'

Thirty-Five

When I finally make my way home from Aaron's, Auntie Mary is sitting in the back porch waiting for me. She's puffed up like a pigeon, vengeance personified. Her pretty face is marred by a scowl. Emily is sitting on the window seat beside her, a worried look on her face.

My aunt stands up, putting a hand behind her to support herself as she draws herself to her full height. 'Come with me!' she says, and leads the way to the dining room.

I follow, with Emily dancing along beside me whispering, 'What drama! Here's trouble for you now, Vic.'

Auntie holds the door so I can pass within, then closes it in Emily's face. She stands with her back to the tall fireplace. 'How dare you?' she says. 'How dare you, Victoria?'

'Auntie, I—'

'Don't you "Auntie" me! No niece of mine'd embarrass me in me own home, in me own village.' In the heat of her anger, her accent is shredding.

'I wouldn't do that. I wouldn't.'

'So why d'you go sneakin' out to the house of that Cotton woman, whose child has just died, they're sayin' now by her own hand. They were already sayin' that about the others that died. She's a bad woman.'

'That's not fair. She's had a terrible life, and lost so many . . .'

Auntie Mary drives on, 'And not satisfied by that, why, you traipse down to the house of that shoemaker and . . .' she pauses at the enormity of the thought, '. . . you helped him feed his hens! I told William you should never have had a single shoe from that man. Too big for his own

168

boots, him. Why, he even writes to the papers! You didn't need boots. Your own were perfectly fine.'

So I've been spied on. Mrs Grey, no doubt. My anger makes me toss my head. 'There is nothing to that, Auntie. Feeding hens! I imagine you fed the hens many times at home at Newfield.'

This mention of her own humble upbringing brings an ugly red flush to her neck and to her round cheeks. 'That's enough! The woman is poisonous. What's she done to you? You come here meek and mild and she turns you into a harridan. I intend to talk to your Uncle William. You'll return to London tomorrow. Mark my word.'

At this the door swings open and the eavesdropping Emily almost tumbles in. She stands up straight. 'Don't send Victoria back, Mama. Don't you do it!' She walks across and stands by me, shoulder to shoulder. 'She's here and she can walk properly now and she's become beautiful, like Guinevere. You can't send her back.' She grasps my hand. 'She is my cousin. She belongs here.'

My aunt looks at us, one to the other and back again, her normal colour returning. Then, to my utter relief, her tight mouth loosens into a slight smile. 'You're alike, you two. You both favour William.' Then she sighs. 'What am I to do with you, Victoria? I am so busy with the house and the little ones, and my condition makes me so tired . . .'

'I know!' Emily pipes up. 'I'll be her gaoler. I'll be with her every minute of the day. I'll watch her for you. I promise.'

This makes my aunt laugh out loud. She looks at me. 'Would you not rather go home, Victoria? To be Emily's prisoner seems rather a tough punishment, even for your misdemeanours.'

I put an arm around my young cousin. 'I embrace her supervision. The last thing I wish is to go home, Auntie. I've been happier here, well, than I've been in all my life. I've become who I am in this place. I don't want to go from here. I will fade away if I do. I would die.' I want to go on to say that even so I would not betray Marian Cotton or stop feeding Aaron Whitstable's hens. I try to frame the words but the door swings open and my uncle marches in.

He looks straight at my aunt. 'There's to be an autopsy,' he announces. 'Can't see much need for it, but the sergeant's keen. He'll see the coroner, but an autopsy's inevitable now.'

Auntie Mary puts a finger to her lips and turns back to us. 'You go now, girls. And, Emily – do not let Victoria out of your sight. Promise!'

169

As I stand very still outside the room with my twelve-year-old gaoler we hear my uncle say, 'I have to say I think there may be problems, Mary.'

My aunt says, 'I told you. It's all about the place that the Cotton woman's up to no good.'

'The rage out there is boiling up like the bubbles in a kettle. And there is a new recruit to the ranks of the accusers. I walked back up with Riley and he was pushing some idea with the sergeant about Mrs Cotton's insurance.' He pauses. Then: 'D'you know, Mary, there's something very strange about that? These vindictive feelings of his about Mrs Cotton. He was always very appreciative of her nursing skills. I hadn't thought that he'd join all that tittle-tattle.'

'Then he's seen the light, William. Just because a lot of people say something, my dear, does not mean it's not true.'

'It might just be as you say, Mary. But this is not a simple thing.' He hesitates. We can hear him move, towards the window, perhaps. 'I have to tell you, Mary, there's a danger that all this fuss might just rebound on me, on my professional judgement.'

We hear a rustle. I imagine my aunt moving nearer to my uncle, responding to his obvious concern. She probably puts a hand on his arm. 'What is it, William?' she says.

'Well, my dear, I have looked very closely at the wasted body of the little fellow. D'you know, Chalmers has seen him three times this week? I was there myself yesterday. I gave him morphia and hydrocyanic acid. And Chalmers was dosing him too. We relied on Mrs Cotton to give him his medicine. And on top of that the woman was dosing him with valerian to make him sleep! And the Lord knows what else. I hesitate to say this but it might not look well for any of us if all this confluence of medicine, good and bad, tipped the child over the edge.'

My aunt laughs now, her voice full of pride and confidence. 'Don't be silly, William. You cure patients. That is your job. You are famous for it. If they don't survive it's because of some other intervention. This is another case entirely. The woman is poison.'

At that point we hear them coming towards the door and make for the stairs. We don't stop until we get to my bedroom and there we flop back on my bed, side by side, overwhelmed by laughter which is half tears. I can't think why we laugh, as none of this is in the least bit comical.

When Emily gets back her breath she says soberly, 'I heard Mrs Grey say Mrs Cotton killed the little boy. It's all over the village. And the others. They say she killed the others.'

'Others?'

'The other children. And the lodger. And the husband.'

'That's wicked, to say all that. I know her and she's not in the least like that. I was at the funerals. They were awful. Mrs Cotton carried the baby's coffin in her arms. Why d'they think she'd do that? Harm them all?'

'For the insurance money, that's what.'

'Well, I believe none of it.'

'How so? How can you know?'

'Because I do. I know this woman. She's my dear friend and I can't bear the things they say. She has suffered all these things. She didn't cause them. I've known her for only a short time but I *do* know her!'

Emily looks at me very carefully. 'You speak of her with such passion, Vic,' she says slowly.

I can feel my cheeks heating up.

She persists. 'I thought it was Mr Whitstable you loved.'

'You might be right.' My voice is so low I can hardly hear it myself. 'But I have this affection for Marian. I can't think how to say it. I feel she is my liberator. I am more alive when I am with her. And as I have spent most of my life being less than alive I think this makes me love her too.'

'But it's different from Mr Whitstable?'

'Oh yes. Very different.'

'I suppose it's a bit like the way I love my papa is different from the way I love Mama. But with more Lancelot and Guinevere about it all.' Emily pauses. 'And perhaps Mrs Cotton brings just a touch of Morgan le Fay into the game?' she ventures.

This is all far too tangled for me. I sit up straight. 'It's no game. Shall we go for a walk, Emily?'

She sits up beside me and puts an arm through mine. 'Do you know, Vic, I was just feeling the need for some fresh air?'

We walk out the back way past the mill and the millrace and along by the river. Emily comes with me right up to Marian's narrow back door. It would be dangerous to be seen at that particular front door today. We knock very hard but no one comes. I call urgently to Marian, saying that it is *me* and she has nothing to fear. She still doesn't come.

We make our way right along to the brewery, then behind the Eden Arms and down the other side of the green, threading our way down the narrow back lanes. Emily is delighted at all this. 'All the time I've lived here I've never been down these lanes. Aren't we just like spies?'

We do not need to knock on Aaron's back door as he's there in the garden, grooming Tilder. He beckons us to him and hands the currycomb to the delighted Emily while he and I go and sit on a bench just outside his back door. It seems that he too has tried Marian's door and failed to raise her. I go on about this, rather, but he's not too alarmed.

'Marian does things her own way, Victoria. Even after so many deaths, she has to mourn. And she'll want to do it in private as she'll allow no one to see her weakness. I did hear from Ma Dodds that there'll be an autopsy and an inquest tomorrow. Bit quick off the mark, if you ask me.'

After this we are content to watch Emily groom Tilder as Aaron tells me of a book he was reading, about The Rights of Man. I tell him a bit more about Miss Cobbe's ideas but struggle to find examples. Her words are fading from my mind in these dramatic days.

After lingering with Aaron for half an hour, Emily and I continue on our way down the backs and out on to the Darlington Road, to return home to Western House. We make a game of doing this without touching the green, thinking we might manage to complete our errand unseen. But the houses have rear windows as well as front, and more than one face has loomed at a window, observing our progress.

Later, back in my bedroom, Emily asks me lots more searching questions about Aaron, and sings the praises of the donkey, Tilder. I answer with only one part of my mind: the other part is busy with the fact that I won't be able to see or help Marian until after tomorrow's inquest. No doubt that will clear everything up and things will be restored to what counts as normal in this increasingly peculiar village.

Thirty-Six

'So what-for d'you think that Kilburn girl and her cousin are lurking down the backs?' Margaret Riley peered through the heavy lace of the rear shop windows at the two girls walking arm in arm down the lane.

'It's a free country,' grunted Thomas, tying on his black apron. He'd given himself the hard task of clearing out old stock to occupy his mind, which was buzzing far too much with the events of the morning. 'Come away from that window, Marg. There's too much peering through windows in this place.'

'Like you say, it's a free country.' She glanced at him, not wanting, today, to be too hard on him. He had the Cotton woman in his sights now and wouldn't let her get away. From being the woman's advocate he'd become her enemy. Something had happened. Margaret was curious about this but would bide her time in finding out just what it was. Time, now, was on her side.

Out in the shop, the bell jangled. Margaret touched her hair, pulled her apron straight and went through the curtain. Thomas could hear the rumble of voices, then a shriek from Margaret.

Marian Cotton appeared through the curtain and marched into the back room.

'Now, Thomas,' she said calmly, 'your missis said you didn't want to see us but I told her you did.'

Margaret's dishevelled head popped round the doorway. 'Thomas! This woman—'

He held up a hand. 'Drop the latch on the shop, Marg, and go upstairs and make yourself a cup of tea.'

173

'But, Thomas—'

'Do as I say.'

Thomas and Marian stood in silence until they could hear Margaret moving around overhead. Then he looked Marian straight in the eyes. 'What can I do for you, Mrs Cotton?' he said in his smooth grocer's voice.

'What can you do? You can call off your dogs, that's what you can do. Call off that doctor and the tame sergeant. It's not right. They'll have me behind bars afore you can blink.'

'The only place good enough for you, lady.'

She stared at him. 'Why is it, Thomas? Why? 'Cause I gave you a bit of comfort, you being so needy? To be honest, I was surprised. Only last night did I see how needy you were.'

'You have a dirty mouth.' No unctuous grocer now. 'Keep it shut or you'll get the worst of this.'

She shook her head. 'How could it be worse, Thomas? Isn't my last bairn taken from me and aren't I left with nothing in the world? And without my piece of paper I don't even get no insurance.'

'Oh, Charlie, so beloved to you that he was the one you wanted in the workhouse, or down with Cotton's brother so you could get shot of him. You had no room for the boy. No room in your heart or your life.'

'My heart? Heart, is it?' She laughed, a strange rasping sound. 'Oh, Thomas, this heart of mine has taken a battering. I had a big heart. So big it could take in the world. Then all around me they drop like ninepins, despite my best efforts. I can keep others alive but I can't do it for my own. In the end my heart has shrunk and hardened and I am forced to take comfort in a bit of love in the night, in a silk dress or a fine shawl. There's little else for me.'

He pointed a long slim finger at her. 'Don't you come all self-pity with me, madam. You are selfish, selfish to the bone, and death to anyone who gets in your way.'

She stared at him hard, holding his eye with her bright glance, then said softly, 'And why-for this soft spot for Charlie, Tommy? He's just another little lad that has hung around my skirts, or in front of your shop. Nice enough. Nice touch with a penny whistle. That's all he is. All he was.'

He dropped his gaze. 'He was an innocent,' he mumbled. 'And he died there while you . . . when we . . .'

She went on as though he had not spoken. 'P'raps he reminded you of your own lad, Tommy? The one you couldn't even save from himself, who was so miserable in this house that he did away with himself.'

He reached out and shook her then. The body that had been so wonderful for him in the dark of the night flopped around like a rag doll. But still she caught his gaze, her own eyes glittering in triumph. She was a strong woman. It was her choice not to resist.

He dragged her to the door, through the back yard, and threw her on to the cobbles. 'Yeh're a whore,' he said. 'Nowt but a tuppenny murdering whore.'

She hauled herself to her feet, adjusted her bonnet, and smoothed her hands down her apron. 'You're not the good man you think you are, Riley. You may be sure that God will judge you for what you've done this day, even if no *orthly* judge will.'

He moved towards her and she backed away through the high gate. He locked it behind her, then went inside, locking the door behind him. He went upstairs. Margaret was sitting at the table under the window.

'Is that a pot of tea, Marg? Mebbe you could pour me one.' He sat down opposite her.

She poured his tea and handed it to him. Then she leaned slightly to one side so she could peer right down to the end of the green. 'Those girls are making their way back to Western House. That London girl sneaks around the place like a thief. I don't care where she's come from, she's not an ounce of breeding. No fit company for the doctor's children. I've said it to Mrs Grey more than once.'

Thomas sipped his tea. 'You might have a point there, Marg. You might not be wrong.'

Thirty-Seven

At Johnson Terrace Marian turned the oversized key in the lock but the back door would not give. It had obviously been securely bolted from the other side. She knocked hard again and called his name. Three doors along Sarah Shaw leaned out of her window to peer down to see the cause of the clamour, then quickly withdrew.

At last the bolts were drawn back and the door opened six inches. 'Mr Quick-Manning,' said Marian with quiet urgency. 'You must let me in.'

'No question of that, Marian. Things are being said. Dr Chalmers was at the brewery today. I was asked questions by my superior . . .' His broad face loomed into the gap between the door and the jamb.

'What are you talking about? This is Marian Cotton, mister. Didn't I bring you back from the brink, old boy? Would you be standing there if it weren't for me?'

The door opened wider and she stepped inside the back scullery, which smelled of burned lard and lye soap. He shut the door behind her, then faced her, not letting her make further progress in his house.

She stared at him for a moment, then said, 'There's trouble brewing for me in this place, my dear.'

'So they tell me. They told me that at the brewery today.'

'It's this devilish place. This village. What say you and me make tracks from here, old boy? Get away before the hounds grab me in their bite? We can find a nice place, get ourselves married, make a home for this bairn inside me here, this child that comes from you and me.'

'Marry?' He laughed, an ugly cracked sound. 'The brewery would never let me go.'

'What are you? A slave? Isn't this a free country?'

'And if what they're saying here is true? That child you say is mine could be anyone's.'

Marian let a silence settle like a choking smoke in the room, then said quietly, 'Do you know me, mister? I have nothing. Nothing! Now they're gunna even stop me getting my insurance, which is fair pay for the trouble I've been through with that child that wasn't even my own.' She waited. 'All right, if that's not to be, if you are really turning me away, you must have something for me, some recompense if I'm to bring this child of yours into the world.'

He put a hand into his waistcoat pocket, hesitated, then withdrew it. 'There will be no transaction between us, Marian. People will say that I connived with you – that I have admitted compliance with what you've done. That I admit the child is mine.'

'What I've done? I tell you on the Bible, mister, that the child is wrought between you and me. That I've done nothing bad. That all this talk is the weaving of others' cracked minds who cannot bear to contemplate the suffering I've had to face.' She stood up very straight and looked at him. 'The child is yours, mister, begot in the hours we spent in joy together here in this house. I'll make sure that is clear when it's registered, whether or not you marry me, whether or not you give me a penny.'

His tense shoulders sagged and he nodded slightly. 'I'm sure you will, Marian. But apart from that there is nothing here for you. My reputation will not stand it.'

'In that case, mister, I'll have my watch back. Didn't I give you the only thing I have that has value? And you'll avail me of nothing.'

He fingered his empty watch pocket. 'It's upstairs on my dresser. I will send it to you.'

She made to move past him and he blocked her. 'Go you and get it now,' she said.

He shook his head. He would not leave her alone. Not even in his back scullery. 'I'll send it. I'm a man of my word.' He reached around her and opened the door wide. 'You must give back my key, Marian. And sadly you must believe that my door from now on will always be bolted against you. Always.'

She threw down the key and it clattered on to the stone-flagged floor. He left it lying there.

'That's it, Marian. It's all finished now,' he said.

She walked slowly past him into the night. After closing the door behind her and bolting it carefully he stood for a moment with his back to it, then took out a handkerchief and mopped his sweating brow. That's it, he thought. All finished now. Restraint was called for. No bad thing.

Thirty-Eight

I find that I have a mission, but to complete it I must wait until well after supper. My aunt has gone upstairs for a rest, bewailing her exhausting day, and Emily is tucked up in her bed with a book. I creep downstairs, make my silent way along to my uncle's study and knock on the door. A bark of welcome penetrates the solid wood and I let myself in. Uncle William sits at his desk illuminated by an arc of light cast by the heavy oil lamp at his elbow. He has his finger on a large book, open before him. His eyes are tired.

'Victoria! Not yet in bed?' he says. 'What can I do for you?' He is really the kindest of men. He sits back in his chair. 'Sit down, won't you?'

As I sit down his face recedes into shadow, so I pull my seat forward to retrieve it from the darkness. 'Will you tell me what happens at an autopsy, Uncle William?'

He glances down at the book before him. 'You mean this business with young Charlie Cotton?'

'I heard you say there would be an autopsy.'

'There will be. The sergeant called here this evening. The inquest will be held tomorrow afternoon. So I will have to carry out the autopsy in the morning. It is all in far too much of a rush, if you were to ask me. The coroner must have a jury in his back pocket.'

'What will you do? How does this affect you?'

He stirs in his seat, closes the book, and reaches for his pipe, which he lights with something of a struggle. At last he says, 'Well, an autopsy is necessary when the reasons for a death are not obvious.'

179

'And are they not obvious with Charlie?'

He sucks at his pipe for a long minute and then casts his glance towards the fireplace. 'They did seem fairly obvious to me. I'm quite confident. Enteritis, I'd say. The signs are all there. I see them all the time. So many of these deaths.'

I am honoured. I know he should not be saying all this to me. 'Then why do they need an autopsy, Uncle?'

He sighs. 'I'm not absolutely, absolutely sure. There is so much talk around the place. The sergeant and Mr Riley, in their diverse capacities, represent that talk. It is a matter of suspicion. Where the death is seen by any responsible person as suspicious, and there is any doubt, further investigation is called for.'

Now I am puzzled. 'Mr Riley? I thought he was Marian's friend. He helped her. With her work. To get that house on the green.'

'All the more reason, dear girl, to listen to what he has to say.'

That seems unanswerable. 'So what will you do, at the autopsy?'

'I will look for further evidence, further causes of death, in the organs.'

'So you will have to cut him open?' I think of the glittering knives and saws in my Uncle William's surgery.

'No need for you to dwell on that, Victoria. Your Auntie Mary would say it's not proper for a young girl even to think of such things.'

'And will you find evidence, do you think, Uncle?'

He shrugs. 'If it is there, it is possible that I may find it. Autopsy is a very inexact process; the science is very shaky, in my view. There are various new procedures, but . . .'.

'They think she poisoned him, don't they? Mrs Grey and the others.'

'The autopsy is not about what people think. It's about what is there. It is science.'

'So in fact your autopsy could rescue Marian from all this gossip? You could save her.' I shudder. 'How can they do this to her? They are the wicked ones.'

'Misguided, perhaps. Not wicked. They are sound people. But biased against her amongst other things because she is a stranger.' He stands up now and comes to put a hand on my shoulder. 'And you are biased towards her because you are so very obviously fond of her. I have to say this is rather a source of worry for your aunt.'

'Auntie Mary is lucky. She has you and this house and all the little ones. Everyone is safe inside these walls. Marian has nothing, no one. Just that miserable little house with ladders for stairs. Everyone has deserted her. Even Mr Riley now.'

'There is the shoemaker.' He's trying to reassure me. 'He seems to be in her corner.'

'Yes, I suppose there's Aaron Whitstable.'

'And most of all she has you.' He leans down to kiss the top of my head and I can smell the dense fruity smell of his tobacco. 'Your loyalty does you credit, my dear. Now, I think you must go to bed. You look tired and your voice is a mere thread. All this excitement is not good for you.'

At the door I turn to look at him. He's back at his desk, his head down over the heavy book, now open again before him. 'Uncle?'

'Yes, my dear?'

'You will not let Auntie Mary send me back to London, will you? I will die if you make me go back. I am certain of it.'

'I don't think that's strictly true, Victoria. But yes, I think you must stay and see this through. Your aunt may not agree with me but you have much to learn from these events.'

Thirty-Nine

The knocking was very insistent. Marian lifted the curtain to see who was there before unlocking the door.

Aaron came in and placed a squat bottle of rum on the table under the window. 'I tried here before but you didn't answer. I thought you might just let us in this time. I came here to drink the lad Charlie safe passage to wherever he'll go next.' He glanced across at the bed in the corner. She had covered Charlie entirely with the blanket and heaped around him dried flowers and herbs gathered from the riverbanks at the back of the house. Their scent mingled with the slightly mouldy smell that pervaded the house and the sulphurous smell of the heaped-up coal that was spitting away in the fireplace.

Marian stood in front of the fire and watched him pour the rum into two china cups from the rack above the fireplace. 'People are saying I poisoned the child, Aaron.' She shook her head. 'But I am in the clear. They say I wanted to put the boy in the workhouse, but that was for his own good, so he could get more sustenance than I could get him, with no money coming in. With him still here underfoot how could I work to scrape any money together? Tell me that? I even wrote to the lad's uncle, up south, to no avail.'

'Down south,' he said mechanically.

'Down south, then.' She took the cup from him and sipped it, then turned to gaze at the fire. She sighed. 'I have to tell you, Aaron, I've had nothin' but trouble from that Cotton family. I rue the day I met Fred Cotton.' She glanced across at the bed, with its still figure under the sheet. 'I have nothing against Charlie. Quite fond of him in the end.

182

But he'll be the ruin of me. I feel it coming. I knew that the minute I saw the look in Riley's eye when he realised Charlie was dead.'

He shook his head. 'It's just talk, Marian, cruel talk. People round here have nothin' better to do. It's their sport.'

She sat down hard in the chair. 'Have I told you about my mother, Aaron? Had me when she was just sixteen. She was pretty as a picture, they say. I had to watch her die.' She gulped some rum and pulled a face. 'Well, anyway, my mother had this Bible in her house at Seaham where she lived with my stepfather. This book had these pictures of Heaven and Hell. I used to look at it. Learned every page by heart when I was a young'n. And when I was older and taught other young'ns in Sunday school.' She held her cup out so that Aaron could top it up. 'It had pictures of Jesus, surrounded by children. "Suffer little children to come to me." At least there'll be no Hell for young Charlie, Aaron. That's something. Just an eternity of playing around the feet of the Lord Jesus with that brother of his and all my others, the ones that are gone.' She laughed: a harsh grating sound, full of grief. 'Charlie'll be sucking his Spanish, I suppose, and staring at the Lord Jesus with those saucer eyes of his.'

With anyone else, man or woman, Aaron would have put out a hand, touched a shoulder. Instead he nodded his head. 'How fortunate are those of simple faith. There's comfort in it.' He held up his cup and drank. 'A toast to Charlie. And to you, for having the grace to imagine him playing around for ever with his little brothers in some warmer, kinder place.'

She drank from her cup. 'But you don't believe in any of that, do you? About Heaven and all that?'

He shook his head. 'Never. I believe that apart from providing a rich mulch for the earth, as have a thousand generations before us, this is all we have. Every day a jewel to be polished, or a waste of time. What I do think is that notions such as you've just expressed help to keep the poor in their place.'

'Then you're bound for Hell, sure as shot.'

He held up his cup. 'I'll drink to that,' he said.

She laughed and sipped her drink. 'You're a funny bugger, Aaron. P'raps that's why I like you.' Then she shook her head. 'Believe me, all those out there round the green'll have us both in Hell as soon as look at us.'

'This thing about an inquest – you've done nothing wrong, Marian, except struggle on in an aggressive world. No one could condemn you for that.'

She laughed too loudly and drank off the rest of the rum in her cup. 'No one? I wish I'd your faith, lad, unbeliever as you are.' She stood up staggered a little, then sat down again. 'Push the kettle on the fire, Aaron. I think I'd like some tea. No good being the worse for drink when we're keeping watch for young Charlie. Wouldn't be respectful, would it?'

Forty

The inquest is held conveniently in the Rose and Crown, the public house next door to Marian's house. I've never been in a public house before, so as I enter, I have to admit that I look around with interest. The most powerful first impression is the smell: a combination of sour beer and tobacco, old sweat and dust, overlaid by the cutting stench of lye soap. The big public room looks clean enough on the surface but the soiled usage to which this place has been put for so many years is difficult to obliterate.

The publican has stacked the few tables at the back and set his benches and chairs in military lines before a long dining table at the front. Behind this are three chairs, one grand and the others rather more modest. To one side of the dining table are two parallel rows of chairs, all empty.

A jury! Of course. I remember now that my uncle mentioned a jury.

Uncle William must have prevailed on my aunt, because I've actually been allowed to attend the inquest with the strict provision that I must be accompanied by Mrs Grey, who is more than sour at this onerous duty. And, as my aunt has told her not to let me out of her sight, every time I stray more than a foot from her she calls, 'Stay with me, Miss Kilburn, stay by my side. Mrs Kilburn commands it.'

So I can do no more than smile and nod at Aaron when he turns round and catches sight of me as I come in. He has a place on the bench seat at the front, next to Marian, who sits staring hard at the large empty chair behind the long table, ignoring Mr Pullman, the innkeeper, who makes a great business of polishing it with a chamois-leather. On

185

the crowded middle row of seats I can see Mr and Mrs Riley. They must have closed the shop or left their son, Patrick, in charge. Beside them is Mrs Garthwaite, the washerwoman who brings our ironing to Western House on a barrow in covered baskets. Next to her is the tailor, Mr White, who mended my uncle's greatcoat when it was ripped on a farm wire. The blind woman who lives at the bottom of the village sits on the very front row at the end of the waist-coated gentry: an honour bestowed, I think, so that she can hear what she can't see. Mrs Shaw, the neighbour of Marian's from Johnson Terrace, sits by Marian's old friend Mrs Dodds on the second row. There's no sign of my uncle or Dr Chalmers.

There is a rustle beside me and Kit Dawson sits down in a vacant chair. 'Some to-do, this, isn't it?' he whispers. 'A real rum do.'

'What're you doing here?' I whisper back.

'Mr Smith, the fellow I work for, is here. He offered me a ride in his carriage.' He nods towards a plump man of my uncle's age at the opposite end of the first row. 'Quite the scandal, ain't it? How about this woman? They say she poisoned this lad and the ones that went before. And now there's talk of more deaths further afield.'

'That's not true,' I say. 'It's all a mistake. Gossip run riot.'

He ignores me. 'The newspapers are here.' He nods at a man in the third row, sitting with a black hat on his knee on top of which is a small black notebook. 'The likes of him can smell a good old story.'

'How would he know?'

Kit shrugs. 'The police get on to the newspaper when there's the sniff of a story. Newspapers like a juicy scandal and this one's very promising.'

Now I look straight at Kit and notice that his smiley mouth is rather thin and his eyes have a sly look in them that makes me uncomfortable. I can't think why I've liked him in these past weeks. I pull inside myself and look forward, determined to ignore him. I make up my mind there and then not to give him the time of day.

A hum of interest in the room heralds the jurymen, who file in down the staircase to take their places. A tall well-built man with a thatch of silver hair takes the big seat behind the long table. 'Mr Dean,' Kit whispers in my ear. 'Deputy coroner.' A small clerkish man with a bald head takes the much smaller chair beside him on one side. Another more obviously important man takes the seat to the other side. 'Him on the left is Mr Dean's clerk. And t'other fellow is Mr Dale Trotter, Clerk to the Auckland Justices, and a solicitor in Bishop Auckland,' whispers Kit in my ear. 'A lot of interest in this case. Quite a to-do.'

Then there's an upset at the back and my uncle, carrying his doctor's bag, threads his way through the rows, followed by Dr Chalmers. They take two vacant seats on the end of the second row behind Marian and Aaron. The room settles, like leaves after a storm.

After some preliminary conversation between the coroner and the two clerks, the sergeant is called. He refers to his notebook and names Charlie and the date of his death and cites the problem of 'doubt'. Then Mr Riley is called and recounts his early morning walk and being called by Mrs Cotton to see the boy. As he tells his story he does not look down at Marian once. Then my uncle is called, as the others have been, to take the seat at the end of the long table and take the oath of truth. He's obviously flustered. His cheeks are uncharacteristically ruddy and his notebook, when he takes it out, has fresh brown stains on it. The coroner asks him about his conclusions.

'Well, sir, I saw the boy yesterday and have made further investigations this morning but I've had so little time to complete the procedures. Barely an hour. I'd not thought the inquest would come so close on the heels . . .'

The coroner makes a note. Mr Dale Trotter makes a note. Then Mr Dean looks at my uncle over his glasses. 'But you have a conclusion, Doctor?'

My uncle looks at his notes, then looks at Marian, who is staring at him intently from her perch in the front row. 'My opinion is that the cause of death was gastroenteritis, sir. The signs are there and this case has a history. My colleague Dr Chalmers and I have been treating this case. Gastroenteritis. The autopsy revealed nothing to the contrary.'

Marian's shoulders relax and she sits back in her chair. Mrs Riley turns and whispers furiously to her husband. The coroner whispers to Mr Trotter.

A member of the jury – a tall man in tweeds with a heavy watch chain dangling over his substantial stomach – stands up. 'Is this your definite, certain opinion, Doctor? Gastroenteritis. Is it iron-clad?' His voice is local but his manner is substantial. A farmer or mine owner, perhaps.

My uncle stares at him. 'Iron-clad? Medicine is not an exact science, sir. There is art in it. Judgement. In my judgement, on the evidence I have seen, and my experience of this case, the child died of natural causes brought on by an illness that I and my colleague have observed in these last weeks.' He refers to his notebook. 'The boy was in a state of emaciation, but he had been ill for some time. Earlier the day before yesterday I gave him ammonia in effervescence but he brought this back. Later, in the evening, I gave him a mixture of bismuth, hydrocyanic acid and powders containing an eighth of a grain of morphia. There were no marks whatsoever on the child, nothing showing physical violence. The autopsy revealed the lungs adhering to the walls of the chest, an indication of long-standing inflammation.'

Mr Trotter offers whispered comment to the coroner.

Uncle William peers at his notebook again. 'The autopsy revealed in the stomach two or three particles of white powder, which I take to be the residue of the powder I gave him earlier. Medical authors would indicate that the post mortem action of the gastric juices would produce such an appearance in the case of death by natural causes.'

Then Dr Chalmers is called and he confirms my uncle's conclusions. In all, he and my uncle have seen Charlie five times this week and evidently he was getting visibly weaker. Death from natural causes was not an unexpected outcome.

He sits down and there is muttering all round the room, among the jury as well as the crowd on the benches. The coroner lets this flow for a short while, then calls for silence and instructs the jury to retire to consider their verdict. They file out and up the narrow staircase in the corner. Mr Dean and his clerks retire to the snug behind the bar parlour.

Now the room is swept with another, more powerful gale of whispering, dispelled for a moment when Marian turns to look behind her at the ranks of faces. She catches my eye and nods curtly. I smile and nod several times, ignoring Mrs Grey's elbow, which I can feel in my ribs even through my corset. Then Marian turns round and sits staring at the chair that until recently accommodated the substantial form of Mr Dean.

The reporter is scribbling energetically in his notebook, occasionally leaning across and asking a question of the sergeant. He even rises from his seat to go and have a word with my uncle and Dr Chalmers. Then he goes back to his seat and starts scribbling again in his book.

Mrs Grey leans forward to speak to Mrs Riley.

There is a dark atmosphere in the room, thick and earthy as mushroom soup.

Kit's voice is in my ear. 'So you know her?' he whispers. 'That woman?'

For a second I want to say no, that she is a stranger to me. To deny her. 'I do. She is an interesting woman. I know her quite well.'

'And d'you think she did this?'

'Never,' I whisper back fiercely. 'Never in this world.' He stares at me a moment. I can tell he thinks I'm an innocent and that he knows so much more of the world than I do. Then he sits back in his seat, obviously dissatisfied that he cannot pursue this conversation and – like so many others in this room – condemn Marian out of hand. Such condemnations, I feel certain, are threaded through the conversations that are buzzing all around me. In the middle of all this I am compelled to sit silent but I am pleased to the point of complacency that I have no part of it.

It's an age before the jury return. An hour at least. They are taking time with their deliberations. Then at last they troop down the stairs. At the request of the coroner the foreman intones the verdict: 'Death from natural causes.'

A groan of disbelief rolls round the room and there are cries of 'Shame!' The reporter writes furiously in his book. Mrs Grey, beside me, mutters, 'Disgraceful!' Down in the front row Marian has sunk lower in her seat. Aaron has his hand on her arm. I so wish I were brave enough to join them but alas I find myself wanting this necessary courage.

I flee, leaving Mrs Grey behind. In her excitement and anger she's forgotten all about me and is edging towards Mrs Riley. Mr Riley's face is mottled with rage. Outside, I have to work my way through a crowd of loitering villagers, who are already buzzing with the news. At the edge of the crowd, I wait for my uncle, determined to show my pride that he had the courage to come to his own just conclusion.

A few minutes later, when Marian makes her way out of the public house, the crowd jeers and shouts at her. Someone throws a clod of earth, which Aaron deflects with his arm. Another clod hits the door of her house as it closes behind the two of them. Thank goodness they have had no further to walk than next door.

Now my uncle and Dr Chalmers emerge, flanked by Mr Riley and the sergeant. Mr Riley is talking furiously into my uncle's ear. Mr Trotter emerges and he shakes hands with my uncle and talks to him, their faces close. Then my uncle catches sight of me at the edge of the crowd, shakes hands again with Mr Trotter and walks swiftly across towards me.

'What? Here on your own, Victoria?' He glances back to the doorway of the Rose and Crown, where Mrs Grey is deep in conversation with Mrs Riley. Then at Mr Dale Trotter, who is mounting his carriage after Mr Dean. He takes my arm. 'Your aunt will be anxious about you, my dear.'

Without a backward glance we make our way towards Western House, only breathing easily when the crowd is fifteen yards behind us. We slow our pace.

'Well, my dear, I fear this morning we may have heard the baying of hounds who have scented a kill,' he says grimly.

'Were the sergeant and Mr Riley very angry with you?'

'I fear so.' He pauses. 'I would never say this to your dear aunt, Victoria, but those misguided gentlemen were threatening me with my reputation. Telling me I had come to the wrong conclusion.'

I have to smile. 'That can't be so, surely. Not you!'

'Never underestimate the power of angry men, my dear.'

'Do they want you to say what you don't believe is true?'

'They think they know better.'

'Well, Uncle, I was never prouder of anyone than when you gave your evidence today. I will never forget it. Never!'

He grasps my arm more tightly. 'Thank you, my dear. You are so very kind.'

Inside the house I follow him into the dispensary. He sets his bag on the bench and removes two wide-necked jars from its capacious depths. They contain items in dark liquid. He puts the smaller of them in a cupboard and locks it carefully.

His glance strays back to me. 'You shouldn't be here, my dear,' he says. But his voice is distracted and I know I can stay.

'What's that?' I venture. 'In those jars?'

'I'm afraid these are some interior parts of the unfortunate Charlie Cotton. They hurried me on so much, but I felt I could not leave them there on poor Mrs Cotton's kitchen table. The woman has had enough to face.'

'What will you do with that stuff?'

'I will look at it more carefully when I have time. The coroner made no request for a chemical analysis. I may do further work for my own peace of mind. In any case, this material may have some clinical interest in understanding the effects of enteric fever on a child of that age.' He picks up the larger jar. 'This I will dispose of. Mere detritus.'

'Dispose of?'

'I'll get Mr Carr or Mr Chalmers to bury it out the back where it will do no harm.' He stares at me and then blinks. 'What am I doing here, talking to you of such things? Those fellows rattled me rather. You go, my dear, and tell your aunt, who is no doubt waiting, of the verdict, before the rapacious Mrs Grey gets hold of her.'

My aunt, who is in the kitchen surveying with satisfaction a row of plums she has just bottled, takes the news calmly. 'Is that what William found?' She places a disc of waxed paper at the top of each jar.

'That's what he said. The jury brought back the verdict "death from natural causes".'

'That's it then,' she says placidly. 'Storm in a teacup. This village is full of seven-day wonders. Now, dear, would you go and tell your uncle that tea will be ready at five o'clock? I thought we could have tea, after which we may all sit in the garden and get the best of this sunshine. He can play catch with the children. And do send Emily to help Lizzie with the table! Did Mrs Grey not come back with you?' She asks this as though she doesn't need an answer. I don't know whether it's her condition, but sometimes I think she goes through life in something of a dream. She's so very nice when she's like this. I wonder if I dare ask her if I can go and visit Marian. I dismiss the thought. I daren't risk it.

Tomorrow will be soon enough.

Forty-One

Marian waved the precious piece of paper under Aaron's nose. 'Now Riley will have to give us money to get Charlie buried. He can't deny us. I'll go across right now and tell him.'

Aaron took the death certificate from her and smoothed it out on his knee. Marian's kitchen seemed to have shrunk to the two chairs before the fire. The kitchen table was unusable because its surface still carried bloodstains from the autopsy. The bed in the corner was now draped like a tent with old sheets, to hide the bloody, invaded body of the child from human sight. Only the two chairs and the fireside rug seemed habitable.

'You want nothing going outside just now, Marian. You should stay right here inside the house. The mood those people are in, they'd stone you as soon as look at you. Why don't you write a note and I'll take it to him and get your relief money? After that I'll go down the undertaker and get you a coffin. You can't stay in this house with that poor child's body in that state. I'll fix up the funeral for Monday, first thing.' He brought her the pen and the small bottle of ink that stood on the mantelpiece, and the Bible to lean on. 'You just write and tell Riley you want your dues.'

She did as she was told and handed him the note.

He glanced across at the tented bed. 'Will you be all right here? Just for a wee while? I'll get back as soon as I can.'

'That child never hurt anybody when alive. He'll not do it now.'

Across at the shop Riley was curt and businesslike with Aaron. He tucked money into an envelope taken from the shop shelf where he sold them in singles. On it he scrawled Marian's name, then thrust it at Aaron and said, 'I'd not see the poor lad with no coffin, but you can tell that woman it's not the last she'll hear from me. She'll not get away with this. Everyone knows about her now. Only a matter of time.'

Aaron tucked the envelope in an inside pocket and then rocked back slightly on his heels. 'I have to say I'm a bit surprised at you, Mr Riley, turning on that poor soul. I'd always thought you to be a reasonable man, above the common herd.'

Riley opened the shop door for him, clanging the bell hard as he did so. 'My advice to you is to watch out for yourself, Whitstable. She's got you in her snare. It's only a matter of time.'

Aaron strolled down to his workshop to pick up a hammer and nails, then made his way down two back alleys to the undertaker, who already had a middle-size coffin in rough pine up on his bench. He took the money from Aaron and counted it out on the pitted wooden surface of his workbench.

'Made it this morning, Mr Whitstable. I did it by eye. Bairn'll fit in there nice and snug,' he grunted. 'Knew I'd be called on.'

'The lad'll need teckin' to St Helen's first thing Monday,' said Aaron, adding a florin to the pile. 'You'll be able to do that?'

'Aye. Syem as last time. I supposed that. At this rate the woman'll fill the graveyard aal on her own.'

Aaron stared at him. 'I was thinkin' of adding an extra shilling for yourself, but I'm keepin' it for the fact that you're just another one of these self-serving sheep that inhabit this village.' He hoisted the coffin on his shoulder and made his way down the alley out on to the green. Then, before the watching eyes of women in doorways and men in clusters making their way to one of the many village alehouses and pubs, he strode across the green directly to Marian's house, carrying the coffin as though it weighed no more than a twig.

Inside the house he found that Marian had taken down the bed-tent and had rewrapped the small body in another, slightly cleaner sheet. She had washed bloody prints from the boy's face, retied his chin-bandage, combed his hair, and replaced his velvet cap.

She smiled slightly as Aaron came through the door. 'There now, Aaron, old boy,' she said. 'The bairn's ready. These old sheets'll have to be burned. I can't see Milly Garthwaite washing them even if I could pay her, which I can't.'

He balanced the coffin on the kitchen table, now scrubbed clean of bloodstains. He took Riley's envelope out of his pocket and handed it to her. 'Took money out for the coffin. I don't know how you do it, Marian. How you can stand all this,' he said quietly.

She opened the envelope and peered inside. 'Death? Why, kidder, I'm used to death. How many times have I been its angel? What I do know is that though the spirit has flown from the body, this earthly vessel has to be treated with some respect, not plundered like some Frenchie pirate ship.' She nodded towards the coffin. 'Take that lid off for us, will you?'

He did as he was told and, with some tenderness, she lifted Charlie's body from the bed in its off-white cocoon, carried him the two steps across the room and laid him gently in the pine box. For the last time she smoothed his hair and adjusted his cap.

'Now, lad, see to the lid, will you?' she muttered.

Aaron put the lid in place and took out his hammer and nails. He looked at her and she nodded. He did not hurry as, one by one, he hammered the simple nails into the soft wood. When he'd finished he looked up and caught sight of a distorted face pressed against the narrow window. He let out a roar and the face vanished. Marian pulled the curtain across so there was no chink of light from the outside. Then she lit a small oil lamp, which she put on the table beside the coffin.

She glanced across at the soiled bed. 'P'r'aps I should steep those sheets, not burn them. Seems a waste.' she said. Then she pulled the sheets off the bed and folded them so the blood didn't show. 'I've been thinking about things. Them doctors've done more harm than good to our Charlie, I'll tell you that for nothing, Aaron.'

'Marian . . .' He put a hand towards her.

She stepped back. 'Don't say nothing, don't touch us, Aaron. There's been too much talk, too much touching. What d'you think has got me into this mess in the first place?'

Forty-Two

Church this Sunday morning after the inquest is full to overflowing. My aunt has insisted I go with the family to Communion today, although she's never insisted before. She is well aware that my parents are Unitarians and long ago departed the bosom of the Church of England. But today, as some kind of gesture, I think, the whole of Dr Kilburn's family occupy a prominent front pew just behind the empty row reserved for the proper gentry. Even Mrs Grey, Lizzie and Jonty are here, somewhere at the back on the crowded benches for the lower orders.

It seems that other people must have shared my aunt's urgent, ungodly desire to attend church. Every seat is taken and at the back it is standing room only. I wonder whether all these people have crowded into the church to repent of their sin of accusing Marian of that horrible deed, or – as is more likely – to call down the vengeance of Heaven on an unrepentant sinner. Perhaps they just came there to feel virtuous, to reassure themselves that God must be on their side.

So many people linger outside the church after the service, clumped together in groups, not moving down the path to return to their homes. I catch sight of the man in the long coat, the reporter who was scribbling so assiduously at the inquest. Today he is moving from group to group, nodding and talking. He talks to Mr and Mrs Riley, who then turn to speak to my uncle. He talks to Mrs Shaw, Marian's neighbour from Johnson Terrace, and Mr Rogers, another neighbour. He buttonholes Mr Drummond, the sexton, who points down the side of the church – presumably to the place where we buried the other children and Mr Nattrass.

195

Later, to my enormous relief, Emily airily turns down her father's offer of a ride back to the village on the family carriage. 'No, Pa,' she says firmly. 'Me and Victoria will walk back the long way. By the river. We need some fresh air after that stuffy old church.'

He glances across at me. My aunt is busy fussing over the younger ones as they mount the carriage steps. 'Very well,' he says thoughtfully. 'Victoria is looking a little peaky. You do that.'

So twenty minutes later I am standing by the millrace, throwing sticks into the swirling water and watching them chase each other downstream. After ten minutes of this game Emily sits on a half-demolished stone wall and looks at me.

'So, Vic! When are we going to see your friend Mrs Cotton?' she says.

'My friend?' I say.

'You know, the woman who so takes your fancy. The one they are talking about in the churchyard.'

I stare at her. 'Well,' I say carefully, 'there's no *we. I* may see her but you . . . not you. Your mother would have me on the next train.'

She twists her face up in some facsimile of wisdom. 'Well, Cuzz, there we have a dee-lemma. I promised Ma to stick to you like glue, to be your gaoler. And if I don't do that she'll have you on the next train anyway. So I'll have to go with you to see the woman and I promise you Mama will not know as I will not mention her.'

I weaken. I do need to see Marian; I want to see her, if only to say how pleased I am that the verdict was a just one, and that I am not merely a fair-weather friend.

This time when I knock on the back door Marian opens it. She makes no fuss at the sight of Emily and leads us under the ladder into the room. Despite it being the middle of the day the room is in twilight. The curtains are drawn and the dingy space is barely lit by the small lamp that sits beside the pathetic pine coffin on the table before the window. The bed in the corner is stripped now, returned to being a backless couch with the stitched quilt spread over it.

Emily clutches my hand and I return the pressure. Marian goes to stand before the window, with her back to the coffin, her arms folded across her chest.

'Good news from the inquest,' I say too heartily.

'Whatever it is, it's bad news for Charlie,' she says, unsmiling.

'We are sorry for your loss, Mrs Cotton,' chants Emily, obviously bursting to say something.

Marian spares her a glance. 'Me too, kidder, me too. Lost everything now. Entirely on me own, except for your shoemaker, Victoria.' She pauses. 'And that lot out there, every last one of them baying for me blood.'

'They'll quieten down,' I say. I am uncomfortable at my hearty tone. 'Now they know they're wrong.'

'You wouldn't know it,' she said drily. 'I've had stones through my upstairs windows and horse-muck through the letter box. That was a bit of a surprise for me, like. I was expecting a note from the insurance man, with my due money, through that same letter box.'

I glance down at Emily. The language has flown over her head but she's obviously enjoying the drama. We approach the coffin. The wood is rough and unfinished but someone has measured parallel lines and written 'Charles Cotton' in fine copperplate on one corner.

Marian catches my glance. 'Your friend Mr Whitstable wrote that. He's been a tower of strength. Would'a stayed all night if I'd'a let him. Kept me company in my dark hour.' She smiles a surprisingly sweet smile and my heart lurches in the old way. 'Couldn't have him tarred with my brush, could we? Too decent a man for that. He's for you, that one. Got to keep him sweet for you. Not for me.'

I try to ignore my hand, which is being squeezed very tight indeed in Emily's.

'The funeral,' I say hurriedly. 'Is the funeral tomorrow?'

'So it is,' she says. 'I sent a lad and I've had a message back from Mr Drummond. Ten o'clock. Like I say, I'm still waiting for the message from the insurance man.' The light tone has drained entirely from her voice, chilling the dank-smelling overheated air of the room. 'I need that money, you know. I have to . . . I need to . . . get away from this place, Victoria. It's not safe here for me. I'll have to sell the furniture to raise what money I can. I gave Ma Dodds some stuff to sell for me but I've never seen hide nor hair of any money from her. Probably pocketed my cash or paid her debt at Halloran's. Never did nothing that was not for nothing, that woman.'

I think desperately about how I might help. Money. I have virtually nothing of my own. My aunt and uncle keep me. They give me an

197

allowance of half a crown a week, a shilling more than Emily. I would never dare to ask them for money for Marian. If I did so I would very certainly be on the next train to London. On an impulse I unpin a small pearl and sapphire brooch from the neck of my blouse and hand it to her. 'Here, Marian, will this help?'

She takes it from me and holds it in the pool of light from the small lamp. I must admit it glitters very satisfactorily. Then she pushes it back towards me. 'No, honey. I don't want your gewgaws. The way you and me are, it's me that gives and you that takes. I give you the stuff that mends your face. I give you the lad Aaron to mend your walk, and for the other thing, the matter of love. It's not for you to give me something in return or it spoils the favour.'

I let that sink in for a second. Then I say, 'Are you telling me that I have to stay in your debt?'

She laughs at that: laughs here in this room with her dead child in a coffin by the window. It's a cold, hollow sound. 'Well, now, child, isn't it a rare thing for the likes of me to hold a debt over the likes of you?' Then she leans over to repin the brooch to my collar. I can feel the back of her hard knuckles against my throat. She steps away and treats me again to that sweet smile of hers, and I know I am not mistaken in my affection for her. 'Now then, I thank you for your words, Victoria, but I think you and this child here should get on your way.'

We retreat under the ladder and out of the room, keeping her in our sight as though it's dangerous to do otherwise. Before I go through the door I say I will be at the funeral.

She shakes her head. 'No, child. This time you must stay away. This is not like those last times. There will be trouble. Things are different now.'

Outside the closed door Emily shivers and hugs my arm close to her side. 'What a strange woman. Storm one minute, shine the next. No wonder they don't like her. You can't see what she's about. Hard to think that you like her so much, Vic. She wouldn't even take your brooch. How . . . strange.'

I pull her along and we walk quickly along the riverbank. 'She is my friend. That's why she's too proud to take the brooch. That's why I like her. I can't quite explain, but she is really special. An unusual woman.'

Emily is obviously struggling with something. 'But why isn't she sorry? Why is she like that? So hard. Why isn't she crying and wailing?'

I try to explain it to Emily and in doing so struggle to find an explanation for myself. 'I think that she feels if she seemed sorry, seemed regretful, she'd be playing into their hands, those people who throw the stones. She thinks it's her job to stay strong. This makes her seem hard and uncaring.'

'Isn't she playing into their hands herself, by being so proud? I felt really angry in there when she gave you back your brooch. I didn't like her at all.'

'So now she's offended you! But why should she feel sorry, Em, if she's done nothing wrong? If all that has happened to her is more cursed bad luck than should happen to any human being?'

'So. They're blaming her because she's unlucky?'

I have to think about this. 'I think they're blaming her because they think she's the author of her own bad luck and brings bad luck on others. And because she is independent and powerful, despite having nothing—'

'But, Victoria . . .'

I loosen my arm from hers. 'Sshsh, Emily. You're giving me a headache with all these questions. I'll race you back. First to the back gate gets a piggyback to the door.'

Forty-Three

The unspoken pressure from my aunt has been such that, to my shame, I felt I could not support Marian at this last funeral but watch from my window as the sad little cortège winds its way down the village and on to the Auckland Road. I might have approached my uncle for permission to go but am deterred by the fact that the house is in something of a ferment. Mr Dale Trotter has called, as has Mr Dean. There have been raised voices in the dispensary between my uncle and Dr Chalmers. All of these men, I am sure, are calling my uncle's judgement into question. All are infected by this brew of passion that is still sweeping this village. How much I admire my uncle for holding firm.

I have been racking my head to find an excuse or genuine reason to leave the house, but my aunt, though watchful, is not well. So I am called on to help Lizzie with the little ones, with Auntie Mary directing us closely from her sick bed. If I examine my heart, this compulsory activity is something of a relief, as just now I don't quite know how I can continue to see Marian. She has rejected my help just as clearly as she rejected my brooch. Soon – perhaps even today – she will leave the village behind. She is right in thinking that this is no safe place for her.

And then there is the matter of Aaron. Whenever my mind comes away from these more pressing dramas it returns to him. Of course I have continued to wonder about him and his astounding proposal, and how it may be taken by the people around me. Most often my mind returns to his physical presence: the coltish length of him, the long planes of his face, the glitter of his eyes, the way his hair springs from his brow. These thoughts run to such a pitch that sometimes I feel as though I am melting inside.

At last, it is three on the Monday afternoon. Lizzie has taken all the children for a walk and I can go to my room and sit with my leg propped up on a chair. It has become very sore for some reason I can't fathom. Perhaps my boots need some further adjustment. There's a thought.

I am almost asleep when there is a knock on my bedroom door. Mrs Grey slips inside, the newspaper in her hand held forward like a parrying sword. I struggle to my feet. She thrusts the folded newspaper towards me, a slight smile on her face.

'Young Jonty went down to the station to get the early editions of the evening paper, Miss Kilburn,' she says. 'I did suggest to him, like, that he should buy a few. Didn't I give him me own money for them? I got one for just you yourself.'

I take it from her. 'Thank you, Mrs Grey.'

She stands in front of me, hands meekly crossed over each other at the thigh level.

I resist the desire to peer at the paper. 'That will be all, Mrs Grey.' I am proud that I manage to keep my voice so steady.

She scowls, then backs away and closes the door with a vengeful click. Only then do I take the newspaper and spread it out on the dresser by the window. It is all there. The headline: 'Suspected Poisoning at West Auckland'. It is filled with a liberal interpretation of the dramas of these last days, laced with lies and malice. Talk in the village that Marian Cotton is a wholesale poisoner with a mysterious past. The unnatural death of an innocent boy. The names of several others who – it is said 'on good authority' – have died at her hand. There are even allusions to deaths in another place where she lived. It proposes a theory that she was not there in the house when the boy died. There are hints of an immoral assignation. The tears roll down my cheeks and splodge on to the paper, smudging the print.

I sit down hard on the window seat, feeling physically winded by these lies. All the rank gossip and bad feeling we have endured in the village is one thing. The writing down of this for many thousands to read, as though cold print makes the lies proven fact, is quite another. There on the page, written in damning, measured sentences, these lies have such *gravitas*, such an illusion of truth about them.

I close my eyes and see Marian again, first as she was on the train, then on the gryphon seat by the manor house, then cradling her baby's coffin in her arms. I see her drinking rum with Aaron and me, laughing at one of his word-play jokes. The Marian I know, and for whom I feel such deep affection, is not the woman they describe here in these pages: cold and heartless, immoral and murderous.

I make my way along the corridor and burst into my aunt's room. She's sitting up in bed, the newspaper spread before her. Mrs Grey's generosity has reached all corners of this house.

'Isn't this terrible, Auntie? How can they say this? None of it's true. Uncle William gave his judgement, didn't he?' There are tears of rage standing in my eyes.

She looks up at me, then slowly closes the paper before her and folds it across. 'This was always a very strange case, dear. Now then! Have you been crying? Now look where your unsuitable acquaintance has led. Crying over a person who should mean nothing to you.'

'It's all lies. I know her. I know this woman. I cannot be wrong.'

She laughs at this. 'Know? How can *you* know a woman like that? She's not of your class and, what's more, is even hated by those of her own class. She is a deceiver, an immoral woman and possibly even a poisoner. It was always so unsuitable that you associated with her at all. I told your uncle so.'

'My uncle did not condemn her. He admired her.'

She swings round in the bed and reaches for her shawl, her bulk making her actions awkward. 'Your uncle, my dear, is an innocent. He sees only good in everyone. He's as easily deceived as are you. Now I fear his inability to condemn her will call into question his own judgement. Then he also will be condemned.'

'I would like to go and see her, Auntie. She will need help, with these lies all over the newspaper.'

'See her? My dear girl, you will not leave this house! Do you hear me?' She pulls the bell rope by the bed. 'Now, if Mrs Grey can get her nose out of her newspaper, I need to talk to her about what she must cook for supper.' She turns a stern gaze on me. 'And I think you should bathe your face, dear. Those red eyes will surely upset dear Emily.'

I back away. Before I reach her door she repeats, 'You will not leave this house, Victoria. D'you hear me?'

I make my way downstairs and, seeing a light under my uncle's study door, walk straight in. The newspaper is there at the edge of his desk. Its folds are rough: it has obviously been scanned.

'Now, Victoria.' He smiles slightly. 'What can I do for you?'

I put my hand on the newspaper. 'You can let me go and talk to Marian. To tell her we don't believe all these lies.'

His smile fades. 'Did you read it?'

'Mrs Grey is giving out copies like confetti.'

'Silly woman.'

'They are all silly. Silly enough to read all the lies. All those lies. They did not believe you, Uncle. They did not accept your verdict.'

'I don't believe they did. But I am the doctor. I told what I knew.'

I throw myself into the chair beside his desk. 'Why can't you get that reporter here, and tell him to tell the truth in his newspaper? Why can't you defend her as you should?'

He taps the paper with his pipe. 'I can't undo this, make this not have happened. The damage has been done.'

'Can you do nothing more?'

'I can resort again to science, I suppose.'

We stare at each other and I realise he is as uncertain and worried as I am. My brain is whirling. 'Could it not have been all the medicine that Charlie was taking before? The stuff you and Dr Chalmers gave him?'

Suddenly his eyes are opaque, distant. Now he's not the jolly, loving uncle I know. When he speaks his voice is icy. 'You have tapped into Dr Chalmers' worry, my dear. But, of course, that could never be so. We were scrupulous. We can take further steps to prove that fact if necessary. Dr Chalmers is urging me. And the coroner. Everyone feels very shaky about this.' His gaze has wandered to the window. He isn't looking at me at all now.

'Another autopsy? But Charlie was buried today, Uncle. In the churchyard.'

He continues to look through the window as though I am not there.

Then it dawns on me. 'You will use the stuff in the jars? The stuff you buried in the garden? That can't be.'

Now he is looking at me. 'Oh yes I can, Victoria. If it must be, it must be.'

I stand up so violently that I flick the newspaper off the edge of his desk. 'I want to go and see Marian.'

He is already shaking his head. 'No. Your aunt and I are agreed on that. You must not leave the house. Any relationship and acquaintance you have with that woman is at an end.'

His reference to her as 'that woman' tells me everything.

'That woman?' I say. ' "That woman"? Well, Uncle, now I understand. You have joined the hounds. I never thought it of you.'

I turn and stride towards the door. As I close it I glance back at him. He is sitting now at his desk, his head between his hands.

As I leap up the stairs I begin to make plans. I can't do anything until after dark, but then I will do something. It's only when I reach my room that I realise that the pain in my leg has gone. I am comfortable again in my boots.

Forty-Four

This village is a different place in the dark. Tonight it's my good fortune that the sky is clear and the halved moon shines down with a second-hand reflected brilliance. The narrow windows of some houses filter into the night dim, apologetic reflections of the miserable oil lamps inside. Other houses are deep in darkness. Here and there illumination from a public house or an alehouse dribbles on to the cobbles. Apart from these fragments of light the village green is a well of darkness, and the countryside beyond the rim of houses sits in unrelieved shadow, full of threat.

My teeth chatter, not with cold on this mild night, but with fear. I have to make my way down the green the front way, as the backs would be too risky in the dark. Even so, it's not entirely safe. I disturb a roosting cockerel and it shrieks upward into the black night. Still, no one looks out. I tumble into a hole dug by some assiduous child mimicking his mining father. My skirt and jacket are covered in sticky black dirt.

I creep down the alleyway to Marian's back door. I knock hard, one, two, three, four, five, six times, but she doesn't come. I dare not shout for her, as I can see the lit interior of the Rose and Crown next door and hear laughter and some carousing. I imagine that another, more informal jury is sitting in there, assessing Marian's guilt. I knock one last time. Then it occurs to me that she's already gone – has fled away, beset by fear of these vengeful, unknowing people.

I make my way back along the alleyway and peer out on to the green again. Across the wide space down towards the bottom I can see a clear light from the window of Aaron's shop. Perhaps he will know where Marian has gone. Perhaps, even, she is thére with him.

Peering through Aaron's long low window I can see the two lamps he keeps on his workbench and an upturned boot on a last. It is patent leather, unfinished: a lucrative order for him. He must have been burning the midnight oil. But then I press my nose closer to the pane and see his front room workshop is in violent disorder. The neat rows of tools have been ripped off the wall; the leathers have been dragged down, slashed to ribbons and pulled towards the fire. The chairs and table have been upset and the fire raked down on to the hearthrug where it has ignited further illegitimate small fires. I press my cheek closer and look sideways to see if Aaron is there on the stone floor beside his leathers. There is no sign of him.

I don't waste time knocking on the front door but run right round the back and down his garden path. I race past the open hen cree where three hens lie among the scattered corn, their necks twisted. Tilder the donkey is lying on the sparse grass, groaning a snuffling groan. I gallop down to the back yard. The scullery door is wide open and in the filtered light I can see Aaron, lying half out of his house, one bloody hand up over his gashed forehead as though to protect it.

I kneel in the mud beside him. His eyes are closed but when I take off my glove and put my hand on his bruised cheek, it is warm. I lay my cheek close to his and I can hear his heavy laboured breathing. I take off my cloak and pull it close around him.

Then I set off to run for my uncle.

I let myself in to Western House using the same back window through which I climbed at the beginning of this night's events. My uncle is not working late in his study as I hoped, so I have to go up to the bedroom he shares with my aunt and rouse them.

My uncle comes to the door in his dressing gown and listens to my babble about the shoemaker being murdered. He looks at me, right from my unbonneted head, down my muddy gown to my filthy boots. My auntie appears beside him and shrieks at the sight of me. Children appear on the landing, and Lizzie and Mrs Grey emerge from the attic staircase in their nightdresses and nightcaps.

'I'll go back and wait for you there. You must come quickly,' I gasp to my uncle, then turn tail. I can't wait for someone – probably Mrs

Grey – to unbolt and unlock the door, so I let myself back out of the same window.

When my uncle, carrying his bag, finally arrives at the cobbler's shop, I am sitting on the back doorstep with Aaron's head and shoulders in my lap. He is still unconscious but I have cleaned his bloody face a little with spit and my handkerchief.

'He's not dead, is he?' I say. 'Tell me he's not dead.'

My uncle kneels down in the dirt and takes Aaron's wrist. 'What has happened here?'

'Someone has been here. The workshop has been destroyed. All his leathers have been slit. Some have even been heaped on the fire. Hot coals have been scattered about the room.'

He sniffs. 'That must be the foul smell.' He takes Aaron's head in his hands and waggles it this way and that. 'Well, the fellow's not dead but tarrying in some other place. Someone's felled him with a huge blow.' He looks round. 'I'll knock up his next-door neighbour to douse those fires, then perhaps we can get Mr Whitstable up to the dispensary. The foul air inside this house might very well kill him where the beating's failed.' Then he looks up, past me, and his face hardens.

I turn and see Marian coming down the garden path. 'How is the lad?' she says. 'I saw you coming over, Doctor, and thought something was up. I thought I might help.'

'We're taking him to the dispensary, Mrs Cotton,' says my uncle coldly. 'You would most help by going home and locking your door behind you. You can see what has happened here to this fellow, probably because he befriended you. Have you not done enough?'

She holds his gaze. 'Now you, Doctor? Are you the last?' She turns to me. 'And what about you, child? Do you also blame me for every ill that befalls this place?'

'No, no, Marian, I do not. And no right-minded person would think that.' My uncle, though, does not add his denial to mine. I look down at Aaron, who is still sprawled across my knee. 'I'll just help my uncle with Aaron, then I'll come across to see you. I did call . . .'

She's already shaking her head. 'No point, honey. I'm not opening my door to no one.' She nods towards Aaron. 'You can see it's not safe. Right dangerous, if you ask me.' Then she turns and walks steadily back down the garden path.

I shout after her, calling her name, but she doesn't turn round again. My heart is like lead at her summary rejection. It is so unfair.

'Leave her.' My uncle stands up. 'I'll get help here to douse the flames and lock the place up. Then I'll go for my trap to move the fellow. You stay here.'

Five minutes later two men whom I don't recognise come with buckets of water from the pump to douse the smouldering heaps in the workshop. They go to the hen cree and from the squawks that emerge it seems some poultry are still alive. When the men come back I hear one say to the other that 'the donkey's a goner', and finally I start to cry.

As they perform their tasks the men step past and over me and my unconscious burden as though we are not here. One part of me wonders whether these two were part of the gang that came here to do this in the first place, to punish Aaron for stepping out of line, frustrated that they couldn't get their hands on their real target.

Forty-Five

The end ward was bleak and functional, merely offering a bed in the corner with a single hard chair beside it, and a washstand set with a bowl and a jug of water. But this ward had a fireplace and was neither as chilly nor despairing as the general workhouse ward next door. The duty nurse had been told that this fellow on the bed, this Mr Whitstable, had some resources, so had not been brought in under parish relief. His bill had been guaranteed by none other than Dr Kilburn, who had brought him in the middle of Monday night, tended his wounds and sewn up a very dangerous cut on his head before he whirled away again in his carriage.

The next day, although breathing well, the patient stayed unconscious, so was not much trouble. The parish doctor came in briefly, read Dr Kilburn's note about the man, and told the nurse to light a decent fire in the tiny fireplace in the corner as the room was far too cold for a paying patient.

On the Tuesday afternoon, the patient had a visitor, a respectable-looking woman who said she was a nurse, sent by Dr Kilburn to check on Mr Whitstable. She said she would stay just an hour. The hospital nurse – hard-pressed with forty ill patients, seven of them children – was pleased to be relieved of responsibility for Mr Whitstable, even for such a short time.

Marian Cotton shut the door behind the nurse, took a washed linen rag from her bag, went to the washstand and wrung it out in the bowl. Then she dabbed Aaron's brow carefully around the black congealed blood of the scar.

'Now then, Aaron. In the wars, are we? Them scallywags did you a bit of harm, I see.' Her low voice was threaded with an uncharacteristic note of warmth like that she had occasionally shown for Charlie. Had Aaron been conscious she would not have been so open with her feelings, even with him.

He muttered and groaned. Then he turned over in the bed and winced. She put a hand on his shoulder. 'Be still now, old boy. Lie still and get yourself better.'

He lay quietly under her hand. She pulled the single hard chair close to the bed and sat down. She had watched a good number of men in their sleep but none had done for her what this man had.

'Poor old lad. Every blow you took, you took for me. If I'd ventured out it'd've been my skull they cracked.' She took his hand in hers 'D'you know, old Ma Dodds came scuttling over to tell us about this? I didn't let on that I knew. She came in the dark. Even she cannot bear to be seen with us. I wouldn't have cared but, d'you know, the old besom hasn't even pawned my stuff yet? And don't I need the money to get out of that misbegotten place? If I don't get out soon they'll have me. She's not to be trusted. Never was. Always scooting down to Halloran's and telling her tale.'

She wet the cloth again and dabbed at his brow. 'I'll have to sell my furniture and all my bits and pieces, Aaron. My nice clock and my carved china shelf. I called on this fellow at Tindale on my way here and he says he knows a fellow who'll give me a price for the beds, the dresser and the chair. Without selling these, I'll never be able to move on. An' if I don't get away I'll end up like you, smashed up on a hospital bed. Or worse.'

She had been forced to creep out of the village the back way, behind the mill and across the fields, to get away without being seen. She had even dodged behind the church to avoid the sight of Mr Drummond, who had brothers in the village and would soon send out signals.

She put her face close to that of the unconscious shoemaker. 'Seems like they've tarred you with my brush, dear lad. They smashed your place to bits. Fired it. I crept out and took a look but they shooed me away. I'd've liked to straighten it out for you, but they'd get me if I ventured across the green again. I suggested to Ma Dodds that she should do it, clean it up for you, but she'd do nothing for no payment. Anyway, she's scared of their wrath, of Riley and his like. They don't just have power in their fists. There are other ways. The only thing is to get away, lad, you and me both.'

If Aaron had been conscious he would have heard a rare thread of uncertainty in her voice. She leaned over him, dabbing the damp cloth down his jawline. 'It wasn't always like this, honey. Those early days down in Bristol with my first husband – on the way up we were. Nice little house. China. Crystal lamp. That's where I got my clock that I still have. He was a kind lad and . . . well . . . satisfying. We had two children there, boy and girl. It was easy – I've always had children easy. You should have seen the girl, Aaron. I called her Victoria after the Queen. She was pretty, like a fairy doll. Then Gill, the boy, he was killed. Knocked down in the street by a horse tram. My man was cast down by that. The lad was the apple of his eye. But I still had my Vicky. Then she got sick. Poisonous fumes of the city. She was so sick. I had doctors. I went to wise old women I knew. I nursed her day and night. Did not sleep myself for five days but still she slipped from me and I came near to cursing God. I tell you, Aaron, a key turned in a lock somewhere inside me when that happened . . .' She pushed the damp hair back from his forehead.

'Get away from him!'

She jumped at the sound of William Kilburn's stern voice behind her. 'Doctor . . .' she said.

He leaned over Aaron. 'Did you give him anything?' he demanded.

'Don't talk soft,' she said scornfully. She met William's bleak gaze. 'The lad's out cold. What do you think I am?'

He stood up. 'That is what I'm driven to consider, Mrs Cotton.'

She frowned at him. 'Seems that they belted poor old Aaron here on the outside and they worked their poison on you on the inside. They've got old Quick-Manning deserting me, running scared . . .'

'What is it that you do, Mrs Cotton, to wreak such havoc?' The doctor's tone was weary, forbearing.

'What do I do? I tell you what, Doctor. I tell you what I don't do. I don't poison no one. Never have. I help them. Isn't that what *you* do?'

'But you do dose them with unlikely potions. Didn't you give young Charlie valerian on top of the medication I prescribed?'

'I told you about that, Doctor. It was to make him sleep. Isn't he just as likely to be knocked over by that stuff you gave him as anything I could give him? Didn't he throw all that up like *it* was poison?'

211

It was the barely veiled contempt in her eyes and her slight, knowing smile that at last made him lose his temper. He took her by the upper arm and pulled her to the open door, shouting for the nurse.

He thrust Marian towards her. 'Did you let this woman in here?'

Marian wrestled herself free of him and stood facing them, her arms folded.

The nurse was flustered. 'She told us you had sent her, Doctor, to take care of the patient.'

William rubbed his hands, one against the other, as though to clear contamination. 'This woman is a liar and worse. You must never allow her in here, Nurse. Never!'

Marian glared at him and turned and walked quickly away through the door at the end of the corridor. The nurse looked after her. 'She seemed like a decent enough woman, sir.'

'You are deceived, Nurse. As others have been,' he said brusquely. He turned back to the room. 'And your patient. How is he?'

'Breathing very well, Doctor, but sleeping too sound, to my mind. He looks fit enough. Plenty flesh on his bones and what skin's not bruised looks healthy enough. You can never tell. Sometimes they wake as though nowt had happened. Sometimes they just slip away.'

William pulled his gloves back on. 'Well, you must take great care of him, Nurse. He has been cruelly treated.'

'All well and good, Doctor. But I'm really short-handed here.'

He put a hand in his waistcoat pocket, pulled out two sovereigns and pressed them into her waiting hand. 'Then buy another pair of hands, Nurse.'

She bobbed a curtsy. 'As you say, Doctor.'

Outside the workhouse, William flicked Patch's shoulder and told him to walk on. He would call up at Bondgate and tell the solicitor Dale Trotter about his decision to carry out chemical tests on the viscera still in his possession. He would assure him of his commitment to double-check on his own judgement at the inquest of young Charles Cotton, and reopen the case if necessary. And that he would leave no stone unturned to get at the truth.

Forty-Six

To say that I've been kept in prison for the last two days might be something of an exaggeration under the circumstances, but I have certainly been under close surveillance. My aunt was so shocked at the sight of me on Monday night that, apart from supervising the removal of my bloody, dusty clothes and the bath that followed it, she did not at first mention the incident with Aaron. However, she has since insisted that, apart from when I am in bed, I stay by her side, whatever she is doing. Emily as well stays close by, making cow eyes at me, frustrated that I won't tell her the whole tale.

The swift turn of events has left my brain whirling. I lie in my bed thinking about Marian and Aaron, the first friends of my own that I've ever made. Of course, there is Emily, who I am sure counts herself as my friend. But now my friend Marian is being pushed further and further beyond the pale and needs to get away from this place. And Aaron is near death. Aaron of the smooth skin, the streaked hair, the wise eyes. And the soft lips. Lying here in bed I lick my own lips very carefully and imagine his lips just touching them.

Then there is the strangest thing. As I lie here half dreaming my visions of Aaron and Marian, they kind of merge into one being. All my happy times of self-discovery with her seem to transfer to him and become part of the reason why and the way that I love him. It is he who now becomes first in my thoughts.

Even in my dream state I have to acknowledge that these recent events will have their consequences. I wonder if this is my last chance to be the person who I have become. Soon my anxious aunt will have me on that train to London. And then the time of friendship, the promise of passion, will be over. I will return to the chaise longue in my father's house; my skin will pollute itself again and this ache in my leg will stop me walking.

This thought impels me to get up, light my candle and check the scrap of paper scrawled with Marian's untutored hand. The instructions for the paste and the potion are there. She has put me in charge of myself. I can mix the potions myself. Now and in the future. Even in London. I will never now return to what I was, even if they make me go back to London.

Now I drag my thoughts away from Aaron to think more closely about Marian: to consider again how so much hatred may be heaped on a single person. Surely there must be a reason. Perhaps someone knows something that I don't know. But then I have my vision of Marian as I first saw her on the train, with Charlie beside her in his little cap. I see again her bright, direct gaze, hear the note of irony in her voice. I feel certain that she is no murderer. I know that her brightness, her difference, has given its own offence in this place. It is these qualities that have allowed them – no, driven them – to make a murderer of her. But stop. Here I am making excuses for them, for Mrs Grey, Mr Riley and his wife, for my aunt, and now even my dear uncle.

Then I have a vision of Aaron, in the doorway of his cottage, with his bloody head on my lap, and feel again the leap of terror I felt when I thought he might be dead. I know now that I truly do love him. No matter how great my affection for Marian, this feeling is greater. Though I do feel great concern for her in her present difficulty, my main concern now is for Aaron. If he doesn't survive then I might as well spend the rest of my life fading away on some couch in London.

The next morning I dare to ask my bleary-eyed uncle how his patient was when he went to see him. I hold my breath and wait for him to tell me Aaron is dead or dying. He glances at my aunt and says quite calmly that Mr Whitstable has no obvious injury apart from a bad cut on his head and bruises from the beating. He does appear to have some concussion, though, as he continues to sleep.

'Who beat him?' demanded Emily, her bright eyes on me. 'Who was it who nearly beat that nice man to death?'

'Sergeant Hutchinson is looking into the matter,' says my uncle. 'It seems there was some drunken brawl. A falling-out among cronies, perhaps. You never know with these people.'

I rush to Aaron's defence. 'Mr Whitstable is not one to brawl. He's not that kind of person. I know him. He is intelligent, thoughtful . . .'

'Know him?' My aunt looks up quickly. 'My dear, I know he made you fine boots but you can hardly claim to *know* him.'

Emily looks as though she is about to speak so I rush in. 'Those ruffians, whoever they were, are no friends of his. His workshop was all broken and set fire to. They killed his chickens. They even killed his poor old donkey.' I look hard at the wide-eyed Emily to stop any reaction from her that might betray our earlier visit to Aaron.

My aunt sighs and goes on. 'Dear Victoria, you are such an innocent. You take to the strangest people. Whatever were you doing there at that time of night? I cannot think what impelled you.'

I bite the bullet. 'I went to see how Mrs Cotton was, after the inquest. She wasn't at her house so I went across to see Mr Whitstable, to see if she were there. I thought she might be there, as he is her friend and has stuck by her in all her difficulties.'

'So that's why they beat him? Because he was the woman's friend?' said Emily. 'I see now. But why would they kill a poor, innocent donkey? That's what I wonder.'

I am obliged to spend the whole day with my aunt. I stand by to help her with yet more bottling. Then I lift sheets down from the linen cupboard, so we can count them and return them to the same shelf. This seems to me to be a pointless, time-consuming exercise. Then she requests that I join with her for the children's afternoon lessons. I end up with young Eric fast asleep on my lap. I am just standing by the nursery window jiggling him awake so he will be able to digest his tea, when I realise I am looking at my uncle at the far end of the back garden under the deep hedge. He is in his shirtsleeves and he is digging the ground with a long-handled spade. My heart sinks. I know what it is that he digs for. He is recovering poor Charlie's stomach.

Eric's eyes pop open and he beams at me. 'I want my tea, Vicky. Where's my tea?'

Later that evening I wait until after supper and excuse myself.

'Where are you going?' demands my aunt.

'I want to talk to Uncle William.' My uncle has had a long surgery and has not joined us for supper. 'He's probably still in the dispensary. I heard him say goodbye to Dr Chalmers half an hour ago.'

'Good!' she says brightly. 'You may take a supper tray for him. He's very naughty, going without supper like this. He needs his strength, as do we all. Especially at this time.'

So I have to wait while she goes to the kitchen and makes a tray of bread and cheese for him with her own hands. Then she cannot resist delivering it herself. She pushes the dispensary door open with her elbow and announces our presence. 'A tray and a niece, William! For inner and outer sustenance. Victoria wants a word with you.'

She crashes the tray on the table where he sits in the light of his oil lamp surrounded by books. Then she waddles out, relieved of the job of being my gaoler.

My uncle tucks into the bread and cheese. 'What is this word you wished with me, Victoria?'

'You saw Aaron again this afternoon?'

'Yes. He's still unconscious but seems fit enough.' He pauses, as though he were about to say something else, then stops. 'Was there something else?'

'I saw you digging in the garden this afternoon. Were you digging up that stuff from the autopsy?'

'I was,' he says.

'Why did you need to do that?'

'I'm going to do some tests on it.'

'Why?'

'Because I am still uncertain about what killed young Charlie.'

'But you gave the judgement. Natural causes. You said natural causes.'

'Other things are emerging.'

'More gossip? Those silly newspaper stories?' Bitterness has seeped into my voice. 'You have already given the judgement.'

The man who stares back at me is not the gentle kind man who greeted me from the train; who gently helped poor Mrs Staincliffe down at the farm. His gaze is angry and frightened at the same time, like that of Mr Riley in the courtroom. 'That judgement makes me vulnerable, Victoria. I fear I gave it with insufficient clarity. Further scientific examination will either confirm or refute my judgement.

216

Either way, we will proceed with more certainty. My reputation hangs on it.' He hands me the tray. 'Now will you return this for your dear aunt? I must read more about this new test, which will clarify matters for good and all.'

I return the tray to the kitchen and climb the stairs to my room with a heavy heart and a sense of foreboding. My mind wanders. I feel in my bones that my uncle will find something, whether it's there or not. It occurs to me that Marian's fate is sealed by things outside herself, and whatever she does or whatever I do, nothing can be done about it.

Forty-Seven

My uncle boiled up the bits of Charlie with hydrochloric acid. Then into his little boiler he put some clear copper. That was when the arsenic showed: a white powder residue on the copper. I know this because I crept into his study that night and read a scientific journal open on a page referring to something called the Reich's test. Then I scratched around and rescued some sheets of paper from his waste-paper basket and smoothed them out on the desk. They were drafts of a letter he had sent that day to the coroner affirming his findings of the presence of arsenic, and advising the exhumation of Charlie's body to facilitate further tests for verification. On the sheet were several crossings out and amendments, as though he was not quite sure how to say what he wanted to say.

The arrest followed the digging up of Charlie and a second autopsy held by my uncle and some medical colleagues in an outhouse of a farm nearby. These results confirmed my uncle's first findings from the Reich's test and he advised that the coroner should consult an eminent forensic scientist from Leeds called Mr Scattergood. (Marian was to refer to him in her last letter to me as 'Mr Scatter*bad*'. Her dark irony did not leave her even at the end. Scattergood's evidence was to be conclusive in her eventual condemnation.)

But I am ahead of myself! Here we are, just after the second autopsy. As a consequence of this Marian is now incarcerated in the cells in Durham Gaol, having been arrested, then held at Bishop Auckland before being sent by train and closed carriage to Durham.

And now this village, the town of Bishop Auckland, even places

218

further afield are in a moral uproar fomented by the vehement articles in both local and national newspapers about what they see as Mrs Marian Cotton's 'obvious guilt'. Much of the information comes from a report from a police sergeant, who has been asked by the powers that be to visit places where Marian has lived in the North. He has sought out people who gather eagerly to say, on reflection, that she probably murdered people close to her in their community. Time and again they say it. The speculative total is now nearly twenty. It seems children and adults have dropped around her like flies (as though people in these places were *not* dropping down like flies anyway). One part of this account states in all seriousness that Mrs Cotton caused the death of their pigs! 'When residing in Walbottle a number of fat pigs died and the place became so hot that they were obliged to leave it and they came to reside at Bishop Auckland . . .'

The sergeant's report, to be sent to the Home Office, has been laid out in full in the *Auckland Chronicle*. So, it seems that as well as going to the magistrates, the policeman's 'report' has gone to the newspapers and is now seen as true as the Gospel. There is even an advertisement:

THE WEST AUCKLAND POISONINGS
Now ready, Carte Photographs of Marian Cotton, St Helen's
Auckland Church and Marian Cotton's house at West Auckland.
Sixpence each.
Published by J. T. Clarke, Photographer
1 Market Place, Bishop Auckland

It says also somewhere in one of the articles that Marian is now 'with child' and there cannot be a trial until she is delivered. My head is whirling with all this barrage of fantasy expressed as fact.

I read some parts of this news reporting to Emily. Then I turn the page over with a dramatic flourish, and tell her I am disappointed there is no account of Marian Cotton flying round County Durham on her broomstick! But there is no such tone of humour in these stories, just the deadly whine of prim certainty and condemnation of a woman none of them seems to know.

There are even similar newspaper reports of the affair – couched, perhaps, in more restrained language – in *The Times*, so the whole country must be agog with this scandal! I imagine my father rustling his paper in his study in Lordship Park and leaning over to pull the bell to send for my mother. I've said nothing of this matter in my letters to them, but my uncle's name is in the newspaper article, so they will know how close all this is to our lives here.

Even worse, thousands of copies of a dreadful song sheet have been sold, with doggerel condemning Marian Cotton, and a satanic cartoon claiming to represent her. I feel certain that at this very moment the good people of the district are singing this song with relish in the Eden Theatre and all the alehouses.

I have scratched my head as to how, in my present rather anomalous position, I might manage to see Marian, even in prison, to talk to her of these things. She is not mentioned in my presence in this house and I have to depend on eavesdropping to glean any facts. I did try to broach this matter with my uncle but he was so severe and forbidding I did not persist. He is still kindly in demeanour but is not the man he used to be.

At last I plump on a plan to use the good offices of Kit Dawson to achieve my end. I don't know what may be done about defending her, but I will consult with him about this. I have missed some choir sessions but have sent a note to Mr Dawson intimating that we might go to tea before choir today. As well as this I am very eager to see Aaron, who is still unconscious in the workhouse hospital. Of course, Emily is my willing co-conspirator and, although she has the instinctive dislike for Marian that is characteristic of people round here, she listens carefully to my pleas of injustice and witch-hunts, and nods wisely. I don't really know what goes on in the child's head, but I imagine our present quest fits in with her romantic sensibilities, fed as they are by her intense reading habits.

Kit Dawson is waiting for us when we arrive at the Kingsway Rooms. He stands up in his mannerly fashion and helps us into our chairs. Even before the tea is served I launch into my tales of injustice, my need to see Marian, and her need for some kind of legal help in her plight.

He whistles under his breath. 'Injustice?' he says. 'The woman's guilty. Haven't you read the papers? Clear as pie. You can feel it in the air. She knows so herself. There has been no peep from her.'

'She doesn't know what to say. How would she? She's knocked over by these events. And what about the law? And argument? Is there to be none of this? No innocent till proven guilty?' My voice is loud. People are staring. Emily's hand is on my arm and even the phlegmatic Kit is looking alarmed.

I breathe slowly to calm myself down. 'Can your Mr Smith not consider this case? Can he not look after her? She needs a solicitor at the very least.'

He dares to laugh. More a smirk, in reality. 'Well, to be honest, Mr Smith is not quite a solicitor. He's that self-important, but is really only clerk to Mr Chapman. But no lawyer with his buttons on would risk being associated with Marian Cotton. The case is open and shut. The woman's guilty. Any lawyer involved with her would get no further work.'

The waitress brings the tray with the silver tea service and the triangular sandwiches and we have to wait until she is clear. Then I try again.

'It is only open and shut, Mr Dawson, because of all those pages in the newspapers. The horrible drawings. Poor Marian is condemned out of hand before she is heard.'

'But so many witnesses have come forward to give testimony.'

'Witnesses? People who talk to a tall-hat reporter who's feeding them with propositions? With an eye to his own fame? Or a policeman on a witch-hunt? Is that a court of law?'

He shrugs. 'My dear Miss Kilburn, your open-mindedness does you credit, but have you thought you might be too carried away over this woman? Even I must admit to a certain dismay at your intense involvement with her.'

I curb my temper, even as I comfort myself with thoughts of how mean and self-satisfied his face is: more than a little prim and humourless. 'Surely she should have some lawyer to defend her, Mr Dawson?'

That shrug again. 'Well, even if Mr Smith or Mr Chapman were to take an interest, there is the vexed matter of money. Who would pay any lawyer, even if they were willing? I can't imagine *that* woman would have the wherewithal.' He sits back in his seat, certain of his logic. For him the question is closed.

'Indeed, Mrs Cotton does not have such wherewithal. That's one reason why all these tales of her doing terrible things for money are such nonsense. All she has is debts. Wouldn't she be a rich woman if what they say is true? She's as poor as any mouse in St Helen's church.'

I risk a gesture, putting one hand on his arm as it lies on the table. 'Would you not just ask Mr Smith and Mr Chapman if they could advise her? Help her in any way?'

He stares at my hand. 'Well, Miss Kilburn,' he says with sudden, explosive heartiness. 'I can see I must try to do *something* for *you*. For your tender-hearted self.' He puts his hand on top of mine and I resist a spurt of laughter brought on by a kick on the shins from Emily.

After tea I ask Emily to give my excuses at choir to my singing companion Miss McCullough as well as similar lame excuses to Choirmaster Kilburn. Then I set off, heart pounding, to the hospital in search of Aaron. According to my uncle the shoemaker is still deeply unconscious so I will not be able to speak to him. But I will be able to see that dear face.

In the dark entry to the building, really the much-feared workhouse rather than a true hospital, I manage to engage the confidence of the nurse attendant by reference to my dear Uncle William's concern for his patient. The fact that I am myself a Kilburn is something of an open sesame.

'You favour your uncle,' she says, leading the way to the small end ward, past the open workhouse ward where patients sit in drab rows. They lie there tidy, silent and watchful, wearing mittens against the cold. The air is so damp that I feel they must die of chill if they are left here much longer. As the nurse opens the door to the end ward I am relieved to feel a gale of warmth. At least Aaron is not fighting the cold as he lies unconscious. My uncle must have paid for the blazing fire in the corner.

My heart leaps when I see that, far from being still unconscious, Aaron is sitting up in bed reading a newspaper, his small wire-rimmed glasses on the end of his nose. His thick hair is drooping over the substantial bandage that still covers his injured brow. He is so pleased to see me that he jumps up, making his glasses fall off his nose and his newspaper scatter in pieces on the bed. 'Miss Victoria!'

'Mr Whitstable! Really!' The nurse bustles across and adjusts his blankets. She restores the newspaper to some order and in doing so manages to elbow me well back from the bed. Then, obviously in the interests of propriety, she moves to stand, arms folded, by the door.

What I would really like to do is to smother him with kisses to express my relief but I have to call to him across the great void that is the threadbare carpet beside his bed. 'When did you wake, Aaron? You have been quite a Rumpelstiltskin.'

He is gazing, gazing at me. 'I woke up with the sun this morning and the good Nurse Copper here gave me a fine breakfast of bacon. And she kindly sent someone for a newspaper, so I'm entirely back in harness.' He tapped the newspaper on the bed. 'Dire news here, I feel.'

I glance at the nurse but she is staring hard at the uncurtained window. 'My uncle sent me to check how you are, Aaron,' I lie. 'He'll be delighted to know you have woken up. We thought perhaps you might slip away from us. Do you remember what happened? How you got your injury?'

'I remember this gang of lads bursting into my shop and them holding me back as they broke up the place and slit my leathers. Then I made to run and after that all is black. But that's naught.' He taps the newspaper with his retrieved glasses. 'What about this? I'm more concerned about this. Have you seen what it says? How has this happened? How is Marian? Looks like they've ganged up on her too, to worse effect.'

I lower my voice to a whisper and say, 'Can you believe it? It is all such a mistake.' I glance at the nurse. 'It is a scandal across the county, and further. It's like heat. You can feel it everywhere you go.'

He shakes his head. 'We must do something, Victoria.'

I tell him about my conversation with Kit Dawson. 'He's not the most pleasant of men, but I think I've persuaded him to ask his employer to visit Marian and see what he can do.'

'Good, good. I will write a letter to her . . . I wonder, are you allowed to send a letter to a person in prison? . . . We need to ask her how she is, what we may do.' Suddenly his eyes are boring into me as though he can see every image set there in my mind, hear every thought that has occurred to me. Thoughts of Marian flee. He fills my vision and my world.

He lowers his own voice to a whisper. 'And how have *you* been in all this, Victoria?'

The nurse coughs. 'Patient needs to rest now, miss. You can tell the doctor how well Mr Whitstable is recovering.' She turns to leave.

I step quickly across the carpet and kiss him on the brow. He takes my hand and kisses it.

'Miss!' calls the nurse from the outer ward. 'The patient needs to rest. Dr Kilburn would not like this.'

Forty-Eight

'We've got ourselves some visitors today, Mrs Cotton.' Miss Douglas, called 'schoolmistress' in the prison, but now assigned with a colleague to keep watch over the notorious murderess, stood quietly by the door and waited for Marian Cotton to put down her embroidery, stand up from her hard chair and follow her through the door.

The rule in prison, that inmates should only speak when spoken to, had been broken early in their relationship. Mrs Cotton's very notoriety had given her status in this rule-ridden place and allowed some latitude. After all, what sanctions could be taken against one already condemned to death by public opinion, if not yet by due process? As well as this, those who supervised Mrs Cotton allowed themselves to be curious about the mind of this woman. The governor, the chaplain, the chief wardress and various matrons had all indulged themselves with conversations with this particular inmate. They had a professional interest, after all. It was said now with certainty that Mrs Cotton had abandoned her own child and had killed more than twenty people. In the quiet hours, over a rare cup of tea, there were quite intense commentaries on Mrs Cotton's demure presence, her fine looks and her well-mannered disposition. The speakers referred to her intelligence and her occasional ironic perception of the world about her. Not one person met her but mentioned their unease in her presence.

In their various careers the governor, the chaplains, the attendants, matrons and wardresses had experienced all kinds of wickedness and despair, madness and innately evil disposition. But this woman seemed not to fit in any category that could make sense to them. They suspected

225

she might be sly, although they could see little sign of it. So they treated her with the restrained kindness they might accord a wild animal that had not yet scratched them.

'Let me guess, Miss Douglas,' said Marian, her breath showing in lacy strings in the chilly corridor. 'It's Mr Robinson, my true husband, who has brought my own son here to see me at last, and wishes to say sorry for sayin' all those things he said about me in the Sunderland papers. He's here to say my letter to him has softened his hard heart.'

Miss Douglas had witnessed Marian's letter, begging Mr Robinson to bring her only surviving child to see her – the boy she had abandoned and left with him in Sunderland – and to stand up for her in court, to say that he knew her well and that she was no murderer.

The schoolmistress shook her head. 'Not this time, Mrs Cotton. No,' she said, 'it's some solicitors, from Bishop Auckland, I think. A Mr Chapman and a Mr Smith. It seems they're to see to your case.'

Marian gave a little skip on the cold stone floor. 'Are they now? Well, it's a welcome thought that anybody may "see to my case", apart from guilty doctors and scavengers of policemen, like.'

'Now, Mrs Cotton, you must not speak like that. These people are your betters.'

'Do betters never do wrong, Miss Douglas? That's what I want to know. It's not so in my experience.'

Miss Douglas was saved the problem of answering this ticklish question by the necessity to pull up her weighty iron ring, select the key and unlock the heavy door of the interview room. Inside, lit by a stray beam from the high window, two men – one young and one middle-aged – sat on leather chairs to one side of a polished table. On the table in front of the older man was an open notebook, a pen and a narrow bottle of ink.

The schoolmistress led Marian to a small, scarred schoolroom chair opposite the men. 'This is Mr Chapman, your solicitor, and Mr Smith. Gentlemen, this is Mrs Cotton,' she announced, then retired to sit on another hard chair just by the door.

There was no shaking of hands. Marian sat on the chair and turned her gaze on the older, portly man. 'Mr Chapman . . .?'

He shook his head. 'No, Mrs Cotton. I am Mr Smith. This is Mr Chapman. I have the honour to be his clerk.' He tapped the notebook in front of him. 'I will make notes of your conversation.'

226

She narrowed her eyes and peered at him more closely. 'I think I recognise you. Weren't you at our Charlie's inquest? The one where they decided, quite rightly, that the poor wee soul died of natural causes?' Marian frowned at the younger man. 'An' *you*'re not very old, are you? More like a schoolboy, to my eye.'

Miss Douglas coughed loudly.

The young man went quite red and put his hand for a moment on his luxurious moustache. Then he cleared his throat. 'I am here for a preliminary discussion, Mrs Cotton. To find out—'

She nodded briskly. 'Good. I can tell you one thing, son. I did none of those things they are saying, and you are to make sure that everyone knows that. A clear mistake and the sooner people know the better. People died around me, aye, like they do around all of us. But people lived round me, too. You ask Dr Kilburn, who's not a bad man, and that Riley, the assistant relieving officer. How many people survived 'cause of my own special care? It's my curse that my special care was not enough for my own . . .' Her glance dropped to Smith, who was staring at her with bulging eyes. 'Are you not takin' note of this, mister?'

Smith tapped his notepad with the end of his pen. 'First things first, Mrs Cotton. We're here at the particular request of Miss Victoria Kilburn to consider whether we may take on your case—'

She interrupted him, a small smile crossing her face. 'Victoria? Aye, there's a good'n. She's very special, is Victoria.'

'. . . one crucial aspect being whether you are able to pay for the services of Mr Chapman.' He sniffed. 'As well as this, payment would be required for a barrister for when the case comes to court.'

'Two men? Can't you do it yourself? Paying two instead of one? Never heard of it.'

'The point is, have you resources to support your defence, Mrs Cotton? These are professional men.'

She stared at him until he dropped his gaze, picked up his pen and dipped it in the ink.

'Well, sirs,' she said, 'I've got no money squirrelled away, though you'd think I have from what they're saying about me out there. But my house is rented now to a man called Lowery. Write this down on your paper. Decent feller. Lowery. He has the use of my bits of furniture and stuff, but I told him he had to sell it if I needed the money and it seems like now I do need it. There is a very good clock and some fine china.

There's one or two other bits worth more than pennies.' She stared at the still-empty notebook. 'Write it down. *Lowery*. Staying at thirteen Front Street, West Auckland. And a Mrs Dodds – *Dodds*, write it down there, sir – she has some good clothes and things to take to the pawn man. You can get them from her.'

Smith looked at her coldly. 'Is that all, Mrs Cotton?'

'There's one more thing. A Mr Quick-Manning, who lives on Johnson Terrace. He has a silver watch of mine, a watch of quality. Worth a bit. You can retrieve it from him and make what money you can from that. Should be a fair penny.' She leaned across the desk. 'Here, I'll sign that to give you the right. That's what you lawyers like, ain't it? Signed papers?'

Mr Smith dipped the pen and handed it over. 'You can *write* then?' he said, lifting his brow towards young Mr Chapman, who was looking towards the narrow window, wishing he were on his new tennis court, warming up for a game.

Marian signed with a flourish. 'Aye. As you see, sir, I can write. I can even read. Could you believe it? Miss Douglas will sign here as my witness. Isn't that so, Miss Douglas?' She cocked an eye at the school-mistress, who came and put her name alongside Marian's looping signature, then went again to sit by the door. Mr Smith blotted the page carefully.

'Now you'll need another sheet, Mr Smith.'

'Why would that be, Mrs Cotton?'

'You'll need a list of the people to defend me from this silly charge.'

Mr Smith moved, to put himself in Mr Chapman's eye-line. The solicitor shrugged and returned his gaze to the window. Mr Smith pulled down another page in his book.

'Right. Dr Kilburn first. He and Chalmers saw Charlie all that week and were dosing him with God knows what. Prussic acid and hydro-cyanic acid. Write that down. I checked with Mr Townend the chemist. That Kilburn, he knows in his heart I am innocent. Good God, I am for the saving of life, not the taking of it.'

'Mrs Cotton!' Miss Douglas called from the door. 'Blaspheming is the wrong way to go about this. And without respect for your betters you'll get nowhere.'

'Anyway. What you suggest is mistaken. Dr Kilburn is a main prosecution man,' said Mr Smith. 'It would be counterproductive to use him.'

'Put him down,' ordered Marian. 'Now put down the assistant relieving officer, Mr Riley. The grocer, he is.'

'Why him?'

'Well, to tell the shameful truth, he was with me in my bed when the boy Charlie died. Riley is haunted by the death of his own son. He can't forgive himself so he points a finger at me because my son has died when he was there. He is a decent enough man but is pursued by demons.'

There was a shocked silence in the room. Mr Smith wriggled in his seat. Mr Chapman folded his arms protectively around himself and kept staring out of the window. Miss Douglas whispered, 'Mrs Cotton . . . Marian. No lies! All this will not help.'

'Write it!' said Marian. 'It's the truth.'

Smith shrugged but did as he was told.

'Now write down Mr Quick-Manning, who is a friend of mine and who I nursed back from the teeth of death, and that old man Mr Lanister that I brought back from death's door, him likewise. They know I'm not in the business of killing folks. They both would have died but for me. Write it!'

His pen scratched the surface of the paper.

'Now, write Mr James Robinson of Ayres Quay, Sunderland. He will tell you those deaths down Sunderland were nowt to do with me. The bad chance of poverty and illness, that's all. The two of us had our differences, for Robinson was a mean man. And it's true that we disagreed over money. Moreover, our life together was hit by tragedy when the children died in the house we shared. But he was fond of me once and I can't believe he'd go for any of this rubbish. I tell you, he's the only man worth calling *man* that I knew in a long time. Except for this shoemaker . . .' Her voice faded a little. 'Write it down, Mr Smith. Mr James Robinson, shipbuilder.'

He wrote down the name and address and smoothed the blotting paper over the second page.

'Now, give me the pen. I'll sign it and Miss Douglas'll witness this one as well. Keep it right. You fellows like that, don't you? All signed and sealed.'

When this was done, Mr Chapman pulled a gold watch from his waistcoat pocket and peered at it short-sightedly. He stood up. 'We should go, Smith,' he said abruptly. 'Too long here.'

'Stand up, Mrs Cotton!' said Miss Douglas from the door.

Marian stood up, her wooden chair scraping on the stone floor. She watched as Mr Smith tucked the notebook into a small case and Mr Chapman pulled on his gloves and picked up his hat and cane from the table.

Unctuously, Smith bowed Mr Chapman out of the door before him. Then he looked back towards Marian. 'Whatever happens, Mrs Cotton, I have one pertinent piece of advice for you.'

'Pertinent?' She cocked her head. 'And what would that be, Mr Smith?'

'When they question you in the police rooms, in the court, anywhere, don't say anything. Say nothing. Do not protest. If the prosecution is false it will be self-evident. If you protest, you will condemn yourself out of your own mouth. You have shown us this here, just this afternoon. You condemn yourself out of your own mouth. Say nothing. That is my advice.'

The two women listened to the men's steps echoing down the corridor. Then Marian sagged against the table. 'By, Miss Douglas, this bairn's trying to kick its way out.'

Miss Douglas came and helped her upright. 'Come on, Mrs Cotton, We have to go back now.' After she had locked the door behind them she took Marian's arm again as they walked down the dank corridor: an unusual intimacy. 'Lawyers!' said the schoolmistress, her mouth pulled very thin. 'Not an attractive breed. But unfortunately we need 'em.'

On their way from the gaol Mr Chapman and Mr Smith turned into the County Hotel to take some brandy and to savour a cigar, before setting off again, Mr Chapman to his Durham office, Mr Smith to the station for his train to Bishop Auckland. Mr Smith drank too quickly and, ignoring Mr Chapman's weary eye, nodded to the hovering waiter to refill his glass.

'I don't know about you, sir,' he said to his superior, who was young enough to be his own son, 'but don't you think a man needs something to get the taste of that place out of one's mouth?'

Chapman made the shadow of a toasting gesture with his glass before taking a sip. 'And the taste of the inmates, eh, Mr Smith?' he said.

'What a frightful woman,' said Smith. 'The language of the gutter.' He took a more measured sip of his brandy. 'Would you consider taking on this case, sir?'

Chapman stared at him. 'Could funds really be raised from those miserable artefacts the woman mentioned?'

Smith shrugged. 'How can you tell? I have heard it said that some of these people have mattresses weighed down with sovereigns.'

'We would have to brief a barrister.'

'And there would be witnesses to call on, briefs to prepare. That would accrue costs.'

'What witnesses?' Chapman asked.

'The people she named.'

Chapman laughed hoarsely. 'Don't be silly, man. We'll be a laughing stock, surely. Have not these people declared themselves her accusers? Naught would be served by that. These are leading people in that community. No one would wish to employ us ever again. No. Clear-cut case, anyway. No need for them. Surely you see that?' He nodded to the waiter, who filled up his glass. He sniffed at the brandy. 'Did you see the woman's condition? Not only is she without conscience, she is without shame.'

'So you would not wish to act for Mrs Cotton?'

'I didn't quite say that. Perhaps we could brief a barrister. Keep her quiet. The end's inevitable, anyway.'

'And take what funds we may?'

Chapman stared at him, then threw off the last of his brandy. 'You might. But think of it, man. Not a penny in it. The pittance you'll rake up will barely cover our costs today.' He took out his heavy watch. 'Now then, Smith, we should make haste, or I will miss my meeting and your train will leave without you.'

Forty-Nine

Aaron has sent me a note to say he's out of hospital and has taken rooms in Princes Street in Bishop Auckland, as he's had his fill of West Auckland and he plans to take a new shop in Newgate Street to ply his trade. It seems he has been back to the village to salvage his tools and his clothes. He says he did hesitate at Western House, thinking he would call on me, 'But I have to admit that my courage failed me at the front door, and something else in me discouraged me from going, like a tradesman, to the back door.' He thanks me for visiting him in hospital, saying, 'The sight of the fair Victoria was enough to bring anyone to life.' I blush here where I'm sitting, at the breakfast table.

'Not a letter from your dear parents, I think?' said Auntie Mary, watching me closely.

I shake my head, put the note back in its envelope and put it under my side plate.

'A Bishop Auckland stamp, I see,' she pursues me.

I am forced to think very quickly. 'An enquiry about some fingerless mittens for my little sister, Pixie, who has a birthday soon. A letter from my mother reminded me. I saw some in a shop in Bishop Auckland but they only had them in white. Now they tell me they have them in blue and I may collect them.' The words come almost too easily. I am amazed how easy it has become to lie. In fact my mother's reminder was a surprise. Pixie – Rollo too – has barely crossed my mind in these weeks.

'Yes. Pixie's birthday! Your father mentioned it in his letter last

232

week.' She pauses. 'He also mentioned the accounts of our nasty scandal in *The Times* and is very concerned about the situation here; thinks perhaps there are risks for you.'

'There can hardly be any risks, Aunt Mary, when the person they suspect,' I glance at my uncle, who has his nose in the *Auckland Chronicle*, 'unfairly in my view, is locked up in Durham Gaol.'

Auntie Mary beams. 'Quite! We said this in our letter to him! Is that not so, William? And the fact that we do not want to lose you as you are such a good companion for our dear Emily.'

Emily shouts, 'Hear! Hear!' but my aunt has to content herself with a grunt from behind my uncle's newspaper. She shrugs and sets about her bowl of prunes.

My aunt, very large with child now, is increasingly placid. I wonder if this is what the Almighty does to women when they are about to go through that veil of pain called childbirth. He makes them calm and slippery so that nothing can touch them. I have tried to talk to her twice about Marian Cotton, but the savagery and injustice of these events do not impinge on her one bit. All she says is that I must trust my dear Uncle William as he is very wise over such matters. And did I note that Mrs Cotton had actually abandoned a child in Sunderland? It said so in the newspaper. No proper mother would do this.

At another time I might have taken her advice, had I myself not been very well acquainted with the special character of Marian Cotton and had I not witnessed my uncle's own uncharacteristic discomfiture over these events. As to the abandoned child, I would need to talk with Marian to know the truth of that, among all those other untruths. I know I must make up my own mind about what is right and what is wrong here. What lengths I am driven to these days! Not only must I put salve on my face each night and walk with a straight back, I must make up my own mind on the way things are and should be, without any recourse to the opinion of the older and allegedly wiser people of my acquaintance. It is no easy thing but I know I have the strength for it.

Whatever its source, my aunt's current dreamlike state allows me a remarkable freedom of movement, sometimes even without Emily as a decoy. Today I am able to make my way alone into Bishop Auckland (on the pretext of the fingerless mittens) to see Aaron, because Emily is having some special mathematics coaching at her own request. She has decided she is too ignorant in these matters and is cultivating an ambition to be a scientist.

My tentative knock on the door of Aaron's lodgings in Princes Street brings forth a short stout woman with a squint. Using only her right eye, she surveys me from my neat feathered hat down to my built-up shoe. I request an audience with Mr Whitstable and she turns away into the dark passage, leaving me at the door. I hear her shout, 'Mr Whitstable! Here's a cripple lass ter see yeh!'

He comes to the door, his soft hat in one hand, buttoning his jacket with the other. He has only the smallest bandage, now, across his brow. He smiles at me, his pale skin flushing. 'Miss Victoria! I am just going to visit my new shop and you must come with me to see it.' He bustles me down the street, away from the eye of his landlady, who observes our hasty escape through her heavy lace curtains.

We talk very little as he strides with me down on to Newgate Street and into a narrow shop, which seems to go back for miles. It is lined with gleaming nut-brown shelves and counters. The air is threaded with a slight perfume. I sniff a little to identify it. 'What was this place before?' I frown.

He takes my arm. 'It was a millinery shop run by a mother and three pretty daughters. The daughters have wed and the mother has stopped with hats and started with grandchildren.' He pulls me the length of the shop to a large workroom behind. 'And see! A very decent workshop. I can make my shoes but as well as this I can sell my ready-made boots to customers. Then buy in leather goods like gloves and belts to sell out in the front.' He points to the ceiling. 'And there above us is a warren of rooms that is more than a house. The milliner has sold me her furniture too, so today or tomorrow I will take up proper residence here.' He drags me further on, through more rooms, to a heavy back door. 'And see! A garden as big as my garden in the village. There are old apple trees here and some fine shrubs. I think this must have been a very old garden and was once a very fine one. If you look at the roof line you can see that the shop, with others, used to be a bit of a fine house.'

The tumbled green space sits smiling at us in the sunlight. I am conscious that between us the air is buzzing with meaning. He pulls me further on, until we are under one of the drooping apple trees. 'See! My chickens can roost here. There is even room, perhaps—'

I am suddenly stricken. 'Did you hear about Tilder? Those bad boys killed him.'

'So your uncle tells me,' he says soberly. 'Those lads were so very angry. Called Marian all kinds of names before they banged me on the head. But what need was there to kill our poor old donkey?'

'Did the sergeant arrest them?'

'I don't think so.'

'Not like Marian.'

'No.'

I look back at the house and down again at the wonderful garden. 'That's really why I've come to get you, Aaron. Kit Dawson says Mr Smith and the lawyer Mr Chapman have at last been to the gaol to see Marian. We need to go and see them and talk with them about how they can help her out of this terrible fix.'

He pulls me by the hand so I am facing him. 'Victoria, Victoria! How I love the way you seem so very certain Marian didn't do all this. There she is, damned out of hand by everyone except you and me.' He pauses. 'Is there a chance we may be wrong, d'you think?'

'I am certain about it. I feel it in my bones. Don't you and I know her better than this? So many others think they know her from the talk behind Riley's counter or the newspapers.'

He nods gravely. 'I've been thinking that I should write to the newspaper about that reporting. There is prejudice all over it. What chance has Marian of a fair trial after that?' He puts a hand through my arm. 'Now, Victoria. Where will we find him? This Chapman?'

'In the Market Place. He has an office there.'

He takes a handful of keys from his coat pocket and locks the back door of the shop. Then he leads down to the end of the garden where a stout gate built into the high wall opens out on to the narrow road that backs all the large houses on Newgate Street. To our right, on a despoiled meadow, tilers are going about their daily work balancing precariously on the roofs of new houses. New houses, fine shops! This modern town is a world away from the narrow medieval ways of the village: the 'bear-pit', as Aaron calls it.

With new heart I take Aaron's arm and stride out boldly, the day, the place and the company making me more optimistic about this encounter with the men who might just save Marian.

Fifty

We knock on a heavy door with a knocker shaped like a unicorn, are admitted, and enter the office of Mr Chapman in the Market Place to find Kit Dawson standing side by side with another clerk at tall writing desks. Kit is copying from letters scribbled on a pad beside him. He turns towards me but his smile falters as it transfers itself from me to Aaron, who stands steadily at my side, his felt hat in his hand. I introduce them and Kit offers Aaron a limp, unwilling hand. He glances at his colleague, an old man who clutches his pen as though it were a weapon. The old man sniffs.

Kit leads the way back out again into the Market Place where the Thursday market is in full swing. Then he turns on me, barely controlling his anger.

'It's not right, Miss Kilburn, that you seek me out in my place of work,' he says coolly.

'Oh, Mr Dawson, we were merely coming to enquire whether Mr Smith and Mr Chapman had been to see Mrs Cotton and what they would do for her.'

'We?' He eyes Aaron. 'Who is this "we"?'

'Aaron is another friend of Marian.'

'A "friend"? What a lucky woman Mrs Cotton is to have such *friends*.'

I rein in my anger. 'Are they to help Mrs Cotton? Your colleagues?' I persist.

'Well, they went to see her . . .'

'How is she?' I say quickly.

He frowns. 'She is a woman in prison. I did not enquire as to her health.'

'What did they decide?'

'Well, Mr Smith is in West Auckland as we speak, trying to raise some funds . . .'

I cannot resist clapping my hands. 'So now you must introduce us to Mr Chapman, so that we can tell him what we know of Mrs Cotton, that she could not have done this terrible thing.'

He puts up a hand as though fending off a physical blow. 'Stay steady, Miss Kilburn. Mr Chapman is out at a meeting of the Board of Health. Something about drains. Then he is going to the Durham office. He and Mr Smith will get on with this matter of Mrs Cotton as they see fit. I'm sure there's no need for him to talk to you or . . .' he raises his eyes to Aaron, '. . . anyone. The evidence will speak for itself.'

He turns his back on Aaron and puts his body between Aaron and me. His face is very close to mine. 'Does your uncle know you are ranging round the town in all sorts of low company, canvassing support for this poisoner?' he whispers.

I step to one side so that Aaron is in my eye-line again. 'Will you tell Mr Chapman and Mr Smith that we will try again, Mr Dawson?' I smile as I say the words clearly and slowly, as though I am speaking to a small child. 'And when they see Mrs Cotton again in that dreadful place, would you kindly ask that they should convey our cordial regards to her? They must say our names. Mr Whitstable is writing to her, so I imagine he will hear of the lawyers' efforts from Mrs Cotton herself.' I step round Kit and take Aaron's arm. 'Thank you for your help, Mr Dawson.'

He swirls away, his jacket lifting at the speed of his movement. Behind him he bangs the heavy door so firmly that the unicorn knocker lifts and clatters back on its iron holder.

'That lad's rather lacking in manners.' Aaron looks down at me. 'You've lost a friend there,' he says.

'That man?' I say scornfully. 'He was never my friend. Never.'

Fifty-One

Mr George Smith was in West Auckland to tackle Mr Lowery about Mrs Cotton's furniture. He got there early and was obliged to wait in the Rose and Crown until Lowery came off shift at the pit. The front parlour of the public house was dingy and quiet at this time of day but the landlord, Mr Pullman, recognised Smith from the inquest, and embarked on a long homily about that day and the subsequent scandalous events. On hearing Smith's particular errand he became so excited that the single plume of hair that covered his head floated up and down in the still air of the stuffy overheated bar parlour.

'The lawyer, are you? I cannot think what the feller wants, living in the house of a murderess, in the room where that li'le one died.'

Smith didn't either, but that was not his business. He decided not to comment.

Later that afternoon in Mrs Cotton's house, Mr Lowery did not seem too pleased that Smith had come to take the furniture from under him, but when he saw the signed paper he nodded his reluctant agreement. He stood by and watched as Smith pointed items out to the cart-man, who manhandled the heavier items through the door on to his cart. Smith told the cart-man to be careful with the rather fine clock, the spindle-backed chair and the carved shelf. He also counted the knives and forks – some of them old silver – before he allowed the old man to take them.

'So how is Mrs Cotton?' said Lowery. 'This place is prickling with talk but – speak as you find – I didn't think her a bad woman. She was kind in her way. She knew her Scriptures, which is more than some of the Godless lot round here.' God was one of Mr Lowery's pre-occupations.

'Which is the bed that the lad died on?' asked Smith.

Lowery pointed to the couch bed in the corner, thinking the clerk would at least leave that behind.

'I'll leave you the one upstairs then.' Smith put a hand on the decorative back of the couch bed. 'This'll raise a few bob, with that murder tale attached. Travellin' shows live and breathe on that kind of thing. A kid acting the writhing child, the screams of pain! Or p'raps a waxwork. Penny a peep. You know the kind of things.'

Lowery gave the cart-man a hand with the bed, and when they were outside alone he said, 'That's a funny gadgie in there, innit? Godless, in my view.'

The cart-man sniffed. 'He never take no more notice of a man than the gelt he stands to gain. An' I've had a few shillin's from that feller in my turn. So I'm not complainin', I can tell yer. He has a bit of a sideline clearing houses from them who's died in debt.' He looked up at the tall narrow house. 'Never yet cleared the house of a murderer, like. Worth an extra shilling, mebbe? I'll try that on the Smith gadgie.'

Lowery went back into the house. 'Are you finished, then?' he said sourly to Smith, who was standing before the small mirror above the mantelpiece.

Smith brushed the rim of his bowler hat and peered into the mirror to ensure it was on at a smart angle. 'I think so. Just about.' He reached out and unhooked the mirror. 'Not a bad one, that. Bevelled edge. I'll tell the old boy to wrap it in a blanket. Can't have it cracking, can we? Bad luck for someone, don't they say that?'

After shaking hands with Lowery, Smith made his way along to the rooming house where Mrs Dodds had a downstairs front room. She handed him the shawl and the dresses, still in their parcel. 'I fear I didn't quite get ter gan down to the pawn man for her, sir. And when they took her down Durham Gaol I thowt there was no point. What use has she now for the shawl and the dresses, nor even the pawn man's money?'

'Well, she needs it now to pay her way in court.'

'They're saying round here they shouldn't waste time in the courts. Just string her up and have done with it.'

'There has to be a trial, Mrs Dodds. This is England, you know. The home of all modern law.'

'And then they'll hang her?'

'Looks like it.'

She went to the door with him. 'Me, I don't think she was a bad woman, you know.'

'Don't you? Second time I've heard that today.'

'She quite liked that bairn, Charlie. She didn't like to be shut in the house but she worked hard enough out of it. She was a good payer. Always paid her dues. Even ran up debt to do that. She wanted to get on in life, and all the time she couldn't. Things pulled her back.'

Outside the house Smith handed the parcel over to the cart-man and told him to go to a certain address in Railway Street, deliver the stuff to a Mr Raine and say he would call later for his money. Then he turned back to Mrs Dodds.

The old woman eyed him. 'She could be funny sometimes. She had this great hearty laugh that you had to join in on.'

'Being funny's hardly a defence against murder, Mrs Dodds.'

She lifted her heavy shoulders in a shrug. 'Just seems unlikely to me, though I daren't say it round here or I'll get a dose of the same medicine. They gave the shoemaker a beating. D'you hear that?' She paused. 'And another thing, she was a good payer. If she had a bit – which wasn't so often – you got a share.'

'I'll be honest, Mrs Dodds. Being a good payer is another thing that's hardly a defence against murder.'

She wiped her hands on her apron and said, 'I hear tell they've dug up the others, now, Mr Smith. The lodger, Nattrass, and the other little'ns. I hear'd they had a job finding them in amongst all those pauper graves. How they know who's who there's no telling. Seems like they looked for Fred Cotton and couldn't find him. That's what I heard.'

'Diggin' up more bodies? That hardly bodes well for your friend Mrs Cotton, does it?' he said, turning away.

She called after him. 'I never said she was my friend. I worked for her, that's all. So where to now, Mr Smith?'

'Down Johnson Terrace to see Mr Quick-Manning.'

'Him? Oh, he had a soft spot for her. She's carrying his bairn, d'you know that? Will he do right by that bairn, think you?'

He looked at her with distaste but said nothing.

'An' will you talk to t'other feller that was after her? Riley the shop-man? Did you know he was after her?'

He turned away.

'D'you know what the worst of her was? Round here, like,' she said to his back.

He was tempted to turn back. 'And what's that?' he said without turning round.

'They're scairt of her, bliddy scairt. She had them on the run. And for that they're gunna bliddy hang her.'

Smith turned heel and almost ran the length of the green to Johnson Terrace, where Quick-Manning handed over the watch – of high value, Smith thought – without any demur. But unlike Mrs Dodds, Quick-Manning would not be drawn into any conversation about Mrs Cotton and shut his door loudly as soon as Smith had turned on his heel.

Walking briskly towards the station, the silver watch safely in his pocket, Smith reflected that, for a woman who was supposed to be destitute, Mrs Cotton was clocking up quite a lot of value. So that was promising, at least.

Fifty-Two

In Martin's drapery, hoping to find blue fingerless mittens, I bump into Miss McCulloch from choir. I am pleased to see her broad, plain face and realise I have missed the unity of our voices, like a conversation without words. I tell her I am so sorry I missed the practice. She beams her delight and says how much she has missed *me* at the recent meetings.

She puts a hand on my arm. 'The contraltos have lost the melody entirely without the blending of our two excellent voices. I have thought I might come down to West Auckland myself to rout you out, to bring you back into our company!' She looks so pleased that I think for a moment she is about to kiss me. She settles for an affectionate squeeze of my forearm and I smile uncertainly, pleased at her friendly touch but not too sure how to handle it. But I like Miss McCullough. I have from the first. These dramas have caused our friendship to falter but it will flourish. I know it.

I have come upon her standing at Martin's long mahogany counter buying six sets of open drawers for her 'young ladies'. 'They are hoydens, every last one, my dear,' she says fondly. 'How a young lady might rend such items into rags I am not certain. I suspect, though, that the laundry has been overbleaching them and weakening the fibres. Whatever it is, it will go on the girls' bills and they will have to explain to their long-suffering parents.'

At a loss for something to say, I ask her more about her girls. 'Do all of them sleep in your boarding house?'

'Not all of them, more's the pity. The school is obliged to take day girls, the daughters of local tradesmen who have much to learn beside the parsing of sentences in French. They join my girls at the house for lunch and I have to tell you, the difference is marked.' She looks me up and down. 'And what brings you into town today?'

'Well, I am making enquiries about some legal matters for a friend.' We stand watching as the assistant wraps up the drawers in an immaculate brown paper parcel. I hesitate, then a stream of words come to my mouth unbidden. 'I had thought I might look for some kind of post, perhaps something clerical. I have lately felt the need to strike out on my own.' No sooner have I said the words than I know they are true, although nothing could have been further from my mind when I came from my uncle's this morning.

Miss McCullough strikes the counter with a heavy hand, making both me and the poor lady assistant jump. 'I have it! I have it, Miss Kilburn! You are sent to me from Heaven! I have it!'

I look at her in astonishment. 'You have what, Miss McCullough?'

'Let me explain. I have just lost my assistant matron – lost! How careless of me!' She laughs rather unnecessarily at her own joke, then calms down. 'A young woman worked for me and has just left. She has become affianced to a young man who is her brother's friend. Another of these importunate farmers. Very inconvenient, I may tell you. Now I am struck by the wonderful thought that *you* could be my assistant matron! Just the type! Genteel, well bred, musical. Show these farmers' daughters some London manners.'

'I have to tell you, Miss McCullough, not only have I never been inside a school, I am barely educated myself.' Despite my denial I am very taken with her idea.

'Nonsense! A blind cat could see you are cultured. And culture, my dear, is education, however it is acquired. Do not fear. I will show you the way. You will lead the girls by your example. You will run a few errands for me. Lead the boarding house choir. There is a very nice room in the boarding house overlooking the river. Wear View House on Bondgate. You can't miss it.' She coughs and actually blushes. 'It may be somewhat indelicate, my dear, but I am driven to say that there would be a salary of thirty pounds a year. Independence! Every woman needs independence.' She takes the parcel from the assistant, who scurries with her to the door and opens it for her. Miss McCullough looks back at me, the feather in her hat bobbing. 'Think about it, Miss Kilburn! I do need you. You are an answer to my prayer. I will ask you again at choir next week. Don't let me down.'

My brain is buzzing. I think perhaps Miss McCullough is an answer to *my* prayer. Astonishingly, it is a prayer I could not have expressed as little as an hour ago.

The assistant scurries back to me. 'Can I help you, miss?'

'You have fingerless mittens in your window. I wondered if you had them in blue?'

Fortunately she does.

Later, as the train chugs through the town and past the pits and the dreary houses, I have the time to savour the astounding thought that I might be in a position to earn some of this vulgar money. My mother would be horrified at the thought of me taking up a post that is, effectively, that of a glorified housemaid. And I know my Aunt Mary would be hurt, seeing it somehow as a betrayal of her rise in society. She goes up, I go down. Like some kind of social seesaw.

Back at Western House I come upon her sitting on the couch in the upstairs drawing room, embroidering forget-me-nots on a nightdress for the new baby. Knowing nothing of my treacherous thoughts, she admires the mittens, as well as some pretty pink tissue paper in which I intend to wrap them. She puts down her needle to watch me tuck a card into the folded palms of the gloves and wrap them in the pink paper. I catch her glance.

'Now then, Auntie, where might I find some brown paper to wrap them for the post?'

Aunt Mary sighs. 'Alas, my dear girl, that won't be necessary. I must be honest with you. William and I have been forced into a rather difficult decision. These new exhumations must have been reported in the London papers and your uncle has had a long wire today from your father. He is now adamant you must return to the safety of London. He will not take no for an answer. Appears to think you are existing in a sink of iniquity. He offers to send your mother's maid to accompany you on your return to London or suggests you might like to take Emily to London with you. He thinks she might find the capital stimulating.' She picks up her embroidery. 'We will miss you so much, my dear, especially Emily, for I could never let her go, even with you. But I understand your father's concern. We are used to the rough-and-ready ways of people round here. Some might see us as rough and ready

244

ourselves. But you, being so used to being protected in your father's house . . .'

These are platitudes. I realise at last that she is weary of me and the extra problems I seem to have wrought. She must feel the new baby is quite enough for her to think about.

Very carefully I put my parcel down on the windowsill and peer out across the green. Mr Riley is up a ladder, cleaning his plate-glass window. Finally I say, 'I do not wish for Joan to come and collect me like a parcel, Auntie. And we should not take Emily away from her studies. I will travel quite happily on my own. I did this when I came and I shall do so on my return.'

She relaxes, obviously relieved that I haven't resorted to making a fuss. I think she expected rebellion. 'Well then, dear, we must make plans. We must write to your father and tell him you will return . . . when, do you think?'

I look down at her with some affection. She is as round as a dumpling and her pretty face is lit by a grateful smile. She is so trusting. 'I think perhaps Friday, Auntie. No doubt there will be a morning train.'

'Good. Dear Victoria! I want you to come back here as soon as this terrible business is all over. And when I'm safely delivered of the next little Kilburn. In the meanwhile, I am sure your father and mother will be so very delighted to see you rosy and well.' She lifts up her embroidery to the light and admires a completed forget-me-not. 'Now then, dear, shall you break the news to Emily, or should I?'

Emily is sitting at the big desk in the schoolroom with a large book open in front of her, poring over a beautifully wrought drawing of the disposition of stars in the universe. She listens carefully to what I have to say, then explodes. 'So you're letting them make you run away? Away from me and that nice shoemaker with the beautiful manners. He saved you, and you saved him – from death, no less. The Chinese believe that if you save someone you are always responsible for them. Did you know that? And here you are leaving that awful Mrs Cotton in the lurch even though you've convinced me there is something all right about her? And worst of all, you're leaving *me* behind, not even letting *me* come with you to find out about London? I can't—'

I cut off the flood of words by the simple expedient of putting my fingers on her lips. Then I go back to the door to make sure it is shut tight. Then I put my face close to hers. 'I am not going!' I whisper loudly.

She leaps up. 'Not going, but you just said—'

'I will act as though I am going, but instead will take rooms in Bishop Auckland until this thing about Marian is settled in one way or another. And, as you say, I would never now wish to leave Aaron behind.'

Her eyes are shining. 'You're running away, going into hiding. Like King Charles from the Roundheads.'

'I am not going to hide up a tree!'

'They will come after you. They will!'

'I will write them letters to explain. Tell them it is only for a time. Until . . . until the matter is resolved.'

'D'you mean until after the trial? After they've . . . done with Mrs Cotton what they're going to do? And will I not even see you?'

She looks so earnest that I have to chuck her under her chin as though she's a very small child, not the oddly ageless, often quite grown-up creature she really is. 'Perhaps we could make an arrangement . . .'

She jumps up and clutches my hand. 'Secret assignations! How very wonderful.'

'You must keep it all a secret. Not blab to anyone.'

'I will. I will! I'll even put on a mournful aspect at your departure. I'll bawl in my bed because I am missing you and they will all be sorry for me.'

I shake her. 'No need to be so dramatic, Em. If you do that they're sure to think something's afoot. They are not stupid.'

I leave her peering at her book of the universe and make my way down to my uncle's study. He is working at his desk, his pen scraping over the paper.

'Victoria!' His smile is tired, his face lined and imprinted with worry. This is not the bluff country face that met me at the station when I first arrived. 'How are you, my dear?'

'I have been talking with Auntie Mary. It seems I am to leave on Friday.'

He nods. 'For the better, I think. Things are difficult here at the moment.'

I take a breath. 'The new exhumations?'

'You will know that we exhumed Nattrass? And now Cotton's other children, Frederick and Mrs Cotton's own very young one, Robbie.

They searched for Mr Cotton but were unable to find him. That graveyard is worse than a battlefield.' He puts one hand up through his hair and sighs audibly. 'Bad news, I'm afraid – or good news for those who are convinced of Mrs Cotton's guilt. The report is that there is evidence of arsenic in each one.' He does not look at me when he says this.

'So it's good news for you, Uncle William.'

Now his gaze is full on me. 'I take no joy in this, Victoria. I know you like the woman. At first I too thought these deaths were mere grisly routine. But it builds up.'

'What builds up? The evidence, or the pressure regarding the evidence?'

He picks up his pen again. 'Is that all, Victoria? I have this report to finish for the Board of Health. There are moves afoot to build a new drain at the bottom of Johnson Terrace. Not before time, in my view.'

I stand in the shadow, outside the arc of light from Uncle William's desk lamp, watching the top of his head, which stays stubbornly down over his notebook. I back out of the room and close the door behind me. One side of me recognises that my uncle's certainty regarding this new evidence should have shaken me. I should now be swayed as to Marian's guilt and should be joining the massed ranks of the accusers. But this does not happen. As I stand in the darkness of the hall it dawns on me that, innocent or guilty, there are two main players in this drama: Marian and my uncle. After these events neither of them will ever be the same again and one of them may not even survive.

Later, in my room, when I have done my face and laid a cloth to protect the pillow, as Marian has taught me, I lie down wide awake on my bed and think about friendship. In my time here I have discovered friendship and affection like the turning of a key. Turn one key and there is Marian on the train. Turn another key and there is my Uncle William in his study. Turn another and there is Auntie Mary at her cooking table. Turn another and there is Emily collapsing with laughter with me on my bed. Turn another and there is Aaron kneeling before me in his workshop. Turn another and there is bulbous, plain Miss McCullough, whose warm friendship, even on so short an acquaintance, is, I know, the key to the next stage of my life.

And I truly know that the turning of all these keys has depended entirely on the turning of that first key when I met Marian Cotton.

Fifty-Three

Having two bay windows and a kitchen as well as a scullery, Mr Quick-Manning's house on Johnson Terrace (rented very cheaply from the brewery), was rather grander than the other huddled dwellings on that particular street. Coming from a similar post in Carlisle, the excise officer had moved to West Auckland three years before when his brother – a bachelor – died and he thought he needed a fresh start. He settled quite well in his new job, and although he missed the pipe-smoking companionship of his brother, he was meticulous in his work at the brewery to the point of obsession, and the simplicity of his bachelor home life had never been a problem to him.

Before he met Marian Cotton, Quick-Manning had been going along quite nicely: working six days a week, buying simple provisions at Mr Riley's, eating each night in the Eden Arms, before going home to read *The Times* from cover to cover and enjoy a pipe before bed. Having enjoyed sound health for all of his sixty years, he had been floored when he was struck down with smallpox. He was pathetically grateful for the careful attention of Dr Chalmers and Dr Kilburn, and touched by the attention he received from the demure, attractive woman assigned to nurse him. From her he had to submit to intimate ministrations last enjoyed more than half a century ago at the tender hands of his mother.

Mrs Cotton had been restrained and not importunate. She had brought her own salves and potions to supplement the medicines of the doctors and, he felt, had brought him right back from the brink. It was when he was nearly better that the basic nature of their interaction changed. She would stroke his hair, press his hand, make him a special tea of her own

248

concoction. She would take off her apron and loosen the top buttons on her blouse so, as she leaned over the bed to pull the blankets to hospital correctness, he could see her full throat in the golden glow of the oil lamp. His head had whirled with the scent of her.

In the end, when he could bear it no longer, he had grasped her hand in his, touched her throat with the back of his hand. That was it. It was as though the plates on the earth's crust moved. From then she took to taking his hand in hers and allowing it to lie there, and kissing his brow on leaving.

When his recovery was fully endorsed by the doctor, Mrs Cotton helped him into his dressing gown and down the stairs, and settled him beside the blazing fire she had prepared. Then, when he was comfortable in his big chair, she eased herself on to his lap and allowed him to nuzzle that full round neck. From then, day by day, the level of their intimacy moved forward so that on the day when he was fully better and ready to go to work, they made love on his large couch and he almost cried with the relief of his pent-up feelings. After that event the intimate part of their relationship became routine. The end of the nursing did not mean the end of Mrs Cotton's visits to his house in Johnson Terrace.

Mr Quick-Manning lived an isolated life but was no fool. He did not imagine that Mrs Cotton had conceived an undying passion for him. After all, he was an old man, twenty years older than she was, and she was a striking woman, very fit for her age. He knew, though, that he had something to offer her. And she could offer him this physical solace on which he had become increasingly dependent. Her life previously had been difficult and oppressive, and he could offer her a glimpse of another life, more secure and genteel than she was used to, but to which he knew she aspired.

Not that he ever thought she was a taker. In fact she often turned down money that he offered her, saying such transactions were revolting to her. She was generous. He was very touched when she'd presented him with the silver watch as though to prove that she was not greedy. It was this that drove him to think that marriage was not out of the question, despite their difference in station. How excited and grateful had she been, when this was touched on. Even his devastation at the notion that she was with child had not quite blighted their plan to marry.

So when the dramatic events of these last months started to unfold, Mr Quick-Manning had at first been disbelieving, incredulous. The condemnations in the papers had been impossible to believe. It was when he finally saw the account in print in *The Times* that he began to accept it as fact. If it was in *The Times* it must be true. Now he had to contemplate the humiliating thought that he must be a very silly old man and she a very clever woman. He must have been mistaken in her. Wasn't she a fine deceiver and, by all appearances, had he not had a lucky escape? This was despite the fact that in the dark of the night he liked to imagine her as her old, apparently innocent self, ministering to his needs in her own particular way. This gave him some relief from the extreme tension of days now when he had to endure sidelong glances at the brewery, and the importunate jocular references by Mr Riley as he bought his daily loaf.

He had been troubled by his possession of the silver watch and was relieved when that oily, overeager solicitor's clerk had come to relieve him of it. He was pleased that he had summoned up the grace to ignore Smith's reference to his 'lucky escape'.

But when in this day's post had come a fat letter with a Durham postmark addressed in a looping, unfamiliar hand, he knew it must be from Marian Cotton. It seemed he was not going to escape so easily.

Deer Old Boy – How are you? I often think in my narrow sell. Forgive the prison paper and the tremblin Hand. I had thought to write love letters on Finer paper. I have not been too well lately and am weary of carrying this baby though I am sure it is well, takin its sustenance even while I Fail with all the pressures on me. The wee thing moves inside me to remind me of the Future. I hope you don't Believe the lies being Put about. You must know me beter than that.

Now then for all we did together and for the sake of this baby of ours I want a favor of you, mister. The baby is due about Christmas, and I will register it with your and my name Together. You can be sure of that. What I want you to do is this. You must go to Mrs Edwards on Johnson terrace. She is Barren and has been coming to me to get potions for it. All in vain, poor wench. She longs for a child. Go to her and tell her if the Worst comes she can have this Baby for her own. She must keep it safe. I have but one other Child of my own left in the world in the care of Mr Robinson of Sunderland and I'd like to think this Special one of yours and mine will see a Good life. Do this even though you won't do anything else for us.

I have told the Lawyer to talk to you so you can say as how I wouldn't do such Things as they are saying about me. But I don't trust these lawyers – not one of them. They all have death in there eyes. Like the police has Hell in theirs. Also dear Mr Quick-Manning will you kindly give the enclosed privately to Miss Victoria Kilburn. I could not send it Direct to her house for Clear Reasons. Do this, I ask you. Your old firend Marian Cotton.

Witnessed by Maria Douglas. Schoolmistress. Durham Gaol.

He looked at the two letters, the opened one Marian had written to him and the sealed one, addressed simply 'Victoria'. He threw his own letter on the fire and watched it burn. Then he tucked the other in his inside pocket and put on his hat and coat. The night air outside had a winter chill. He must take care of himself or he would come down with sickness again, and who would nurse him then?

He decided that he would make the effort to call on Mrs Edwards and her husband. He supposed the least he could do was to find carers for the child. He would offer the couple some money. That would deal with his own responsibility in this embarrassing matter and bring the whole affair to an end once and for all. And then he would make enquiries about another post. He would write to an old acquaintance in Carlisle who worked at the brewery there. It was time to get away from this place. No doubt about it.

Fifty-Four

I lean out of the train window to wave to the dramatically tearful Emily and the impassive Mrs Grey, whose figures are now melting into wreathing steam. Then I sit back in my seat until the brakes of the train creak, the wheels start to roll on the iron rails, and the train chugs on its journey. Luckily I have the first-class carriage to myself; my small luggage is in the rack, my boxes are in the guard's van. At last I can open the letter that has been burning a hole in my pocket.

After breakfast, Em, tears in her eyes, waylaid me in the passage, accusing me of telling tales of staying nearby just to allay her fears. 'Tell me it's not a trick!' she whispered.

'It's not a trick!' I assured her, even while I was wavering myself at the audacity of what I was planning.

Then, just half an hour ago, an old man, respectably dressed, puffed his way across the green when he saw Jonty loading the gig with all my luggage. Jonty was busy with his task and Emily was not yet out, having rushed back for her green mittens declaring it was 'just *too* cold'.

The man thrust the letter in my hand. 'Miss Kilburn? I think this is for you,' he gasped, and turned on his heel and fled.

My aunt, looking down from the upstairs drawing room, must have seen the exchange, but I didn't look upwards to see. I stuffed the letter into my muff and said something to Jonty about making sure the big box was the right way up. Then we were all aboard and I was waving to Auntie Mary as though nothing had happened.

I know this letter is not from Aaron, as these days I recognise his neat schoolboy script. And it can't be from Kit Dawson or he would have sent it more conventionally, straight to the house through the post. Peering closer, I recognise the writing from the list of herbs that Marian gave me. From this letter rises the smell of old clothes and carbolic soap, alien and eye-prickingly unpleasant. The smell of prison. My hands shake as I smooth the sheet out on my knee.

Deer Victoria

The spelling for your name is easy as it is the spelling for the Queen. And it is the name of a child I once had and lost. I trust you are Well and still taking the Stuff for your face. There is a herbalist on Tenter Street in Bishop who will sell you the ingredients when mine runs out.

I sit here at the Bottom of a deep well and there's no climbing out. Things happen very Fast but as well as this things go very slow in here, and where usually once I was able to order things in my Life there is no ordering here. The Women who guard me are not bad, considering the nature of their job. But I do as they say. It must be done.

I have seen lawyers about my case but they give me no Faith. They say I must say nothing on me own behalf. This makes no Sense to me but they have me so scairt that I am driven to obey. I have to try to move things along for myself but it is Hard, watched as I am Day and Night and with no voice to shout out for me. Mind you, the good woman who minds me today has let me write this to you and send it by Mr Quick-Manning and sees no harm in it. That's something. The good Lord has some mercy. There are plenty priests here who beg me to recant – that's what they say RECANT – they <u>Are Worried for my Eternal Soul!</u> I'm a bit more Worried for my Earthly Body at the minute to tell you the Truth. But like I say to them, how can I recant if there's nothing to recant? Sometimes I want to say the words to make them feel better. But telling that lie would be a sin. I know my Bible. The point of this letter, honey, is to tell you to get together with Mr Whitstable and to go to Sunderland for me to Ayres Quay, Pallion, and talk to Mr Robinson. He was a husband of mine and a real man, though fearful Mean with money. I was married to him one time and left a boy of mine with him for safekeeping. It was the right thing to do as me moving to plague-ridden places has meant the loss of all my other children. I have written to him to ask him to come here to See Me to let me see my own child and also to plead for me to the Powers and say I may be a lively Woman and have a quick mouth but I am Decent and would never hurt anyone. But there is silence coming back from him.

This is what you have to do for me Victoria. You and dear Aaron W must go to Sunderland and seek out James Robinson and persuade him to Speak for Me. Time is very short. They delay my trial till this child is born and that will be soon after Christmas. I dread to think what will happen then. I tell you honey I am drowning at the bottom of this well. Such Wickedness. I see they have even said I despatched my own mother and I loved no one better in this world. Had I my mother still I should not be seen here. But thank God she is I hope in Heaven. But you are decent, Victoria and I trust you to do this. Please give my best wishes to Aaron W. He wrote to me that he also had Trouble from the Beast in recent times. Write me when you have Talked to Robinson.

Cordially Your loving friend, Marian Cotton

I read the letter, close my eyes and lean my head against the headrest. My heart and body are full of feeling. All at once I smell the honey and almond smell that struck me the very first time I met Marian on this very train. I feel good and warm. I can feel Marian here with me in the compartment, as she was on that first day. What a strange, compelling feeling there was between us even then. I needed her help that day on the train and she gave it in her own way and with a whole new world attached. Now she has shown that she needs my help and, though I will do what I can, I know my powers fall far short of hers. I screw my eyes tight and try to conjure her up again, there in the carriage with me.

Then my eyes snap open and instead of seeing Marian with Charlie beside her, his velvet cap perched at an angle on his head, all I see is the empty seat, red plush gleaming.

At the railway station I deposit my case and boxes in Left Luggage and go in eager search of Aaron. His squint-eyed landlady keeps me at the door again and tells me with evident satisfaction that Mr Whitstable is no longer her lodger, that he is at his shop in Newgate Street. She adds that perhaps it would be better if he stopped writing to the papers and stuck to his last.

'I should have known. Cobblers are trouble,' she says sourly. 'Always were and always will be.'

The front shop, still smelling of women's perfume, is empty, although there are sounds of hammering from the workshop at the back. I go and stand in the doorway. There he is. His leathers are hanging on the far wall. Shelves on the side wall buckle under battered cardboard boxes, the familiar tools and the serried ranks of the custom-made lasts he has made for his special customers. His books sit on a newly built shelf. His long table is set under a long low window that looks down the garden. Through the windows I can see the trees, stripped of their leaves, spread clear and black against the dense white of the winter sky.

He is there, cutting away at the sole of a long leather boot. His hair falls on his face as he leans over his task, his sharp knife almost an extension of his hand. How I wish I could draw. Then I could express his sense of complete, almost religious devotion to the task in hand.

'Aaron.' I say it softly, not wanting to disturb him.

He swings round, a smile spreading across his serious face. 'Victoria!' He stands up. On his brow I can see the deep scar, so expertly sewn up by my uncle. There is no bandage. 'What a surprise.' He takes my muff and drags a chair to the orbit of the fire that flickers in the iron range. 'Sit down here and warm yourself. Cold, it is, outside. There was flower-frost inside the windows when I started work this early morning.'

I sit down and look carefully into each corner of the room. 'So you've brought all your work things from West Auckland?'

'Aye. What stuff was untouched by the marauders. I have closed up entirely down there. Don't care if I'm never there again. So I am started here. I've written to my big customers to tell them where I am and three of them have called on me already.'

'Started again, so soon!' Through Aaron I'm now learning how much what a person *does* may be bound up with what he *is*. My father's work in the City of London has little to do with who he *is*. *The Times*, his friends at his club, those things signify who he *is*, but his work does not define him.

'Well?' Aaron is smiling at me and I realise I must have been staring. 'Have I got a smut on my face?'

'But what about the shop itself?' I say hurriedly.

'Ah. That'll take a while longer to set up. It will need stocking and organising. I'll have to take on a retail journeyman of some sort to make a start on that. In the meantime the shoes and boots are my daily bread.'

He pulls a chair up beside me and puts his hand over mine. 'So, Miss Victoria, what brings you into Bishop Auckland on this wild and stormy day?'

I breathe slowly to cool down the heat that is flaming my cheeks. Still, I leave my hand where it is. I like the reassuring feeling of the pressure of his palm. It is a thing I wish to become accustomed to. 'I was supposed to be getting the next train to London to go back to my parents. There's so much fuss about these events to do with Marian, even in the London papers. Now they all believe this package of lies.'

He sags in his chair. 'They're terrible indictments, Victoria. They list children, even adults. All now dead.'

I snatch away my hand. 'Don't say that even you believe these lies? Don't we know her? Would she do all that?'

He grabs my hand and does the most extraordinary thing. He turns it palm up and kisses it, making some energy stir, very deep inside me. He holds on to my hand tightly so I can't wrest it away. 'I do think we know her, Victoria. I do think all this is wrong. Haven't I written to the newspapers, complaining of the prejudicial material they're printing, before Marian is even at trial? Haven't I talked to the clerk to the court here? But it's like blowing against a prevailing wind, believe me. Even people I thought quite reasonable will not look at this thing clearly. They keep muttering about smoke and fire.'

'We must do something. She has written this letter to me.' I extract my hand from his, reach across to my muff and produce the letter. 'She's thought of a way we might be able to help her. At least we must try to do this for her.'

He pulls out his glasses, perches them on the end of his nose and reads the letter carefully. Then he sighs. 'Poor old girl. If anything would convince you she believes she is wronged, this would.'

'Then we must go and find this Mr Robinson and convince him to speak on her behalf.'

'Would he do this, though? He talked to the newspaper. I read the account of his involvement with her. He says she stole money from him. And she left him with an abandoned child.'

It all sounds so bad. 'Well, she says there that Mr Robinson is a mean man. Perhaps they had . . . er . . . different feelings about money. Or if he were keeping her short of money, being an intelligent and forceful woman, she would work out a way to get round that . . .' I waver. I am really not quite certain of what I am trying to say. 'But even so, taking money is not at all like deliberately taking a life.'

'And what about this child who she's supposed to have left behind with him, like a forgotten parcel?'

'Well, the child was lucky. At least he's still there, not like Charlie and the others. She thinks it must be healthier in Sunderland than in West Auckland. Perhaps the sea air,' I venture hopefully.

'Her enemies would say that it is healthier away from Marian.'

'Those enemies don't know her as you and I do.'

'But the people who are quoted in the reports knew her. They lived close by her.'

'Ah, but they are reflecting on her now, when they are in the spotlight. They have heard these scandalous lies about Charlie and Robbie and Mr Nattrass. If Marian were so bad when she lived close to them, why didn't they report her to the police? They may not have liked her, that's for sure – even loathed her. We've seen that in West Auckland, haven't we? A person either likes Marian a lot or dislikes her intensely. And if, as in the case of Mr Riley, you first like her then come to loathe her, woe betide you! He has pursued her like one of the three Furies. If anyone is the architect of this disaster he is the one.'

Aaron sits up straight again. 'You remind me of my principles, Miss Victoria. That bang on the head must have banged a few of them out of me.' He tucks away his spectacles. 'Now then. When do we go to Sunderland to see this Robinson? We'll go together.'

Now I have to tell him the tale about me not going to London. In effect, running away. He listens without comment.

'What now then, Victoria?'

'Well, first I have to find somewhere to live and must write letters both to my aunt and uncle to tell them what I have done. And, of course, that I am safe and have not been stolen away by ravening wolves.'

He looks at the door of the kitchen, and at the ceiling. 'We-ell,' he says uncertainly, a spot of colour on each cheek, 'there are rooms aplenty here . . .'

I have to laugh at his discomfiture. 'No, no!' I say. 'That would not be the thing. You know that and I know that.'

He relaxes. 'Perhaps Mrs McGurk on Princes Street would rent you my old rooms.'

I thought of the malevolent half-straight gaze of the little woman. 'I have no money, so that is out of the question. I have an idea about finding work. I have been offered a post.'

'You? Work?'

'Well, things change. I could barely walk straight six months ago, and I had a face like dried porridge. Now I walk straight and my face . . . well . . .' I turn my face towards him. 'What do you think?' I am willing him to touch me.

He runs a finger down my cheek. 'Peaches and cream,' he says softly.

I shake my face free of his hand. 'Well, now I have discovered that I may be able to earn money through my labour. Such revolutions.' I tell him about Miss McCullough's amazing offer. 'I only know her through the choir, but we took to each other from the first moment. She said I would have a room and a wage and would be teaching the girls their manners, drying their tears and all that kind of thing.'

'That's it? You'll be a school matron? But you told me you'd never been to school. What do you know about schools?'

'I can't think there's much that one should worry about. Miss McCullough seemed to think I could do it. Anyway, it is a respectable lodging, and will do while I think what I can do for Marian.'

He kneels down before me and kisses my cheek. 'What *we* can do for her. We'll do this together. Now! I have waited too long. May I kiss you properly, Miss Victoria?'

It is fortunate that later in the day when I call at Wear View Miss McCullough is at home. A young maid in a white frilled apron leads me straight up the winding staircase to the first-floor sitting room. Miss McCullough listens gravely to my stammering explanation for running away from my kindly aunt and saintly uncle, and my keenness to take up her kind offer of the post as assistant matron. I am sensible enough not to mention the name of Marian Cotton; just say that I wanted more independence in my life.

'Independence!' She relishes the word. 'I did something similar myself, Miss Kilburn, at the even tenderer age of sixteen. I ran away and made my own life with my sister, and I have never regretted it.'

We sit in silence for a second. Perhaps she will shoo me away for being so importunate. I hold my breath.

'Well,' she says finally, 'this is rather swifter than I had hoped, but why not? I took to you from the first and trust my own judgement. I have worked with young women now for fifteen years and I have never been wrong. Not once.'

I sigh my relief. 'You can be sure that I will do my best—'

'Now!' she interrupts. 'We must keep things right. You must write to your uncle and your father on our school notepaper, saying you are taking up the post of assistant matron. I will write also, securing the bona fides of your new situation. Now if we write our letters straight away we can go off in the gig to get your luggage at the station and drop these letters off at the post office on the way. Your uncle will receive your letter in the four o'clock post today, so he won't think you've jumped off the train at Crewe.' She paused. 'And your father – is he expecting you off a certain train?'

'Well . . .'

'We can send him a telegraph wire so he will know you are not to arrive then, and must expect a letter.'

My admiration for Miss McCullough grows by the minute. But even as I agree with her suggestions I know I must be careful with her. Being taken under her wing could work out to be a feathery kind of prison.

'There is just one thing, Miss McCullough. It's really important.'

The energy and delight in her demeanour fades a little. 'And what would that be?' she says quietly.

'I have some errands I must do, Miss McCullough. Private matters, which will, unfortunately, take up some time in the next month or so. For instance, tomorrow I must go to Sunderland for two days on a particular errand. Then I will return and afterwards there may be other days when I have such errands. I assure you that this is just at the very beginning. Perhaps I should take up the post in a month's time . . .' I pause for a second under her unrelenting gaze. 'These are matters to attend to regarding my independence . . . well, my *independent* judgement on a certain matter.' I play my last card.

She gives a tiny nod. 'It is better that you are here. Apart from the days when you are on these . . . errands . . . you may go out after lunch and should be back for tea at four. It may be possible that by arrangement you could be back at the house by seven p.m. We have formal dinner then, and the doors are locked. You would be expected to supervise the young ladies then, play cards with them, perhaps charades. Supervise their sewing. I have to tell you, my dear, I have been fulfilling this role in the last two weeks and, to be honest, it is unutterably boring.' She leans over and pulls the bell by the fireplace. 'There, that's it then. Now we shall have tea.'

I smile at her frankness and want to blurt out the whole truth to her. But I hold back, fearing that she might throw me out on my ear before I manage to embark on the next part of my mission for Marian.

Fifty-Five

As the cab from the station makes its way through the streets of Sunderland towards Pallion, the strings of tall well-built houses and glimpses of green remind me of Stoke Newington. Then as we draw nearer to the docks the streets become narrower, the houses are lower and more packed together, and the air over everything is dark and sulphurous. The river begins to loop towards us on our right and we begin to squeeze past warehouses the size of palaces, and cranes clustered together like long-legged birds. At last we come down the street towards Ayres Quay, its work suspended in rustling and creaking silence on this Saturday afternoon. At the bottom of the cut created by two narrow rows of houses we glimpse a looming slice of a great ship under construction, its prow higher than the tallest house.

We make our way to Rosannah Street where Mr Robinson, alerted by Aaron's note, is waiting for us. He's a tall, well-set-up man, good-looking in a certain way, with an abundance of crinkly fair hair that he keeps under control with some kind of gleaming pomade. His house is bigger than the others in the mean street, its interior clean and well appointed. A brass-faced grandfather clock ticks away in the corner and a dresser in an alcove groans under the weight of fine china.

Mr Robinson makes no pretence of entertaining us. There are no cups of tea or glasses of port.

'This is quite a business,' he says, gesturing us to sit down. He stands with his back to the parlour fire, rocking on his heels and occasionally lifting the back of his jacket to facilitate a draught of heat. 'Quite a business. A bit of a surprise for me, like. I was putting it all behind me, that business with Marian.'

'You were surprised?' I say quickly. 'Is it hard to believe? What they say of her?'

'Well, she was a bit of a scoundrel, I knew that. Without conscience in a certain way. But I was surprised when I read all that stuff. The grim reaper certainly followed the lass around, didn't he?'

'So how did you know her, Mr Robinson?' says Aaron.

'Well, my own wife, Hanna, died, leaving me with five little'ns. I advertised for a housekeeper and along came Marian. A bit afore Christmas that was. Then right away my lad John fell ill and went to his Maker. Joined his poor ma, if you like. But Marian was barely into the house then.'

'So how did you find her, mister? What kind of person, what was she like?' asks Aaron.

'Well,' he says slowly, 'she was lively, bonny. Had a bit about her. Outspoken. I liked that brightness but, to tell you the truth, that didn't suit me sisters. They did have a bit of a say about the way things changed round here, as they'd been caring for the bairns after Hanna died. No, their noses were put out when she came. But me and Marian settled in nicely. She had a touch about the place.' He nods towards the china. 'Could never resist a bit of nice china. Then one time she went off to see her sick mother in Seaham and came back with some linen and bits and pieces when the old woman died. Marian was real cut up about her mother going like that. Wept on my shoulder. But now I see from the papers she killed her own mother—'

'That's not true,' I say angrily.

'Victoria!' warns Aaron. He turns to the shipwright. 'Marian seems to have made a good impression on you, sir.'

Mr Robinson moves a step forward from the hot fire. 'To tell you the truth, she was like a breath of fresh air. Anyway, as well as the linen, she brought back her own daughter from Seaham, little Isabella that had been staying with the mother. But Marian started to say the air in Sunderland was bad and before long we lost my own little James and Elizabeth, as well as her young Isabella in a single month. Marian was heartbroken herself but sustained me in me own misery at the loss of me own two children. Marian went down with the fever herself but just picked herself off the ground. It's like she got better by an act of will.

She always seemed a very strong woman. Hard as iron at the centre. To be frank, that's what appealed to me about her.'

'You didn't suspect anything? Losing those young ones seemed a normal tragedy to you?' My head is whirling, trying to add up all these deaths.

He shakes his head. 'Unthinkable. And, anyway, lots of families in these streets lose one, two, even four bairns. These diseases spread like wild fire.' He pauses. 'Like I said, me sisters couldn't stand her. But I didn't care what they thought. Then afterwards, after all this business broke, you begin to add things up differently, don't you? They've been on to me about her now, all right. How they were right in the first place.'

'But you were loyal then? When you were with her?' Aaron prompts him. 'Despite your sisters?'

'Aye. We had a bairn of our own, Mary Isabella. Marian was pleased, and wanted me to be pleased. She said it would make up for the others. But then that bairn went to her Maker only days old. Marian was so cut up.' He takes out a handkerchief and wipes his brow. 'It was all too much. Marian wanted to leave me. Took up a job at the infirmary for a bit. For a change, she said. I think they liked her up at that infirmary. But she came back after a time.'

'So what was the problem between you?'

'Marian liked money. She liked nice things. China. Clothes. She bought cloth and made real nice things to wear for herself and the bairns. She loved ornaments.' He glances round the room. 'Some of them are still here. She'd pay people to clean and wash for her, like, so that took a bit of money. Liked to live the life of a lady. I used to have her on about it.

'But things got bad. She'd been through my savings behind my back and got me into debt, dirtied my reputation. I couldn't have that. My sisters were livid. I was livid. I wanted her out then. It was hard, like. By this time we had another bairn between us, a lad, as well as my own last two.'

'But,' says Aaron slowly, 'you wanted her out because of the money, not because of the children dying?'

Robinson shakes his head. 'That didn't occur to me. I was stompin' mad about the money when I found out. So when that police sergeant a month or so back came asking his questions and sayin' my children here should be dug up I was put out, I can tell you. He asked me about insurance and I remembered Marian had tried to get me insured but I wouldn't agree to that.' He pauses. 'No special reason. Waste of money, in my view. Then I got to thinking that mebbe they were right about her. My sisters are right hot on it now, saying if I'd insured myself I'd have been in Bishopwearmouth Cemetery alongside Hanna and me own children.'

I have to push him. 'But you didn't think so at the time?'

He shakes his head slowly. 'It seemed then she was too lively for such a thing. And she was really bad with grief when the bairns died. You had to be here to see it.'

I take the letter out of my muff. 'Mr Robinson, I have a letter here from Marian asking me to beg you to go to the prison to see her. To take her son to see her, for what might be the last time. She asks for you to speak up for her at her trial, to tell them that in spite of the tragedies in her life she is not the kind of bad person they are portraying. You could—'

He is already shaking his head. 'I could never do that, hinney. Whatever she has or hasn't done, she's caused deep grief in my life. My sisters, my neighbours, they'd feel betrayed, they'd tar me with the same brush. I'll keep my son away from her and that place, never mind what she says.'

I am impelled to push further. 'Then you're telling me that you do think she killed your children?'

He shakes his head again. 'Of that I'm not sure. But the trial will show if she did, won't it? Truth will out. The courts know what to do about these things, don't they?'

'Would you not just take her son to see her for one single time?'

'No. That least of all.'

After that there is nothing to say and he shows us out of his parlour into the narrow hallway. Standing in a doorway that must lead to a back place – a kitchen perhaps – I catch sight of a child of five or six, britched like a boy although, with his full head of dark curly hair, and his pale skin, one might take him for a girl. My downward glance fixes on him as his brilliant eyes – so familiar to me – pierce mine, before a female hand pulls him back into the kitchen.

Robinson meets my gaze. 'Aye. That's her bairn. A fine lad – and clever too – that'll not be blighted by his inheritance, if it's anything to do with me. She left him, you know. Abandoned him with a neighbour after she left me. Whatever else she may be, she is a woman of no conscience.'

Robinson, though genuinely puzzled by our quest, is genial enough. He tells us where to find the tram that will get us to the hospital, and gives us the name of a man for whom Marian worked after she left Pallion. 'She always liked to work outside the house, did Marian, never cared much for sticking at home.'

He kept track of her. I wonder whether this was through fondness or fear that she would take the boy away from him. There is no doubt that he is fond of the boy.

At the hospital a heavy-set gatekeeper guides us to a ward where Marian once worked. The ward sister puts us in a small room with two nurses who worked with her and are eager to talk. These two are like Jack Sprat and his wife: the younger one thin as a rake, the other built like a ship in full sail. They tell us Mrs Marian Robinson was a good worker, with lots of energy. That she was 'nipping clean'. She cared for the patients, and often stayed longer than her shift when a patient needed it. She was good on night shift, where she wasn't averse to making a long night go quickly with her tales of her times down south, where she had seen many a strange sight. And she could tell the cards, though – the thin woman glances cautiously at the half-open door – of course, that was forbidden and could only be done in the lost hours in the middle of the night. She gives a wolfish grin. 'We paid her to tell our fate. Mebbe she couldn't tell her own.'

'Still, it did pass the time on a long shift,' says the other nurse, whose two chins are held in check by her starched ribbons. 'Mrs Robinson was strong meat, I could see that. Sure of her ground, like, and confident. Not everyone here liked that. She wasn't even half-trained, after all. But see her with them patients and you could tell she had the feeling! Me, I've been nursing for twenty years and I know it, I can tell that look. Folks got better round her whatever the doctors could or couldn't do.'

'But she left?'

'Aye. She took on this feller next death's door and brought him round. Then she went off with him. Married him, I believe. Keen for a treat. But then I heard he died. She did have bad luck.'

'And it goes on,' says the thin nurse. 'Think of all this stuff in the papers.'

265

The other nurse nods her head, her chins wobbling. 'It's just, we two have talked together and we don't see it, her snuffing folks out. It goes against . . . well, what we saw, what we knew.'

'Can you write?' says Aaron suddenly.

'Aye. Not everyone here can, but me, I know writing and reading.'

I catch Aaron's thought. 'You should write to the court and tell them what you said of her. There is no one to speak for her.'

The woman frowns. 'Where would we send a letter?'

I close my eyes. 'Address it to the magistrates' court at Bishop Auckland. Someone there should know who to give it to.'

The thin nurse looks hard at us suddenly, from one to the other. 'And what's here for you? Why do you come and plead her case? You're an unlikely pair.' She nods at me. 'I'd think you'd be too grand to be bothered about such as Marian Robinson.' She turns to Aaron. 'And you, what are you?'

'I'm a shoemaker. Miss Kilburn here and me are friends with Marian. We want to help.'

'It's like a ball rolling downhill,' I add, not very helpfully.

'So no one can stop it?' says the thin nurse.

'That's not what I mean. I mean we must—'

'Kilburn!' says the fat nurse. 'I knew I knew it from somewhere.'

'In the paper,' says her colleague.

'It's the doctor what dealt with this case.' Victoriously said.

'My uncle,' I say lamely.

'Doctors!' says the thin nurse. 'Robinson loved doctors. They liked her too.'

The chair creaks as the fat nurse stirs in it. 'You want to go and see the nurses at Smyrna House – that's a kind of hospital for fallen women. She worked there. And go and see Mr Backhouse, the Quaker gentleman. Lives in a big house called Ashburne out on the Stockton Road. Robinson – that is, Mrs Cotton now – worked there for him after that poor fellow died – the one she got married to that had been the patient. This Mr Backhouse liked her, gave her presents. I saw her one Saturday night at Coggan's Music Hall. She told me about him, what a good old boy he was. A Quaker gentleman. Like I say, he gave her presents.'

Later, walking by the busy main road back into the town to find some lodgings, we examine the picture of our friend Marian that is unfolding

266

before us. We know there were three husbands before Mr Cotton, and that she seemed always on the move. This, of course, is at the core of the lurid newspaper accounts. Moving about seems to be a very suspicious thing to do. (It *is* odd for a wife to outlive her husbands. So often it is the other way round, like that farmer my uncle was called out to.) But then hearing Robinson and the nurses talk quite warmly of her as a person known to them lessens even further thought that the accusations are just. Instead I have this growing impression of monstrous coincidence, as though indeed the Furies are after her, and Mr Riley is only one of them.

We stop at the post office in the big main street and write a note to Mr Backhouse. It is not difficult to find where he lives, as Mr Backhouse is known in the town, and to the man in the post office. In the letter we say that we are friends of Mrs Cotton, formerly Robinson. We will call on him at eleven in the morning and take the chance that he will be in and would like to discuss matters to Mrs Cotton's advantage.

The man in the post office gives us some addresses of respectable hotels and lodging houses and we come out on to the big wide street, which is abustle with crowds from all walks of life, from the sailor to the milkmaid, the lady to the beggar. I stop Aaron then and there, and present him with my sapphire and pearl brooch.

'What's this?' he says, frowning.

'There is the matter of money, Aaron, and the fact that I have none. I cannot take money from Miss McCullough for these days I can't work. I want you to pledge this for me and obtain what money you can for it.'

He tries to thrust the brooch back at me but I resist. 'I have money enough for both of us on this adventure,' he growls.

'That's not good enough,' I say firmly.

'I know. How terrible! The charity of a cobbler!' He sighs and puts the brooch deep into the pocket of his heavy coat.

I know we must look an odd couple, me every inch my father's daughter and he most clearly an artisan in his Sunday best. But it seems not to matter here. Even though a variety of people walk this street they all walk their own distinct pathways and see little of the people around them – the very opposite of the bear-pit that is village life.

'Now!' I command. 'Go now to pledge it! There must be such a place here. This must be the street with everything.'

He looks around. 'Will you wait?'

I look into the window of the draper's shop outside which we are standing. 'I will go in here and spend an interminable time choosing a bolster case, by which time you will be back.'

In fact I find a hundred faults with the bolster cases presented to me and come out half an hour later with none, which is very convenient, as, indeed, I have no money.

Aaron is waiting outside and my heart lurches at the sight of him through the etched glass of the double doors. This adventure is all about Marian, but I know it will bind us together in a way few people have ever been bound together. And I am glad of it. My concern for Marian is somehow dissolving into my passion for Aaron.

His face lights up when he sees me. He looks me up and down. 'What? No bolster?' he grins.

'Too expensive,' I say, 'being more than one and threepence.'

'Well, now.' He pushes a carpetbag into my hand. 'You are a rich woman. The money is in there, and other things that a kind woman in a shop told me a young lady would need to stay overnight. You can't arrive at a hotel with a reticule. They would turn you away.'

I blush at the thought of the contents of the bag. I thought this errand might take more than a day but have not gone so far as to provide for it. I am unused to such adventures.

'Did the brooch raise a good amount?' I ask, relieving him of the bag.

'The man was more than generous. Twelve guineas. Said the sapphires were good.'

I accept this, although I have no idea in the world of the value of the brooch, a present from my father on his return from a pleasure trip to the Paris Exhibition of 1867. He gave us all brooches, although my sister Lottie got a necklace and a small tiara as well.

'Now,' I say brightly, rescuing myself from the moment. 'Where shall we stay?'

'*We* will stay nowhere, Miss Victoria. You will stay at the Excelsior Hotel. A very respectable hotel, according to the lady in the dress shop. And I will stay at Mr Sneddon's Boarding House for Men, which is round the corner. We will meet after breakfast and go to see Mr Backhouse. The lady in the shop said it was only a short walk down the Stockton Road. Then after that we will get the afternoon train back to

Bishop Auckland. No doubt your Miss McCullough will be waiting for you in her schoolgirls' eyrie.'

I stare at him very hard. I have to admit to some secret thoughts about what would happen between us here. It crossed my mind that it would still be virtuous to dine together and talk into the night before retiring (reluctantly, I thought . . .) to our separate bedrooms. But then no respectable hotel-keeper would tolerate that. Then I had the fugitive thought that it might be nice to get a less respectable hotel-keeper, who would be complaisant about this.

I had not contemplated separate hotels.

He is holding out his arm. 'Well, Miss Victoria, shall we go?'

I take his arm and pinch it as we walk along. 'You are infuriating, really horrible.'

He grins and puts his other hand on mine, where it is lying on his forearm. 'We're breaking enough rules as it is, Miss Victoria. Today we are on a mission for Marian. There is time enough for breaking those rules that just encompass you and me.'

We stroll along. 'One thing!'

'What's that?'

'The next time you call me "Miss Victoria", with that glint in your eye, I will swing up this bag and hit you so hard you'll be scarred on both sides of your head.' Where does this come from? In my very joking and coquetry I feel that Marian is here not just beside me but somewhere inside my head, speaking through my mouth. She is all around me even in this strange place.

Fifty-Six

'Seems as though they'll try you at the February assizes.' Miss Douglas sat down and took out her knitting from a linen bag she carried over her shoulder. She rooted round the bottom of the bag and emerged with a needle, threaded through a strip of flannel, and a small, half-made child's silk cap.

Marian took this up eagerly, shaking it down, smoothing out the creases and holding it up to catch the light from the narrow prison window. 'This'll make a nice little cap for the baby. I'll need a bit of pink lace to trim it.'

'You're sure it will be a girl?'

'Sure of it, the way I'm carrying it. Anyway, she speaks to us, you know. So I know it's a girl.' She pleated the edge of the cap with her fingers. 'I tell you what, Miss Douglas, I could have done with this work to keep me busy through the night. The nights in here are so long. I'm not one for such things but the long nights make even me turn to thinking and regretting.'

Miss Douglas shook her head. 'You know the rules, Mrs Cotton. No sharp implements.'

'They think I'll do away with myself, don't they? Save them the bother?'

'It's a rule for the whole prison, Mrs Cotton. Not just you. No sharp implements.'

'Well, they've no fear of me getting rid of myself as I've nothing on my conscience and I know that one way or the other the court'll recognise that. Truth will out.'

'Like I say, it's February, your committal date.'

'Well, this baby'll be born some time after Christmas and they say I'm to have her and wean her, so you're right. That takes us to February for the committal. It'll be good to have the baby by me then. Then they'll see what a good mother I am in spite of what they say. She won't be weaned then. That should take till March.' She paused. 'Then, if things go ill, they'll take her off me.' She bit off some silk thread with her fine teeth and held the needle up to the light to thread it. 'That being the case, I've got someone to take her on, like. There is a couple I know that can't have a bairn. I thought I'd make them happy if only for a while. I've had it fixed up by Mr Quick-Manning, who's the father.' She nodded at an opened envelope on the table. 'There, Miss Douglas. You see for yourself how the father of this baby tells us of his fine arrangements. The governor knows, 'cause he's already read my letter.'

Miss Douglas put down her knitting and picked up the envelope. There was no address.

Mr Quick-Manning would beg you to inform Mrs Cotton of arrangements for her child to be placed with Mr & Mrs Edwards with financial arrangements set in place.
    Signed Quick-Manning

Marian completed the last bit of satin stitch on an embroidered rose on the cap's brim and bit off the silk thread. 'White on white. Then a bit of pink lace. I always liked that. Refined. I first saw it in a house I worked in, in Sunderland,' she said. 'Aye, Miss Douglas, what kind of note is that? Not so much as a God-bless-you-how-are-you-Marian-how-kind-you-were-to-me.'

Miss Douglas stared at her. 'But at least it's a decent home for the child,' she suggested. 'That's something.'

'At least that. Only for the time being like. This little one will be there for us to collect when all this is over.'

Miss Douglas shook her head slightly and took up her knitting needles. 'Did you hear from your lawyers?'

'I did not. I had a letter from Mr Lowery saying my goods had been collected. So the case is that fellow Mr Smith has all my stuff and must be selling it. But I've not heard nothing from him, nor his lord and master.'

271

'But you have other letters, I see.' Miss Douglas nodded at the neat pile on the table.

'Well, Lowery wrote, like I said. And there's one from my friend Miss Victoria Kilburn. Perhaps you remember you signed up the letter I sent to her? I told you about her. She has the same name as my first child. Both named for the Queen. Young Victoria walked like a cripple till I showed her to a good friend of mine. A shoemaker. Those two were made for each other. A real love job. And she wouldn't have seen it were it not for me. There's satisfaction in that. Anyway, she's walkin' well now and looking good. Passion. The flies in the sugar, hey?' She chuckled openly for a second, making Miss Douglas put down her crochet hook and stare at her. She had noticed more than once that Mrs Cotton liked to order things. She obviously took satisfaction in the happiness of her young friends whom she had brought together, as she had at the thought of the Edwardses with a child to care for at last. The woman had a radical effect on everyone who came in touch with her. It seems that she made grown men weak at the knees and made some women hate her. Miss Douglas herself had felt invigorated by her presence even in this place, and came to look forward to her shift when she was on duty with the notorious prisoner. At night in the staff dormitory she prayed on her knees for her: that, guilty or innocent, she should obtain mercy.

Marian caught her gaze but went on, 'Seems those two lovebirds went out to Sunderland for me to see that old husband of mine, but he's not biting. But they have got some other women I worked with to write to the court. And today they are going to see a fellow I worked for to ask him as well to plead on my behalf. He wasn't a bad old fellow. Mr Backhouse. P'raps we'll get a bite there.'

'Those two do seem to be your very good friends,' said Miss Douglas. She knitted her way to the end of a row. 'Is there *really* nothing, Mrs Cotton, that you regret?'

Marian looked at the door. 'Is the chaplain on his way? Do we have to talk about regrets now?'

Miss Douglas shook her head. 'It's just that you talk with such energy about your life. About what you have done, the people you have known. Like it was a great adventure.'

'You're only here once.' Marian rethreaded her needle with the white satin thread. 'To tell the truth, it was no big adventure. It was often nothing but pain. Being cast down and scrambling to your feet again. I had good times in those early days, with my first husband down in Bristol. A rare, special man, he was, and we were both young. But no luck seemed to stick to us there. He lost work and we lost some bairns between us.' She frowned. 'Three, I think. I did most of my crying then, and perhaps later when that house of Robinson's seemed cursed. I felt that God scowled at me in those days. Then one morning I woke up and knew I had to accept whatever He sent to me. It was like God had spoke to me in the night. After that there were few tears. I always tried to take precautions after that. I got my loved ones insured so they weren't buried like paupers. But they're holding even that against me now. Can't do right for doing wrong.'

'But your marriage with Mr Robinson, you say that was a good one . . .'

'I was a fool! You talk of regrets? I have a real regret there. He was a fine man, James. Good-looking, strong. I tried to make things nice for him. The house, the food. I made nice clothes for myself and all the bairns. I made his shirts with the best cloth from the market. But the money seemed to run away from me. That didn't matter, as James was a prudent man. He had savings. But I didn't tell him about what I was spending and all his money slid away. And there were deaths. Then there was no money left and James had the most towering, cold rage on him. That was him and me finished, even though I liked him most of any man I've known. Perhaps even better than Mowbray, my first true love that I went to Bristol with.' She executed three tiny parallel stitches and looked closely at her work. 'Robinson put locks on the door so I couldn't get back in.'

'But they say you left a child with him? The last survivor?'

Marian shook her head. 'Not quite. I left *him* with an acquaintance while I went off working. I promised her money. But then I couldn't get back to get him, as circumstances were, so she took him through to James Robinson. And once the bairn was in that house, there was no getting him. I've often wondered about him. His smile and that.'

'It all sounds so logical when you say it, Mrs Cotton.' Miss Douglas, whose most passionate moment was her regret when her only sister married and went to Australia, sighed.

'Aye, it might be logical to me and you, but those beasts out there see

273

no logic in it. And when I think about it – my life – it has had its bright bits, but believe me, Miss Douglas, it was no fancy adventure.'

Miss Douglas, who had spent many hours with Mrs Cotton in the months of her imprisonment, detected for the first time a thread of regret in her prisoner's voice. But it was not by any means the regret which the chaplains plagued her for, a repentance for the ghastly sin of murder. Rather it was a distilled rage against a life where even a person of her undoubted powers was no match for a malevolent fate. And Miss Douglas, brought up in a strict nonconformist tradition, which viewed one's fate as ordained, now found herself in profound sympathy with Mrs Cotton. This was so whether or not the woman was guilty of the terrible thing of which she was accused.

Fifty-Seven

I managed to get a letter off last night to Marian, using the good offices of an elderly bell boy at the hotel. He raised his eyebrows at the prison address, pocketed the penny, and gave me a fine salute before racing off to the post office. I imagined Marian's sturdy satisfaction at her wishes being carried out in this way. And the fact that I'd had to run away from home to do it, and had only accomplished it in the close, unsuitable company of a working man, signified the radical effect Marian had on everyone who came in touch with her. There were no half-measures with her; I know now that this was why, wrongly perceived, she could draw hatred like a magnet.

Despite the strange bed and the dingy surroundings of the small hotel, I slept well. I did have a dream about being stuck with Marian in the folds of a cliff while the tide surged on and up around us. I woke up from this dream and identified its location as near Falmouth in Cornwall where my family took their holidays. It was the spot where I once sobbed my heart out when Lottie and Pixie and Rollo left me at the top of a cliff in my Bath chair while they went exploring. Here in Sunderland I drag myself out of the nightmare and sit up. Though still very much alive, Marian is haunting me, awake and asleep.

At nine o'clock, as we arranged, Aaron is loitering at the entrance to the hotel. He beams at the sight of me and he sweeps off his hat with a flourish. 'Miss Victoria! How fine you look on this very fine morning!'

He pulls my arm through his as we walk along the Stockton Road and we draw glances, perhaps because we are a fine, distinguished couple. Or perhaps because I am lame. Or perhaps there is something entirely unsuitable about us: we are somehow an unmatched pair. But I care about none of this. I love him. We love each other. And despite the seriousness of our errand, I relish spending this time with him.

When we find the house, we are obliged to go through fine wrought-iron gates and up a long sweeping drive and make our way round a huge ash tree before we reach Mr Backhouse's wide black-painted door. I pull the knob and we can hear the doorbell clang right through the house.

The butler looks rather askance at Aaron but tells us Mr Backhouse is expecting us. He leads us into a wide hall with bright tiles and a skylight that floods the floor with winter light. The newel post of the carved black staircase has a cast-iron sea nymph holding a lamp aloft. The staircase winds up to a landing lined with mirrors and, as far as I can see, paintings of ships in full sail. The hall where we stand has only one set of furniture: a round polished table graced by a silver letter tray and four matching chairs set against the dark walls.

Mr Backhouse, a tall, heavy man dressed in black, with a fringe of silver hair and a very distinctive nose, ambles in. He has a patrician manner, obviously used to being in charge of those around him. He does not indicate that we should sit or relax, but stands before us as we explain our errand, looking from one to the other as though he can see our story in our faces as well as hear it with his ears.

'I have read of the case,' he says abruptly. 'Of course I knew her as Mrs Robinson. Found her a fine servant. Quiet, efficient. Refined in a way, despite her local accent.' He glances at Aaron, as though he too is guilty of this heinous crime. 'Incredible to think she has left this trail of disaster wherever she has gone.'

'Nothing more than savage coincidence,' I say urgently. 'I am sure of it.'

'The woman's been unlucky, not malevolent,' says Aaron gruffly. 'Like you, we know her, and we don't think it's true. It's the way they're putting it all together. Like a tide gathering.'

Mr Backhouse glances at him and gives him the barest of nods.

'You knew her, Mr Backhouse. She lived in your house.' I look around the gleaming hall. 'Was she ever any harm to anyone here?'

'Never,' he says, glancing round himself. 'And I consider myself a good judge of men . . .' his glance slides back to me, 'and women.'

276

Now I know he has believed us. I can feel my shoulders, my whole body relax. 'Well then,' I say, 'the ladies at the hospital are writing to the Bishop Auckland Court giving Mrs Cotton a good character. Perhaps you would be kind enough to do the same.' I try to hold his gaze firmly in mine. 'Only this way may this awful tide, this unfair torrent, be stemmed.'

He nods, vigorously this time. 'I will give the matter some thought, Miss Kilburn, Mr Whitstable. I have it already in mind that I may write some letters to others who may help. So I may do this for her as well. Thou art good friends to the woman. I honour that. How old art thou?' he says abruptly, turning to me.

I am surprised, both by the question and his Quaker style of speech. 'Eighteen and nine months, sir.'

'Thou art a credit to thy people.' He glances at the butler, who is standing by the door, and the servant comes forward. Our visit is obviously at an end. On his doorstep Mr Backhouse suddenly shakes us both very heartily by the hand, all at once amenable and not very patrician at all.

Outside, hidden by the trunk of the huge ash tree, Aaron pulls me to him and holds me tight, then kisses me on the lips. Then his lips are on my ear. 'Thou art a credit to thy people,' he whispers.

In this moment I forget about Mr Backhouse. I even forget Marian. All I know in this world is Aaron, and all I want to do is to raise my lips to his and to stay kissing him until the day goes and the light fades.

Fifty-Eight

Marian has had to stay in prison for the birth of the baby before any further legal actions. There are now to be further committal proceedings regarding the earlier deaths at West Auckland as well as the trial at Durham Assizes for young Charlie's murder. These six months have whirled by almost too quickly for me. My work with Miss McCullough at the school boarding house is never onerous and is made better by the fact that I like the girls with whom I have to work: daughters of farmers and tradesmen whose families desire us to give them the lick of gentility. I have enjoyed working with them, learning alongside them of matters and ideas that I myself would have grasped had I had the privilege of school, and sharing with them snippets from my eclectic self-education, not least the works of Miss Cobbe, which I have rescued from Aaron, who has read them carefully and announces that Miss Cobbe had an interesting point of view, and was somewhat prophetic.

I have started a small choir in the school boarding house, which takes place twice a week in the dining room. We sing songs from the lighter repertoire, even descending sometimes to gems from the music hall, much to the delight of the girls.

My good relationship with Miss McCullough, so summarily embarked upon, has gone from strength to strength. It has become a small bedrock in my life. I am continually surprised by her remarkably tolerant attitude to my comings and goings. I realise that no normal assistant matron would have had such freedom. She doesn't explain her attitude but I have come to understand that it is a combination of her peculiar affection for me and her own regret for a life first tied to her

278

parents, then her sister, then the school, all of which have conspired to expunge her own well-conceived ambitions for independence. As well as this, at heart she is a romantic soul and looks with tolerant warmth on my friendship with Aaron.

Aaron has joined with other tradesmen trying to establish some kind of just defence fund for Marian, although it still seems to go on in a very dilatory fashion. He has also been campaigning to raise objections to the horror of hanging, which he calls 'judicial murder', should the unthinkable guilty verdict be arrived at.

To my delight he and I see each other most days of the week on one or another pretext, all the time forging a deeper and deeper mutual bond, which can only express itself, for this time, in the most exquisite kisses. I am subject to a kind of blind hunger for something further but Aaron – groaning sometimes – saves me from myself and talks of a time when, for good or ill, we can begin to make our own future.

He is on my mind when I wake up in the morning, and his image is the last thing I call up before I go to sleep. Of course, my deep affection for Marian continues unabated but I regret to say that without her dynamic presence she has become something of an idea, a cause, rather than a real living being. It is Aaron who now fills my world as I, I am sure, fill his.

Marian herself continues to write to many people and conduct her own urgent campaign from inside the prison walls, but this typical expression of power has sadly faded in time and a note of bitter helplessness has begun to permeate her letters to me. Even without seeing her, I know at last she is changing. I think the people inside the prison – religious and otherwise – have been pressing her hard but, even so, she will never show any guilt by a statement or an action. Of course, I am with her on this. I know she is not guilty. If she were guilty, isolated and unsupported as she is, she could not resist their pressure. After all, she is a cradle Christian with a real notion of hellfire.

The moral temperature in the town is going up again now, as they are to bring her back to Bishop Auckland soon, for these further committal proceedings for the murders of the other two children and Mr Nattrass. This is fuelling further commentaries in the newspapers. Almost worse, each Saturday in the market place two market men in long coats vie with each other to sell the most song sheets and savage caricature portraits of Marian in the guise of murderess.

279

Towards Christmas I went carolling with the girls from my boarding house choir. We were accompanied by day-girls and supervised by a gaggle of teachers from the school but it was still good fun. As well as this I have enjoyed singing with the town choir in the company of Miss McCullough under the baton of Nicholas Kilburn. These times too are an opportunity to see and talk to my dear Emily, who is as loyal and funny as ever. Auntie Mary has had a baby boy and is recovering well.

The only down note in choir is the sight of Kit Dawson, who avoids me now, and only mumbles when I ask what Mr Smith and Mr Chapman are doing about Marian.

Miss McCullough and I have thoroughly enjoyed singing our hearts out at the Christmas concerts at the splendid new town hall. Mr Nicholas Kilburn rehearsed us and conducted us with Messianic fervour and received great acclaim at the performance. I am proud to be his kin.

Aaron came to all the concerts and I was touched to see the pride with which he applauded our efforts and thrilled at the special way he came up in public to grasp my hand after it was all over. My uncle and aunt and the children were in the audience at the main concert, but were gone before the choir came out front.

Emily told me at the next practice that Auntie Mary thought I looked very well and said how unfortunate it was that I had estranged myself from them. This brought to mind her kindness when I first arrived in the North and I indulged in a small flood of tears when I was alone with Aaron as I contemplated how much I missed them all. So much I'd willingly sacrificed for my friendship with Marian. He dried my tears and told me I was a better person for the sacrifice and it would all come right in the end.

Of course this makes me treasure all the more the hurried conversations I have with Emily at choir practice. I know she has asked her parents if she may come into town to meet me properly, but this has been refused. However, her father continues to ask her quite kindly how I looked in choir. But more generally, Emily tells me, he goes around with a face like a thundercloud. I would not be surprised if Marian's forthcoming trial weighs as much on his mind as it does on mine. He is a genial and good man, and this is a dark time for him and, in my view, his conscience.

When my candle is out and I lie quietly in my narrow bed, I have begun to dwell on an idea that my Aunt Mary and Marian Cotton are connected in a negative fashion by these new babies. On the one hand there is my aunt, surrounded by her children, all of whom have been cherished and have survived. On the other hand there is Marian, who has given birth so many times but with only one child – the bright-eyed boy from Sunderland – surviving the rigours of her class, her situation and her own disaster-ridden life. And then there is the child who is to be born: even this one will be taken away from her.

During these night-time hours I also ponder on the reasons why I still cling on to my certainty that Marian is being ill dealt. Even further, that she is not guilty of what they say with such confidence. Surely if she had done what they say, she must be mad. But I have known her intimately and I know she's not mad. She's unusual, but that does not make her a murderess.

The school rules allow me to venture out on Wednesday, Saturday and Sunday afternoons as long as I return by four o'clock, a deadline sometimes interpreted rather generously by Miss McCullough. Of course these are the times I go to see Aaron, most usually to his shop, which is now such a success that he can afford to employ two assistants, both rather red-eared young men. When I visit him we usually talk in his workshop but occasionally if it is fine we go out and about for an hour, to tea in the Kingsway Rooms, or a matinée at the Eden Theatre.

When Aaron and I meet we always touch on matters regarding Marian but there remains little fresh to say, other than protesting our disbelief. We tend to talk in circles. We wonder who next we may see or write to, to urge them to protest. Aaron has talked to a solicitor and has the name of a man in Darlington (a Quaker and a man of conscience like Mr Backhouse), who may move things to action there.

But often we talk of other, more immediate things, like events in his shop and the tradesmen with whom Aaron is becoming acquainted. I tell him tales of the naughty ways of the schoolgirls in my care. Nowadays, by tacit agreement, we always meet in the presence of others, either in Aaron's workshop or in the public social places of Bishop Auckland.

Aaron is very careful of me. I sometimes wonder whether, if he were a younger man, he'd be more impetuous in his courtship. Perhaps it is I who wish for the passion rather than he. But then I see the look in his eye and feel the urgency of his occasional touch, and I know this is not true.

281

In my saner moments I know it will not always be like this. It's as though we're holding our breaths until this business with Marian is settled and real life can start again. But then, of course, a kind of guilt sets in: thinking such thoughts infers that we are hurrying Marian's life away.

But still I truly relish the teasing and laughter between us, the surreptitious kisses and the holding and stroking of hands and wrists and cheeks. With every word, every action we become closer, more certain of the way we love each other.

And there are practical outcomes from our strange life in suspension. I've become something of an expert in the principles and processes of cutting and trimming leather, if not the practical skills of making fine shoes and boots. Aaron has also shown me the simple rudiments of his book-keeping, with an eye to . . . what? The future, of course, but neither of us says it out loud. Not just now.

At the boarding house I have received postcards from Pixie and Rollo, several letters from my father and even one from Lottie. Those from my father talk of his disappointment with me and deliver some ruminations on the fact that I seem to have lost my way in life. That said, he seems somewhat relieved that I am under the downy wing of Miss McCullough, who sends him fortnightly reports of my virtues in the role of assistant matron and my promise as a teacher.

In fact, Miss McCullough is my co-conspirator. She knows of my attachment to Aaron and our faltering and frustrating campaign on Marian's behalf, but mentions none of this to my father.

So, although the outward quality of my life is unthinkably inferior to the life I could have led as the invalid sister of the beautiful Lottie, my parents have, in the end, come to accept my work in the school as an act of charity and goodness on my part: a second-best thing to being a missionary in China or darkest Africa, perhaps. The letter from Lottie – extolling her own overblown domestic bliss – echoes these views. She intimates that, as my disability has put me outside the pale of normal human intercourse, turning to Good Works must be a consolation. As I read her letter my thoughts go back to the previous afternoon, spent in Aaron's workshop, our laughter punctuated by kisses and warm words. I know that Lottie could never have such times with her dark, intense husband.

My family's hypocritical admiration for my virtue does not extend to

282

sending money to support my Good Works, so I have to stumble along on advances in my paltry salary and the nest-egg provided by the sapphire and pearl brooch. Still, money is the least of my worries.

What is clear in all this is that my parents have no expectations of my returning to London and are quite relieved that I have taken my fate out of their hands. However, my spy Emily tells me that this same fact has caused trouble in the doctor's household. Both my aunt and uncle wish heartily that my father had come here hot-foot and hauled me back to London to rescue me from my independent life. Paradoxically, their disapproval of my father warms my heart, as I feel that this disapproval at least shows the strength of their own affection for me. However mistaken, my aunt and uncle are fond of me: they want me out of what they see as harm's way.

As I say, Miss McCullough, my tacit co-conspirator, knows I am 'walking out' – for want of a better term – with the highly unsuitable Mr Whitstable. He has given me a silver locket, which hangs round my neck on a thong of the finest silvered leather. Inside it are tiny portraits of him and me, executed by a very talented man who lives next door to the herbalist on Tenter Street. As well as this, Aaron has made me a fine new pair of boots from a high-quality Argentinian hide that he brought home from Hartlepool docks.

And the letters keep coming from Marian. She was pleased at the news from Sunderland Hospital, Smyrna House and the good Mr Backhouse, although very disappointed in Mr Robinson's unbending demeanour. She tells me about the fine robes she has made for the baby and the fact that she – she always calls it 'she' – should arrive any day. 'Then woe is Me, dear Lass, as the Fates will roll over me at that Time. I'm to go to trial as soon as the baby's safely weaned. Then she'll go to Johnson Terrace and Mrs Edwards, and I will face my tormenters.'

I have now confided my views on the scandal to Miss McCullough – how could I not? Although very sceptical and leaning towards the mob's view of Marian, she is sympathetic with me and somewhat admiring of my loyalty.

'Would that I had a friend like you,' she said one night, patting my arm. 'I'd be set up for life.'

It is Christmas Day, and we have just had a very decent dinner with the ten girls who have remained at the house over the holiday, owing in some cases to their orphaned state and in others to the fact that their parents are Doing Some Good for other children across the sea in the Colonies. After a fine repast, just before three p.m. Miss McCullough sends the girls upstairs for their afternoon rest. At precisely three o'clock Aaron calls at the house to take sherry with us and give us presents: an exquisite new pair of indoor shoes for me and a pair of soft green leather slippers for Miss McCullough. She is delighted by these and remarks on their fine fit, obliging me to confess that I borrowed an old pair of her shoes so Aaron could take a pattern.

My Christmas present for Aaron is a new soft felt hat, a fine woollen scarf and a silk necktie. He puts all these on at once, making us laugh. Then, after an hour, he takes his leave in his usual mannerly fashion. Inside the closed door he kisses me with great passion and we murmur of our love for each other, but I am distracted by the giggles of girlish spies on the landing and go to rout them. When I return I stamp my foot in frustration as he is gone.

Back in the parlour Miss McCullough, who has settled down with *The Mill on the Floss* on a cushion before her, looks at me over her glasses. 'Your Mr Whitstable is one of nature's gentlemen,' she says. 'How fine it is that we know him.'

It's a paradox under the circumstances, but Christmas this year has been the best Christmas I have ever had in my life, marred only by Marian's ever-present living ghost. Although Aaron is now at the centre of my life, behind and beneath my own delight I am still haunted by the thought of the bleakness of the Christmas Marian is experiencing behind her grim prison walls.

Fifty-Nine

Marian Cotton's child, a girl as she predicted, was born in prison in the middle of a cold winter night. She was attended at the birth by two women from the prison hospital, the chief matron and Miss Douglas, who had sat up with her when the pains started early on the previous evening. Mrs Cotton had assured her then that she would see the birth that evening, as she never 'went long' with the labour.

But she did 'go long'. The pains, which she endured with her usual stoicism, came and went and after three hours they went away altogether. The chief matron sent the hospital women away. Miss Douglas refused to go off shift, and stayed on with Miss Davies, her replacement. They gave Mrs Cotton a new nightdress and clean sheets, settled her down on her bed in the corner before retiring to their small table to sew.

After an hour Marian turned and twisted, then hauled herself so that she was sitting up. 'She doesn't want to come,' she said quietly. 'She doesn't want it, this life.'

'What's that?' said Miss Davies.

'This baby is not like the others. Having the others was like shelling peas. This one doesn't want to come. She knows that when she comes, it's all up for me.'

'Well,' said Miss Davies. 'She . . . it will come, Mrs Cotton, sure as the sun rises in the morning.'

Just then Marian shouted, 'Ouch!' and arched her back with the pain. 'You're right, miss. Here she comes!' She threw the sheets right off the bed and drew up her knees.

The two women raced across to her.

'Now!' shouted Marian.

Miss Douglas pushed at Miss Davies. 'Go and get them. Get the matron, get the hospital women,' she shouted. She closed her eyes and said a quick prayer then turned round. The prisoner was grunting and groaning. Then she was still. Miss Douglas moved towards the bed.

'There,' said Marian softly. 'There she is, Miss Douglas.' And there the baby was, a pinkish purple curled-up little thing, with a skullcap of black greasy hair. 'Pick the baby up, Miss Douglas, and make her cry. Let her breathe the breath of life.'

Gingerly Miss Douglas lifted the baby in her two hands, conscious of how warm and slippery, how surprisingly heavy she was.

'Not too far,' gasped Marian. 'She's still joined, you know. Jiggle her a bit.'

Miss Douglas leaned nearer and did as she was told. The baby opened her mouth and protested: a high-pitched, piercing cry. The sound made Miss Douglas shudder with deep pleasure. Afterwards she was to write blasphemously in her diary that on hearing that sound she heard the voice of God.

Marian hauled herself up in the bed. 'Here, miss, give us a look.'

She held the baby towards Marian and the baby's eyes snapped open. They were big and round and very dark. 'I've never seen such a new baby,' whispered Miss Douglas. 'Never.'

Marian ran a long slim finger down the baby's cheek. 'No sight like it, miss. Isn't she a beauty? If I had my way – which I probably won't – she'd be called Victoria. Like the Queen. And after her own first sister and my good little friend Victoria Kilburn.' Then she looked up at Miss Douglas, her eyes blazing, more alive than they had been in months. 'There you are, Miss Douglas. You know and I know something for a fact, don't we? No woman could bring forth such a wonderful thing and want to hurt it. Am I right?'

The schoolmistress had no time to answer her. The door crashed open and the room was suddenly full of the hospital women and matron. The baby was taken from her hands and Marian vanished behind a wall of starch-clad backs.

Miss Douglas looked down at her greasy blood-streaked hands and fought the desire to cry. Then she made her way out of the room and down the corridor, looking for somewhere quiet to wash her hands and compose herself.

Later, looking out of a barred window to the prison yard below, she thought how much she would miss her prisoner when she went from this place, as inevitably she would. And she hoped that the black-haired baby with the large eyes would have a quiet, happy home with her new parents, despite this dramatic start in life. She deserved that, after all, for her mother's sake.

Sixty

The birth of Marian's child has brought a flurry of articles in the papers that rehearse yet again the earlier calumnies regarding Marian's character and asserting her 'certain guilt'. Aaron has done stalwart work with his pen, protesting to the newspapers at the injustice of such condemnation and the impossibility of a fair trial. There are others – many of them Quakers like Mr Backhouse – who share his concern and humane revulsion against Marian's fate should she – as seems inevitable – be found guilty. All this protest has brought no change whatsoever regarding the slanderous articles, and there are letters in the papers condemning such people of conscience as fosterers of evil.

Aaron has suffered the more direct criticism of a stone flung through his shop windows. He lost three good orders, but his boots are so fine that his more thoughtful acquaintances have put his recalcitrance in the matter of Marian Cotton down to cobbler's madness and have, they tell him, 'made allowances'.

All this, of course, makes me love him all the more.

And my aunt's baby is to be called Edward. Emily told me at choir that, though rather shrunken, her mother is now much more her old, jolly self. To my great sadness I was not invited to the christening at St Helen's church. Emily, to her transparent delight, was made godmother.

Tonight at choir she has just finished telling me all about the christening tea when Kit Dawson – who has been avoiding me of late – sidles up to tell me that Mrs Cotton is to be brought to Bishop Auckland next week to be charged, then no doubt committed to Durham

Assizes, for the further murders of Mr Nattrass and two other of the children.

'Marian Cotton murdered no one,' I say mechanically. 'She would never kill anyone.'

He shrugs. 'Whatever you say, Miss Kilburn.'

'And will your Mr Smith and Mr Chapman be speaking for her? Have they worked out something about this case?'

Again, that careless shrug. 'I can't think so. There was some talk of their briefing a barrister for the first case, that of young Charlie Cotton next month at the Durham Assizes. But of course there are no funds.'

'But your Mr Smith gathered all her things and sold them. Marian said so in a letter. There must be something. And there are some people raising funds.'

'I don't think so, Miss Kilburn. Mr Smith makes no mention of it.'

His expression is so smug that I long to raise my hand and slap it against his face. But I need his help, so I desist. 'Which day will it be, the committal here at Bishop Auckland?'

'Next Friday. The twenty-first of the month.'

'Will it be possible for me to attend?'

'You'd need a ticket from the solicitor Mr Dale Trotter. He's clerk to the magistrates and in charge at this stage. He will be doing the questioning in the hearing.'

'Can you get me a ticket?'

'We-ell, Miss Kilburn, I don't know how suitable . . .'

Then, from inside me comes this new fierceness, this strength that I never knew I had. I do not even raise my voice but I feel that everyone within three miles hears my words. 'Mr Dawson, I *will* be there. I will create such a commotion at the door, I will mention your name in a very loud voice, I will protest Marian's innocence and—'

'If you feel so strong, Miss Kilburn,' he interrupts, 'I will see what I can do. The tickets will be at a premium, so many people want to take a look at the woman.' He pauses. 'You're looking very fine these days, Miss Kilburn. I hear you are an independent woman living in the town.' He is so smooth he is in danger of flowing through a crack in the floor. 'What say I try my best to get you a ticket and you go out to tea with me again?'

I stare at him, trying to blank the rage out of my eyes. 'Perhaps I will, Mr Dawson.'

'Right,' he says briskly. 'I will get you a ticket.'

'But I need—' I want Aaron to come with me.

He is already shaking his head. 'Only one is possible. As I told you, the tickets are at a premium.'

'Miss Kilburn!' Miss McCullough has been waiting at the door for me. 'I think we should go, my dear.'

Kit touches my arm and I resist snatching it away. 'Meet me on Thursday, three o'clock in the Kingsway Rooms,' he says, 'and I will have your ticket for you.'

Sixty-One

Marian Cotton adjusted her baby's shawl so that she could suckle properly. 'They're saying now that it's to be Friday at Bishop. This lying accusation about the others, about Nattrass and the children. Who is to go with me, Miss Douglas? I shall not go without the baby. I'm telling you that.'

'Mr Thompson,' said Miss Douglas. 'You know him. He's talked with you. He's in charge here.'

'I remember. Not a bad fellow.'

'And Miss Wilkinson.'

'That's all right then.' Marian had met and dealt with the senior matron who took turns in guarding her. 'Nothing to complain of with her. But it would've been nice, perhaps, if *you'd* come with us, miss. We've got to know each other here, haven't we? And the baby is happy with you.'

Miss Douglas shook her head. 'I'm too lowly a person for such a public task. The world's eye will be upon you.' She leaned forward to look at the baby burrowing away at Marian's engorged breast. 'She seems to be enjoying her breakfast.'

'Oh yes. I never had any problems feeding my children. It's keepin' them that's always been my problem.' The words were said with the dry detachment that Miss Douglas had become used to. It was part of the puzzle of this woman. She was always polite although she had not been humbled, as many would have been, by her prison experience. Her protests of innocence were threaded with calm certainty; the progress of the accusations was met with dry contempt and eventually a kind of

291

resignation. She retained a kind of personal power, even in here. And Miss Douglas, who had seen her with her baby, did not now believe her to be cold and unfeeling. She was powerfully reserved and resolutely determined. Even in here that gave her a brief power. The letters she shot off around the place seemed to galvanise some people into some kind of action.

'Miss Wilkinson says you must take the baby, as you are still feeding her.' Miss Douglas sat back in her chair. She nodded at two envelopes neatly laid out on the table. 'I see you have more post.'

'Take a look.' Marian moved the baby to the other breast. 'No good news there. One from the Newcastle barrister fellow with nothing to tell. The other, from that Smith fellow – the one that came here with Chapman that day – makes no sense at all.'

The one from Blackwell the barrister said:

Mr Blackwell duly received Mrs Cotton's letter. He has been retained by Mr Smith, acting for Mr Chapman, Solicitor, Durham, to defend her at the ensuing assizes, but regrets that up to this time he has not received instructions from either of the above gentlemen.

The other said:

Madam,
     You will be brought over to Bishop Auckland on Friday first on the other cases when I will see you. I wrote Mr Blackwell the other day about the Case.
     Yours truly
       Geo. F. Smith

Miss Douglas frowned. 'So this next week is about new cases?'

'Aye. Like I said, now they blame me for the deaths before this happened to Charlie. All false.'

'I see. And the case to which Mr Blackwell refers is the one here in Durham, the accusation about little Charles Cotton?'

'Aye, another false charge, as you know.' Marian paused. 'I have it that some good folk have now written to the Court to tell them that I'm not the person as'd do such things.'

Miss Douglas shook her head. 'There's no guarantee in that, Mrs Cotton. And the legal advice you're getting from these two gentlemen seems careless, to say the least. To my knowledge you've had not one jot of advice from them at all.'

'Oh yes I have, Miss Douglas. If you remember, the only advice I've had is to keep my mouth shut. Not to say a thing. Mr Smith was very strong on that.'

Sixty-Two

On Friday 21 February, after seven months' incarceration, Marian came out of prison with her baby in her arms. She was escorted by Mr Thompson and Mrs Winifred Wilkinson to Durham railway station to catch the 8.28 train to Bishop Auckland. Members of the public were most anxious to catch sight of the notorious woman. They gathered at Durham station and all the stations *en route*. In Bishop Auckland they lined the streets.

My ticket, extracted from Kit Dawson yesterday, only allows me to stand in the crowd at the back of the courtroom, behind the two rows of chairs provided for chosen ladies and gentlemen. A cluster of men – perhaps more than fifteen – have the notebooks and long coats of gentlemen of the press.

Marian is led in between a burly man and a bonneted woman who have an official look. The baby in her arms is bundled in a black-and-white checked shawl, on its head a satin cap trimmed with the pink lace that reminds me somehow of the glengarry cap that young Charlie Cotton always wore. Marian is pale and thinner than she was but this makes her look elegant and refined, a world away from the coarse, cruel caricature that has been the public's image of her these last seven months. Her dress and bonnet are black, her shawl black and white, similar to that which wraps the baby. Her face has a blind, enclosed look, and my heart sinks when they lead her to a seat facing the magistrates, all old men. She has not seen me. She does not know I am here. She is Daniel in the lions' den.

At times, as the day proceeds, she gives the baby to the matron to rest her arms, but seems eager to have her back after a few minutes. Now and then, in the middle of the proceedings, the baby mews some protest and Marian breast-feeds her under her shawl, quietening her down in an instant. This is an accomplished, caring gesture, not the action of a child killer.

I watch the proceedings during all that Friday. Marian sits there, rocking and occasionally feeding the baby. Those West Auckland people, familiar now to me, are paraded before the magistrates to rehearse and conveniently embellish their version of the circumstances in which Marian Cotton planned and executed a devious plan to kill not just Joss Nattrass and Freddie Cotton, but her own baby Robert too. Nattrass' workmates George Vickers and Thomas Hall tell us how she came into the sum of £10. 15s at his death. Her neighbours Janet Hedley, Phoebe Olson and Sarah Shaw describe the obsessive, possessive style of nursing that Marian favours. (This is said as criticism, but one would have thought it a positive sign in a nurse.) They even wheel out a Mr Detchon, a chemist's assistant from Newcastle, who says he identified her in prison as a person who had bought an arsenic bug repellent. This is years ago! There is an insinuating veiled allusion here to probable deaths in Newcastle and Sunderland.

Then comes the unchallenged assertion (which I *know* to be untrue) that Marian delayed the burial of the baby until Nattrass died so she could save money by burying them together. I stare hard at the back of Marian's head to get her to challenge this, but she says nothing. And there is no one – no Mr Smith or Mr Chapman – to challenge it for her.

Step by step, in response to Mr Trotter's questions, these witnesses contribute to the already existing myth of a heartless, manipulative woman. In the room there are murmurs of astonishment and suppressed pleasure as each damning point is made with no denial. I have to bite my lip to stop crying out, urging Marian to speak up in her own defence. I am frustrated that I cannot do so myself.

In fact on the first Friday, when she is committed for trial at the forthcoming Durham Assizes for the murder of Nattrass, the chairman of the magistrates actually asks her if she has anything to say.

Her voice comes back into the court, low but clear. 'I have nothing to say at present.'

'Will you wish to have any witnesses bound over on your behalf at this trial?'

Here now she can say something. She does. 'I have some witnesses.' Her voice is low and strong.

'Are there any here?'

'There are three here.'

'Do you wish to have them bound over in your defence?'

'Yes.'

'Do you wish to call them now?'

'No.'

The sergeant stands up and asks the names of these people.

She says, 'Bernard Hedley, Janet Hedley and Eliza Atkinson.'

'These people are witnesses for the prosecution,' the sergeant frowns. 'They have stood up for the prosecution here.'

A whisper goes round the room.

Trotter stands up. 'Now, Mrs Cotton.' His tone is quite kind. 'As you hear the sergeant say, these people are witnesses for the prosecution. You have heard their testimony today and this testimony has assisted the court in deciding you must go for trial. They are against you. It becomes a question whether we can bind them over for your defence if they are not examined here in your defence before the magistrates.'

There is a long silence. The baby cries again and Marian attends to her. The chairman of the magistrates leans forward and fixes Marian with his eye. 'Are we to understand, Mrs Cotton,' he says brusquely, 'that you do not wish to call witnesses at present for your defence?'

'No, sir.' Her voice, though still clear, has become thin and weary and I realise she is confused and uninformed now about what is really happening here, or what all this means. And this is only about Mr Nattrass. On Tuesday we will go through the whole thing again in the matter of the children.

But today the chairman explains that if she won't call and question witnesses in her defence now, then they can't be bound over for such a purpose when this case comes to trial. I think I am not the only person to be outraged at this. Mr Trotter himself looks uncomfortable and cross.

As she is led out of the room she glances up at last and catches my eye. She smiles briefly and nods, and I lift my hand in desperate greeting.

Sixty-Three

There had been a small drama at lunchtime over the magistrates' pedantic concern regarding the feeding of the prisoner. This was solved by Sergeant Hutchinson, the one who wrote the damning report on the personal history of Mrs Cotton that mentioned the killing of pigs. He suggested to their worships that they take the prisoner to the Sun Inn next door to the police station. The obliging publican, Mr Leng, would clear the snug to provide privacy. Hutchinson told their honours that he could recommend the food. He himself had enjoyed many a fine repast put on by Mr Leng.

Mr Leng served them himself: lamb chops, potatoes, carrots and a steamed raisin pudding to be washed down with fresh-drawn ale for the sergeant and Mr Thompson, and with pint mugs of water 'for the lady and the prisoner'.

Miss Wilkinson took the sleeping baby in her arms and sat in the corner while Marian ate her food. Mr Thompson and Sergeant Hutchinson sat at their table by the window, devouring their repast with smacking sounds of appreciation. Mr Leng, standing by the door, watched Mrs Cotton with some astonishment as she ate her food in a steady and genteel manner. A rational, jovial man, he had expected a woman of dark visage and beetling brow, with those sly eyes so familiar from the posters. But here was a slender creature of long bones and quite refined looks. Her gaze was open and bright, and when he put her plate before her, her murmured 'Thank you' was quite mannerly.

Back in the crowded bar parlour the place was abuzz. The murder hearing had been very good for trade. In addition to the usual customers

297

from the police station, there were reporters and tradesmen and gentlemen of the town, many of whom had forsaken their professional obligations to be in the courtroom. They were agog that the woman was actually here in the room next door, eating her dinner. One wit called down the bar, 'You should have slipped a dollop of arsenic in there, Mr Leng. Saved the hangman a lot of trouble.'

A growl of assent gravelled its way through the bar.

One man shook his head so violently that his ginger beard lifted in the air and glinted in the firelight. 'The law must take its course,' he intoned. 'This ain't the Middle Ages, man.'

'I'd say it has quite a look of the Middle Ages,' said another, older man in a black suit and white stock, who was drinking water. 'Mrs Cotton had no counsel. What thou saw in there was all indictment and no defending voice. The woman's as guilty as sin but what thou seest in that room is not the law in process. Not at all. More a hanging party. I was told that fellow George Smith, that works for the lawyer Chapman, had been assigned, but there was no sign of him in that court.'

A man at the end of the bar called, 'Smith? Chapman's clerk? I saw him this morning, just by the Market Place.'

The man with the beard was listening intently. 'Then the feller must be got to come here, and the magistrate should see what he has to say. We should do something about all this,' he said. 'Have you seen the commentary in *The Times*? They'll pick this drama up all over the country and we'll be a laughing stock up here. As though we're out of the ark.'

This was met with nods of agreement. No one here in the bar parlour would deny their avid interest in this dramatic case. But there were those who liked to see themselves, and be seen, as civilised men. The questionable role of George Smith in the affair offended them, and would stir one or two of them to action.

Sixty-Four

After that first Friday hearing I hover outside the court and manage to catch Mr Dale Trotter as he leaves. He holds a black umbrella up against the encroaching rain and his cloak reaches his ankles. I step right in front of him. 'Mr Dale Trotter?'

He looks up with astonishment. 'Yes?'

'You don't know me, Mr Trotter, but I am niece to Dr Kilburn. Would you be so kind as to have a word?'

He relaxes. 'Miss Kilburn!' He touches his hat with his free hand and lifts his umbrella to allow me to move inside its protection. 'What is it, my dear?'

'Mr Trotter, I am a friend of Marian Cotton.'

In the dingy light of the afternoon I can feel rather than see his straggling eyebrows rise. 'Are you, now?'

'I thought I should remind you that Mr Smith, who works for Mr Chapman, has been engaged by Mrs Cotton. Or so she thinks. But he was not there today and I venture to say your questions raised as fact more than one thing that I know to be untrue. And in the matter of her witnesses, which you raise, he should surely have advised her. She was very confused over that. Anyone could tell.'

'Is that so, Miss Kilburn?'

'I wondered perhaps whether you think it would have been more just if she had someone to challenge those points for her? And help over the issue of witnesses and whether or not she can speak.'

'Quite possibly. I may tell you, Miss Kilburn, that their worships also raised this with me. You are not alone in your concerns. I have promised to look into it. You can be sure of that, Miss Kilburn.' He lifts his hat and quickly sidesteps me with his umbrella so that he is talking to me now through a veil of rain. 'I must hurry on to tea. My dear wife ensures it is on the table at five thirty precisely when I am in court.'

I am so absorbed in watching his receding back that I jump when I feel a hand on my shoulder. It is one of the long-coated reporters. 'Seems you are a friend of the poisoner, miss.' He guides me into the protection of a shop doorway and takes out a notebook. 'I write for the *Northern Echo*, miss. I noted that Mrs Cotton greeted you in court.'

'I am her friend, but she is not a poisoner. What we saw in there was a travesty. A terrible thing. I know she has not done these things and she sits undefended. A lamb to the slaughter.'

He writes something down. 'May I ask how someone like you, a refined lady, if I may say, comes to be friends with a woman like her, a common woman, who they say is the biggest poisoner in history? Twenty at the last count.'

I stare at him. 'What she is is the victim of a life lived hard, in hard places, of jealousy and hatred by those who see her sense of self, her confidence as hubris and want to bring her down.'

'Hubris, is it?' He writes that down. 'And what did you say your name was, miss?' His pencil is poised.

Who knows how this report will spread, given the journalists' talent for sensationalism and gossip. I think of my father reading *The Times* over his breakfast. 'I didn't tell you my name.' I push past him out of the doorway and stride away.

He calls after me, 'Stop.'

I stop and turn towards him.

'Will you be at the Durham Assizes next week for her trial for the murder of young Charlie?'

'I will.' The confirmation slips out, despite my determination to tell this man nothing.

'So what do you think of the fact that the Government has assigned Charles Russell, QC, to prosecute her? He's a big cheese. A big gun. Set for high things, they say. That's despite being a Catholic and an Irishman.'

'I know naught of that, except that if it is true, it is a greater travesty and we should all be ashamed of ourselves.'

He looks down to note this in his book and I flee from him, and all his nauseous, predatory kind.

I race down Newgate Street as fast as my poor feet will allow, keen to boast to Aaron about my courage in tackling Mr Dale Trotter. Of course, by the time I get there I'm as wet as any cat left out overnight. Water is dripping from the feather in my hat and my feet are squelching in my Spanish leather shoes. Aaron's assistants watch me blandly from behind their counters as I create foot-puddles on their polished floor.

In the workroom Aaron leaps up from his bench with a broad smile. 'Well, dear lass, you look like a drowned rat.' He leans down and kisses my nose. 'A wonderful bright-eyed rat, no less.'

He makes me sit down by his fire and removes my shoes and stockings, hangs the stockings over the fireguard, then stuffs newspaper in my shoes and sets them in a cooler place. My coat he hangs on the drying-line over the fire and he shakes the raindrops from my hat before tying it to the line with a leather shoelace. Then he sits cross-legged on the floor and takes my curled foot in his hand and pats it with a cloth.

He looks up at me. 'This is how I first knew you, Victoria – through this little foot. How thankful I am to this little foot.'

We both laugh and laugh, and there is a lake, an ocean of sympathy and good feeling between us. This is good after the conflict and bad feeling I have endured today. I put a hand on his shoulder and he kneels up so his face is level with mine. I put my arms round him and pull him towards me. Now our faces and breasts are together, bound tightly by our eager arms. His face is warm and I can feel his heart beating loud against me, my own heart thrumming in my ears. The kiss is only a completion, a sealing together of our two selves into one. It goes on such a long time I lose my breath and have to pull away to breathe, then our open mouths are together and his tongue is flicking round just inside the soft flesh of my mouth, along my teeth, charging my whole body with feeling. We are inside each other. An amazing inside kiss. I have never thought of such a thing.

Now he groans and pulls back, and I lean forwards and run the very tip of my tongue over the edges of his lips. He stands up away from me, making me feel cold and bereft.

We are silent then, both steadying our breath. I look at him steadily. If he swept me up at this moment I would do anything, anything that men and women do, to take that kiss to the place where it was leading, a mysterious, unknown land to me.

He lets out a short gasp of air, almost a snort. 'Well, Miss Victoria, I think we must part for ever or marry soon, or I will go mad.'

A vision of my father rises before me, not his face or his form but the powerful scrawl of his writing on a letter. I sit back in the chair.

'Would that be possible? My father . . .'

'You can choose for yourself, Victoria. Scotland. We can be married in Scotland. When we've seen this through for Marian, we can go to my friend's in Morpeth and stay overnight, and from there we can go to Scotland and be married by our own say-so, no others involved. Would you do this? Do it quietly so we can start a life together?' He waits. For me it is a foregone conclusion, but there is the edge of uncertainty in his dear voice.

I stand up and place myself again in the circle of his arms. 'How wonderful, how tidy that would be! Of course I would do it.' I put up my face, hungry for another inside kiss.

His jaw goes rigid and he takes a step back, ensuring I am at full arm's length. 'You are the most savage temptress,' he says softly. 'I'll not do wrong by you.' He wrenches my heart with his tenderness. He goes on, 'First, Marian. Then Scotland.' He kisses the corner of my mouth. 'Then the rest of our lives.'

His red-eared assistant charges through the door then swerves to a halt at the sight of us standing so close. We leap apart as though this is some ridiculous melodrama at the Eden Theatre.

'A traveller, Mr Whitstable,' the boy gasps. 'Come to see you about a line in men's attaché cases.'

I retrieve my coat from the rail. 'Dry now, I think, Mr Whitstable. And now I must go or Miss McCullough will be looking for me on the highways and byways of this blessed town.'

Sixty-Five

Marian is brought again the following Tuesday from Durham for the resumed hearing regarding the children. I nearly applaud when Mr Dale Trotter stands up and states that there is information, verified by Mrs Cotton, that Mr George Smith, clerk to Mr Chapman, has sold furniture and other effects on Mrs Cotton's behalf to procure money for her defence. And Mr Thompson, the chief warder, asserts that Mrs Cotton had given Smith money. He says Mrs Cotton was surprised when Mr Smith was not present on her behalf last Friday, although he said he would be there. However, Mrs Cotton has made no complaint. She has written to Mr Smith but has had no reply.

Mr Trotter expresses his professional regret that the case is undefended, and says that Mrs Cotton should have all possible assistance. He also goes on to state, to my amazement, that there are many points of evidence that might be got up in her defence.

'I have passed a letter to Mrs Cotton assuring her that a Mr Richard Murray, who has been observing these events and collaborating on a defence fund, will at least find a counsel for her at the Durham Assizes.'

The chairman also leans forward. 'You do realise, Mrs Cotton,' he says, enunciating very clearly as though he thinks she might be deaf, 'that at the Assizes you will have a counsel assigned to you by the Crown?'

She nods slightly at this, taking in this information. I know that, like me, she must think what poor creatures they all are, running around now like chickens who have seen a fox.

But what has happened here in these two days at the magistrates' court cannot be undone. The long-coated men will see to that. Smith's underhandedness has rendered Marian defenceless in this preliminary court and this could warp any future hopes she may have for justice. Undefended against these accusations, she will now appear through the newspapers to be culpable to whoever contemplates these events in the future.

Sixty-Six

The second hearing is very cold and snowy. I have to squeeze through crowds of people in the street to get back to my place in the rows behind the chairs. One good thing is that when Marian is led into the courtroom with her baby she catches sight of me again. She smiles thinly and raises the baby to me in a kind of offering, before sitting down in her place at the front.

I nod and wave, and people in all parts of the court turn and twist and peer to see who has received such a greeting from the murderess. I keep my face forward, staring at the back of her head, trying to force my good wishes through the very bone of her skull.

They have tracked down Mr George Smith. He cuts a mean figure, slithering and writhing with assertions that Mrs Cotton may have given him money for him and his employer to watch the very first case that will be tried, and retain counsel, and he has done so. But this is not so for this case. It is for the case of Charles Cotton at Durham.

This is taken as explanation and nothing further is done about it. But what terrible men they are, he and Mr Chapman! Taking Marian's money and doing nothing for her. Had they made a decent fist of defending her against this purely speculative and circumstantial case, they might have made themselves a great professional name. As it is, they are too lazy to bother, and too convinced of her guilt, if I am to believe Kit Dawson, to feel any prick of conscience. There is a murmur of disapproval all around Mr Smith in the court and it is reassuring to see that Mr Dale Trotter at least is evidently disgusted at his deviousness and lack of professional responsibility.

I sit there with my heart in my boots. Marian, powerless as she is, was compelled to trust that Messrs Smith and Chapman, professional people, after all, would do their duty by her. But they have done nothing. If they had not been cynically holding on to her money and her confidence, perhaps someone else would have taken her case. A genuine defence might have slowed, if not stopped, the landslide of blame and rumour, speculation and ignorance, medical hubris and prejudice that has constituted the case against her.

Above all, that terrible man Smith has stopped her speaking and questioning on her own behalf. Her voice, which I know to be dry, intelligent, perceptive in a way not usually evident in one of her class, would, I am sure, have pricked the balloon of prejudice from which this whole case hangs.

I wait for Smith to be admonished by the court but this does not happen. Even so, he turns and slinks out, looking neither right nor left. In this way he misses the cold looks of the magistrates and the piercing, accusatory gaze of his victim, Marian Cotton. Beside me the men in long coats scribble away.

Smith having been dealt with, the second session sees a parade of doctors before the magistrates: my uncle and his colleague Dr Chalmers, a Dr Richardson, who attended Mr Nattrass, and the forthright Dr Scattergood, an important expert from Leeds.

At first I am reassured by their talk of the commonness of babies dying of teething convulsion: Dr Chalmers seems certain that the baby died of that condition. There are some references from my uncle, and Doctors Chalmers and Richardson, to the similarities between death from arsenic poisoning and death from typhoid. Despite a good deal of pressure, Dr Richardson refers back to Mr Nattrass and still asserts that he died of typhoid or Bright's disease. He rather sticks to that view.

My uncle and Dr Chalmers tell the court of their work attending patients and the comfort of offering the usual diagnoses, prescriptions and nostra for the regrettably familiar and death-dealing illnesses common in their practice in these deprived working-class districts. Compared with the case of Charlie Cotton, in these earlier cases of Nattrass and the two children, it seems clear here in court that the doctors had never given murder a thought. It is only now, in retrospect, that they are struggling with the possibility of murder and the evidence reconstructed from the exhumed bodies. This personal struggle is evident in each of them.

I am beginning to feel that if these are indeed suspicious deaths, one might argue that the doctors could be held to be complicit in the deaths because of their careless doctoring. But I have a twinge of sympathy here, knowing as I do the dedication and selflessness in my uncle's vocation. But I cannot escape the notion that as, with their help, the court moves towards a more certain assumption of Marian's culpability, they provide some easement in their own guilt. After all, isn't poisoning such a secret deadly process, the essence of wickedness? And might it not deceive even a dedicated doctor?

Following these doctors' professional tentativeness, and scrupulous reserve, the certainty and authority of Dr Scattergood, as he analyses each of the three cases, comes to dominate the whole proceeding. To Scattergood's mind all his analyses point to arsenical poisoning. You can hear a pin drop in the room: Scattergood holds forth with the quiet authority of a priest or a magician: it is as though we are at prayer.

Then Marian's baby mews and a small hand flails from its confining shawl. Everyone relaxes. Marian quietens the baby by putting out her hand and cupping the baby's head, as though to protect her from the calumnies outlined in the dour, clipped voice of Scattergood.

Scattergood is the only expert offered by the court: no other expert is called to confirm his findings or to qualify the shaky uncertainties of the doctors who have preceded him as witnesses.

It's inevitable too that, undefended as Marian most certainly is, such confident, unchallenged evidence as that of Scattergood will ensure that these two further cases will go to the Durham Assizes as indictments of murder against Marian.

Marian looks up at me one last time as she leaves the court. I try to smile with the most profound sympathy, to show her I am contemptuous of these proceedings and am on her side. She returns my wave and nods as she walks out, frail but straight, between the man and woman from the prison. I can feel the eyes of the reporter from the *Northern Echo* on me again. He smiles and nods.

Outside the court he says, 'Was that all you expected, miss?'

'No, it wasn't. I expected a fair trial where my friend was defended against lies. That certainly didn't happen. Did you see that terrible Smith man?'

'So I did. Old Trotter gave him a bit of a roasting, don't you think? I swear I felt a flicker of sympathy for Mrs Cotton around the court when he was lying his way out of a fix.'

'Will you write about it in your newspaper?'

He shrugs. 'Worth a paragraph, I suppose. That man's mendaciousness is offensive to anyone's sense of justice. Even in a cut-and-dried case like this.'

My heart sinks yet again. 'Cut and dried? Cut and dried? Have you been sitting in there asleep?' And for a second time, I run away from him, this time up the hill towards the boarding house, where I know Miss McCullough is waiting for my detailed resumé of the day's events.

Outside the court and in the road leading away there are still crowds waiting in the snow. They stand stolidly to catch a glimpse of the notorious Mrs Cotton on her way back to the station. They do not shout or throw things but my friend is seen as a show, as shocking as any freak paraded in a circus. As I force my aching leg to haul me uphill I consider the strangeness of it all. Although I don't agree with them, these people think Marian is touched with evil and has taken away many lives. You'd think, therefore, they would *not want* to see her; they would hide away from her, to preserve themselves from that evil. But no! They are fascinated by her, as though the mere sight of her will provide some comfort as they come to terms with the lesser evil in their own puny lives. It's as though she, like Scattergood, is some kind of magician, to be handled carefully and observed roundly before she is sacrificed to keep the dumb, waiting people snug in the sense of their own normality.

Sixty-Seven

My Dear Child,

Me and Miss Douglas thought it nice of you to attend that Court room and show a Friendly face in my hour of Trial. Your sweet face looked at me all clear and Bright and I thought for a minute there might be a bit justice in the world. It was a hard enough Time for us Coming Through to Bishop in the train, the snow clagged on either side, making light of the pit heaps and making cob-webs of the black pit wheels. At every little railway station, Croxdale, Tudhoe, Spennymoor, Coundon, then Bishop, people were gathered in the Snow, some of the children too ill clad to be out there in the Cold Wind. They just stare at me and I don't no what they expect. Perhaps me to have horns and cloven Feet or to be as ugly as sin like on the pitcher someone drew for the paper. At one place – Coundon I think – someone threw a clod of Earth at the window. Mrs Wilkinson, the wardress that was with us, she tutted her teeth and said people should No Better. They are not bad, the women in here.

The chaplain comes but he is a bit High Church for me and keen on Confession and the Shriving of souls. I've asked the women here if they can find me a Wesleyan Minister. My dear Mother was a member of the Wesleyan Society and, me, I taught in the Sunday School and never missed at chapel. So why do they say these Things about me? And tears I have shed for how they bring my Mother into it! There will be no more Sunday school teaching for me now.

The Babe is fine and thriving, drawing lots of looks and interest here as she is bonny. The women in Here says they never saw so good a Mother. The babe's name is to be Margaret Edith Quick-Manning Cotton. A long name for the little rosy Scrap that lies beside me. I thought perhaps of giving her <u>Victoria</u> but could not Without your say-so.

Some Folks have shifted themselves now and they say some good men have got together money to get me a lawyer for the assizes. A lawyer visited me. A good one so Far as I can see. Very quick and Sharp. He was on a lot about how much arsenic I kept in the house and I said no more than any Housewife whose house is rife with them Bugs and Germs which I hate. Sergeant Hutchinson certainly found no arsenic in my house, nor nothing of any harm. This is so even though I had no warnings they would come for me that Morning. Trouble is, this new Lawyer fellow is hard pushed for time to Understand what Really happened here and the women in here tell us that the newspapers is rife with stories of the Bishop court that repeat the lies as truth. What chance can a Woman have?

Like I say time and time again, the biggest fault lies with that Smith who led me wrong. Told me not to speak a single words if I Was Asked Ever so hard or Ever so much. I was not even to say if it was wrong. Smith never brought forth one witness for me yet I Want nothing but the Truth from any one of them. Smith says wait for the Assizes but there is no sign of him here over that and the Assizes happens next week. If it had not been for Smith I should make 5 or 6 of them stand with their tongues tied and that would have made a different story for the newspapers.

I need you to do Some thing for me, child. Will you get down West Auck. And get to Riley and ask him about the <u>arrowroot</u>. I have been begged in here time and Again to confess guilt though I am guilty of Nothing, Have been racking my brain and the only thing I come up with is the arrowroot. I always use arrowroot to settle the gut. Always have. The arrowroot I got from Riley, and he mixed a new Box with an Old before he weighed it out. All of My sick ones had this from me when they got the gripes from whatever sickness it was that attacked him. I give it to every last one of them except baby Robbie that had Teething convulsions that did for him. The arrowroot is the only thing I can think and I willed no one any ill and the only ill came to me myself. Talk to Riley and help me. Tell him to speak up for

    your friend

      Marian Cotton

Witnessed by Maria Douglas. Schoolmistress. Durham Gaol.

An interesting thing has happened. Despite the bad feeling locally against Marian there is this headstrong growth of people in the wider world who are now revolted by her defenceless position. Tradesmen, including my beloved friend Aaron Whitstable, have set up a fund for her defence. They have advertised for donations to the fund in the *Auckland Chronicle*, 'contributions to be sent to John Leng of the Sun Inn'. I have given Aaron £3.10s from my own little nest egg to help it along. It seems they are looking to a certain Mr Campbell Foster, a very good barrister of the Northern Circuit, to defend 'this unfortunate woman'. This must be the man to whom Marian alluded in her letter.

Worse news is that the government is taking an interest in the case and has appointed a famous lawyer, Sir Charles Russell, to prosecute. This must be the man the reporter mentioned. Aaron tells me he is a coming man in the government despite his Irish Catholic background. His appointment has ruffled a few feathers in Durham of those who thought this juicy case was theirs. It seems to me that such an appointment is another sign that the outcome of the trial is almost a foregone conclusion. Such a well-thought-of man would not be secured unless they wanted a conviction at any cost.

Despite such bad news, the appointment of a proper defending barrister makes me feel the faintest thread of hope. He must be the man who has been, according to her letter, questioning Marian in prison. Yet there is only a week to go and Aaron agrees with me that it will need a very vigorous defence to countermand the slander, the lies and the overexcited hatred that have filled the air these seven months.

Aaron says all this is the talk among these gentlemen who are offering help from as far afield as Darlington and Stockton. He also says that if the authorities had tried Marian before Christmas instead of postponing the trial because of her pregnant condition, there would not have been time for this accumulation of hysterical moral opprobrium and there might have been a possibility of true justice.

So much is chance. I do so wish to stay optimistic but it is hard.

Sixty-Eight

Mr Riley's wife is none too pleased to see me in the shop and says dourly that 'he' is out the back with the lad, loading up the delivery cart for the dale. She is just this side of surly but, like many of the commercial class, cannot quite bring it off with the gentry.

'Would you kindly ask Mr Riley if we may speak?'

She stares at me hard, then lifts up the counter flap. 'Mebbe you'd better come through, miss.'

'Here's Miss Kilburn for you, Tommy.' She leaves me standing in the back room and slams the door behind her as she goes inside.

Mr Riley's pencil stays poised over the book as he looks towards me. 'Good morning, Miss Kilburn,' he says with thin politeness. 'If you'll give me a moment.' He completes the last entry, then says, 'Now, Miss Kilburn, it's a while since we've seen you round these parts. What can I do for you?' Unctuous grocer's politeness. 'How are you? I did hear you were living in Bishop these days.'

'Yes. I am helping at the girls' school.'

'And how is our Mr Whitstable? He was a loss to the village. No doubt you are in touch with Mr Whitstable.' He smiles slightly.

I ignore the insinuation. 'I have a query for you, Mr Riley, from Mrs Cotton.'

His face stiffens to a lardy white. 'Mrs Cotton? The woman's where she should be, behind bars.'

'She has written a letter—'

'Ah. She sends out her tentacles . . .'

'How can you refer to her like that? A woman you've known.'

'Me? Excuse me, Miss Kilburn. Have you been deaf and blind as well as—'

'Crippled?'

He has the grace to flush. 'The woman is poison.'

'Not so long ago I thought you liked Marian. I know she had a soft spot for you.'

'Liked? Well, I helped her through hard times. I gave her leeway. Her credit was up to thirty pounds when I finally stopped it. I found work for her. But I was blind to her true nature. She pulled the wool over my eyes like she still pulls it over yours.'

I stare at him, trying to figure out just what it was that drew him to Marian here in the village. One would never know from her. She is the keeper of secrets and in her days here showed her power over people. See how she wove her relationship with me out of just about nothing. She changed my life. She affected Aaron, she affected Mr Quick-Manning, and Mr and Mrs Edwards. She certainly changed the life of my uncle and Mr Riley. Anyone who has known her in this village will probably never be the same again.

'Miss Kilburn?' He penetrates my meditation. 'I can't see why you bother with the likes of her.'

'She changed my life,' I say slowly. 'And in her agony you persecute her.'

His colour is high again. 'You see, Miss Kilburn! You are under her spell.'

'Spell? Ah, is that what you think? That she's a witch?'

'That's not what I said.'

The back door clicks and Mrs Riley peers out and says, 'There's customers pilin' up, Tommy,' before going back into the shop.

'What is it, Miss Kilburn? What do you want of me?' he says irritably, the grocer's mask slipping.

'It is about arrowroot, Mr Riley. Mrs Cotton wrote to me of arrowroot. She's been going over everything in her mind and wonders whether perhaps there was something in the arrowroot she got from you, whether that worsened her patients' condition rather than helped them.'

'The woman's mad. And, like I say, she's infected you.'

'She says you mixed arrowroot from two boxes.'

'Is she accusing me now?'

314

'No, no. She is just trying to find a reason, even from her prison cell, for the terrible things that are happening to her. Surely that's only human. She wants you to speak up to the court about the arrowroot.'

'You are mad? You should tell Mrs Cotton that the things that are happening to her are due to her own wickedness. The court in Durham will see how she caused the death of that fine little lad and there are all those others before this child, clearly her victims. She is selfish, cold, without care. That, Miss Kilburn, is your friend Mrs Cotton.'

I find myself staring at him again. 'You liked her,' I say slowly. 'You really liked her, just as I do. At one time you saw her power and were not afraid. Then the table turned and she produces the opposite of that affection in you and you become frightened and craven like other people around here.'

He opens the back door very wide and stands to one side. 'You should go, Miss Kilburn,' he says. 'And if I were you I'd watch my step.'

I move past him and he crashes the door behind me.

Outside the shop my eye travels across the green to Western House and my feet move towards it almost without my will. My hand is raising the big knocker on the door before I even think of the action. Mrs Grey comes to the door and for a moment I think she may leave me there in the road while she backs into the house to make her enquiries. But she mutters, 'You'd better come in, I suppose.' She steps back and I move into the hallway, with its familiar smells of food, babies and medicine. To my consternation my eyes fill with tears.

'I'll get Mrs Kilburn,' she says, marching towards the dear, familiar staircase.

In minutes my aunt is coming down the stairs, her new baby in the crook of her arm. To my relief she is smiling. 'Victoria dear, how good of you to call.' She holds up her cheek for my kiss and I can feel nothing but goodwill from her direction. She holds up the baby, who has a tiny bullet head and a face like a rosy pickled walnut. 'See my little Eddie. Is he not fine?'

She looks back at the hovering housekeeper. 'Mrs Grey, would you go and tell Miss Emily that her cousin is here, and then serve some coffee upstairs?'

In the drawing room Emily rushes to my side and clings to me like a limpet. When reprimanded by her mother for being a fusspot, she sits quietly beside me, holding my hand.

My aunt looks me straight in the eye. 'It's very generous of you to come, Victoria. We have missed you.'

I squeeze Emily's hand.

My aunt cups the baby's fine head with her hand. Only last week I saw Marian do just the same thing with her baby in court. 'I think there are matters, dear, on which we don't agree. On those we must agree to disagree.' She looks at me very directly.

I stay silent.

'So we must not speak of such things here. But despite this would it not be civilised to return to our old way of being together? You were such a fount of pleasure to all this family, not least to Emily there. I swear she has eaten no more than a bird since you left. She is quite, quite thin.'

In fact Emily looks much the same, although she is rather stretching her mouth by grinning from ear to ear.

I realise that I am being offered a bargain and that bargain involves my keeping quiet about my obsession with Mrs Cotton and my friendship with Aaron while I am under this roof.

'Please!' says Emily, pressing my hand.

I nod slowly. It dawns on me that many people must make such strange hypocritical contracts merely in order to live together. Marian, of course, rejected such hypocrisy when she went off courting Mr Quick-Manning, even when she had Mr Nattrass living with her. And perhaps she was rejecting such hypocrisy when she tried to fob Charlie off on his blood uncle, or to get him into the workhouse. In these matters she denied the comfortable lie that she had been transformed into his mother merely through a short-lived relationship with his father.

'Well!' says my Auntie Mary brightly. 'Tell us about this school where we are told by your father you do such good work.'

'Are the girls very naughty?' asks Emily, grinning.

It is an hour before I get away from the fuzzy warmth of the Kilburn drawing room and make my way back down to my uncle's surgery. There is a queue of people in the corridor, and through the dispensary window I glimpse Mr Carr and Dr Chalmers mixing their potions.

My uncle is not at his desk, but in his deep chair, smoking a pipe and staring into the heart of his fire. He frowns at me for a moment as

316

though he doesn't recognise me. Then his face clears. 'Victoria!' He coughs. 'Something of a surprise.'

He does not ask me to sit down.

'I was upstairs talking to Auntie and Emily.' I try to keep my voice steady. 'So I thought I would come down to see you.'

'They mention you and regret that our ways seem to have parted.' His shoulders sag and he flings out his hand. 'Sit down, why don't you? There must be a reason for your coming here on this bitterly cold day?'

I move a pile of papers from a hard chair and sit opposite him. 'To say what I want to say, Uncle, I would have to break a pledge I have just made to Auntie Mary, about not mentioning certain things if I'm to be welcome again here in your house.'

'We'll suspend all pledges for half an hour. Say what you have to say.' He relights his pipe.

'There are actually two things I mustn't talk about. Either of these things might make you forbid me this house for ever.'

'Do go on, Victoria!'

'The first problem is that I continue to be the friend of Aaron Whitstable. We are bonded together and will, I think, marry one day.'

He raises his thick brows. 'You must think a good deal of him. He's a sound enough fellow.'

'He makes me feel entirely special, that I enhance his life. Marian started that feeling and he completes it.' My cheeks are burning at the forthright way in which I am driven to speak. After a long pause I say, 'I knew you would think him unsuitable.'

To my surprise he laughs and shakes his head. 'I was just thinking that he was about as unsuitable for you as your dear aunt was seen to be for me. You should honour him, my dear. He will take care of you, just as your Auntie Mary has taken care of me.'

A rattling knock shakes the door. Dr Chalmers' head appears. 'I'm just going out to see Mrs Leader, Doctor . . .' His glance freezes as it settles on me. 'I'm sorry . . .'

My uncle waves him off with his pipe. 'Thank you, Chalmers. I'll see you when you return.' The door clicks and he turns back to me. 'I'm afraid Dr Chalmers thinks it's all a matter of sides, my dear. If you're not with him, you're *agin* him.'

'That is the other matter.'

'I thought it might be.'

'I have just called on Mr Riley at Marian Cotton's request. I was asking about arrowroot. Marian said she bought arrowroot from Mr Riley and dosed all those people with it. The ones who died. Except for the baby. It seems Mr Riley mixed an old and a new box before he measured out what he gave her. She says this might—'

He is already shaking his head. 'No. Arrowroot would not have that effect.'

'Did you look for arrowroot at the autopsies?'

'No. But if we had we would just have found a harmless substance.'

'Could you look again?'

He shakes his head again. 'Impossible. We'd have to re-exhume; there would be further vexed questions about reliability. In any case, the coroner, I feel sure, would not allow it. And Mr Riley—'

'Like everyone else, for Mr Riley Marian's guilt is a foregone conclusion.'

'That was not the case for me, my dear. I was shocked when the truth began to emerge.' His gaze returns to the leaping flames of the fire.

I will him to raise his eyes to meet mine. 'What is strange to me, Uncle, is how, in trying to get the truth about Charlie, we proceeded so quickly from your confidence that his death was from enteric fever to a certainty that it was poisoning. And then suddenly it was extended so conveniently to all those other bodies.'

'It was proof. Science.' He drags his glance back to mine. 'Dr Scattergood is a very good authority.'

'Are there no other authorities?'

'There may be, somewhere in England, but it's a very young science. But we did not need another authority.'

'Mrs Cotton needs another authority, though, doesn't she?'

'That is a point of view, my dear.' His voice is ragged, strange. 'But our facts are as we have shown them.'

I get up to go and he stands up to put a hand on my arm. 'I liked her, Victoria, just as you do. I appreciated her difference. But she is a secretive woman, enigmatic. Who knows what goes on in her head?'

I look into his eyes. 'You became frightened of her, Uncle, like the others. A poor bereft woman. What power you accorded her! You began to feel that, whatever the evidence, she was guilty.'

His hand drops. 'Don't be ridiculous.'

He follows me through the house to the big door and opens it for me.

'Come to see your aunt and Emily, Victoria. They have missed you.' There is sincerity in his weary voice. 'And you should bring Mr Whitstable. He is a sound man. I see he adds his name to letters regarding a decent defence for Mrs Cotton. An honourable man, if mistaken. You will be welcome here.'

He does not finish with 'when all this is over, when Marian is dead', but the words hang in the air between us.

As I walk the familiar road to the railway station I begin to understand that I will never really be able to visit Western House as I did in those early days, when I first felt like a member of a real family, where I made those first steps to my new self. As I walk through the village to the station I mourn as well my first vision of the village as a clean simple place full of kindly people and sturdy country morals. The truth has been so much darker than that. But perhaps that is so in every village, every community. Only strangers see simplicity.

On the train I decide that my family in these days must be Aaron. And, of course, Miss McCullough. But my visit has left me with a peculiar sadness at this new distance from my aunt and uncle, and my lost ideal of country village life.

Later that night I share these overwhelming feelings with Aaron as we sit in Miss McCullough's parlour. He blots my tears with my own handkerchief and says that for Marian's sake we shouldn't feel sorry for ourselves. Beside her troubles, ours are puny.

Sixty-Nine

I have had to ask leave from Miss McCullough to attend the Assizes. After a bit of humming and haa-ing to make the favour clear, she says I may take the days I use as my year's holiday, although I'm not due for holiday at all this year. Of course I know that she doesn't mind me going, as she will love my stories of the proceedings in Durham as she did the earlier events at Bishop Auckland.

Aaron has left his shop in the charge of his young men and we have travelled here together on the train. As we make our way through the alleyways of Durham and the bridges over the winding river, we catch glimpses of the rearing cathedral and its attendant castle, sure signs, Aaron says, of the moral and political power represented in this county town.

Then, when we reach it, the bulk of the prison echoes this massive power of the state. How very far this is from the narrow houses of West Auckland, where, in more normal times, simple people live and die almost without being noticed at all.

We have to fight our way through the waiting crowd and show the tickets Aaron obtained for us through his committee. The court room itself is bigger and more impressive than that at Bishop Auckland, though much of the crowd is a similarly seething mixture of gentry, general public and reporters. A grand gallery is filled with what look like rather affluent ladies of the city and the county. There are even some grandees seated alongside the Judge, Mr Justice Archbold, who sits on his bench like a medieval king in his court. And down at the front there are clusters of men – lawyers, by their garb – craning their heads and muttering away: no doubt keen to observe this historic case.

The rest of us are squashed on the benches right at the back.

The buzz and sense of expectation reminds me of the Eden Theatre in Bishop Auckland, just before the curtain goes up. The raising of the curtain is the arrival of Marian, led by her gaolers to the front of the dock. Today she has no baby on her knee to comfort or distract her. She is paler, and stumbles a little against a stick that she carries, so that one of the matrons has to help her to her place. It occurs to me that my uncle and those cynics who believe as he does will think that this is all an act, as was her tenderness towards her baby in the committal: even her reserved, fine appearance will be held against her. They will count this as another drama of her life's lie. For them she is the sneering, satanic woman of the newspaper portraits.

There is an actual photograph of her now in the papers, taken, I am told, in prison. In this photograph she has on her familiar checked shawl and the black bonnet she wore for the funerals. Her thick black hair is smoothed down, her large eyes are shaded and deep-set and the set of her full mouth is wistful. This photograph does not show the sparkle in her eye or the humorous curve of her mouth, so familiar and beloved to me. But even so, she looks much younger than her forty years.

Sadly, the Marian that sits in court today, looking neither left nor right, is a shadow of the woman in the photograph. Even her lovely hair is loose and unkempt, falling on to her face in a wild fashion. I will her to look towards me but she keeps her eye on the rail in front of her.

In a whisper planted close in my ear Aaron points out to me the man who will prosecute: Sir Charles Russell, tall and fine-featured, with his thick fair hair swept back, the theatrical jut of his chin giving him the look of a storybook hero. He is an impressive figure. How I wish he were defending Marian rather than prosecuting.

Mr Justice Archbold asks him whether anyone appears for the prisoner.

'No, my lord, it appears to the contrary.' Russell's voice, as he stands up to speak, is slightly highly pitched and nasal, but has the distinctive rounded tones of the Anglo-Irish. 'I am told that the learned counsel who has been mentioned as likely to be instructed has received no communication.'

'The money was raised.' Aaron's voice in my ear. 'Where is the dratted man?'

The judge frowns, and calls to his side a clerkly man for consultation. He calls Sir Charles across and they talk. Though his voice is low, the Irishman's clear voice penetrates the four corners of the court. 'I've been told this is not a popular brief, my lord. Set for failure, professional suicide.'

'Nevertheless,' grunts his lordship, 'this is a disgrace.'

He then adjourns the court until one o'clock and says gloomily that by then he expects to see a defender, or he will be looking for someone to cite for contempt.

As she stands up to leave Marian lifts her head, looks round the court and catches sight of me and Aaron. For a second her eyes lighten and she turns to the woman at her right side and says something. In her turn the woman on her left looks across and sees us. Then all three of them melt into the fabric of the building beneath the dock.

At one o'clock Mr Campbell Foster is introduced to the court, and the judge announces that the case of *Regina versus Cotton* will begin on Wednesday. A sigh of disappointment flutters round the court. No fireworks today.

It is on the following Wednesday that, after experiencing the same preliminary gathering ritual, the fireworks start in earnest.

The defendant is asked how she pleads. Mr Campbell Foster speaks to Marian and she rises from her chair to speak low and clear and to plead not guilty. She is tidier and more composed today. I want to clap my hands in support but can't because Aaron is grasping my left hand under the folds of my skirt.

Sir Charles Russell starts with a damning summary of facts constructed from the assumption that the defendant is guilty. He commits himself to bringing evidence that Mrs Cotton was intensely cruel to Charlie. He uses words like 'depraved' and 'morally weak' in reference to her motives. This time Aaron has to grab my arm to hold me down. The other people in the row turn to look at us, to find the source of the disturbance.

But when Sir Charles tries to bring up the other apparently related deaths, asserted as 'possibly true' in the newspapers, Mr Campbell Foster leaps to his feet protesting that such extraneous evidence is inadmissible in this trial, which is concerned only with the death of

322

young Charles Cotton. But the judge does not accept this and pushes Sir Charles on.

Then the prosecutor goes on to discuss the arsenic and its acquisition, blandly ignoring the fact that no arsenic was found in Mrs Cotton's house when it was searched. As his beautiful voice sounds through the court the details of the case are so familiar that I feel I can recite them: he focuses on the most damning interpretation of the facts that could exist. He wheels out people Marian worked with in Sunderland, to bring out their vague assertions that she had access to the poison there.

Then he puts Sarah Shaw up to rehearse the tale of the West Auckland deaths as though they were all one. She recites them earnestly, with relish. There is an intake of breath in the court. Again Mr Campbell Foster objects to bringing in these earlier deaths but no notice is taken of him. The death toll is rolled out as though prejudice were truth.

Old Mrs Dodds is called. Marian lifts her head and examines her old friend from head to toe. Mrs Dodds tells what sounds like a true tale of Charlie's journey to death, but she is pressed to talk about the presence of arsenic in Mrs Cotton's house to clean the bed. Sir Charles encourages her to remember that there was some left over. At least Mr Campbell Foster gets her to describe how kind Marian was with Charlie but Sir Charles sweeps on, getting her to criticise Marian's decision to have the boy's bed downstairs when he was ill. She goes on to describe the green fluffy wallpaper and carpet in the bedroom Marian shared with Charlie.

'Like her other house. She had that there,' she offers. 'Very fond of that fancy paper she was. Bought it though she couldn't afford it.'

Mr Townend the chemist is called to verify the purchase of arsenic and soft soap from his shop. In fact, he gives conflicting evidence of the amount he dispensed. I write it down. At one point he says he gave her half an ounce, which is two hundred and forty grains, at another point he says it was only three or four grains. I don't think Mr Campbell Foster makes enough of this, although he does point it out.

Then Mr Riley takes the stand, a sturdy figure, the very essence of respectability. This time Marian leans forward and holds him in an unblinking stare for the whole of his testimony. He avoids her gaze but in a firm voice he damns her here in Durham just as he did at the earlier hearing. He repeats gossip from the shop about Marian and Mr Quick-Manning, but says he is not swayed by gossip. He talks about Marian trying to persuade him to get rid of Charlie to the workhouse; of her trying to fob the boy off on her brother-in-law in the South. No one asks him whether he really thinks that Marian's stepson of about a year was truly her responsibility or how stepchildren fit in his workhouse jurisdiction.

Riley's voice lowers in pitch as he talks of the morning of Charlie's death and dwells on his increasing suspicions of Marian. He is a very steady, reliable-looking witness, and speaks earnestly as though he is speaking the actual truth. To my dismay I realise he thinks it really is the truth.

As he gets down from the box Marian stands up and speaks to him in a low voice. 'Your God will judge you, Tommy Riley. Be sure of that.'

The judge gives her a withering look and admonishes Mr Campbell Foster that he should control his client or she will be taken down. Campbell Foster whispers to her and, after a hard glance at the judge, she nods her head vigorously and sits back in the seat.

Sir Charles calls other witnesses, some of whom I don't recognise, to give evidence that Marian treated her children cruelly – particularly Charlie. One woman asserts that it was common knowledge in the village that she abused the child. Marian shakes her head through all of this and I find myself doing the same.

Then my Uncle William is called and this time both Marian and I are leaning forward, examining the witness. He goes through his part of the sorry tale, now so familiar to me. Mr Campbell Foster makes him reiterate the fact that at first he judged Charlie's death to be natural. He also takes him through his own prescribing for Charlie: bismuth, hydrocyanic acid, prussic acid and morphia. Uncle William agrees that they are all irritant poisons, but, he assures the court, when given in proper doses, they can be very effective. He also agrees that they do require great care in administration.

Campbell Foster challenges my uncle at every point regarding the presence of arsenic in everyday life, but he stays steady and does not get flustered. He says that yes, arsenic is sometimes found in the soil in churchyards, that yes, the fluffy green wallpapers are said in some learned articles to be arsenical although he has never seen that effect. And yes, he has read that arsenic would throw off fumes in a very hot room, but again he has never seen that effect. Through his questioning Campbell Foster ensures that the people in court know that people have died of chronic arsenic poison while living with this wallpaper and that in Prussia – a very scientific country – such wallpaper is banned.

I think this is all very convincing, and Marian is watching my uncle closely, nodding at every point made by her lawyer.

But very clearly the judge, Mr Archbold, is not convinced. He taps his pencil impatiently as Campbell Foster proceeds with the questioning and finally brings him to a stop. 'Mr Campbell Foster! Your question is very speculative and can hardly be asked. Your cross-examination is of an extremely speculative nature.'

Campbell Foster then asks my uncle about the presence of powdered arsenic in his dispensary but my uncle says very firmly that the only arsenic in his dispensary is in solution. There is no powder on his shelves. My brain starts to race. I know this not to be true.

The barrister then turns to the fact of Charlie's high temperature as he lay in his bed in the hot room, and the fact that the turned mattress underneath him had been lying on a framework treated with arsenic and soft soap. He pursues with my uncle the notion that arsenic has been found dissolved in water in places with bad or non-existent drains. My uncle firmly denies that these factors would cause the presence of the poison that he had observed and analysed, in the case of Charlie Cotton.

Sir Charles Russell gets to his feet. The sigh of satisfaction in the room when this distinguished man stands up is palpable. In his soft, convincing tones he goes again through these issues of the soil, water, the wallpaper and the medicines and, with a confident flourish, appears to dispose of them all. The judge allows him to hold forth and does not, as he did with Campbell Foster, stop him and say that much of this is speculative.

Even so I think Mr Cambell Foster has put up a good show here. Surely he has said enough to plant some real doubts in the minds of the jury. The possibility of arsenic being in the domestic environment to be absorbed through daily life was, I think, well argued. And above all, the domestic environment that Marian carried around was unique to her. She kept her rooms hot, was obsessively clean, hated bugs, liked fancy wallpapers, and liked to be nurse and dose her patients. It looks to me that Campbell Foster has shown the potential for savage domestic accidents where arsenic is concerned. Surely here is reasonable doubt that she wilfully murdered Charlie or anyone else.

The cross-examination of Dr Chalmers follows the same pattern: Campbell Foster's tentative but determined questioning cast on one side; Sir Charles' skilled assertions of obvious guilt.

Mr Campbell Foster asks Dr Chalmers about the dispensary and the disposition of the drugs. His most interesting revelation is the matter of the existence of powdered arsenic in the dispensary. This is despite the fact that my uncle gave evidence to the contrary. I know from my own experience that there was powdered arsenic there. Now I have the question in my mind of why my uncle does not want to disclose this. My only conclusion at this moment is that he is indeed worried about the extreme nature of the medicines he routinely offers as treatment. I contemplate, then loyally reject, the thought that at the end my uncle was in a position through the autopsies to make sure powdered arsenic was found.

Still, I feel that Mr Campbell Foster's dogged questioning must be at least casting some doubt on the false certainties we have lived with all these months. If the jury has any openness in their minds they must be thinking afresh now.

But my heart sinks again when Dr Scattergood takes the stand. His authoritative demeanour, with its side-allusions to the other cases at the earlier hearing, is accepted as admissible by the judge. He is very convincing. Mr Campbell Foster tries, but cannot penetrate his certainty. Most importantly, Campbell Foster's protests about the inadmissibility of the evidence regarding the deaths of other members of Marian's extended family again go unheard.

As the day goes on Marian seems to shrink further and further inside herself. Her face becomes bony and her eyes become blank, like grey slate. When the death of her baby Robert is mentioned, tears well up in her eyes and drip unnoticed on her cheeks. There is one chilling moment when she glances sideways, back at the crowded benches. Suddenly she bears an eerie resemblance to the horrible creature who has been caricatured in the papers.

As the jury troops out I address my thoughts to the detail and the doubt in the arguments we have heard. It will certainly take many hours for the jury to consider them. I wonder if any one of them, like me, is sceptical about my uncle's protests about the arsenic. I wonder if they will argue over the conflicting accounts of Marian's kindness to Charlie. Perhaps more than one of them will not be able to reconcile the image

326

of the frail woman before them with the amoral, scheming person Sir Charles has so ably described. All of them will understand that if they say she is guilty, this same frail woman will be hanged to death.

Some people move out of the court to get some air, but Aaron and I stay put, worried about the scramble for places when the jury returns. He says in a low voice, 'That old Mr Campbell Foster was not half bad, considering he had barely minutes to prepare. He built a proper defence. He asked good questions. Pity he didn't have time to bring an expert witness to refute Scattergood. The thing about the water and the wallpaper was going somewhere until that judge encouraged Russell to dispose of it. Obvious bias, that.'

'So those men who you write to will be satisfied?'

'Well, at least Marian has been defended here. For a bit, it looked like she wouldn't be. Cold comfort, maybe, but there you are.'

'But why couldn't Campbell Foster stop the whole thing to get time to prepare? Then he might have called another expert, perhaps called people like me and you, those nurses in Sunderland, and Mr Backhouse, to vouch for her as a decent person. Did you hear those lies about her hurting Charlie? I couldn't believe that.'

We are still sitting there in the cold room, our breath rising in the air, when a bell sounds somewhere and people begin to stream back into the court room, some climbing over benches to make sure of their seats. 'They've decided,' says Aaron quietly.

They have been out less than an hour. I cannot believe it. There can have been no hard discussions and fine argument. My heart sinks.

Guilty! Simply said. Marian collapses into the arms of the wardresses, who help her to stand while the judge puts on his black cap and intones his sentence. Somebody at the back of the court cries, 'Yes! Yes!' and there is a low growling cheer. The judge stops to look sourly in the direction of the noise.

The policemen lead Marian away. I will her to look at me but she looks neither right nor left. As we struggle to make our way out Aaron has his arm around me and I use his shoulder to quieten my sobs. Outside in the large crowd, there is intermittent cheering. A mixed crowd on the corner by the prison have been celebrating what I am sure they saw as a foregone conclusion. They have their arms round each other's shoulders and are chanting the rhyme that has become so familiar in these past months.

'Mary Ann Cotton
She's dead and she's rotten
She lies in her bed
With her eyes wide open.
Sing, sing. Oh what can I sing?
Mary Ann Cotton is tied up with string
Where, where? Up in the air
Sellin' black puddens a penny a pair.'

Their song pursues us as we hurry as fast as my poor feet will go, through the town to the station. Aaron is already talking about an appeal and what that might cost, and that his correspondents would definitely move to that. He – and they – are aghast at the abhorrent thought of a woman, guilty or innocent, being hanged – the 'judicial murder' they speak of in their letters.

As for myself, I cannot think of anything except my dear friend Marian collapsing into the arms of those women. I am powerless, entirely powerless to do anything about it. What kind of friend am I?

Seventy

Miss McCullough has kept me very busy since the day Marian was sentenced. There has been a sick pupil to keep watch over; another girl to take by train and cab to her home in Middleton-in-Teesdale for her grandmother's funeral; the whole of the linen closet to reorganise and document, and our little choir to rehearse for a competition to be held at the town hall and judged by the excellent Nicholas Kilburn. This will be quite a challenge as the Nonconformist chapels in South Durham have wonderful small choirs. The male group from the Welsh Chapel is held to be of national class and has performed in Leeds.

I acquit myself quite well in all this, despite sleeping little and battling against a dead feeling at the pit of my stomach. Aaron calls most days to have a cup of tea with Miss McCullough and myself but I find myself distant from him. Our contact is more formal and polite than it has been recently. He brings the news of an appeal for a retrial.

The newspapers tell us that Marian has had to give up her baby girl to Mr and Mrs Edwards. How I feel for her now. This is the very last of her children to be taken from her. When we hear this, Aaron holds me close but there is no kissing.

He tries to comfort me by saying that there is, ongoing even now, a campaign by good men who urge the reduction of the terrible sentence to imprisonment instead of judicial murder. I feel too numb to rise to real anger about all this and I see Aaron and Miss McCullough exchanging glances at my blank inability to react. One day I overhear Miss McCullough say to him in the hall, 'It's not over yet, Mr

Whitstable. We need to watch over Miss Kilburn. We must wait this time out with her.'

Another day Aaron sits with me and helps me write a letter of friendship and support for Marian. 'We both know what has happened to you is unjust, and treasure the friendship and warmth that you have brought to us and know you will go to the Heaven in which you truly believe and will there be surrounded by those loved ones who have gone before you. We will never, never forget you, dear Marian.'

This gives me a degree of comfort but Aaron finds the Heaven bit hard to agree with, as he believes in none of that. I don't know what I believe but, despite my lack of churchgoing, I can't think that there is an end to life with death, that this is all there is. More importantly, I do know that Marian believes in her early religious teaching; she managed to combine all that with her pagan ways to her own satisfaction. So this point about Heaven is perhaps a comfort for me more than for her. Marian is beyond comfort except from the Wesleyan minister she mentions in her letters. She says she likes him and he 'makes a lot of sense even to a woman in my dire position'.

Seventy-One

The appeal put forward by Marian's lawyers has been turned down flat!
They cannot have considered it at all. The sentence is to be carried out
only two weeks after the judge put on his black cap to make his
pronouncement.

All hope is lost. I am devastated. Miss McCullough tries to keep me
busy but there are still moments when I am on an errand for her in
Newgate Street when thoughts of Marian in her cell overwhelm me.
Newspaper headlines shriek the loss of the appeal. Her savaged image
peers at me from newsagents' posters. Children cheerfully chant that
awful song to accompany their innocent games of skipping or two-ball.
The town is in a low ferment, a state of waiting.

On the day before Marian is due to be hanged, a vast cloud sets itself
over the town, befogging the streets and reducing the day to darkness at
noon. When the cloud breaks, the water washes down like a waterfall
before steadying to a drenching downpour, which empties the streets
and pavements and drives everyone under cover.

Our girls come in from school like drowned puppies. They are
allowed to change to their dressing gowns before supper and Miss
McCullough insists we draw the curtains, build up the fires and have an
extra singing practice. She insists that we choose the jolliest tunes in
our repertoire, which pleases the girls, who soon forget about the rain.
As for me, I carry out my tasks numbly, driven on by leaden duty and
fear of the image that lies like a snake at the back of my mind.

Aaron arrives after the girls have gone to bed and we drink hot
chocolate with Miss McCullough beside her fire. We talk about the

terrible rain and the trouble it has caused in the town, but none of us mentions the subject that is uppermost in our minds.

Before he leaves, Aaron reaches for my hand. 'I will call for you at six o'clock in the morning, Victoria.' He glances at Miss McCullough, who nods her head. 'I think, rain or shine, we must go for a walk.'

The next morning is fine and bright, although the buildings and the gutters still reflect last night's deluge. True to his promise, Aaron calls for me at six o'clock. We travel to West Auckland on the train and it is still half dark as we make our way through the mill yard, along the backs, past the end of the garden of Western House, past the millrace, past the back of Marian's house, out to the river reaches and woodland where, in those early days, we heard the fox and discovered the stray donkey. This time Aaron guides me closer to the river and stops me at one point where a hillock rears up and overreaches the riverbank.

'Look,' he says. 'Just look at that.'

I catch a glimpse of one sleek dark shape, then another, sliding through the water; two faces turn and round eyes gleam up into the morning. 'Otters.' I breathe, rather than say the word.

'We missed them that first morning,' Aaron says. 'Do you remember? Marian said we should look for the otters.' We walk on and this time Aaron takes my hand rather than my arm and I focus my mind on that soft warm touch, keeping at bay thoughts about that horrific thing happening twelve miles away. They will be getting her from the cell.

It starts to rain again and we come upon a low hut, once a cottage, I think, but now used by a farmer as a barn. Aaron pushes open the door and guides me in to the low tar-smelling space. Just inside the door he draws me to him and I start to cry, my face against his. And I can feel his tears on my cheeks. Then we kiss, sadly, gently at first and then with a frantic urgency that comes from very deep inside. I put my fingers inside the collar of his soft shirt, and he tips off my hat and unpins my hair. Then we are half-sitting, half-lying against a heap of dried grass and his shirt is open and he is unbuttoning my blouse so that we are skin to skin.

What happens next is very elaborate and strange. I was always curious about this man-and-woman thing and now it is happening to me. Even as it is happening, this surprising, powerful, raw coming-together, it strikes me that *this* is what my mother and magisterial father do together! It's what Auntie Mary and Uncle William do. How very strange. I start to laugh. Aaron catches my humour and starts to chuckle, and by the time he finally makes his way right into me (after me gasping that such a thing is impossible) we are both laughing with delight, with astonishment, and finally with a frenzied kind of sadness.

Then he rolls away from me and takes out his watch and shows it to me. It shows eight o'clock exactly. I hear her voice in my ear, in my head. '*Now, honey,*' she whispers. '*Isn't that a good thing?*'

Then Aaron stands up, facing away from me while he does up his breeches, giving me privacy to do up my blouse and pull down my skirt. I use one of my petticoats to clean myself, then roll it up into a tight ball and stuff it into my bag. When he turns round I am quite decent, although my struggle with my falling hair goes on. He helps me with this task and places my hat firmly on my quivering mass of hair.

'You are a lovely, lovely lass. Now you will have to make an honest man of me.' He kisses me on the nose. 'You are all right, my sweet-heart?'

'Well. That was a bit of a surprise. Astonishing. But yes. I am all right.'

He runs his fingers through his hair and then pulls out his silver watch again. He shows me the dial: 8.15. 'It's over for her,' he says soberly. 'She can suffer no longer.'

I wait to cry but there are no more tears.

'We had better go back, love. Your Miss McCullough has been that worried about you and what today has brought into your life.'

I take his hand in mine. 'I really liked Marian, you know. I will never, never forget her.' The words, as they burst out of me, sound ridiculous, childish.

'Marian really liked you,' he says. 'I always thought that. Both one-offs in your own ways. You had sommat to offer each other. And, in a queer way, she'll always be part of you and me, of the two of us, whatever we do.'

As we walk back along the riverbank we talk of Marian, of the things she said and did before that toxic dam of hatred spilled over on her. At the millrace Aaron puts his arm through mine. 'She would have been pleased about all this, you know.'

'About what?'

'That we weren't sitting around waiting for her death knell. That we were . . . well . . . doing what we were doing. Making love, making life, instead of taking it. She was very open about all that.'

I manage a laugh.

'I have always realised that Marian wasn't all good, you know. No more than any of us,' he says slowly. 'She made her own rules. And she could be a bit liberal with the truth when she wanted to be. I had this thought once that she made up who she was, each time she moved on.'

'She was hard to read. She liked to be the giver, not the taker.'

'Liked to be in charge. Sure.'

'Yes, so she did. But did you ever doubt her, Aaron, ever think that she did those things? The things they say, and will always say about her?'

He turns me to face him. 'No,' he says. 'Never.'

Later that day, as I move about the school house doing my work, I feel lighter than I have felt in all these seven months since they took Marian away. I do feel wretchedly sad and lost, but each time I try to think closely about what happened today to Marian I am stuck with the image and the feelings of making love to Aaron in the hut by the river. Her savage death will not haunt me as it will haunt others for years to come, so much so that she needs be transformed into a monster to justify the tissue of untruths that has grown up around these events.

Aaron comes back for tea and is at the school house at six o'clock when Miss McCullough and I have a visitor: a tall thin woman with a plain, unlovely face and tired eyes. She introduces herself as Miss Douglas, the prison schoolmistress who witnessed some of the letters that Marian wrote to me.

She hands me an envelope. 'The last letter,' she says. 'She asked if I would bring it for you myself.'

I take it but do not open it. 'This is kind of you, Miss Douglas.'

'I looked after Mrs Cotton all these months. I had some time for her. I was there when her baby was born. She was a good mother,' she says. 'And she was nobody's fool.' She lowers her voice and glances around as though there might be spies. Perhaps it is a prison habit. 'Mr Henderson, the Wesleyan minister who looked after her in these last weeks, became convinced of her innocence, you know.'

The words hang drily in the air.

Aaron coughs. 'Victoria and me, we always thought her innocent. We are her friends, her supporters.'

Miss McCullough stirs in her chair. 'Myself, I am not sure. Even if the woman weren't innocent, though, that trial was a travesty.'

'Some people are saying that now. But it is immaterial. Nothing can make any difference now.' Miss Douglas sounds desolate.

I find myself staring at her really hard. 'How was she? How was Marian?'

She knows what I am asking and offers me something. 'Mrs Cotton was quiet, resigned, but so very afraid. Who would not be afraid? But she most definitely had her faith and I suppose that was something. Whatever people say, she knew she wasn't going to purgatory. That should tell you something about whether she . . . well, you know.'

I still stare at her.

She shakes her head. 'You want to know about it? It was dreadful. Barbaric. I saw very little because I fainted. Miss Wilkinson fainted too. Mr Dale Trotter from Bishop Auckland was there, and he looked very seedy indeed. It was a terrible thing. I may tell you the hangman himself is bound for purgatory if anyone is. What a nasty man he was.'

Miss McCullough stands up. 'Tea! We haven't offered you tea, Miss Douglas.'

Miss Douglas gets to her feet. 'No time, I'm afraid. I have to make my way to West Auckland to see Mrs Cotton's child. I promised to take a letter to Mrs Edwards and take a peep at the baby. Have you seen her? She's very fine. I became quite fond of the little one in the months she was with us. Did I tell you I saw her born? Yes, I did.'

When she has gone I sit and read Marian's letter out to Aaron and Miss McCullough.

'My Dear Child, How fitting that my last letter to you from this dark place . . .'

It is a wonderful letter, full of Marian's own particular energy and self-knowledge, although often bitter. It is a kind of explanation of her life and how she saw it. And it shows faith in herself and her maker. It ends: 'in sorrow I must leave you . . .'

By the time I have finished reading it I am sitting on the couch with Miss McCullough close on one side of me and Aaron on the other. There are even tears in Miss McCullough's eyes.

'Poor woman,' she says slowly. 'How easy is our life compared with hers.'

I think what a good woman Miss McCullough is. How lucky I am in knowing her.

We sit there in the light of a single lamp for what seems a very long time. Then Aaron stands up. 'Miss McCullough,' he says, 'I think it would be good for Victoria to have a change. I thought perhaps I might take her to visit my friend in Morpeth. The air is very good in Northumberland.'

She turns to me, the light from the lamp edging on to her dear lugubrious face. 'And will you come back to us, Victoria?' She is very shrewd.

I put my hand on hers. 'We will come to visit you, Miss McCullough.'

'We?'

'From Morpeth we intend to go on to Scotland and be married.' I glance up at Aaron, 'On what Aaron calls "our own say-so".'

'Will you, now? And what am I supposed to do about that?'

'You could wait a week and then write to my father. Tell him I am doing the right thing.'

She smiles. 'I'll be glad to. I must tell you how lucky I feel to have come upon you in the choir. You have told me your friend Mrs Cotton had a spark of light, of energy that she brought into your life. I have to tell you that you have brought such energy, such light into my barren life. I think we sang in tune.'

'And will continue to do so,' I say. 'When we get back.'

The next day Miss McCullough waves us off at the station with tears in her eyes. I sit back in the empty carriage and look out through the rain streaming down the windows as the train pulls out of the station. My mind is filled to the brim again with thoughts of that very first journey to West Auckland.

Aaron places his hand on mine, his lips come close to my cheek. 'It's over now, sweetheart. Don't you worry about Marian,' he whispers. 'She wouldn't want that, would she? Wasn't she a great one for moving on?'

Epilogue

... So, child, in sorrow I must leave you to this earthly toil.
Sitting in this place, it has dawned on me that at the very end at
last my heart has flowed with love again, and that love was for
you. For that I thank God and in that I am redeemed. But I'll not
see you again. Not in this world, anyway. My gaolers here whisper
that what's to come will not be easy and I must stay strong.

A Woman Scorned

Historical Afternotes

Although a work of fiction, this novel was inspired by the real people and events surrounding the trial and execution of Mary Ann Cotton in 1873. As well as newspapers, census and contemporary documents, my main source for the public facts of the story has been the meticulously researched *Mary Ann Cotton* by the late Arthur Appleton (County Durham Books, 1973). Mr Appleton concluded that Mary Ann probably killed fourteen or fifteen people. Tony Whitehead, whose well-documented account *Mary Ann Cotton, Dead but not Forgotten* (self-published, undated) is presented in rigorous style, almost drifts to the conclusion that Mary Ann was guilty at least in three cases.

Interestingly Appleton comments that in some programmes put out by the BBC in 1975 the actress playing Mary Ann found her role difficult because she believed Mary Ann to be innocent. Derek Hebden's *Murder at West Auckland*, a more summary account (History Snapshot Series, 1987), was also useful.

Well researched as they are, in all these writers' accounts the terms 'may have', 'perhaps' and 'probably' tend to be used in the absence of true connective evidence. So, whether Mary Ann was guilty or innocent appears to be a matter of *belief*.

Tellingly, Appleton says in his conclusion, 'The Mary Ann Cotton family spanned the lifetime of the Durham Coalfield. The underworld of coal was explored and known far better than the underworld mind of Mary Ann Cotton.'

The writing of this novel was inspired by the thought that perhaps the 'underworld mind' of Mary Ann Cotton – transformed to 'Marian' in my novel – might be further explored through the rich, sinewy medium of fiction.

What Happened to the People?

Margaret Edith Quick-Manning Cotton, Mary Ann's daughter, born in prison on 7 January 1873, was paid a halfpenny a day for life to compensate for being born in prison. When her foster parents Mr and Mrs Edwards brought her home to West Auckland, crowds came to the house to view this daughter of the 'murderess'. In her very long life Margaret Edith travelled to America, became blind at thirty, had two marriages and a daughter and three sons, two of whom were killed in the First World War. Her surviving son told Arthur Appleton she was 'an angel'.

George Robinson, the son Mary Ann left with her husband James Robinson in Pallion, became a manager at Short Brothers Shipyard at Sunderland, and eventually lived in a comfortable style to which Mary Ann would have aspired.

Dr William Kilburn continued to be a much-loved and respected local doctor. When he died at fifty-six in 1886, a window in St Helen's church was dedicated to him by his appreciative friends.

Nicholas Kilburn, the choirmaster, became a nationally known music entrepreneur who was a friend of Elgar. Two coincidences: Nicholas's granddaughter married the eminent archaeologist Sir Mortimer Wheeler, who is great-grandfather to my own son-in law, Sean. And in 1870 Nicholas's uncle built the house where I now live and gave it to his daughter. There is a passage in the novel where Victoria notes these 'new' houses being built in 1872.

Thomas Riley continued to be a pillar of the community, eventually calling himself 'merchant' on the census. In 1874 he was co-trustee with Sir William Eden for the new school, contributing £100 himself.

In 1889, seventeen years after this case, **Sir Charles Russell**, Mary Ann's prosecutor, defended the middle-class Florence Maybrick against a charge of poisoning her husband with arsenic. Amongst other legal strategies he touched on some of the arguments employed by Mr Campbell Foster in the Mary Ann Cotton case. He seemed to be on the verge of securing an acquittal when Maybrick destroyed her own case by making a statement admitting a degree of culpability. Maybrick was not hanged. She served fifteen years in prison and lived to an old age in the United States. Russell later became an MP, then Attorney General in Gladstone's ministries of 1886 and 1892, ending up as Lord Chief Justice of England in 1894.

Finally, a year after these events, after much discussion, a new drain was installed at the bottom of Johnson Terrace in West Auckland.